GHOSTS AND MADMEN

JAMES TARR

Vinci Books

vinci-books.com

Published by Vinci Books Ltd in 2025

1

Copyright © James Tarr 2023

The author has asserted their moral right to be identified as the author of this work in accordance with the Copyright, Designs and Patents Act 1988. This work is a work of fiction. Names, characters, places and incidents are the product of the author's imagination or are used fictitiously. Any resemblance to actual persons, living or dead, places and incidents is entirely coincidental.

All rights reserved. No part of this publication may be copied, reproduced, distributed, stored in any retrieval system, or transmitted in any form or by any means, including photocopying, recording, or other electronic or mechanical methods, nor used as a source for any form of machine learning including AI datasets, without the prior written permission of the publisher.

The publisher and the author have made every effort to obtain permissions for any third party material used in this book and to comply with copyright law. Any queries in this respect should be brought to the attention of the publisher and any omissions will be corrected in future editions.

A CIP catalogue record for this book is available from the British Library.

Paperback ISBN: 9781036707149

Printed and bound in Great Britain by Clays Ltd, Elcograf S.p.A.

By James Tarr

James Tarr Conspiracy Thrillers

Failure Drill

Splashback

Splits and Transitions

Whorl

Waiting for the Kick

Ghosts and Madmen

The Subsection

PART I
OUTLIERS

Chapter One

El Paso, Texas, was situated at the tip of the far-west-jutting arm of America's second-largest state, driven like a spike between Mexico and the American state of New Mexico. It was almost directly south of Albuquerque, the two cities linked by a four-hour-drive along I-25. Across the border from El Paso was Ciudad Juarez, which occupied the northern-most point of Mexico east of Phoenix. It was a sensible spot to cross if you were heading anywhere in America other than California or Arizona.

More than two million people lived on either side of the border there, twice as many in Ciudad Juarez as El Paso. The cities shared nearly twenty miles of border, which followed the winding path of the Rio Grande—El Rio Bravo (del Norte) as it was known in Mexico. The El Paso border crossing was the second-busiest between Mexico and the United States, second only to the San Ysidro crossing between Tijuana and San Diego.

The street was named Broadway, in the Thomas Manor neighborhood of El Paso, in the middle of the city, and it seemed particularly ill-suited to the grandiose name. Barely wide enough for three cars, the asphalt was so cracked and faded it looked like the desert floor. Dry grass sprouted in random tufts along the low curbs and occasionally pushed through the cracks.

The houses lining the street were little better. They were small, single-storied, brick and siding, all done in light colors —white, peach, and various shades of pink—and yet still looked dirty and faded. There were occasional trees, but most of the low roofs were open to the baking sun. A few of the houses had carports, but most of the vehicles belonging to the residents squatted in the short driveways, in full sun, soaking up the heat. If it wasn't clear from the dilapidated condition of many of the houses, or the age of the vehicles parked in front of them, the bars across almost every window told the tale.

Directly behind the houses on the west side of Broadway were the six lanes of Texas State Route 75, Cesar E. Chavez Border Parkway, running nearly north/south, and directly behind that was the Wall. Although, technically, here it was more of a fence, constructed of square steel beams with almost no horizontal cross-supports, so few people short of accomplished gymnasts and mountain climbers could get over it at all, much less quickly.

The Wall wasn't the border; the border was the shore of the Rio Grande some four hundred feet from the Wall. Depending on the time of year, and the rain, the river here was sometimes less than twenty feet wide. Three hundred feet west of the Mexican riverbank was Blvd. Cuatro Siglos, a six-lane highway running along the northern border of Ciudad Juarez. There was a six-foot-high berm running along the shoulder, so the locals driving along couldn't see the river, or the border, but everyone knew it was there.

Clouds didn't keep the moon out of the sky; its gravity still turned the tides.

On the west side of Blvd. Cuatro Siglos were the kind of businesses you would expect—gas stations and industrial parks, for the most part. The Ciudad Juarez neighborhoods sat to the south and further inland, including the Parceles Ejido Jesus Carranza, which stretched for a mile and sat almost directly across the border from Thomas Manor. From the houses on Broadway on the American side to the buildings sitting along Cuatro Siglos on the Mexican side was barely more than three hundred meters in a straight line.

Thomas Manor hadn't been a good neighborhood in years, and with the situation at the border at its worst since The Republic of Texas had been at war with Mexico, For Sale signs dotted both sides of the street.

The house they were interested in was on the west side of the street, near the south end of the block. There was no For Sale sign in front of it, and no vehicles parked in the driveway. Since they'd had it under surveillance there'd been no sign of life.

The drone had been circling over it for hours, so far overhead it was practically invisible to the naked eye. It was equipped with night vision and thermal cameras, both of which were useless in the baking Texas summer heat. The house was a plain one-story that was indistinguishable from its neighbors. The person who owned it was a ghost; the name went nowhere, and the property taxes were paid out of a business account. It was a shell company, owned by another shell company, but the company which owned that one was a known entity. So that gave the intelligence they'd received more weight.

However, it was time sensitive. They'd gotten the drone

parked over the house in the early hours of the morning, minutes before the ground team was even in the air and en route. They studied the real-time feed from the drone during the flight, working up several plans.

There were a lot of ways to do it. All of them had risk.

Pike was lead on the team. He didn't need to tell any of them that. As soon as he identified himself to the group—a formality, as four of the five men already knew who he was, and three of them had worked with him on various missions—he got respectful nods. And a few penetrating, wondering stares.

Pike was a legend, as much of a legend as you could be in a profession where most of what you did was secret, classified at the highest level. The more successful the mission, the less anyone knew about it. It was only massive screwups which made the news. But whether you were talking military, CIA, or private contractors, the top-tier spec-ops community was small and closed-knit, and everyone knew everyone, or you knew a guy who knew the guy. The accepted background story was that he'd started out in Special Forces, before the date Nine-Eleven had any meaning, and he'd been in his current position for at least five years, but between those two postings was over a decade of mystery, rumor and innuendo. Most of the whispered stories about his "greatest hits" were so outrageous that they couldn't be believed…except the people who were telling them had no tolerance for tall tales, not about the shit that mattered.

Pike was, by far, the oldest man still in the field. Most guys his age were in management, sitting behind desks or watching, on monitors, the action taking place elsewhere, usually across the world, directing the action. Not Pike. He was still shrugging on the armor, lacing up the boots, and hitting the skids. Or, in this case, the leather recliners, as they were travelling in style. Nicer than most of them were used to—the G5 was undoubtedly registered to one of the countless shell companies the government had on paper and used whenever it needed insulating layers.

"We don't have anything that can see through that roof?" Fancy asked. It was a rare man on the teams who didn't use a work name. You didn't want to shout a guy's real name during an op, only to have surviving bad guys try to track him down. Fancy was a former Navy SEAL, lean and dark-haired.

Pike shook his big head. His head was nearly square, with a big jaw. His dark blonde hair seemed to be fading rather than turning to gray. He was of average height, and thick everywhere. At his age, most people would assume it was fat. That he was, perhaps, a 'former jock'. "Not on that Reaper. And as soon as that sun's been on that roof for half an hour, the mirage is going to fuck everything up, thermal will be useless. We'll know who's in there when we get inside. For what it's worth, it's supposed to be empty."

That got snorts out of the team members. "That's worth exactly nothing," Cherry said, which is what they were all thinking. He'd started out in the Rangers, and during his first combat tour in Afghanistan had met up with a bunch of trigger pullers from the operations side of the DIA. They'd had very cool toys and been doing some wicked stuff, and it didn't take much to get him to change lanes.

They looked at the slowly rotating image of the house. "There's hardly any back yard. Or front yard, for that matter. Is that a fence or a wall that runs along the back?" Boot asked. He was of Italian descent, but depending on his haircut, facial hair, manner of dress, and how much tan he was sporting (as he got very dark), could pass for Arab, or Israeli, or Greek. Or Mexican.

Fancy pointed at the second laptop, which was displaying an image from Google Earth, taken from the northbound lanes of the Cesar E Chavez Border Highway, running just behind the house in question. "Both. There's a six-foot wall, concrete or cinderblock, that runs along the edge of the sidewalk. But it looks like the city put it there to block noise. It's not the property line. See?" He leaned in and tapped the screen with his finger. "There's a chain link fence that runs along the property line. Of all the houses. But that's, what, two, three feet between the wall and the fence? Should be able to fit between that easy. Completely out of sight of anybody driving by. And that chain link is waist high. Once you're over, looks like you're about twenty feet from the back door."

"Easy to get over," Cherry said, "but you're exposed as fuck to anybody in those houses. We've got to cross behind one or two before we get to the target house."

"Two."

"We're going to get there, what, early afternoon? How long can we wait?" They all looked at Pike.

"We can't."

Boot nodded. That was the answer he'd been expecting. "I can walk right up and knock on the front door. I won't look out of place in that neighborhood. If they're already in the house, there's a good chance, a real good chance, that they'll assume I'm a contact or something. Dropping off, or picking up. Whatever." He looked at Pike. "I'm fluent, and dressed in civvies they wouldn't know I'm not a local." He had on a plaid work shirt over faded jeans and boots.

Pike shrugged his big shoulders. "This is me not saying no. But whether it works or not, we need to get all of us, six guys, into that house. ASAP. Which means not waiting until dark. The only way to do that is to walk right in the front door, or go over the back wall. A next-door neighbor might see us going in the back, but somebody is bound to see us going in the front door."

"Like a fucking chorus line," Tommy said. Tommy was short for Tomboy, or sometimes Tomcat. "And you have to assume there's at least one person on the block paid to watch, if they're not in the target house."

"The mission's the mission," Cherry said, shrugging.

Fancy looked at Pike. "And then once we get in, if the house is empty, we sit and wait? For how long?"

"For a day or a week, until something happens or we're called off. But they're supposed to show up around dinner time, late afternoon to evening. So if we can get in without causing a scene, we shouldn't have long to wait." He crossed his arms around his chest, displaying his huge forearms, and tilted his head down. It looked as if he was trying to nap, but they knew better. After a minute, he looked up. His eyes roamed around the expectant faces. They stopped on Fancy. "*¿Como 'sta tu Español?*" he asked the man. How's your Spanish?

"*No malo,*" Fancy responded without missing a beat. Not bad. "*Tengo un poco de acento.*" I have a little accent.

"*¿Como carajo no tienes acento?*" Boot demanded of Pike. "*Eres mas blanco que la leche.*" How the fuck do you not have an accent? You're whiter than milk.

Pike just smiled, and looked at the second-in-command of the team. Dog—named Doug by his parents—had done two combat tours in Special Forces, then started contracting for Blackwater and the companies that came after Blackwater's fall from grace. When the contracting started drying up he wasn't ready to retire, and had run into a number of spooks during his time in country, so he knew who to call. "What kind of vehicles will we have when we get there?" Pike asked the man. "Find out. Make, model, color, year."

Dog nodded, and pulled out a satellite phone. "Not that I give much of a shit for the formalities, but will there be someone from Border Patrol or whoever there when we touch down? FBI? Home game, they prefer to have someone from a domestic agency attached, like the CIA has to roll."

"This is officially a joint operation between CBP and us," Pike told him. "Ask the colonel, he'll tell you the same. The bigwigs are looped in."

Dog frowned. "Yeah, but aren't they supposed to have someone actually on the ground? With us? Participating? Or at least watching?"

Pike gave him a look, and then shared it with the rest of the team. "The rules don't seem to be the rules anymore."

"You can say that again. Okay, well, I had to ask." Dog walked to the other end of the aisle to make the call, grabbing a Gatorade out of the mini-fridge on the way.

The rest of them looked back at the laptops and other intelligence and site data spread atop the table. "What are you thinking?" Cherry asked Pike.

Pike shrugged. "Nowhere to hide on this one. So you work with what you've got. Magicians can't do magic, what they do is make you look over here," he stuck is right hand off to the side, "while they're doing something over here." And he wiggled his left elbow. They saw he'd stuck his left hand in his pants pocket, and while they watched he withdrew it, like he was pulling something out of his pocket, and turned his hand up so they could see him flipping them off.

Ghosts and Madmen

The car was a small sedan, a tired Hyundai whose paint had faded under the brutal Texas sun until it was somewhere between silver and gold. It pulled to the curb across the street from the target address. Boot climbed out the passenger seat and stretched, looking around, up and down Broadway. He was in no hurry as he walked across the street.

Behind the tint and the glare, Fancy, at the wheel, was little more than a silhouette. Anyone looking at him wouldn't have been able to see more than his black hair, which is why Pike had picked him.

Boot clomped across the street in his boots, feeling the heat through their soles. His thick navy-blue cotton work shirt was untucked, but the collar was buttoned, and the sleeves were rolled all the way down. He had a flat-brim Texas Rangers ball cap—with the reflective sticker still on the brim, of course—pulled down low on his forehead. He walked up the concrete path to the front door without hesitation and banged on the steel burglar door with the palm of his hand. "Yo! *¿Estas ahi?*" You in there? He waited about ten seconds, then banged again. "Hey! *¡Hola! ¡Pendejo! 'Stoy aqui.*" Asshole! I'm here. He tried to peer through the door, but it was too dark. He moved to the side and looked through the front window, which was also covered by bars. "So far I've got nothing," he said quietly into his mic. "No sound or movement."

"Roger that," Pike said into his ear. "We are inbound. Do your thing."

Fancy rolled his window down half way. "*¿¿Qué carajo?*" he shouted across the street. What the fuck? Boot threw his hands up theatrically in response. He stepped back onto the small square concrete slab that served as a porch and banged at the door again. Half a dozen good hits with the side of his fist, then he kicked the door as well. "*¡Despertar!*" he shouted. Wake up.

"*¿Deberíamos irnos y regresar?*" Fancy called out. Should we leave and come back?

Boot frowned and pulled a cell phone out of his pocket. He angrily punched at it with his thumbs, then held it up to his ear.

"*¿Estamos en el lugar correcto?*" Fancy called out. Are we in the right place? Boot waved at him to shut up, then started a loud conversation with his phone, talking to nobody in loud Spanish—hey, where are you, answer your damn phone, we're here, call me back.

In his ear, Pike said, "In position. Give us cover in three, two, one…"

On one, Boot went back to kicking the front door with his heel, cursing, making a lot of noise. A dozen good kicks, the clanging metal echoing up and down the street. He thought he heard another noise, a faint crunching thud, but it barely registered over the noise he was making.

"*Vamos, esto es una mierda,*" Fancy called out to him, still invisible inside the car. Let's go, this is bullshit.

Boot waved at him, and pulled his phone out again. He acted like he was texting someone while listening for noise inside the house. He'd could hear them moving around, then Dog's voice came over the comms. "House is clear."

"*Jodan estos tipos,*" Boot called out to Fancy, and stepped off the porch. Fuck these guys. Fancy rolled up the window. Boot walked back across the street, feigning irritation, and climbed into the passenger seat. He landed a little too hard, and winced. "Shit, right in the dick," he said, and as soon as his door was closed he reached down and adjusted the rig stuffed down the front of his pants—a Glock 17 in a Safariland IncogX holster, with a spare magazine caddy right beside it. The spare mag had a TTI extra capacity basepad, and between the two he had forty rounds of 9mm+P onboard to solve any problems. You could hide a big damn gun down the front of your pants with just a loose shirt for cover, but you had to remember to be careful sitting down. He hadn't.

Hand on the grip of the pistol, he looked at Fancy, then out the windshield. He spotted nothing moving on the street. "Anything?"

"No, but…" Fancy shrugged. There could be a lot of eyes out there. He drove away.

"We're clear. Didn't spot anything," Boot said into his mic.

"Roger that," Pike said quietly in their ears. "We're set up. Park it on Playa Lateral and ruck in."

"Copy," Boot said.

They parked the sterile sedan several streets over and threw backpacks over their shoulders before heading out on foot. Across to the highway, then along it for a hundred yards. The sound-blocking wall drew closer. It was broad daylight, with cars passing every few seconds, but there was nothing they could do about that. They just stepped inside the wall like they belonged there, behind two dirty, cluttered yards, literally hopped over the low fence, and jogged up to the back door of the target house. It was mostly closed.

Boot pushed open the door, and they quickly went inside, shutting the door behind them. There was a metal frame, but it had been bent in exactly the right place for the bolt to pop out. Just inside the door Boot saw the long crowbar that had done the deed. He and Fancy knelt down and ripped open their backpacks and began assembling their rifles.

If they had to do anything it was going to be up close

and personal, and noise would probably be an issue, so every man there had a SIG MCX Rattler in his backpack for his main weapon in addition to the pistols they all carried. The rifle had a comically-short 5.5-inch barrel, so with the skeletonized stock folded it was barely over a foot long. They unfolded the stocks, shoved loaded thirty-round magazines into their guns, chambered a round, and then grabbed the sound suppressor and ratcheted it into place using the QD mount. The Surefire SOCOM300 SPS was designed to be the quietest "silencer" on the market for subsonic 300 AAC Blackout ammunition. It wasn't short or light, but it was definitely quiet—even on full auto, the guns were nearly Hollywood quiet, and with the sound of passing traffic in the background it was likely even the neighbors wouldn't notice the sound of shooting.

There was hardly any furniture in the house, as if it was vacant and awaiting sale. The team had their Rattlers up and trained on an open door in the center of the small house. It led to a very small room, a closet or perhaps a pantry, barely four feet wide and six deep, with a few shelves high up on the walls which were bare. When Boot and Fancy had their guns hot Pike raised his hand to get everyone's attention and moved forward.

Pike stood in the open doorway of the pantry, squatted down, and very slowly pulled back the carpet covering the floor inside the small room. He spotted the drilled hole, big enough for a finger, before he spotted the seam in the plywood flooring. Carefully and quietly he laid the carpet back into place, and as he backed away from the room, moving toe-to-heel, he jabbed a knife hand at the open door. He retreated to the furthest corner of the house from the pantry and let the Rattler hang from its single-point sling, one hand loosely on the pistol grip.

"Command, this is Gargoyle," he murmured into his comm. "We are in position. No activity."

"Copy that, Gargoyle. Stand by." There was a very brief pause. "Gargoyle, new orders. You are to capture any wildlife you encounter. Capture, and do not allow any to rabbit back home. Please confirm."

Pike frowned. He didn't need to look around to know identical expressions were on the faces of the rest of his team, who'd heard the conversation. "Command, Gargoyle copies, but…we didn't bring any of the toys we should have for that kind of play date."

"Understood. Make it work."

Pike's frown deepened. "Command, any additional intelligence for us? Numbers, gear…timeline?"

"Negative, Gargoyle. Check back in top of every hour."

"Roger that, command. Gargoyle out." Pike was pleased to see his men weren't looking at him but rather at the pantry, guns held at the low ready, but he could tell they weren't happy. He stared at the closet, and thought. It was nearly in the exact center of the house. To the left was the kitchen in back, and a living room in front. It sat at the end of a short hallway which led to the bedrooms on the other side of the house—three of them, although one was tiny, not much bigger than the pantry/closet in question. If you stood just around the corner, in the kitchen, that was the only spot anywhere close to the pantry where you could position yourself and not be seen by someone in the small room. He switched over to the team channel. "Anyone got any zipties?" he quietly murmured. "I think I've got a couple in my pack."

"I've got two," Dog said. He was talking so quietly that even though he was standing just a dozen feet away Pike could only hear him through the earpiece. "Pretty sure. I'll check. No gags or hoods though, I didn't pack for date night."

"So what's the plan, boss?" Cherry asked.

Pike looked around. Six heavily armed men arranged in a semi-circle, in an enclosed space. They'd needed to blend in, so nobody was wearing armor, but hopefully that wouldn't make a difference. "Stay out of sight, somehow take 'em one at a time as quietly as possible, and when something goes wrong," because it always did, "try not to shoot each other."

"And if they rabbit back the way they came?" Boot asked.

Pike shrugged his big shoulders. "Command said do not allow any to escape."

The first indication they had that their efforts might have some payoff was a soft thump, and a vague noise that might have been someone talking very quietly. Then a faint creak, sharper, louder, and closer.

Cherry and Boot were in the first bedroom, the open doorway just a few feet down the hall from the pantry. The rest of them were stacked up in the kitchen. The creak was followed by a thump. "Okay, good," they heard a man say, with a thick accent. "Let me check out the windows, but we should be okay. You understand? *Coños. Pendejos. ¿No?*" More thumps, then a man stepped into view. He was wearing a dusty navy-blue work shirt over black pants and Nikes. He straightened up with a groan. Putting a hand on his lower back, he glanced at the brightly-lit windows running across the front of the living room, the south Texas glare cut by gauzy curtains and window bars. Then he turned leisurely turned toward the kitchen and took a step before his eyes even registered what he was seeing.

Dog, who was at the front of the stack, took half a step and hit the man with a textbook-perfect jab to his solar plexus. The man's eyes opened wide even as he woofed softly, then Dog had an arm around his neck, dragging him through the doorway into the kitchen.

Dog locked his arm down, tucking his face in tight to take the wild punches to the top of his head as the struggling man's face turned deep red, then purple, then he was out, unconscious. Fancy moved in, and they had his wrists ziptied behind his back barely thirty seconds after Dog had thrown the punch, with only a few vague scuffling noises for their efforts. Everyone in the kitchen froze, listening for more sounds from the pantry. Tommy was now in the lead, at the door. He edged out, leaning, his eye clearing the kitchen doorway, but there was nothing to see.

They waited. Fifteen more seconds passed. There was some very quiet discussion, barely audible, then they heard a man hiss, "Hey. Guy. What do you see?" There was a pause, then a brief, heated argument, the words impossible to make out. There was another pause, then they heard movement. Tommy pulled his head back behind the corner, and they waited.

As soon as he heard the man step out of the pantry Tommy came around the corner, Rattler up. He saw the man was unarmed, and had his back to him, so he reflexively dropped the Rattler on its sling and wrapped a big arm around the man's neck—and all hell broke loose.

The man shouted as he saw the arm, instantly spinning with an elbow up, and kicked backwards and sideways. There was a dull crunch, and Tommy was going down, his mouth opening to scream in pain at his broken knee. Before

Tommy even hit the floor, desperately trying to hold onto the man he'd grabbed, another man was scrambling out of the pantry and he charged at Tommy. Fancy tackled him, but the second man violently twisted in midair and threw Fancy into the front window, the sound of shattering glass loud. Two more men jumped out of the pantry. Boot and Cherry ran out of the adjacent bedroom, guns up and shouting, but the two most recent arrivals didn't back down, instead charging the guns. A wild burst from Cherry's Rattler ran up the wall and the sound of meaty impacts echoed down the hallway. Cherry went down, wrestling with his man. Boot slammed the end of the suppressor into his man's face, stunning him, and another brutal impact of the steel cylinder into the man's forehead sent him down, but as he fell he wrapped his arms around Boot's knees and brought Boot down as well. A fight commenced on the floor of the hallway, four men in nearly one pile, elbows and knees flailing.

Tommy was keening like a dog hit by a car, holding his knee, and Fancy was stunned after his impact with the window, which had sliced up his leg badly. The two men who'd done that damage climbed to their feet as Dog and Pike came out of the kitchen.

Without a sound one of the combatants leapt at them in a flying kick. Pike dodged to the side, and Dog took the foot in his chest with a yelp and went hurtling backward into the kitchen with his attacker. Pike closed with the other man as the fighting raged all around. Pike blocked a flurry of blows to his face and head with his forearm and the Rattler, and lifted his leading leg off the ground as the man tried to kick out his knee but telegraphed the move. The foot bounced off Pike's shin without doing any real damage. Pike blocked a throat punch with the Rattler as his own foot flicked out.

It hit the side of the man's knee hard enough to make him stumble, and one arm dropped. Pike slammed his fist into the side of the man's neck, then punched him in the face with the receiver of the Rattler hard enough to crack bone as he swept the man's legs out from under him. Loud crashes sounded from the kitchen as Dog fought his man. Then a figure was charging Pike from the hallway, both Cherry and Boot on the floor there in a messy tangle, trying to get to their feet.

Pike spun, far too quick and light on his feet than a man his size should have been, and flipped the running man over his hip with far more force than necessary. A surprised look on his face, the attacker flew through the air, rotating, and hit the far wall upside down hard enough to crack the drywall. Pike darted after him, and as the man slid down the wall and hit the floor on head and shoulder Pike kicked him in the face. As the man flopped to the floor Pike planted a knee on the back of his neck. He grabbed his Rattler and aimed it at the room, but the fighting was over. The four combatants were down, semi-conscious, but his team was hardly in better shape. Tommy was rocking, holding his broken knee. Fancy was bleeding heavily from cuts across his back and thighs from window glass. Dizzy, he crawled over to the man whose face Pike had cratered with his Rattler. Fancy flipped him onto his face and pulled out a ziptie. Dog staggered out of the kitchen, a long cut above one eye pouring blood. Cherry was using one arm to hug the other, his face scrunched up in pain from what felt like a hairline fracture. Boot looked dazed from a bad blow to the head. Everyone was panting and sweaty. And, frankly, bewildered at the ferocity of the resistance they'd encountered.

Pike stood, Rattler up, and glided to the pantry. The

carpet was thrown back, and the trapdoor was open, revealing a black rectangle in the floor. Pike aimed his gun down the hole. He saw a short wooden ladder, and dirt walls, but no movement. He jumped through the hole, dropping eight feet and landing in a crouch. His Rattler was up, the red dot of his optic glowing brightly.

He found himself at the end of a tunnel, four feet wide and almost six tall, running straight away from him. It was dimly lit by light bulbs running along one side, spaced every fifty feet along an insulated power cable. The tunnel angled gently downward, but seemed straight as an arrow, pointed perhaps a few degrees off from true west. Pike tried squinting, but that didn't help—the tunnel was so long, and so poorly lit, that he couldn't see to its end. But he estimated he could see at least a hundred yards, and he was alone. No one was close enough to have heard what had happened in the house. He climbed back up the ladder, closed the trap door, and lowered the carpet over the top of it.

"What the actual fuck just happened?" Boot gasped.

Pike walked over to the man he'd flipped into the wall and ziptied him. "These guys were good," he said appreciatively. He could feel he'd have some bruises in a day or so, but at the moment was flying on adrenaline.

"Command gave us charges to blow the tunnel, we still going to do that?" Boot asked, leaning against a wall. He'd noticed Pike had closed the trap door. Upstairs had seemingly known everything about the tunnel—how long it was, how it was constructed, that the other end of it came up in the back room of a gas station on the opposite side of the border, and roughly when this group was going to use it—but they hadn't know the guys coming through it were going to be serious motherfuckers? Talk about an intelligence failure.

"I'll check in," Pike said. "Wouldn't surprise me if they've changed our orders. Again."

"Command could have warned us to look out for ninjas," Dog said, exploring his head wound with tentative fingertips. He'd need stitches.

"No shit," Boot agreed.

"That wasn't karate, that was *wushu*," Pike said. He got a lot of confused looks. "*Gōngfu.* Kung fu," he finally said, giving it an American accent. "Literally translates to bitter work in Cantonese. Karate is Japanese," he said. He dragged the guy he'd just ziptied away from the wall and flipped him onto his back. He was in generic work clothes, a button-down cotton shirt over jeans. All of the men were dressed similarly. Pike pointed at his features. "These guys are Chinese."

"I thought they were Mexican," Boot said. He'd seen the compact builds, and the black hair.

"The guy in the kitchen is," Pike said. "The coyote. The rest of them are military-aged Chinese males. At least one of them has good English. I wouldn't be surprised if they all did."

"And they've had some serious hand-to-hand training," Dog said, pressing a palm to the cut on his head. Head wounds always bled heavily, and half his face was covered with blood. He looked at Pike. "You think command knew? I was thinking they would be cartel guys. Mules, or maybe higher-ups. This is…something else entirely." He looked over his shoulder, toward the freeway, and the wall, and the foreign country just beyond. "What the fuck is going on at the border?"

"Like I said, the rules don't seem to be the rules any more," Pike observed. He didn't look or sound happy about it.

Chapter Two

"This is a really bad idea," Dave said, staring out the windshield. "A really, really bad idea." He clenched his hands nervously. They didn't sweat, not any more, not after the third-degree burns and skin grafts, but if they did, they'd be dripping.

"Why?" Lori said, sitting behind the wheel. "You don't think it's a good boost for…public morale, or whatever the Sheriff said?"

"No. I mean, yes. I mean…I don't know." The crowd was big. Bigger than he'd been expecting, but of course it was going to be big. Not only was Sheriff "Shotgun John" Osterman there, and the mayor, but so was the freaking Governor of Arizona.

Lori was parked halfway across the lot, which was packed with cars, but through a freak of luck they could see past all the vehicles and the people to the front of the Cracker Barrel. The Sheriff was standing on the sidewalk there, accompanied by his fireplug of a wife on one side and the governor and mayor on the other. There was also another woman; Dave didn't know who she was, but he guessed either the manager of this restaurant, or perhaps a district manager. Maybe a Cracker Barrel corporate rep. And hundreds of onlookers. News media. Everyone but the local high-school marching band.

They'd been planning to close the restaurant. Demolish it. It has been the site of a horrific terrorist attack, as the news media described it. Technically it had just been a distraction, an assassination attempt by a cartel on a very high-profile Sheriff while another team went after a witness hidden at a nearby motel. Three cartel soldiers had died in the Cracker Barrel, one inside the gift shop. Four citizens had been injured in the gunfire, not including the sheriff, who'd been shot three times in the chest and abdomen with an AK-47. Now, six months later, he was still using a walker or cane to get around, but he'd left all of that in the car for the ceremony today. Which had all been his doing. He'd reached out—to someone at Cracker Barrel, Dave presumed, but he didn't really know—and talked to them. The city had taken a huge psychological hit—the incident at the Cracker Barrel, the bomb and random shootings outside the sheriff's department, another distraction, and the gunfight at the Pima Motel. People didn't feel safe, not nearly to the extent they used to. The bomb crater outside the sheriff's department had been filled, and the damage to the building repaired, but the Cracker Barrel had sat dark and closed, the yellow crime-scene tape fluttering in the wind.

Until the sheriff had talked to someone. Maybe a lot of someones. Probably using motivational phrases like "You can't let them win" and "Fear only works if you give in to it." He could be very persuasive.

They'd turned the grand re-opening into something

more. Dave was glad to see it...but it made him nervous, too. Uneasy. He'd practiced his draw for an hour at his house, trying to burn off some energy, and Lori had just let him be. He rubbed unconsciously at the throbbing spots on his hand—the inside of his middle finger knuckle, which pressed against the underside of the trigger guard, and the web of his hand, which pressed tightly against the rear of his pistol's frame. Which was now on his hip. And there was a spare magazine on the opposite side. It still didn't feel like enough.

Dave saw several vans with brightly-colored logos plastered across their sides, and at least three camera crews. And a shit-ton of deputies. There were a dozen of them, in uniform, helping to keep the crowd back, and also keep an eye on everyone. There was no reason for the cartel to go after the Sheriff again, but that didn't mean anything, and he was there with the mayor and the governor. None of the deputies were carrying rifles, but that was only because the Sheriff thought it would send the wrong message, one of fear. However, Dave did spot a lot of familiar faces in the crowd, cops in plainclothes. And he saw one unmarked Sprinter van parked right beside the building—he assumed it was full of officers in full tac gear, armed to the teeth, just in case.

It looked like the sheriff was speechifying for the cameras, smiling and gesturing while his wife stood by his elbow, looking up at him, smiling. Dave cracked his window. He could hear the talking but couldn't make out the words.

"He looks good," Lori said. Dave thought he looked pale and weak, but compared to how he'd looked in the hospital for weeks, in an induced coma with tubes everywhere, he was vastly improved. But the man looked old. His age had finally overwhelmed his force of personality.

After a short speech the sheriff and mayor and governor moved closer to the building, where a wide yellow ribbon was strung across the front door. Someone produced a giant pair of scissors, and all four of them, awkwardly holding onto the oversize handles, cut the ribbon. The cheer from the crowd was deafening, and rolled across the lot like a wave.

"God, everyone loves him," Lori said, a smile curling the corner of her mouth. The sheriff's wife, taking those short quick steps of hers, moved up to his side and firmly gripped his elbow. They followed the governor and the mayor inside the building, the sheriff walking like he was atop black ice. After a brief delay, the deputies doing their best to organize the crowd, the public followed after. The Cracker Barrel was open for business.

"You either love him or you hate him, there's no middle ground," Dave agreed. "I'm actually surprised there's no protestors."

"Today, here? Everyone knows he killed one of the cartel guys in the gift shop. Even though they never released that video." Unlike the video of the citizen gunfight with the cartel hit squad at the Pima Motel, just a mile down the road, retrieved from the security cameras and sold to the cable news networks. That had been seen. By everyone. Dave front and center, running a liberated AK, covered in blood.

"Yeah, well." He'd never thought the people who protested as especially discerning. More like kids who needed attention. And a spanking.

They sat and watched for a while as the crowd slowly filed into the building. Everyone was smiling and laughing. It was a party. A celebration.

"There's no way everyone's going to fit," Dave said. He

saw the reporters and camera people were not being allowed into the restaurant.

"Then they'll sit on the porch in the rockers and wait their turn," Lori said. "I heard there was memorabilia inside the gift shop."

He frowned. "What, shirts that say 'I survived the cartel attack'? I bet most of them weren't even fucking there."

She punched him in the arm, hard. "Don't be an asshole."

He glanced at her. One of the photos of the incident, taken by a diner with their phone, was of the sheriff on his back on the sidewalk outside the front door. His shirt was dark, so the blood soaking it from collarbones to belt wasn't so obvious, but it was bright red where it covered the hands of the woman putting pressure on his wounds. And was smeared all over the front of her white shirt. It had taken weeks before Lori had been recognized. "Sorry." He rubbed his arm. She knew how to hit.

"So?" she said. She tilted her head toward the restaurant and raised her eyebrows. He made a face.

She frowned at him. "You're a part of this." A big part. He'd killed two men inside the Cracker Barrel, including the one who'd shot the sheriff. Killed at least three more at the Pima Motel, driving there at double the speed limit, two motivated armed citizens in his wake, and they'd prevented the assassination of the young woman in witness protection through a by-God gunfight with the cartel hit squad in the motel parking lot. All caught on camera. "And everyone knows it. Plus, you were invited. So was I. If you're not going in, fine, you can wait in the car. I'll crack a window."

"Fuuuuck." He tilted his head back and closed his eyes.

"Besides, I want to meet the governor."

"I don't know if she wants to meet you. Knowing the

sheriff, how he feels about her, he neglected to mention he invited us. You."

"Me?" she said. "Hey, you're the one under FBI investigation. And he knows. And doesn't care. Well, maybe it's not that he doesn't care, but…"

"Oh God. This is a really bad idea," he said, but he opened his door.

He'd been sitting in the car too long, and his leg had stiffened up. He'd been shot in the hip, and the leg, and had been beaten nearly to death, although he was healing nicely. Could even jog a bit, although he wasn't going fast, or far. The scars across his face were still pink, but thin, and his beard covered most of them up. If you weren't looking, you might not notice them.

There was a party atmosphere outside the restaurant. They were hardly noticed as they walked up, a slender young man in his late twenties hand-in-hand with a pretty but unremarkable blonde. The news vans were parked at the curb nearby, and Dave forced himself to not look in their direction, as they had cameras set up on tripods. Several deputies were standing nearby, positioned to make it look like they were assigned to watchdog the media rather than posted outside the door on guard.

Inside, the gift shop-slash-lobby was packed with people, literally jammed in shoulder to shoulder, talking at the tops of their lungs. Dave traded a look with Lori and then pulled her along. Moving through the crowd was like wading through waist-deep mud. Finally, they reached the hostess stand. Just past it was the wide doorway into the dining room, and there was a deputy posted there, hands on his belt.

"Hi there," Jack said.

The hostess had vaguely been aware of his approach.

"Oh, honey," she said apologetically, shaking her head. "I can put you on the list, but it's going to be two hours at least."

"Supposed to be a couple of seats for us at the sheriff's table," Jack said as quietly as he could.

The hostess, a middle-aged woman, blinked at him and her eyes squinted, then widened. Her mouth worked a couple times, but no sound came out.

"He's in the back, Cujo, he's waiting for you," the deputy said to him. "And you're damn lucky you didn't stand him up. She would have been quite offended."

"She?" Lori said.

"His boss," the deputy said wryly. He didn't mean the mayor, or the governor.

Smiling, Jack nodded at the man, who looked vaguely familiar, and headed into the dining room. After the densely packed gift shop the dining room seemed airy, even though every chair at every table was filled. Dave spotted the Sheriff immediately—the last time they'd been in the Cracker Barrel, he and Lori had been seated with the sheriff just inside the door. This time, he'd taken command of a large round table against the back wall of the restaurant. Like a king occupying his throne. It was meant to send a message, him eating brunch at the same place where he was shot showed that he was unafraid.

Dave and Lori wove between the tables filled with chatting diners, the noise level quite loud. It was mostly families and large groups he saw, some with kids. Quite a few people had their cameras out, discreetly (or not so much) taking photos and videos of the sheriff and mayor and governor.

As he and Lori drew near the sheriff spotted them, and with some difficulty rose to his feet. His wife did the same, and hurried around the table to them, as the mayor and governor turned to see who had arrived. There were two empty chairs at the table. "You look good, it was so nice of you to come," Lillian Osterman said warmly. She was nearly a full head shorter than Lori, who wasn't tall, and Lori bent down so the woman could give her a peck on the cheek. Lillian reached out and warmly squeezed Dave's arm. He was vaguely aware that the noise level inside the restaurant dropped to zero, then resumed in a frenzy of whispering, as everyone there recognized him. Up close, Dave thought Osterman looked like a shrunken, pale, old version of his former robust self...but then again he was in his seventies, and recuperating from being shot three times with an AK-47 at point blank range. Most men who'd suffered that would likely have died.

Osterman nodded his head. "Governor, mayor, this is Jack and Lori. The last time I was here I was dining with them, and this young lady ended up with my blood on her up to her elbows trying to save my life, beside a cardiovascular surgeon recently retired out of Boston. I consider her family, and would be offended if you don't as well." The corner of his mouth twitched as he looked at Dave. "And Jack, well, he was here too."

Both the governor and the mayor shot the sheriff disbelieving looks. Osterman had told them he was expecting two more, but hadn't said who. But everyone in the state knew who Pima Jack was. He'd killed two cartel soldiers at the Cracker Barrel, not twenty feet from where they were sitting. Bitten the nose and lips off a third man who been beating him in the face with an AK-47 inside the gift shop. Raced over to the Pima in the sheriff's car and killed more at the motel in a massive gunfight. And became a huge, unequivocal local hero, for a few months—then men from Detroit, with ties to organized crime, showed up and reportedly tried to abduct him, and he killed them too. And the mobster that they worked for was murdered a day later in Vegas. Now 'Pima Jack' was under investigation by the FBI, although that wasn't common knowledge. The Arizona electorate still considered him a hero, but...

The mayor was blinking erratically, a hesitant smile flashing on and off his face. The governor couldn't decide to smile for the onlookers, or frown. She turned her face toward Osterman, who looked absolutely delighted at her discomfiture. "I've heard of ambush journalism," she said. "Is this an ambush brunch?"

"This is a celebration, of life and its many wonders and endless surprises," Osterman said. He sat down with some difficulty, grabbed a plate, and held it out to her with a look of childlike innocence on his face. "Biscuit?"

Chapter Three

Gogolak much preferred physical files. Hard copies in his hand. Pages he could turn. With hardcopies it was so much easier to flip back and forth, find that one quote or interview note or the one specific crime scene photo. Spread them around a large table, or an entire room. But physical files just weren't as convenient, especially when they grew from bulging folders to filling boxes. So, for the trip east, he had everything on his Bureau laptop. Much easier to deal with on the road, especially when flying.

He had a bit of room to spread out, make notes—one seat back table for his laptop, another for a pad of paper—as they'd bumped him into first class. That happened a lot; as a gun-carrying federal agent he was required to carry his gun onboard, to serve as an ersatz air marshal. Not that they really had those anymore. Nobody in the federal government seemed to care about terrorism anymore, unless it was domestic terrorism, and those guys never bombed or hijacked airplanes. They never did much of anything, not that you'd know that from the huge amount of money and manhours the FBI was throwing at them.

For this trip he didn't just have folders or boxes worth of material he could review, there was a literal warehouse worth of stuff, dating back thirty years. More. And he'd read it all, at one time or another. But for this trip he concentrated on the material generated in the last five years and pertinent to his investigation, which was comparatively narrow in focus.

He was only supposed to be in Detroit for twenty-four hours, but he remembered a twelve-hour trip to Cleveland early in his career that had turned into a five-day marathon of surveillance, interviews, and arrests, so he'd checked a bag. He grabbed it off the luggage carousel, after waiting what felt like an hour for them to unload the plane, then jumped into the front passenger seat of the waiting Bureau car. The yawning agent behind the wheel looked like a teenager to Gogolak, but he was getting close to mandatory retirement age.

The young man drove them to the FBI headquarters in downtown Detroit, where Gogolak checked in with the ASAC, then grabbed a bland G-car and drove northwest for his appointment. He arrived in the area almost an hour early, and drove around, checking the place out. Spaced every mile north or south, east or west, was a main road, ruler-straight and usually two lanes in each direction, with a center left turn lane, but between them was nothing but narrow, twisty turny residential streets, green with spacious lawns and looked over by mature trees. There were a number of lakes in the township, and all the streets seemed to curve this way and that, like the lakes were exerting gravitational pull. The houses visible from the street were larger than average, and the ones set further back on big lots, mostly hidden from view, appeared to be bigger still. Most of the neighborhoods didn't have sidewalks—the well-manicured lawns stretched down to the streets, where no one parked. Very few vehicles were visible in the driveways, as every house had an attached two- or three-car garage. While he didn't see as many Mercedes or BMWs or Audis as he was expecting, most of the cars he did see were new.

He had an address memorized, and his phone got him there without incident. It seemed one of the nicer areas, with every house set on a one- or two-acre lot. The house was mostly out of sight behind a hedge. Gogolak turned in his seat and looked around. Most of the neighboring houses were hidden from view but for a sliver of roof or brick or siding visible above or between manicured hedges and mature trees. If anyone came down their driveway he and his G-car would be plainly visible, sitting on the street, but apart from that he was as hidden in plain sight as you could be in upper-middle-class suburbia. The streetlights looked like new LED models, but were spaced quite a distance apart, and he guessed that at night the street would be dark.

He left the scene and arrived at his ultimate destination twenty minutes early, sat in his car for fifteen minutes staring at his laptop, reviewing his notes, then stuffed the laptop and what physical files he had into his leather briefcase and headed in.

There was one uniformed officer at the elevated front desk, sitting relaxed behind armored glass. He took note of Gogolak, but one middle-aged white male in a suit didn't ping anything on his threat radar. He barely paid attention when Gogolak reached inside his suitcoat.

Gogolak stopped before the desk, and flipped open his badge wallet. "FBI Special Agent Gogolak," he announced. He tried a smile. It felt awkward on his face. He'd never been good at smiling. They rarely felt natural, and from people's reactions, they didn't look natural either. "I've got an appointment with Detective Dixon."

The officer nodded, and reached for a phone. "Hold on a minute."

West Bloomfield Township Police Department Detective William "Billy" Dixon commandeered a small conference room for their meeting. While Gogolak pulled out his laptop and folders Dixon brought two cups of coffee, then carried in his own files. There wasn't a box of them, but there were a good eight inches of folders packed with incident reports, surveillance logs, crime scene photos, witness statements....

Dixon saw the FBI agent eyeing the stack. "I'd like to close this case before I retire," he said. "I'm coming up on my twenty." Dixon was short, but looked like he might lift weights. Unlike Gogolak, whose thin hair was balding, and whose pale blue eyes were tucked behind glasses, Dixon had a full head of thick brown hair and Hollywood looks.

Gogolak asked, "And then to greener pastures?"

Dixon shrugged. "I've got an ex-wife, one kid in college, and one about to be. A corporate security gig with that private sector paycheck, on top of my pension, would make me breathe a little easier."

Gogolak nodded. His laced his fingers together on the table in front of him. "Well, I've reviewed everything you've sent us. Read and re-read it. Since I was in the area I did a drive-by of the scene of the original hit-and-run. Do you have anything new that we're not aware of?"

The veteran West Bloomfield Township detective breathed deep, through his nose, and worked his neck. Talking, even thinking about David Anderson made him tense. "Okay, I agreed to this meeting with the understanding that you'd be sharing. Yes, you have every report this department has generated investigating the murder of Paolo Bufonte. I like Anderson for it. He's my only hard suspect. I've turned up circumstantial evidence that shows he might have had Big Paulie under surveillance prior to the man getting run over—twice—in front of his house, but that's it. He's got motive—Paulie killed his parents in a DUI, and then got off on a technicality—and he doesn't have an alibi. He's never cooperated with us and lawyered up immediately, which is somewhat suspicious. Everything about this kid is suspicious. The FBI—supposedly, according to all the news reports—working for the father, Pietro Bufonte, the head of organized crime in Detroit, twice tried to have him killed, the second time using Detroit SWAT cops out on bail, that they'd just arrested—"

"Not the FBI," Gogolak interrupted him, his voice soft. "An errant, compromised special agent."

Dixon had been trying to get confirmation, and jumped on that. "So you're confirming that? Because that's never been officially confirmed. And it never sat right with me."

"Really, why is that?"

Dixon shook his head. He knew all the interrogation techniques, and he wouldn't be manipulated. Distracted. "Are you confirming that? That your special agent was working for Bufonte?"

Gogolak paused, then shook his head. "No. That recording, it's real, we've authenticated it, and it's incontrovertible proof FBI Special Agent Peter Hartman enlisted Paul Wilson of the Detroit Police Department, out on bail for his arrest related to a string of strip club robberies, to murder David Anderson. In exchange for making certain evidence disappear. But there's no proof that it was for Bufonte. For whatever reason. That Detroit organized crime was involved at all. That's just been the assumption. But let's be honest. No other explanation seems plausible, you have to admit. Twenty-five year old kid—who'd applied to the FBI, if you hadn't heard—with no criminal record, no known criminal associates, working for an armored car company, and a private investigator. Why would anyone want him dead? Why would a senior FBI agent risk his entire career to arrange his murder? Mob involvement is the only thing that makes sense, because Bufonte blamed him for his son's death." He peered at Dixon. "Do you know something that I don't?"

Dixon paused and thought. He looked at the wall behind Gogolak, then said, "I know someone. Not quite a confidential informant, but he knows a few things. Told them to me from time to time. And he assured me that Bufonte had nothing to do with those attempts on Anderson's life."

A dubious look settled across Gogolak's face. "Well, then, it seems clear that this source is lying to you. After what happened in Arizona? All four of those men were associates, employees of Pietro Bufonte. And they didn't show up at Anderson's house at dawn, in a car filled with firearms and duct tape, for a book club meeting."

Dixon shook his head almost violently. "At that point Anderson had been in the wind for, what, a year? And that whole time, the entire world thought Bufonte had already tried to have him killed. Twice. And Bufonte was dying of cancer, or so I heard. So what did he have to lose?" Dixon frowned, and leaned back. "So what the fuck happened in Vegas? That's mostly why I agreed to this meeting. Quid pro quo. Four men dead, including Pietro Bufonte, in his mansion in Vegas. Murdered, it was announced shortly thereafter. Normally, something like that, you'd assume it was rivals. An inter-family dispute, or whatever you would call it on the organized crime side. But it happened less than twenty-four hours after his four men show up at Anderson's house. And Anderson burned them down before half of them got out of the car or got a shot off. That fucking kid, every year it seems like he gets into a gunfight and walks away. He's killed I don't know how many people, and he's never even been *charged*. He's been living under a fake name in Arizona since he left Detroit. Isn't that illegal?"

The FBI agent paused, considering. "Not when the new identity was issued to you by law enforcement, as part of an ersatz witness protection program."

That was news to Billy Dixon. He blinked in surprise. "Osterman?" The Arizona sheriff had been all over the news reports from down there. He'd been the one to bring the recording of FBI Detroit office Assistant Special Agent-in-Charge Peter Hartman soliciting murder to the media. How he'd gotten it…no one seemed to know. After being suspended, pending an investigation, Hartman was found in his home at the end of a rope, so no one could ask him any questions. Pretty much everyone involved in these incidents, other than Anderson, was dead, and Anderson wasn't talking. Gogolak nodded. "Well…shit." The news made him think. He peered at the FBI agent. "What does the FBI have to say about that?"

Gogolak shrugged. "Officially we don't have a position on it."

"Okay. And Vegas?"

"Four dead. Two shot, two bludgeoned to death with a hammer, and then the house was torched, using alcohol as an accelerant. Pietro Bufonte was shot in the face, sitting behind his desk. The fire was put out before it completely destroyed the house—turns out marble doesn't burn so well, and he loved his white marble—but no useful physical evidence was recovered. The gun used was found at the scene. Registered to one of the dead men. Not believed to be a perpetrator, he was a known associate of Bufonte. The hammer used was left at the scene as well. In someone's head, actually. No fingerprints on the pistol or hammer."

"A hammer? Like a regular hammer? Is that weird? It seems...weird."

Gogolak shrugged. "Weapon of opportunity, maybe? Nearly as many people killed by blunt force objects every year as gunshots. You grab what's at hand."

"And do you like Anderson for it? I mean, Vegas is only a few hours from where he was in Arizona."

Gogolak made a noncommittal face and shrugged. "He is on the suspect list, but...he's not former military. He's never even been a cop."

"Maybe not, but do you know how many people he's killed? I know you know, if you're looking into him."

Gogolak frowned as he thought, doing the math. "Sixteen. Confirmed." Which didn't include the half-dozen bodies found around Anderson's Arizona cabin. The details of what exactly had happened there were still murky. But most of the men who'd died there had extensive military records, with documented time in combat.

Dixon gave him a pointed look. "I know guys who did tours in Iraq who don't have that many confirmeds. You try to talk to him? Let me guess, he's lawyered up, and isn't talking."

"Correct." In fact, traffic cameras had picked up Anderson's Jeep entering the city earlier that evening, but they had absolutely no direct evidence tying him to the murders. Couldn't place him within miles of the house. They'd attempted to interview him, but he'd refused to cooperate in the investigation, as he assumed—and rightly so—that he was a suspect. His high-profile defense lawyer —on loan from Osterman, it seemed—had stated that Anderson, distraught over the attempt on his life earlier that day, had driven around for hours in an attempt to clear his head, including through the city of Las Vegas, to look at the lights of the Strip, but until the FBI had enough evidence to charge his client, that was all they were going to get out of Anderson. He would not be sitting down for any interviews.

Anderson—clearly—was a person of interest for the murders, but many of the higher-ups in the Bureau simply couldn't believe he had done the deed. One guy, who was still suffering from wounds received in a terrorist attack, had somehow gone all ninja and taken out four guys by himself? Quietly enough that the neighbors hadn't even been sure they'd heard any shots, before the smoke started billowing out the windows of the house, and a passing dogwalker had called 911. The FBI brass thought it was much more likely Bufonte had been taken out by one of his rivals, or by the organization itself because they considered him a liability. Especially since Bufonte had died sitting at his desk, on the second floor of his house, like he was talking to someone he knew. Gogolak had no opinion, and would follow the evidence, wherever it led.

In truth, Bufonte's death cleared up a big mess, a big headache for the FBI. Whether it was true or not, the man was thought to have co-opted a senior FBI agent. Been involved in arranging a murder through the FBI, or so the story went. With both Hartman and Bufonte now dead, that story should now fade away.

"How many times have you met with him?" Gogolak asked the detective.

"Anderson?"

Gogolak shook his head. "Bufonte."

Dixon hadn't been expecting the question. He frowned as he thought, eyes moving back and forth. "Total? I have no idea. His son was killed in the only unsolved homicide we've got in this town. And I mean the *only* one, we're not exactly a hotbed of crime. If you drove around, you saw. Generally, the most serious crime we've got here is stolen cars, and once or twice a year somebody—usually from Pontiac—robbing one of the gas stations on Maple or Middlebelt; we're gated communities and golf courses. My investigation's been open the whole time, and I'd go back to it from time to time, but rarely got anywhere with it. And, you know, Bufonte's not a regular guy. He or his people would check in for updates. I know I met with him personally at least two or three times. Here, I think. I believe I talked to him more on the phone. Him and his people."

Gogolak raised his eyebrows and cocked his head. Dixon nodded. "I know what you're thinking, but I didn't give them any more information than I would give the average person. Not on an active, or at least open, investigation. But, I mean, the last year or so, I didn't need to tell him anything, did I? His face and name were all over the news, how he'd used the FBI to arrange the murder of Anderson. He was tried and convicted in the court of public opinion. Did the FBI ever talk to Bufonte about that?"

Gogolak nodded. "He denied it. He denied everything, including even knowing who Hartman was. But, generally, these guys deny everything as a reflex when talking to us."

"Okay," Dixon said forcefully. "That happened, the FBI as murder-for-hire by the mob was splashed all over the news. I don't need to tell you. So what did you do? The FBI. Don't tell me you didn't do anything. I know you had to have wiretaps all over his phones already, and once all that shit with Hartman happened I imagine you had to be up on all of Bufonte's electronics, his houses, his cars. Well, maybe not everything, if you'd had a bug in his Vegas house you'd have heard everything and would have already made an arrest, but what about that? You ever hear him admit to hiring Hartman?"

"Pietro Bufonte has been in organized crime his entire life, since he was a teenager. He was well aware he was under surveillance, electronic and otherwise, and frequently employed countermeasures."

"That's not an answer."

"I can't comment on an ongoing investigation."

Dixon gave him a dirty look.

"Can I speak with your source?" Gogolak asked.

"My source?"

"The man who told you Bufonte had nothing to do with FBI Assistant Special-Agent-in-Charge Hartman arranging the murder of David Anderson. Your source, who's not a CI, but who knows things."

"No." Dixon shook his head. "Because he was Tony Gianucci."

Gogolak blinked twice, which was all the time it took him to place the name. "Anthony Gianucci. One of the three men found dead in the Las Vegas home of Pietro Bufonte, along with Bufonte himself."

Dixon nodded. "You got it. He and I...well, we didn't become friends, but he was the guy Bufonte had call me for updates on the investigation, and he liked me, so I cultivated him as a source. Occasionally he'd tell me things. Like how Bufonte didn't have fuck-all to do with Hartman."

"Unless he was lying. Everyone lies to cops."

Dixon nodded. "That they do. But good cops learn how to spot liars."

Gogolak stared at him through his glasses, his pale blue eyes steady. He made a noncommittal grunt.

"I'm surprised there's just one of you," Dixon said, after a beat.

Gogolak sighed. "Victims of our own success. I'm probably the lead guy in the Bureau who specializes in American, domestic, organized crime. In the sixties, seventies, and eighties, I'd be a rock star, meeting with the Director, my arrests splashed all over the front of the New York Times. But we're victims of our own success. Between wiretaps and RICO and forcing cooperation using immunity, we crushed the five families. Gotti was the last real big fish, and he died twenty years ago. In custody. You go onto the FBI website, look at the page on our organized crime task force, we don't even talk about the mafia in this country, it's all about transnational organized crime. Smuggling and human trafficking, cybercrime, money laundering for terrorists. The only mention of the mafia is in Italy. I'm not saying organized crime in this country doesn't exist, or isn't still a problem, but after Nine-Eleven the Bureau forgot about it to jump on the anti-terrorism action, and never really came back to it."

"So...with Bufonte dead, and Anderson not cooperating, and it sounds like you've got nothing on him, what are you doing? Trying to clear the FBI's name in all this? Prove you weren't involved?"

Gogolak tried another smile. "Something like that."

Chapter Four

"Well, that was as unsatisfying as prison sex without the reach-around," Dog pronounced with a frown, as they watched their visitors file out of the room. That got a lot of wide eyes in response, and Fancy burst out laughing.

"That's an oddly specific and disturbing comparison," Cherry said. He was working his arm again. The humerus hadn't been broken in the fight, as he'd initially thought, but it sure hurt—ached—as much as a hairline fracture. The bruise went down to the bone. He'd be favoring it for a week, at least. "Anything we should know about?"

Dog smiled, the line of stitches above his eyebrow stretching. "Ask me no questions, I'll tell you no lies."

"That was the least amount of reporting I've ever done for an after-action report," Pike agreed. The fact that they'd wanted nothing in writing wasn't so unusual, for a classified mission inside the U.S. border, but the—what was a good way to describe it?—forced disinterest? the debriefers out of the DIA's Directorate for Analysis had shown toward the ethnicity/nationality of the four men who'd used the cartel tunnel to cross the border was curious. Unusual. Perhaps, if he looked at it from a personal viewpoint…concerning.

Fancy leaned back, and stretched his legs out. He had stitches and sutures across the back of both legs from the window glass, and would likely be out of rotation for a month. "How's Tommy?" he asked Pike.

Pike frowned and shook his head. "Lateral break, or whatever the medical term is, of his left knee. Right now, the best they're hoping for is that everything will heal right and he'll be able to walk normally, without a limp, after six months to a year of physical therapy. Chances are he's done."

"Fuck," Boot swore. He glared at the team leader. "Have any of these assholes, Higgins, anyone, told you who the fuck these guys were?"

Pike spread his hands. "You know everything I do."

"Fucking kung fu shaolin monks," Cherry said.

"More likely Chinese special forces," Pike said. "Pretty sure I heard them speaking Mandarin down in the tunnel. Twenties, in shape, highly trained…hopefully whoever has them is asking them a lot of pointed questions."

"Mandarin?" Fancy said.

"There are two main Chinese dialects, Cantonese and Mandarin," Pike told him. "Mandarin is far more common, it's the official language of mainland China. The coyote's more likely to talk, if they haven't already tossed him back, but I doubt he knows anything."

"You speak Chinese?" Dog asked him.

Pike gestured at his blonde hair and skin which, even though he was as tan as he ever got, was still pale. "Yes, for all the times I went undercover as an Asian hooker in massage parlors." Boot coughed out a laugh. But they noticed that his answer wasn't really an answer.

"Anyone else get the impression that either they weren't expecting these guys to be Chinese, or they didn't care that they were?"

"Those guys," Pike said, nodding his square-jawed head at the closed door, "likely don't know anything more than the questions they've been told to ask."

"But you've been doing this a long time, right? Don't you get the feeling there's shit going on here?"

Pike frowned and made a noncommittal sound. "This isn't the first time I've heard of this."

"What?"

"Chinese guys—military-aged males—at the border. Chinese, Arabs, guys from north Africa. You name it, any country that is hostile to us. Border patrol is arresting guys on the watch list every month, some of them with guns or even fucking IEDs, and for every one on the watch list there have got to be ten who should be, but aren't. And what are we doing? At most we're just sending them back. I don't even think we're interrogating them. These guys might be different, but…" He shrugged. "Have you watched the news at all, the past few years?" Pike asked him. "What we're seeing is the fall of the republic, in real time. I mean, it's job security, but…"

"Yeah? I never took you as political," Dog said.

"I'm just a fucking observer," Pike said with a frown. "With a front row seat at the show."

"What was that you used?" Cherry asked Pike. "Kung fu?"

"What?"

"Those guys were fucking us up, and you took out two of them without breaking a sweat."

Pike shrugged his big shoulders. "We've all been trained in hand-to-hand."

"Yeah, but when the fuck have any of us ever used it?" Dog said. "I'm carrying two guns every mission. And a knife. And I've never used the knife."

Pike just shrugged again. Cherry peered at him. He'd never worked with Pike before, but he'd heard of him. Everyone had heard of him. Heard the stories. And the man had taken out two of the tangos like it had been easy, while the other two were fucking up the entire rest of the team. "It true, how you got your work name?"

"What?"

"Rumor is you cut off some guy's head in the sandbox in front of the locals, threatened to stick it on a pike."

Pike looked around the room. He had everyone's attention. Saw a lot of speculative looks. Apparently Fancy wasn't the only person to have heard that story. "That sounds an awful lot like a war crime," he said pleasantly. "I did something like that, you'd think I'd have been court-martialed. Locked up."

That got him a number of loud derisive snorts. Every single man there had done things in combat that could be considered war crimes. You didn't win wars by obeying stupid rules the bad guys didn't follow. The only real crime in war was losing. The true warriors understood that. And they noticed—again—that he didn't deny it.

"The fuck's a pike?" Fancy asked.

"A spear," Cherry told him.

"What about the other story?" Fancy asked.

"Which one's that?" Pike said.

"That you've got a radio station in your head."

Cherry frowned and snorted. "What?"

"K-PIKE?" Boot said, laughing.

"No, that one's true," Dog said, chiming in.

Cherry looked back and forth between them. "What," he said to Pike, "like you pick up a radio station on your fillings?"

Pike sighed. "No." He gave Dog a dirty look for confirming the story, but the man just shrugged. Everyone else was looking at him. "When I was younger, just starting out, I was on a mission that…well, I was going to say didn't go so well, but we completed the mission. And killed a lot of assholes. But we got fucked up pretty bad, me worst of all. I died. Heart stopped. Coded out on the table twice. Three times, if you count them doing CPR on me in the middle of the street. I'm not sure how long I was actually dead, but apparently it was a not-insubstantial amount of time." He looked at them. "You know how you get a song stuck in your head?"

"Sure," Fancy said.

"It's kind of like that. I thought maybe it was brain damage from having my heart stopped. No blood flow, no oxygen to the brain, brain cells die. But I've had a few CT scans and MRIs, and they don't show anything. Whatever it is, it's not brain damage. Don't have any other physical or mental problems. And I'm not the only guy that's ever had this, officially the medical term is musical ear syndrome, but usually it happens to people who have hearing loss. My hearing's just fine."

"So you hear a song playing in your head?"

Pike nodded. "As clear as if I was listening to the radio."

Cherry frowned. "The same song? That would drive me nuts. What do they call that, an earworm?"

"No, thank God, that would drive me insane too," Pike

admitted. "No, I hear all sorts of music. Anything I've ever heard. And it's..." He cocked his head. He didn't like talking about himself. Especially his secrets. But the story of this had gotten out. "It's like my subconscious is picking the soundtrack. I can't control it directly, pick what I'm hearing, but I can shut it down. Not shut it off, but turn the volume down, to just about zero."

"Lady Gaga? Taylor Swift?"

"Ah, fuck you."

"No, I'm serious. Curious. What kind of music?"

Pike shrugged. "A lot of classic rock. It depends. Mostly mellow stuff. I'm a mellow guy."

Dog snorted, eyeing the man. Cherry wasn't wrong about his hand-to-hand skills, Pike had gone through those two Chinese SF operators and made it look like he wasn't even trying hard.

Fancy looked at him. "Are you hearing it now?"

Pike shook his head. "No, I keep it shut down almost all the time. Locked down so there's only a tiny murmur."

"And how long have you had this shit going on?" Dog asked him.

"Twenty years," Pike admitted.

"Damn."

"What's the DJ spinning right now?" Fancy asked.

Pike sighed, and concentrated. "Enya. *Orinoco Flow*."

Fancy made a face. "The fuck is that?"

Cherry knew. "I was you, I wouldn't admit that shit. You should have lied. AC/DC, *Thunderstruck*. Metallica. Pink Floyd, maybe."

Pike shook his head. "I told you, I'm sweet and gentle and kind. A harmless lovable little fuzzball. DJ Pike tries to keep me that way. I start hearing rock and roll in my head, guitar solos, shit's popping off. *Thunderstruck*, *Fade to Black*,

Kashmir? Anything by Ted Nugent? We're in a fucking gunfight if that's in my head."

"Did you see God?" Boot asked.

"What?"

"Well, you died. Did you see God?" He was half-joking, half-serious.

Pike blinked twice, then shook his head. "Just the President." They laughed at the joke. "That would have been something, though." He frowned at the closed door again, then sighed. They'd probably never get any answers. He looked at the remaining members of team Gargoyle. "We've all got a week off. Report back next Tuesday. You should be good to go by then," he told Cherry. "Fancy, don't tear those goddamn stitches. You'll be on light duty when you get back, until you heal up."

"You going to do your usual disappearing act?" Dog asked him.

"What?"

"Any time we get more than four days off and don't have to be on call, you go dark. Phone's shut off, no answer at your door, even Higgins doesn't know where the fuck you are. And I get the impression he's tried to find you."

Pike just shrugged. "I like my privacy. And we're not married, the company doesn't need to know what I do on my time off. As long as I pass my semi-annual polygraph they can fuck right off."

"Why do I get the impression you could tell them you're vacationing on the moon with your pet dinosaur and the polygraph would tell them every word out of your mouth was the truth?" Dog said. Pike didn't say anything.

"Listening to K-P-I-K-E, where we've got all the hits!" Fancy crowed. "Traffic and weather at the top of every hour!"

"He's going back to the monastery, to practice his kung fu," Cherry said. "Everyone knows monks aren't allowed cell phones."

Pike smiled enigmatically at him, and the rest of them, and said, "*Méiyǒu sháozi.*"

"Yeah, and kung pow chicken to you, too."

Chapter Five

Osterman sat stiffly upright in the chair, face mostly devoid of expression, neutral, but his eyes darted around the room. Sam Wheaton sat beside him, both men in their uniforms. Wheaton had been with him for decades, and even though the four Division Commanders technically outranked Captain Wheaton, everyone in the department knew Sam Wheaton was the number two man. He was taller than Osterman, slender, with a big bushy graying moustache that drooped over his mouth and probably would not have been tolerated for a second by Osterman if it didn't make Wheaton look the spitting image of an old west cowboy, and sometimes a bit of theater was called for. Especially down near the border.

The room they were sitting in was a bland conference room in a government building, but it was situated in El Paso, and El Paso was as central to the "border crisis" as Berlin had been to the Cold War. Osterman and Wheaton were in the third row, center, and had arrived early.

The room slowly filled up. Occasionally newcomers

would spot Osterman and nod. Or deliberately look away and ignore him. A few came over and shook his hand, said nice things. Wheaton left, and returned a few minutes later with steaming cups of coffee from one of the urns set up on the side of the room. There were pastries as well, but Wheaton left those untouched. He eyed Osterman as he handed over the cup and sat down. "How are you doing?" he asked quietly, blowing at his coffee and taking a sip.

The corner of Osterman's mouth dipped slightly. "I was twenty years old the last time I was shot. The body tends to forget pain; I have no doubt it is a defense mechanism, dreamed up by the Lord, so young men can continue to do stupid things. And young women shove aside the memory of the pain of childbirth to do it all over again, to bring life into the world. But if I don't remember how much it hurt the first time, I do know for a fact that I was quicker to heal. It has been months, and I still can't sit in an airplane seat for a few hours, or this plastic monstrosity of a chair, without something hurting." They'd flown down the night before, and would be flying back to Prescott later that afternoon.

"Lesser men than you have succumbed to far less grievous wounds," Wheaton observed.

Osterman turned his head, an eyebrow going up. "Listen to you, sweet-talking me. You must be worried."

"I know what you're like when you're cranky," Wheaton said. He nodded at the chairs around them, filling up. "I'm worried about *them*. Especially considering why we're here. This topic always gets you…excited."

Osterman's thin smile darkened. "Yes. Well." He glanced around. With just two minutes before the scheduled start of the monthly briefing, the room was nearly full, and he recognized over half the people in the room, and could guess at the origins of most of the others. He saw representatives from the FBI, DEA, BATFE, and Phoenix, El Paso, Tucson, and Albuquerque police departments, in addition to their hosts.

At five minutes after the hour one of the men at the front of the room moved to the podium. He flicked the microphone, to make sure it was on, then double-checked that the laptop was working, and clicked forward and back through a couple slides of his Power Point presentation. He introduced himself, and the rest of the men and women up on the low stage with him, then launched into his presentation, a monthly status update. As he spoke, the words washed over Osterman. He heard them, they registered, but he wasn't listening, not exactly. The hum in his head grew constant, and louder. Like bees. Angry bees. Sam kept glancing over, reading the look on his friend's face. Finally, after nearly half an hour, the speaker finished the presentation, and asked if anyone had any questions.

Two dozen hands went up, including Osterman's. Then the whispering started, and people looked around. Nodded and pointed at the sheriff. And, gradually, all their hands went down, until only his remained. He'd earned the right.

The man behind the podium was Theodore DeMille, Acting Executive Associate Director of U. S. Immigration and Customs Enforcement. He was based out of Washington D.C., but spent quite a lot of time at the El Paso field office. He looked at the sheriff, sitting there patiently with his hand up, and a wide smile split his face. If you didn't know better, it looked sincere, but the knuckles of his hand gripping the podium went white. His other hand waved warmly at Osterman.

"Sheriff! It seems you have the floor. And let me say, on behalf of everyone here, how happy we are to see you back at these meetings. It's been a while, and we're all so pleased to see how well you've recovered from your wounds."

Osterman lowered his hand as he climbed to his feet a little stiffly, and he got a round of applause. Just from the volume he could tell only half the people in the room were applauding, but that didn't hurt his feelings. He'd made a career on brutal honesty, something quite rare in a politician, which he also was, in addition to a sworn law enforcement officer.

Osterman treated DeMille to a small smile. "I know exactly how happy you are to see me, Ted, trust me. But I am happy to be seen. The Lord apparently didn't think I was quite done down here, I just wish the delivery of the message hadn't been so painful. Still, I can't complain— imagine my shock when I discovered the AK-47 which that cartel soldier shot me with *wasn't* actually provided to him by the ATF through their Fast and Furious gunrunning operation." He turned his head and smiled in the direction of the BATFE representatives, who were staring at him. "Such a wasted opportunity."

Beside him, Sam Wheaton lowered his head a tiny bit and, almost imperceptibly, muttered "Dear God," behind his moustache.

Osterman looked back at the ICE representative on stage. Osterman truly found himself agog at the staggering numbers being admitted to by the government representatives. And, he knew, if they were admitting to those numbers, the actual numbers were even worse. And what were they doing with them? Catch and release. Or bussing them into so-called sanctuary cities in highly publicized PR moves. Which was idiotic. Transporting them deeper into the interior? That was the exact wrong thing to do. He straightened up as much as he was able. "Having sat here and listened to your presentation, listening to these staggering numbers, has me a bit at a loss. The Tucson sector alone is seeing two thousand people illegally crossing our border a day? Two thousand. A day. In any other time, in any other place, an…incursion of this magnitude would be considered an invasion. And the response would be military." He remained standing, clearly not done.

DeMille nodded. "I understand your concern. We all do. Of course we do. But the military has been deployed along the border, at various times and places. And CBP," he nodded at the representative of U.S. Customs and Border Protection standing on the stage with him, "has the best kind of gear for dealing with this situation. Training and gear superior to what you probably had when you were in the military."

Osterman ignored the not-so-subtle dig at his age and expertise. "But they are not authorized to use force to repel the invaders, to protect our sovereign territory. And I do not use that term—invaders—lightly. What percentage of illegals crossing into this country are military-aged males? Fighting-age males with no wives, no children, no family. What percentage of illegals taken into custody are coming from nations hostile to the U.S.? Yemen, Syria, China, Iran. Or have ties to terrorist organizations? And what percentage are deported? I know you know, it's a rhetorical question, and the percentages are sickening. Like I said, I use the term invasion deliberately. Yes, we have a bit of military presence down at the border, but they are not being allowed to operate as a military. The purpose of a military is to kill people and break things, and they are doing none of that. Ideally, to prevent the loss of American life, we should be using drones. Armed drones to patrol the skies over the border. If you show a willingness to use them, you will rarely have to, much like spanking a child. But no one in this country seems to have the stomach for that, our Presidents will only drone people in the Middle East. I wonder why that is. For all you standing up there telling us everything that you've been doing, in fact the current government of this country seems to have no interest at all in securing this border. Texas built a floating wall in the Rio Grande to keep out illegal aliens. Arizona built a border wall out of shipping crates. The federal government sued both states to force them to take down those barriers. The largest illegal alien settlement in America, Colony Ridge, just north of Houston, is upwards of seventy-five thousand strong, and they're being offered low-interest mortgages subsidized by the federal government." Osterman peered at the men and women standing on stage. "Those are not the actions of a government that cares about national sovereignty or foreign threats," he said in disgust. "And I don't know what's worse, that you're lying to my face, or that you think I might be stupid enough to believe what's coming out of your mouth." He took a deep breath and shook his head. "I don't know what the hell happened to the country I used to live in, but all of you standing up there should start defending it, or quit in protest. Or disgrace."

"Well, that went well," Wheaton said, as he drove their rental car back toward the Phoenix Sky Harbor Airport. Beside him, in the passenger seat, Osterman was scowling. Wheaton waited a bit. When he got no response, he said, "I guess that means you're feeling better, picking fights with everyone. Did I hear that you sat Anderson's girlfriend next to the Governor at the Cracker Barrel grand opening?"

Osterman glanced over, a light in his eyes. The corner of his mouth twitched. That was all the confirmation Wheaton needed.

"At what point did the Governor discover that she was sitting next to and talking with a porn star? With a very unique skill. Everyone snapping photos with their phones."

"That woman wasn't elected to anything, and you know it," Osterman growled. "I knew we had some corruption in our elective process, but I didn't realize just how deep the rot went. Judges and the state attorney general simply ignoring the rule of law. Honestly, it makes me tired. You know I love a good fight, and goodness knows our good Father does, he made me like this, but it seems like we're losing ground everywhere. And I am…not the man I used to be. The decades have a weight."

"Aren't you the person who likes to say you fight the good fight because it is the right thing to do, even if everyone's against you, even if it looks like you might lose?"

"Using my own words against me is a vile, despicable thing to do."

Wheaton smiled behind his moustache. "Thank you very much."

Osterman sat up a bit. "That young lady—who is a *retired* adult film actress, thank you very much—has more truth and honesty about her than the person currently occupying the governor's office. I may—and do—completely disagree about the morality of what she used to do, but she has never lied about it. Never hid who she was or what she'd done, or engaged in false contrition. And, in truth, the current governor is giving this state more of a brutal heartless fucking than that young lady ever received on camera." He saw the look Wheaton gave him. "Or so I presume," he quickly clarified, having not looked at any pornography since finding the Lord during the Vietnam War. Wheaton snorted, but he couldn't help but notice that was the first time he'd heard the sheriff use profanity in years.

Most men might have called it a day, and headed straight home from the tiny Prescott Regional Airport, as it was late in the afternoon. John Osterman was not most men. He smiled at Sally, his secretary, as he passed her, then settled into his desk chair with a sigh at two minutes after four, not looking forward to the emails stacked up in his inbox, but he knew whatever business he took care of before he went home he wouldn't have waiting for him in the morning.

There was a knock at his open door, and he looked up to see Sally peering at him. "Is the rumor true?"

"Which one?"

"That you're thinking about retiring." Sally Harrison had been his secretary for a dozen years. She sounded put out that she hadn't heard the news from him, rather than having to listen to rumors.

He frowned. "This department is like a small town, all the gossip flying back and forth," he grumbled. "But yes, I am thinking about it. I have been in office since before most of the young men in my command were born. And getting shot does tend to tire one out. But I've got over a year left in my term, so don't think you'll be rid of me that quickly."

"Would Captain Wheaton run for the job?"

"Sam? No. Likely when I leave he's gone too."

"Well, Sheriff, it will be the end of an era, whenever that happens." And she was gone. Her announcement, however true, did not put him in a better mood.

Half an hour later he was leaning back, carefully

stretching his neck and back, when his phone rang. He saw it was an inside call. He took it, and three minutes later Maria Flores and Norm Hill were standing in front of his desk. Flores was small and dark, not much over five foot tall, and Hill was big and pale. Between the two of them they made his office feel crowded. Osterman didn't need to ask why the detectives wanted to talk to him. Flores had a stack of paper and folders in her hands two inches thick. "Anything new?"

Norm Hill was nearly six and a half feet tall, but he looked to Flores, as she was the lead. And by far the more aggressive of the two. She shook her head at Osterman. "Even if there wasn't anything else going on outside of the actual crime scene, this would be a weird one. Middle-aged white guy shot dead right there, one round to the chest, with a ghost gun on his hip and twenty grand worth of night vision goggles on his head. No serial number on the gun. No serial number on the goggles, which the manufacturer, Steiner, can't explain. Or won't. Used night vision goggles like that model cost eight or ten grand. New, they're double that. And then there's the silencer."

"Silencers are perfectly legal to own in this state," Osterman said, playing the devil's advocate.

"And, legally, they're treated like firearms," Norm Hill told him. "They have a serial number, registered with the federal government. Not only did this can not have a serial number, it was plastic. Entirely. I've never heard of a plastic —polymer—suppressor, and did some research, including with the ATF, which was mostly a waste of time. Talking to the ATF, I mean, the average gun store clerk knows more about guns than those clowns. Near as I can tell it was 3D printed. It's disposable, consumable—won't last more than a magazine or two, but I guess that's all you'd need. I found an online forum where somebody said the government, on the spook side, was looking into doing this, so they could have sound suppressors anywhere around the world they wanted, as long as there was a 3D printer, but that's all I got. But if that's not a clear indication that this guy was some sort of a spook, I don't know what is."

"But running his prints…?"

"Got us nowhere," Flores confirmed. "No hits. And that driver's license he's got, it's real, but that address on it goes to an apartment in Phoenix. We served the warrant on that, and if anybody's ever lived in that place I'm a koala. I don't think anyone's ever slept in the bed, or sat in the chairs. It's a…safe house. Maybe."

"Who pays the rent?"

"An LLC out of Kansas City. Dick Murphy dug into it, and the paper trail went nowhere. Same with the credit cards and other stuff in his wallet. It was a…what was the term he used?" Flores looked up at her partner.

"Cover identity," Norm Hill said.

"Objectively, that's fascinating," Osterman said, leaning back.

"It's frustrating as hell is what it is," Hill said. It had been over a month, and they were no closer to solving it.

"But it didn't happen in a vacuum," Flores said, frowning at the sheriff. "With everything else we've had going on in the area…" She gave him a very direct look.

"You think Pima Jack Burton was involved?" The sheriff's tone was neutral.

"You mean David Anderson?" Flores growled. "The guy hiding out here from the Detroit mob? That you got a driver's license for in a fake name? And, a day before Mr. Robert Cooper of Phoenix was found dead, Anderson shot and killed four men not even a mile away? Anderson, who has killed how many people? In how many separate incidents? What do you think? I know he's your friend or something, sir, but…"

Osterman's eyes moved from Flores to Norm Hill. The big man shrugged. "Anderson's style seems more a full mag dump than a single shot, but you can't disagree that his habit of stacking bodies in our city seems to make him a prime candidate for this."

Osterman blinked twice. "Well, you can't both be right," he said slowly, a hint of a smile on his face.

The detectives exchanged a look. "Us?" Flores asked.

Osterman shook his head. "You and the FBI. At the time Mr. Cooper was taking a round to center chest, Jack Burton—David Anderson—was in Las Vegas. Spotted on traffic cameras, and he, through his lawyer, confirmed he was there. The FBI suspects he was there killing Pietro Bufonte and his bodyguards."

"The Detroit mobster guy. Who sent the four assholes after him the day before, and Pima Jack burned them down." Hill was frowning. They, of course, had heard about Bufonte's murder. But they'd assumed it was a competitor who had taken the man out. Or his superiors, as he was garnering unwanted attention with his actions. "They like Anderson for it?"

Osterman shrugged. "He is on the short list of suspects. Or so I've been told, on the QT. His vehicle was spotted in Vegas that night, but other than that they have no evidence. He admits to being in Las Vegas, driving around, trying to clear his head, but from what I hear, the *federales* have no direct evidence tying him to the crime. Just loads and loads of motive. But," Osterman pointed out, "that's a four-hour drive. You like him for the mysterious Mr. Cooper, but Cooper was killed, according to the ME, within two hours of Bufonte's death in Las Vegas. Summerlin, actually, which is on the north side, even further away. As lucky or talented as that young man is, he can't be in two places at once."

"The FBI likes him for the Vegas thing?" Flores shook her head. "Of course they do, he smoked four of Bufonte's guys in front of his house. Justified, apparently, but…" She chewed at her lip. Then she looked up at the sheriff, concern on her face. "Sir," she said tentatively, "I understand that he saved your life. Saved a lot of lives around here. He's Pima Jack, the hero of Prescott, who killed half a dozen cartel terrorists. But if the FBI suspects him of murdering someone…*four* someones, a quadruple homicide…shouldn't you keep your distance?"

"I wasn't there, I was still in the hospital, but I hear he was still limping badly when they came for him at his house. He was still recuperating from his wounds. You think he was in any kind of shape to assault a Vegas mafia compound, like…" He searched for an apt descriptor. "Chuck Norris?"

The two detectives exchanged a look. Hill took the response. "Sir, pardon my language, but have you watched the fucking video from the Cracker Barrel where that guy is ragdolling him, punching him in the face with his AK, like a piñata? He ate that guy's face. He fucking ate his face, sir, in the Cracker Barrel gift shop, fighting for his life. The guys around here call him Cujo. Or the Pima motel, where he ran *into* gunfire? He soaked up bullets, his face hanging half to his chest, and kept running. And shooting. Pain just seems to make him angrier. The only thing that stopped him at the Pima was his heart running out of blood to pump. Literally."

Flores set her folders down on Osterman's desk. "Sir," she said, "can you talk to him about Cooper? I don't know what he would admit to, he won't talk to a meter maid without a lawyer, but…"

"I have," Osterman said. "Even not at my full capacity, it didn't pass beneath my notice that this man was shot in close proximity to Anderson's house. So I asked him about it." He heaved a sigh, and leaned back in his chair. "This young man and I have a…unique relationship. I know things about him that, well, you don't. And that even at this point would surprise you. He won't lie to me. He would just refuse to answer. So I asked him about this shooting. He didn't know anything about it. Hadn't heard about it, in fact, until I brought it up."

"And you believe him?" Hill said dubiously.

"Yes. Absolutely."

"Did you ask him about Vegas? About Bufonte?" Flores asked sharply.

"No," Osterman said with a shake of his head.

"Why?"

"Hmm." Osterman reached out and pulled the top folder toward him, turned it around, and flipped it open. He flipped through the reports for a short while, formulating a response. Finally he said, "I guess that's a question *I* won't answer, and leave it to you to muse about my reasons why." He looked at the crime scene photos of Cooper, the man face-down in the dirt, a dark, almost black stain in the middle of his back. He'd seen the photos before. If he hadn't been recuperating from gunshot wounds himself he'd have been at the scene. Present at the man's autopsy.

He flipped through the crime scene photos—hardcopies in the file, but everything was digitally recorded as well and stored on the department's computer—until he reached the autopsy photos. They were always so sad, really. And graphic. The ME just carved people apart in death, to find out how they'd ended up that way. Necessary, of course, but functionally little different than what most people did to a turkey on Thanksgiving. He—

Osterman sat up so suddenly he hurt, and gave out a small gasp.

"Sir?" Hill said, concerned.

Osterman pulled the top autopsy photo closer to him. A photo of the deceased on the table, visible from the waist up. Naked. Osterman squinted closely, dropping his face down near the photo. He took off his glasses, and pulled the photo close until his nose was nearly touching it. He slid his glasses back into place, then grabbed at the other autopsy photos. He found the one he was looking for, a closeup headshot of the man, before the ME popped his skull open and peeled his face back.

"I know this man," Osterman said.

"Sir?" Flores licked her lips in confusion.

Osterman leaned back. "I know him," he said distantly, thinking. "I've seen him."

"Robert Cooper," Hill said, trying to confirm.

Osterman shook his head. "I don't know the name, but I know his face. I don't know that I've ever looked at the autopsy photos before, just the crime scene photos. His face. I—" He gave a little start. "Well son of a…" He peered down at the photo again, just to confirm. "Sam!" he said. He looked around, looked at his phone for a second, trying to figure out which button to hit, then just shouted out, much more loudly, "Sam!"

They waited. Ten seconds later Sam Wheaton appeared. His office was down the hall, and Osterman's voice carried. "What is going on in here?" he asked, looking from the detectives to the sheriff.

Osterman gestured at the photos spread out on his desk. "You recognize him?"

Wheaton came around the side of the desk and looked at the photos for a while. Moved them around with his fingertips. Finally he shook his head. "Can't say that I do." He looked up at the detectives. "This your DB?" They nodded at him.

"Picture him in a suit. A gray suit, if I remember correctly. In a hospital setting." Osterman paused. "You sang to him. If it's the same man, which I think it is." The two detectives exchanged a confused look as Wheaton glanced at the sheriff, then bent over the photos. He studied them closely, then cocked his head.

"Yeah...maybe," Wheaton said. "It's been almost two years. But yeah, it definitely could be the guy." He glanced from the sheriff to the detectives and back. "And he was found dead near Anderson's house. With all that spook shit on him, right? It has to be the same guy."

"Sir?" Flores said.

"David Anderson first came to our attention after that incident at his little cabin up in the hills."

Flores frowned. "Incident? Seven private contactors shot, burned, and blown up, and Toby Johnson took a rifle bullet through his vest. Supposedly hired by Bufonte, right? To take out Anderson."

"I came into possession of that recording you've all heard, of the FBI agent hiring a Detroit police officer, and his corrupt SWAT-team cohorts, out on bail, to murder Anderson. Officially, publicly, this was done on behalf of Pietro Bufonte, in revenge for Anderson killing his son, which in turn was done in revenge for Bufonte's son killing Anderson's parents. Bit of a Shakespearean tragedy, actually. While

Anderson was in the hospital, recovering from several gunshot wounds and bad burns to his hands, this man," he jabbed a finger at the headshot, "showed up with a full tactical team and a federal warrant to take him into custody."

"Cooper," Norm Hill said. "Robert Cooper."

"I don't know if that's the name he was using at the time," Osterman admitted. "Maybe. I don't know. It has been a while."

"FBI?" Flores asked.

Osterman shook his head. "DOJ. I think."

"No," Wheaton said. "Department of Homeland Security. They had DHS on their vests." He pointed at his own chest.

"I think I heard something about this," Hill said.

"And you didn't turn him over?" Flores asked, frowning. "Why?"

"Because I suspected, at the time, that there was more going on. And the last thing I was about to do was turn him over to representatives of the same federal government that had been recorded arranging his murder. He—Cooper, or…whoever he was that day, was very insistent. Threatened to arrest me."

"And you politely responded by flicking the safety off your shotgun and offering to go meet Jesus with him," Wheaton said, with an admiring smile, remembering the scene.

"I did hear about this," Hill said. "I thought it was bullshit. It wasn't? You singing a funeral dirge to the man? Jesus, Sam. Do we have a copy of the warrant?"

"I do not believe so," Osterman said, trying to remember. The Department of Homeland Security was an umbrella organization formed after 9-11, designed to ensure cooperation of several existing federal law enforcement agencies. While DHS had their own credentialed agents, most of the badge carriers working under the aegis of DHS were employed by other federal agencies, usually ICE or Customs and Border Protection. Identifying yourself as with the DHS was a good way of muddying the waters. "We went in to see Anderson together. The boy was still in an induced coma. He looked over his wounds, and then…left. Just gave up on his mission. And we never heard from him or anyone else about that. No angry calls from AUSAs or SACs or the governor's office." He peered up at the two detectives. "But that might be something you can follow up on. Use to try to track down this man's true identity."

Flores was frowning as she thought it through. "So this Cooper was working for the mob? Taking another run at the kid?"

Osterman shrugged. "What other explanation could there be?"

Chapter Six

Winston Elliott had moved up; he was no longer the Deputy Director of Operations for the Defense Intelligence Agency's Defense Clandestine Service, a title that would fill up a business card without leaving room for a name. He was now the Director of the DIA itself due to one retirement, one firing, and one odd death that had officially been ruled a suicide. One of the most powerful people in the U.S. government...whose very agency most people had never heard of. People knew of the CIA, of course, and the NSA (thanks to Edward Snowden), but after that the nation's intelligence community was a murky web of interconnected allegiances and overlapping responsibilities. There were literally dozens of agencies inside the U.S. government doing intelligence work, their three-, four, and five-letter acronyms a confusing mishmash of consonants and vowels no one outside of Washington could decipher. And those were just the official numbers. Unofficially there were a myriad of different detachments, teams, contractors, NGOs, and "work groups" which showed up on no agency's flow chart, their operating expenditures covered by black funds usually hidden inside the general defense budget.

Officially the DIA did all its work in support of the Department of Defense and the U.S. military. Most people thought of it simply as an intelligence agency, providing data and running covert operatives, providing cover identities (through their Defense Cover Office) for any intelligence officer working for the DOD, but in fact the DIA was also a "combat support agency", providing trigger-pulling men and material support to the DOD through its Defense Clandestine Service. The DIA DCS used to be a very small, and work closely with the CIA's Directorate of Operations like a little brother, but with the unlimited budget most agencies enjoyed during the global war on terror, the size and scope of the DIA DCS had grown exponentially under Elliot's tenure. That was changing, the warfighting budgets had shrunk drastically, but the DIA would never be as small as it once was. Government never shrank, not really. And there would always be another war. Ukraine, Taiwan, maybe someplace in North Africa. Until then, Elliott enjoyed being in charge of an agency with more power than the CIA had during most of the Cold War.

As many people as he had in his employ, he remembered the ones he came up with. One of those was Roger Colman; or, at least, that had been his work name for so long Elliott had trouble remembering his real name. Colman had started with the DIA at the same time as Elliott, and while Elliott had gone into management, Colman stayed in the field. He had a gift for it. For the nasty work, done in the shadows. He'd been one of the best in the business. Until… Until.

Elliott had no medical background, but unlike most people he wasn't an idiot. If he didn't know the exact definition of a term, he could usually figure out what it meant in context. But the autopsy report in his hands from the Tohono County Medical Examiner's Office in Arizona was pretty simple and straightforward. As was the accompanying police report, liberated from the computer system of the Tohono County Sheriff's Department.

Colman had been found dead early one morning, face down on the ground, outside a warehouse, shot once. Elliott had full-color glossies of the crime scene photos. Colman had an Arizona driver's license on him in the name of Robert Cooper, one of his regular cover identities, which is how Elliott came to learn of his demise so quickly, within just a few days. But it had been a month since the man's body had been found, and Elliott still had no answers. The detectives were still investigating it as well—not just because it was a homicide, but because it was so strange. Colman had been found with a pistol on his hip, a professionally-made but unserialized polymer silencer for the pistol in his pocket, and PVS-21 night vision goggles on his head. Which meant, clearly, this hadn't been a robbery; a thief would have taken his gun, and those PVS-21s cost as much as a good used car. The gun had no serial number. The sound suppressor—silencer—had the detectives baffled. Elliott could have educated them, had he cared to, but he had yet to acknowledge any government interest in Colman's death. The sheriff's department had sent Colman's prints in to the federal database, the military, everywhere, and got nothing back. The man had been single, and really had nothing other than the job, so Elliot wasn't sure he'd ever claim the man. There was nothing in it for the DIA to get involved—officially—in his death. Officially, he had been on a leave of absence, as the mission he'd been tasked with was so sensitive.

Cause of Death: Gunshot Wound.
Anatomical Summary:
I. Forty-five year old male shot in center chest
II. Gunshot wound #1, center chest, perforating, fatal.

A. Entry: sternum, anterior center chest, half an inch left of midline, two inches above xiphoid process, uniform round defect. No soot or stippling.

B. Direction: angling slightly upward and right

C. Path: sternum, pericardium, through heart at junction of right atrium and superior vena cava, through spine, damaging T4 and T5 vertebra

D. Exit: center back, half an inch left of midline, 12 ½ inches from top of head

E. Projectile: none

That was the meat of it, although the entire coroner's report was thirty pages long, the detectives' report, including supplementals, nearly that. Colman had been shot once, from sufficient distance that there was no gunpowder stippling on his clothes or his flesh. Likely from between twenty and thirty feet away, based on how the lot, where he'd been found, was laid out. Elliott had both photos and diagrams of the crime scene to look at. From the blood spatter analysis, Colman had maybe crawled a few feet, but had died where he'd been shot. Whoever shot him was directly in front of him, so likely Colman had seen him. But maybe not seen it coming, not perceived a threat, as his pistol was still holstered? Elliott had a lot of unanswered questions. The wound was immediately fatal, traversing his heart and shattering his spine. The bullet had traveled straight through the man and ended up…somewhere. A search had not recovered the bullet or a casing. So…maybe a revolver. Or the shooter had policed his brass. The coroner stated that, due to the lack of damage to surrounding tissues, he suspected the wound had been caused by a handgun rather than a rifle, but that was simply an educated guess and no guarantee. No one had heard a shot, although it was an isolated business park located outside the city limits. Time of death was very late night or early morning, depending on your frame of reference. The police, in fact, had no leads. No witnesses, no suspects, and no physical evidence. Until some new evidence came to light, or a witness came forward....

Elliott knew what had happened, though. Well, not exactly the sequence of events, but he'd set Colman loose to track down David Anderson. Determine whether Anderson's pesky fingerprints, which happened to match those of two other people, were still an issue. Anderson's hands had been badly burned during an earlier attempt to remove him from the playing field using contractors—and Elliott still wasn't sure how that had gone awry, how six combat vets had ended up dead with Anderson still alive. The police reports on the incident, including photos and diagrams of the scene, were wildly incomplete, perhaps deliberately so. After that Anderson disappeared, and after a time Elliott had sent Colman out to track him down. And apparently he had, because his body had been found less than a mile from Anderson's residence in Prescott Valley, Arizona. And that proximity couldn't be a coincidence. Colman had clearly found Anderson, and Anderson had killed him. Any other conclusion after examining the known facts would be idiotic.

Dispassionately, he tried to examine his thoughts on Anderson. If the man no longer had fingerprints matching those of other people, then he was no longer a threat to national security, and thus of no interest to the DIA. Even if —as seemed highly likely—he had killed Colman.

But…he had killed Colman.

And Elliott, to his surprise, after a lifetime in an environment where he shoved his personal feelings and morals aside, into a box, and closed the lid on them, found he'd taken Colman's murder personally.

The question was…what was he going to do about it?

Chapter Seven

Everything he did hurt a little bit, but he was back to full range of motion, and every week the pain was less. At this point it was just a dull ache in his legs and hip and occasionally in his face, which—compared to what he'd endured previously—was practically nothing. He was jogging and walking (mostly walking) four miles every day and doing a paltry few pushups and pullups. It wasn't great, but it was something. It was progress.

The windows were open, in part because the weather was beautiful, and in part to air out the room, thin the smell of the latex paint Dave was rolling on the walls. Using the roller to paint the walls could in no way be considered exercise, but he appreciated that it had him up, and moving.

Lori was in the kitchen, taping off all the trim and cupboard edges and light switches with blue masking tape. She had a Bluetooth speaker set up on the counter, connected to Spotify on her phone, which was tuned to an eighties playlist on the music streaming service. In addition to watching all sorts of movies and TV shows from the

Reagan era, she and her mother had spent time every day listening to the eighties music which made Grace Hoskins think of better times. The minor home remodeling needed to be done, but it was an emotionally fraught exercise, and there was nothing he could do about that, so Dave was keeping his distance. From time to time, when the music grew quiet, he could occasionally hear a sniffle out of Lori. The Cure's mellow and atmospheric *A Forest* ended, and the quintessential 80s pop tune *Bring on the Dancing Horses*, by Echo & the Bunnymen, rolled out of the speakers.

He finished the last wall, then stood in the doorway for a while, watching her. She had her back to him, and was bent over, taping along a piece of wood trim. She was in a tank top over silk boxers, and probably thought she looked horrible. Girls had no clue. He fought the caveman urge to march over there and yank down her shorts, grab her hips, and get to work.

He shook the image out of his head and cleared his throat. "Hey, you want to look at this? First coat's on, but it's probably going to need a second."

Lori straightened up and turned, blowing a lock of blonde hair out of her eyes. "Yeah. I think I'm done in here. Remember, it's not the same color as what's going to go in the kitchen."

"I know, I was there when you spent an hour looking at paint samples, remember?" He felt a small sense of pride he'd actually spoken to her face, and not her chest. That she was not wearing a bra under the tank top was very obvious, and even though he saw her nearly every day…it never got old. He moved to the side as she came into the room and looked around. Her eyes were a bit pink from weeping, but at the moment they were dry.

"You think you'll need a second coat?"

"Maybe. Wait until it dries, then we'll know for sure."

"Okay. Hey, when you get a chance, can you look under the sink? I think there's a leak. The floor underneath is damp. It looks discolored, and warped a little bit, like it's been leaking for a while."

"Have you looked under the crawlspace?"

"The what?" She frowned up at him.

"The crawlspace. You do know these houses aren't sitting directly on the ground, right? They're about a foot-and-a-half, two feet up, on supports, and there are skirts around the outside to cover the gap. You didn't know? What did you think the trap door was for?"

"What trap door?"

"The one on the floor of the hall closet." The floorplans of their houses were identical, just reversed. Dave walked over to the hall closet, which Lori's mother had used to store linens and cleaning supplies, and opened up the door, which folded in the center. And pointed.

"Oh, I didn't know that was there."

"Well, you could go under, see if that leak has actually soaked through the floor, damaged the wood."

"What? No, gross. With spiders and scorpions and spiderwebs and bugs and dirt? No. Ick." She shivered. "Don't you laugh at me. Why are you laughing at me?"

"Girls," he said, a big smile on his face. "And…people are fascinating." He shrugged. "You're grossed out by bugs and dirt, but in your previous occupation you regularly did things a lot of people think are disgusting."

"You mean butt stuff?"

He barked out a laugh. "I didn't, actually, but…"

She blew a lock of hair out of her eyes. "Well, I'm all gross and sweaty, so I'm going to get in the shower. You want to go out to eat after?"

"Yeah."

"You want to join me in the shower? We can explore how you think I'm fascinating…" Her mother had an oversize shower installed, with a railing along one wall, and it had apparently helped quite a bit when the brain cancer started to affect her mobility. Dave and Lori liked it for completely different reasons.

He couldn't keep the smile off his face. "Absolutely. Give me a minute to clean up."

He poured the extra paint from the tray back into the can, and tapped the lid into place. He stood up and was about to head toward the master bedroom when he heard the doorbell. He reflexively swept back the long sleeve plaid shirt he was wearing untucked and unbuttoned and his hand closed on the grip of the TTI custom Glock 17 he had on his hip. He didn't draw it, but he was moving silently toward the front door before the doorbell even faded, face blank. But his brain was in overdrive, and…the doorbell had been a little quiet. Faint, almost. A peek out the window showed him that nobody was on the porch outside the front door. Dave opened the door and stuck his head out, hand still on the grip of his pistol. The sheriff was standing next door, at Dave's house. His new vehicle, a black Chevy Tahoe, was sitting at the curb. His previous vehicle had been totaled—it would cost more to repair the damage from the bullet holes than it was worth. What was worse, the insurance company had refused to cover the damages. Osterman had given Dave the keys specifically so he could drive off to the rescue of a witness against a notoriously violent Mexican drug cartel. The vehicle subsequently getting shot to shit could in no way be described as an accident. Osterman had chosen the Tahoe simply because it was easier for him to get in and out of in his current semi-impaired condition. "I'm over here," Dave called out.

Osterman turned, saw Dave's head poking out, and slowly made his way over. "I wasn't sure if you'd be up yet," the sheriff said as he carefully stepped up onto the porch.

"I still can't sleep late. I'm up at four some mornings." He moved aside and the sheriff stepped past him.

"Hmm. I smell paint?"

Dave nodded. "Lori felt it was time to redecorate. Her mother's been gone a few months. She's still not sure how long she wants to live here, but either way the place needed a bit of work."

"I imagine that could be a bit emotional for her." Osterman cocked his head and looked closely at Dave.

Dave shrugged. "I'm happy to help."

"Well, I was in the area, and stopped by. Lillian is down in Phoenix visiting her nieces, who detest me, as I am 'mean', because the facts I recite to back up all my opinions hurt their feelings. I thought maybe you might be interested in breakfast somewhere? And of course that invite extends to your girlfriend."

Dave opened and closed his mouth twice before he said, "You do remember the last time you stopped by here unannounced, to invite me out to brunch, we both had to shoot people?"

Osterman pursed his lips. "Well, perhaps we shouldn't go to Cracker Barrel, then."

Dave laughed at that. "Yes, that'd be great. Lori's in the shower, let me ask her."

Osterman held up a hand. "I don't want you to rush her. I'm in no hurry. I know how long women take to get ready, shaving their legs and putting on makeup and…" he waved a hand at the mysteries of the feminine.

Dave paused, and treated the sheriff with a wide smile. "You truly are the man you present yourself to be."

That statement made the sheriff tilt his head back and regard the young man in front of him quizzically. "Why do you say that?"

"Because any normal, regular man would have watched a few of her movies, if only out of sheer curiosity. But I know you haven't. When it comes to your faith, you walk the walk."

"And how do you know that? That I haven't snuck a peek at some of her unmentionables caught on film?"

"Because if you had, you'd know she's got nothing to shave anywhere. Laser hair removal. Hold on." And Dave left the sheriff blinking in the living room, speechless in a way he rarely was.

Dave walked into the master bedroom, and opened the bathroom door. Steam billowed out. She was a vague curvy shape behind the frosted glass. "The sheriff's here," he called out, loud enough to be heard over the water. "Invited us out to breakfast."

She opened the door and stuck her head out. "I wondered what was taking you so long. I'll just be a couple minutes. Do I have time to put on makeup?"

He rolled his eyes. "You don't need it."

"You always say that."

"Because it's true."

"You always say I don't need makeup. Or a bra."

"Is there a question there?"

With a frown she disappeared back inside the stall. "I'm putting on a bra," she called out to him over the sound of the shower. "I won't be responsible for him having a heart attack."

"Are you still going to physical therapy?" Lori asked him as she waited for the sheriff to climb out of his big SUV after parking.

"Twice a week. And doing a bit of it on my own, at home."

"Likely not enough, or long as you're supposed to, because you're working too much," she scolded him, taking his elbow. He gave her a bemused look—she was not only exactly right, his wife had said the same thing to him. On more than one occasion.

Dave got the door for the two of them, and walked with them up to the counter. Mike and Matt, the owners, were behind the counter, moving swiftly as they filled orders. Matt was a redhead who moved with a slight limp as he'd left a foot in Iraq. Mike had scar tissue running up his left arm out of sight under his sleeve and reappearing again above his collar on the side of his neck, also earned overseas. The name of their establishment, the Aloha Snackbar, had earned them a lot of enmity from people on the left side of the political spectrum, and earned them even more fans on the right. Their coffee and pastries were also damn good, which was actually the only important thing.

Matt handed his business partner a finished drink, and as he stepped over he said, "Good morning, what can I get you folks?" His eyes came up, and he saw Lori. Not only did he recognize her as a semi-regular, he knew exactly who she was, or rather what she used to do for a living. Military veterans were usually very familiar with porn stars, and she'd been an A-lister when they were overseas, and not by accident. "Oh, hi," he said, his professional smile widening into a real one. His eyes moved over and saw the man he knew as Pima Jack. He knew they were a couple. "Hey there," he said, his smile growing even wider. Then his gaze lit on the third person in their trio, and his eyes bulged. "Oh, shit," he said, before catching himself. "Sorry. Good morning, Sheriff." His partner at the register looked over and did a comical double-take.

Matt cleared his throat. "So we've had a few menu changes, mostly with our coffee. Would you like a rundown of your options?" At their nods he said, "We've got a few flavored coffees from Dark Canyon in South Dakota, and the rest of our roasts—from mild to dark, including decaf— come from Minutemen Coffee." The Aloha Snackbar had severed ties with their previous coffee supplier when it became known the owner supported political candidates and parties who wanted to ban black rifles, despite the name of their company. Matt and Mike respected opposing viewpoints, and freedom of speech. After all, you couldn't claim to support the Second Amendment without supporting the First, and vice versa. What they couldn't stand was hypocrisy and lies.

The three of them placed their orders, and as they moved to the register with their coffees and locally-made pastries Mike said, "On the house."

Osterman made a small sound. "If you refuse to take my money I will be deeply offended," the sheriff said politely. "You earned it. And, after all, you are paying my salary."

"I think you fucking earned it, sir," Matt said. His eyes darted over to Dave and back. It had been the deadliest day in that area of the county since at least the days of the indian wars, perhaps ever. The assassination attempt on the sheriff, the bomb set off outside the sheriff's department along with two men gunning down pedestrians, all (mostly) done as a distraction while another team tried to take out the witness hidden at the Pima Motel. Six dead and twenty-seven wounded, not counting cartel members, and fuck those guys. It could have been a lot worse. He looked at Pima Jack again. It should have been a lot worse.

"Nevertheless," the sheriff insisted firmly. Frowning, Mike took the sheriff's credit card and ran the sale, then, as the sheriff stood in front of him, took the same amount of money out of the register and stuck it in the donation jar in front of the register while staring defiantly at the sheriff. The recipient changed every month; this month it was the Disabled American Veterans.

Osterman nodded. "Fair enough," he said, fighting back a smile.

"Um, Sheriff, are you dining in?" Matt asked him.

"Yes, we are."

"Um, okay. Uh…" His eyes darted back and forth between Lori and Osterman. His mouth worked. It was clear he was trying to figure out how to politely, delicately say what was on his mind. Or if he should say anything.

"He knows what I used to do for a living," Lori told Matt, putting a hand on the sheriff's arm. "He is hoping, if he hangs around long enough, he can help guide me to Jesus."

"Oh, okay. Good. I mean, no, not good, um…" Lori laughed, and even the sheriff had a small smile on his face. She wasn't wrong.

Osterman looked from Matt to Lori and had to shake his head at the wonders and mysteries of life. "You know," he said, to the both of them, with both Dave and Mike listening in, "I'm known as 'Shotgun John' Osterman, and have killed people across four decades, dating back to my time in Vietnam, and yet here everyone is trying to protect *me* from *you*." He treated Lori to a raised eyebrow.

"It's…fascinating," Lori said, throwing a smirk at Dave.

They moved to a table, and Lori automatically took a seat on the side where her back was to the door. Osterman saw Dave was going to sit next to him, not her, and opened his mouth in brief confusion, then realized it wasn't rudeness. Both men sat facing the door. As she knew they would.

By that time they'd gotten the attention of all the other customers in the coffee shop. Osterman was in a suitcoat over slacks—he never went out in public dressed sloppily, and even on his days off his attire counted as business casual—but still everyone recognized him. He'd been in office longer than most of the people there had been alive. And had a fresh kill on his gun, which you didn't see with a lot of septuagenarians. At least half the dozen people in the restaurant came over to talk to the sheriff, say hi or shake his hand. Perhaps a quarter of them also recognized Dave, not because they really recognized *him*, but rather the scars, mostly healed and halfway hidden under his beard, across his face. In context, seated next to the sheriff, it was clear who he had to be. However, once the whispering started almost everyone got up and came over. Shook his hand. Asked him questions, some of which were stupid, but Dave smiled and suffered through. It happened from time to time, and it was still surreal to Dave, who usually put on a baseball cap and tried to keep his head down.

Lori was once again amused that she was forgotten and ignored. Before she'd met Dave, met the sheriff, whenever she went anywhere there was always the chance she'd get recognized by fans. But she'd been retired for a while. Put on a little weight. And it was hard to compete for attention next to a guy who, when he was last caught on film, was bathed in blood, his face hanging in flaps as he ran toward the camera, firing an AK-47.

After not much more than five minutes everyone went back to their seats. Osterman was happy to find his coffee was still hot. He blew on it and took a sip, his eyes roaming the restaurant. "So," he said, and his eyes came to rest on Dave. "What's your plan for the rest of your life?"

Dave barked out a laugh. "You just dive right in with both feet, don't you?" Dave remembered that during the ill-fated brunch at Cracker Barrel, Osterman and Lori had talked about both sex and religion. And maybe politics, too. His memories were a little fuzzy, as the conversation had been interrupted by gunfire, and someone hitting him in the head repeatedly with an AK. Sixty-seven stitches, most of them in his face.

Osterman shrugged innocently. "Well, provided you aren't arrested by the FBI, you'll need to do something to bring in a little money and support yourself, at a minimum." His eyes darted toward Lori.

Dave took a deep breath. "Oh, you heard about that?"

"I'm the walking wounded, but I haven't been in a coma for a while. Surely you didn't think I was that out of it? That I would miss something like that? Or that I don't have people in the FBI who talk to me? There are still a few people in that organization committed to truth, justice, and the American way." Behind her coffee cup Lori smiled at him, because he wasn't using the phrase ironically.

Dave sighed, not sure how to respond. "It's been over a month," he said finally, staring out at the other patrons. "They haven't arrested me for anything." He turned his head finally to look at Osterman. Wondering if the man would finally ask the question. Wondering what he'd say if he did.

"As I said," Osterman said slowly, picking his words carefully, keeping his tone and face neutral, "presuming that doesn't change, and I have no reason to think it will…what are your plans?"

"Well, I still have a decent amount of money in the bank from when I sold my house in Michigan. And the inheritance. I could get by for another couple years, if I was careful. But I…I have no idea. What could I…? I mean, I was trying to get into the FBI when all this started." He laughed bitterly, so loudly several people looked over.

"That door is likely closed to you," Osterman admitted.

"Even if I wanted to go into law enforcement, be a cop, I don't think I'd be hirable with my history. I don't think even you could get away with it. Sure, I'm Pima Jack, but I'm also under investigation by the FBI for murder. Four murders. And you know how many bodies I've got on me. Maybe if they were in Iraq, then they'd be a resume enhancer. You think the mayor or the city council would greenlight me after seeing just what's in the public realm?"

"Likely not. But you have to do something. Even if you had enough money on hand to live the rest of your life comfortably, a man needs a purpose."

Dave gave a little nod. "I have been thinking about it," he admitted. He glanced at Lori. They hadn't talked about it, not exactly, but they'd talked around it. He didn't have any answers yet. But he was starting to ask the questions.

"Well, good. Listen, I wanted to talk to you about something. I mentioned that body found in the industrial park not too far from your neighborhood. Killed the same night you were driving around Vegas, according to traffic cameras. Or so the FBI tells me."

"Is that how they knew I was there? They never said. I wondered."

"And it sounds like traffic camera footage of your Jeep is the only evidence they have to tie you to the incident in Las Vegas. Beyond motive, of course." Osterman quickly held a hand up. "I'm not here to talk about Vegas. I will happily admit that I have not sorted out my conflicting personal and professional opinions on the matter. If my suspicions are true. I'm here to talk about the man shot in the industrial park."

"I don't know anything about it," Dave said. "Really. I wasn't here. Didn't get back until morning. If I knew anything I would tell you. Or keep my mouth shut. But I won't lie to you. I don't know anything about what happened."

Osterman nodded. "I've been getting regular updates from my detectives. We have no leads. And it is an odd one. The man had a pistol on him, still in the holster. He also had a silencer on him, for the pistol. And night vision goggles on his head. Either no serial numbers on the pertinent pieces, or they're dead ends. His ID, his driver license, while it is real, appears to be a...cover identity, I believe is the correct term. Like Jack Burton." He inclined his head toward Dave.

"What?" Dave jerked upright. "Why didn't you tell me? You don't think...?"

"While I admit all that is suspicious, he wasn't found in your front yard, he was found most of a mile away. I was still in the hospital when it happened, so I haven't been as hands-on as I might otherwise have been. Still, the detectives couldn't help but think of you, given your history of decorating the county with corpses, but other than location there was nothing linking you to this. It was only yesterday when I was looking at autopsy photos of the man, and realized I knew him. You remember me telling you about the government agent who showed up at the hospital, after the attack on your cabin, trying to take you into custody? Had a whole team with him. This was that gentleman."

Dave's mouth opened and closed. His eyes darted back and forth as he thought.

"He claimed to be with the Department of Homeland Security, but I can't remember his name, and we don't have a copy of the paperwork he was waving around, so tracking him down so far has proved problematic. And of course there is no guarantee he was who and what he claimed. You were unconscious at the time."

"You think he was working for the mob?" Lori asked.

"Suppressor? Night vision goggles? Fake ID?" Dave shook his head. "I think this is that other thing."

"The...?" She lifted a hand off her coffee cup and wiggled her fingers.

He looked down at his hand, at the scar tissue covering his fingertips. "Yeah. Just like those guys who came to my cabin. And killed Mickey." Mickey had been the FBI fingerprint tech who'd originally discovered Dave had prints which perfectly matched two other people. Dave sat and thought for a bit. Osterman let him. "Was he here to kill me? Because they don't need to." He spread his hands, palms up. He had no fingerprints left, not really. "And I haven't said anything, to anybody. You two and Aaron are the only people who know."

Osterman shrugged, a frown creasing his face. "Maybe they don't know that. Maybe they don't care."

"You said he was shot. How? With what?"

"Once, center chest. No bullet or spent case recovered, but it looks like it was a handgun, maybe a magnum caliber as it punched right through his sternum, heart, and then went out through his spine without seemingly slowing down." Lori made a face and stuck out her tongue. "But without any of the hydrostatic shock you'd get from a rifle round. Or so the ME says, and he knows his stuff. But that's just a guess. We might have a partial footprint. Might have a partial tire track. If we ever have a suspect, person or vehicle, to compare them to, that might get us somewhere."

Dave shook his head and shrugged. Glanced at Lori before he looked at the sheriff and said, "Like I said, I was in Vegas."

Forty-five minutes later they were back at her house, waving at the sheriff as he drove off. Lori waited until the Tahoe was out of sight. Then she turned, and stared at him. Long and hard. "Okay, you were right," he told her.

"I told you. I told you so."

"There was no way to know for sure. It might have been unrelated."

"Bullshit. I told you Aaron was here that night. Panicked. Looking for you. Looking for a middle-aged guy. Government guy, or something like that, was what he said. Who never showed up, not that I saw. And neither did Aaron the next day, he was just gone. And what's that big gun he wears on his hip? Is that a magnum?"

Dave's former partner while working for Absolute Armored in Detroit—and current friend—was Aaron Abruzzo, and he wore his stainless-steel Colt Delta Elite 10mm everywhere.

"Pretty much. Well, I thought there was a small chance, but this pretty much confirms it. But he hasn't called me."

"You're under investigation by the FBI, there's no way he couldn't figure that out, that Vegas thing was all over Fox and CNN for days. If he did do this, he's probably trying to protect you, in case he's a suspect. Which it doesn't sound like he is. If it was him. Have you called him?"

He shook his head. "No. I figure they might be on to my phone."

"You use a burner."

"That won't make much of a difference. Not to the FBI. Or whoever it is. Shit. Maybe it is better that we're keeping our distance." He gave her a look. "I thought this was all over. FBI can't prove anything in Vegas. If they could, I'd be in jail. But this guy, whether or not Aaron killed him, this is something else."

"You think they'll send another guy, to do whatever that one was supposed to do?"

"Fuck, I don't know." He chewed at his lip. "Maybe I shouldn't spend so much time over here. Maybe it's not safe."

"Maybe it is. It's been a month. More. Look at me. I don't want you going down that rabbit hole again. The despair. Waiting to die. Waiting for them to come for you. You can't live like that. That's not living."

He growled, deep in his throat. Scowled. His face darkened. Finally he took a deep breath, and seemed to come out of it. "Fine," he said. "But I'm going to go back to practicing more. And...I need to get a rifle."

"You do what you need to do."

Later that afternoon Dave parked his Jeep in the parking lot of a strip mall and walked across the lot to the building. The Personal Defense Institute of Prescott—"P-Dip" to all the students—was sandwiched between a hair salon and a pet store. Physically the exterior of the place was as unimpressive as the rest of the strip mall, but he'd attended classes there for months, and the owner, Mackie, was excellent.

It was an off-time, and as he peered in the windows he didn't see anyone. The door was unlocked, though, and he went in. Mackie did everything he could to keep the place from smelling like dirty socks, but with all the mats and punching bags soaking up sweat every day it was a constant battle, and the air was a mix of faint sweaty musk, bleach, and some sort of lavender scent. "Hello?" he called out.

A few seconds later Mackie popped out of the back. "Good afternoon!" he said brightly, then recognized Dave. "Zombie. Shit, man, good to see you. Haven't seen you in forever."

They met in the center of the room. "Yeah," Dave said. "Sorry about that. I got pretty banged up in a car accident, and needed to do some rehab. I was wondering—"

"Car accident?" Before he'd started P-Dip Mackie had been a U.S. Army Ranger who'd seen a little bit of combat in Iraq. He'd recognized that Dave had PTSD long before Dave had. He gave Dave a dirty look as his eyes were tracing the pink scars on Dave's face. "Zombie, I watch the goddamn news. You don't think I know how you got fucked up? I watched it. The news played it non-stop for weeks. Took me all of half a second to recognize you under all that blood, not giving a shit about the pain, as usual. I know guys in the sheriff's department too, I've seen the video from Cracker Barrel that still hasn't been released."

"Oh."

"Yeah, fucking *oh*. You forgot everything I fucking taught you about counters, blocks, holds, leg sweeps... But you didn't quit, did you. Not for one goddamn second." He stepped close and looked in Dave's eyes. "How you doing?"

"Pain's not too bad. I'm stiff more than any—"

"No, not that. How are *you* doing?"

"Okay, I guess. Good."

"Yeah?" Mackie kept looking in his eyes.

"Yeah. Better."

Mackie nodded. "Yeah, I can tell. Good."

Dave said, "I don't know if I'm up for any sparring, but I'm wondering if I can jump into a beginning class. Get back into stretching, maybe start practicing techniques. I'm mostly healed. Only hurts a little bit, and pain doesn't really bother me. I'm more worried about flexibility and range of motion than anything else right now."

"I don't want you ripping yourself open on my mats." Mackie frowned. "Didn't you get shot like three fucking times? In addition to that guy doing a number on your face."

"Yeah. Thigh, hip, and chest, but none of them were that bad. Broken nose and eye socket. Lost a tooth. Sixty-seven stitches. Concussion. But nothing serious, and like I said, I'm mostly healed."

Mackie rolled his eyes. "Jesus, and you wondered why I called you Zombie. Sure, you can sit in. But don't bleed on my mats, and try not to scare any of the cherries in class, although you don't have that dead-eyed look anymore. Somebody might figure out who you are, so be prepared for that. Let's go look at the class schedule."

Chapter Eight

Victor Ybarra, head and founder of *La Fuerza*—"The Force"—cartel, had most of his cabinet, as he thought of them, at the ranch outside Torreón in north central Mexico to discuss strategy. Current affairs, and future moves. Carlos Guerrero—Chuy—was his wicked smart number two. Miguel Aponte ran a lot of the combat operations. Alan Iglesias was in charge of drug production and distribution—mostly cocaine, but also meth, heroin, MDMA, and marijuana.

A number of other men hovered in the background, for when they were needed. Timotéo Sandoval, a very young lieutenant who'd proved himself in the turf war against Los Zetas and CJNG, which was not going as well as Ybarra had hoped. Two-front wars rarely went well, but CJNG and Los Zetas had already been at war when La Fuerza jumped in. CJNG, *Cartel de Jalisco Nueva Generacion*, was, after all, originally known as *Los Mata Zetas*, "We kill Zetas" or "Zeta killers". Still, the efforts of La Fuerza to expand its territory were struggling.

Beside Sandoval was Nelson Santiago, who'd been under a little suspicion just for surviving the disaster that had been the operation in Arizona, at least until Rogelio Ramos returned home and talked up the man's efforts, and laid all the blame—or at least as much of the blame as he could—on police and armed citizens disrupting their plans to kill the witness against Roberto Muñiz, Ybarra's number three, arrested trying to get back to Mexico. For what it was worth, Ramos had an excellent record, and Ybarra believed every word he said. Still, he couldn't let the man live, not after such a public failure. Especially after Muñiz was murdered in jail by deputies (officially he 'committed suicide') in response to the deadly but failed attempt to eliminate the witness. But Ybarra had spared Nelson. The man's skill with electronics, and explosives, was too valuable to waste. Standing beside Nelson was Munio Molina—MM, pronounced *emmay-emmay*—who had been promoted to Ramos' position.

They'd been discussing strategy for two days, taking breaks to eat and drink and spend time with the women lounging around the big pool in bikinis or nothing at all, while heavily armed men patrolled the grounds. Then Ybarra, while on the toilet and scrolling through the internet on his phone, had stumbled across the video, and it had stuck with him. It was now playing on loop on the laptop sitting on his desk, for everyone to see.

He'd found the video on YouTube, but it had originally been part of a broadcast by a local TV news crew out of Phoenix. The news report, on the grand reopening of a restaurant, featuring many prominent Arizona politicians, was just two minutes long. Ybarra frowned at it, thinking. Chuy was seething. Growling death threats. Ybarra shook his head.

"Don't let the uniform fool you—the sheriff is a politician. And going after politicians always makes for more complications." Not that they hadn't done it before, although almost all their efforts were focused on this side of the border. "I've heard from a few sources that he is thinking of retiring. The wounds are bad, and he may never fully recover. If we go after him now, kill him, will he be an example to the others… or will we only make him a martyr? America is not Mexico, and this man is unique. From what I have read and seen, the last thing we want to do is make *him* a martyr. Things at the border are the best they've ever been for us. *Los norteamericanos* are in the process of destroying themselves, and the best thing we can do is get out of their way. Or help."

Off to one side, Nelson Santiago was trying not to sweat. He still wasn't convinced Ybarra wouldn't change his mind and kill him, and he was wracking his brain trying to think of ways he could make himself more valuable to the cartel. He had one, but it was a bit risky. Still, he was there to do a job, and the more trusted he was in the cartel, the higher up he moved, the better. He'd spent four years getting to this point, and now he was here, with the heads of the cartel, discussing strategy. He cleared his throat. Ybarra and Chuy looked his way. "Osterman might be an unwise target. You're right, he's not just a politician or a police officer, he's almost a…folk hero. More so now than ever. But you could still send a message." Nelson hadn't just been there, he'd done a lot of research after the fact as to exactly what had happened. What had gone so wrong. "Osterman didn't stop your men from killing the witness. That was a citizen. A local hero, now, to be sure, but not a police officer or a politician. Just a regular guy who got lucky. He killed at least five of our men."

Ybarra nodded. He was no stranger to the details.

"If we go to the trouble of killing him, we need to make sure everyone knows we did it," MM said.

"That still could cause us problems," Ybarra pointed out. Which wasn't a no. "Especially at the border. The Americans don't care what we do, as long as we do it in Mexico."

"A murder up there could be messy," Nelson said. "But what if he just…disappeared from there? If we grabbed him, and brought him down here, we could do whatever we wanted. Tell everyone or no one. And while the American authorities might shout, if it happens inside Mexico they will do nothing. Except maybe cover it up. But we can make sure everyone who needs to knows what we did."

Ybarra thought. "Hmm. That is not a bad idea," he said slowly. "But it could easily become messy. Maybe it would simply be better, easier to kill him up there. Nothing sends a message like murder."

"I can look into it," Nelson volunteered.

"Your James Bond gadgets won't help hogtie a man," Chuy said dismissively. He thought Ybarra should have executed the man simply for being part of such a disaster.

"Shouldn't I handle this?" MM said. After all, he had taken over Ramos' position in the cartel. "I should be on the one handling this."

"Then why aren't you?" Chuy demanded.

Ybarra looked back and forth between Chuy, MM, and Nelson, a hint of a smile on his face. A little competition was always good.

Chapter Nine

Aaron awoke with a jerk, panting, his heart racing in his chest. He was covered in sweat.

The bedroom was quiet. Well, quiet except for Arlene's constant low growl of a snore. She was amazing—she both could and would snore no matter what position she slept in, on her back, on her side, face down—but it was a constant drone that he'd learned long ago to tune out. Like white noise. The sound of the surf. He'd thought only fat people snored, but she was lean as an overcooked chicken wing. He glanced over at her. She was on her stomach, her face turned toward him but mostly out of sight beneath her mane of blonde hair. A clump of hair twitched every few seconds as she snored. It was the only sound he heard.

He sat up slowly, trying not to disturb her. He'd mostly soaked through his undershirt, and his boxers were damp as well. He heard snuffling, and saw Peanut on the floor beside the bed, her paws twitching as she chased something in a dream. He shivered in the dark and stood up. He grabbed his heavy Colt off the nightstand and tiptoed out of the room.

Gun down along his leg he moved to the front door and checked that it was locked, then peered out the window. There was never much to see in the trailer park, but of what he could see, nothing seemed out of place. No strange vehicles. No guys in ninja hoods creeping up the concrete parking pad. He checked his watch, a Timex Expedition with glow-in-the-dark hands, and saw it wasn't even four a.m. But he knew he wasn't getting back to sleep. "Fuck," he swore softly.

He grabbed a can of Coke out of the fridge and sat down at the kitchen table. He cracked the top and took a sip, the pop so cold it made his teeth ache, and the bad tooth he'd been nursing for weeks decided to send a lance of pain into his jaw. He winced and hissed and fought back a curse, trying to stay quiet. The throbbing tooth did not make his mood any better.

Aaron looked around for a pack of Marlboros, so he could light one up. Then he remembered he was trying to quit. "Fuuuuck," he growled. He set the can down on the kitchen table next to his Colt, and eyed the pistol. Colt Delta Elite 10mm, stainless steel, with the factory black grips sporting the red triangle on each side. The gun was all original, but for the barrel. That was new. A Scheumann, fit by a gunsmith in Rochester Hills who specialized in 1911s, who Dave had previously recommended. Aaron had bought the match barrel for cash at a gun store downriver, and the gunsmith had been happy to fit it to his gun for a not-so-small fee. Aaron had been ready to tell the guy all about how he wanted a more accurate gun, that's why he bought a new barrel, the factory piece was getting a little loose and shot out, but the guy hadn't asked. Hadn't cared. The pistol's original barrel Aaron had wiped down with his shirt, after making sure it didn't have a serial number on it, and then hurled out the open passenger door window of his rental car, down the side of a mountain, as he drove south on I-17 from Prescott Valley toward Phoenix. A mile later he'd thrown the spent 10mm case. When he'd got home to Michigan he'd started wondering about his shoes, if he'd left prints in the dirt, so he'd thrown those out too, into a Dumpster somewhere in Detroit.

After that there was nothing, no physical evidence, tying him to the body, the secret government agent cocksucker Colman he'd left in the Arizona dirt with a 10mm hole right through the middle of his damn chest. He'd finally remembered the guy's name, or at least the name he'd been using when he'd shown up at the hospital, trying to take Dave into custody...likely to never be seen again.

No evidence whatsoever. As far as he knew.

However, the world was full of things he didn't know, or understand. Why did so many dudes want to dress up and pretend they were chicks? What idiot at Ford decided a twin turbo V-6 was a better choice for the Raptor than a V-8? Who the fuck would put pineapple on a pizza? And were there any security cameras near where he'd shot the guy? Had he somehow left a trace of DNA evidence behind?

If anyone had spotted him or his rental anywhere near the spot where it had happened, you'd think that—at least—an asshole detective would have stopped by the house to ask him questions. It had been a month, and no SWAT team had knocked down his front door with a battering ram, so he was probably free and clear of the authorities.

But, still....

Unlike his friend and former partner Dave, who couldn't seem to take a shit without some assholes trying to kill him, in groups of three or more, Aaron had never shot anybody. Never killed anybody. Sure, he'd pointed his gun at two dozen assholes and idiots while working for Absolute Armored, rolling through the mean streets of Detroit, but he'd never had to pull the trigger. Until now.

And the thing was, nobody knew. Nobody.

He hadn't told Arlene. Not that he thought she'd give two shits, if he told her the guy was a government asshole who'd been going for his gun she'd be like, 'Good riddance' and try to find his grave so she could spit on it. But he was protecting her. She wouldn't have to lie about anything if she didn't actually know anything. And murder was a big deal. A big fucking deal. And they weren't married, so if she knew anything she could be, what did they call it, 'compelled' to testify against him. Better she didn't have to lie. Technically it was self-defense, and if the sheriff had anything to say about it Aaron probably wouldn't have any worries, but Colman had been CIA, or something like that. You didn't just shoot one of those guys and walk away.

He didn't have PTSD, he hadn't been in combat, he'd only shot an asshole who needed to get shot, and the world was definitely a better place without him, but Aaron definitely was having nightmares. He figured that was just because he was worried about getting caught, the CIA or FBI or whoever booting in his door in the middle of the night, not because he'd popped Colman. The guy definitely deserved to get got. Walking back through the desert late at night, night vision goggles atop his head, he'd obviously had Dave's house under surveillance. Maybe he'd been planning to kill him, if he'd been home. No way to know, but the guy's hand had twitched—Aaron hadn't imagined that—and when he flipped the guy's jacket back there'd been a pistol on his hip. Aaron was just faster. And he'd hit him dead center, a perfect goddamn shot, straight through the heart and out his back, if the guy had fallen onto an operating table in a hospital they probably couldn't have saved him. Aaron carried a 10mm for a reason, and he'd shot the guy with an honest-to-God Winchester Black Talon, which the anti-gunners loved to hate and had been out of production forever. It was probably a collector's item. Worked like a fucking charm.

Not telling Arlene made sense. But…he also hadn't told Dave. He'd wanted to, and almost had several times. He could call Dave on the burner he'd been using, and he almost had, two days after he'd gotten back to Michigan, but checking the news once again (to see if there was any more news about Colman, other than the initial report of the murder) he saw Pietro Bufonte, the man himself, whose asshole kid had killed Dave's parents on his third DUI and walked away, and who had sent a carload of guys to kill Dave…had been killed himself. Shot, and his whole house torched. The same night Aaron had killed Colman. The same night Dave…hadn't been home.

Aaron wasn't stupid. He knew what that meant. Exactly what that fucking meant. And he knew the FBI would be all over it. So he stayed away from Dave. He didn't even trust the burner anymore, went out and bought another one, although he hadn't used it yet. Used either of them. He hadn't heard about any arrests for Bufonte's murder, so that was good news. However Dave had done it, he'd been smart. If the FBI had anything on him, he'd be in custody.

He couldn't fly down there; not only was he a bit short on cash, he didn't have any more goddamn vacation, after heading down to Arizona three times in as many months to check on Dave, before, during, and after his hospital stay, courtesy of the cartel assholes who'd torn up Prescott.

It had been a month. So…it was time. To reach out to Dave, and let him know. Because whatever Colman had been doing, whoever he was working for…maybe they'd send a replacement. Shit, it had been a month, maybe they already had. Workers at that shop had found the body just a few hours later, and the sheriff's department was investigating. And likely whoever Colman had worked for was investigating as well, behind the scenes. Aaron was pretty sure Colman's presence there had something to do with Dave's fingerprints, Colman had very definitely keyed on that when Aaron brought it up, but Dave didn't have any fingerprints anymore. Maybe the federal government—FBI, CIA, whoever—hadn't heard that news. There was no inefficiency like government bureaucratic inefficiency.

Aaron didn't trust even his new burner, not completely…and he also didn't have the money to fly out to Arizona to talk to Dave in person. And the lack of sleep from the nightmares was pissing him off. And his tooth was killing him. And Peanut—Peanut had something going on, she wasn't eating. He was worried. She was eleven, which was getting up there in age for a dog her size. All of which was giving him heartburn. Or maybe a fucking ulcer. It never rained 'cept it fucking poured.

"What time did you wake up?"

Aaron jerked his head up. Arlene shuffled into the kitchen, yawning. It was bright, and he saw that the sun was up. A glance at his watch showed he'd been sitting at the kitchen table for an hour and a half. Shit.

"Fucking yesterday, practically." He got up with a sigh. "I'll make coffee."

"Why do black guys love big asses so much?" Aaron asked, staring out the window at the well-padded scenery walking past them in the Kroger parking lot.

Eddie Rogers was behind the wheel of the armored car. He was watching the women walking by as well, and didn't turn around as he answered. "Because that's what black girls got. Most all of 'em start out curvy, and end up thick. If you cain't learn to love what you got, that's a sure way to be miserable your whole life."

Aaron blinked. "Well shit, who knew you were going to lay some philosophy on me this run."

"Like motherfuckin' Gandhi," Eddie agreed, bobbing his round head. He threw a smile back at Aaron.

"More like Buddha."

"Hey now, I've dropped some weight," Eddie complained.

"You still look like you're over-inflated, dude. You got high blood pressure?"

Eddie shrugged. "A little. Runs in my family."

Aaron gave him a look. "Keep an eye on that shit. Aren't heart attacks the number one killer of black guys? My family, it's cancer." He bent down, and peered out the grimy windows, all around the armored truck. "You see anything?"

"Sheeeit, even with half the stores closed there's always so much shit going on in this parking lot you can never be sure." The Kroger was in the elbow of an L-shaped strip mall on Greenfield Road in Detroit, and most of the other businesses inside the run-down structure had closed. "Ain't nobody screamin', runnin', or wavin' a gun."

"Yeah. Well, honk if you see something. Other than big asses." With one last careful look out the small window Aaron popped the door and jumped down. He had his clipboard and single bag of cash—a paltry $16,000—in his left hand, and nothing in his right. The big Colt Delta Elite, shiny stainless steel, sat on his hip, the hammer cocked provocatively. Anyone who saw it, who didn't know anything about guns, assumed Aaron was just looking for an excuse to shoot someone. And he was just fine with that misapprehension, the fewer people thinking about robbing him the better.

Two stops later, Eddie was pulling out of the parking lot of a Popeyes Chicken on Joy Road when he said, "I think someone's following us."

"Yeah?" Aaron turned and looked out the window in the back door. There was a lot of traffic.

"Yeah. Black car. Black or dark blue. All these fucking cars look alike these days, I swear. Kinda like a cop car. You see it back there? Four cars back, next lane over. But I don't know if it's the same one. If it is, it's been on us for two stops."

Aaron squinted. "It's a Charger. I think. You're right, all the goddamn new cars all look alike. And it's the government's fault."

"You always think everything's the government's fault."

"No, I'm serious. It's the regulations on gas mileage. They keep getting stricter and stricter, so all the cars just get smoother and smoother, like eggs, to be more aerodynamic."

"Well they gotta do something about global warming, man."

Aaron rolled his eyes. "Don't even get me started on that bullshit." He looked around. "Take that next turn. We can loop around our next stop from the back. See if this asshole follows us."

Eddie did. The dark sedan hung back, the driver invisible behind the glare off the windshield, but it made the turn behind them. But it didn't make the next.

"I guess not," Eddie said, looking in his rearview mirror.

"Or he saw everything he needed to," Aaron said. This wasn't his or Eddie's usual run, and he tried to think. "This is a three-day-a-week run, right? Remind me when we get back, I'll mention it to Joe. Find out who's scheduled for it day after tomorrow, and tell them myself, because Joe'll probably forget. They'll probably still drive around with their head up their ass, but I can't hold everybody's fucking hand."

"You know, you talk a lot of shit for somebody who's never been robbed."

"And you know why?" Aaron shot back. "Because I pay fucking attention. I had my head up my ass, I woulda been robbed at least three, four times that I can think of. But I saw it coming. Or Davey did. You see 'em coming, and you eye-fuck 'em, you pull your gun out and let 'em know you're ready to rock and roll, they fuck off down the street. Which, I guess, means only the guys ready to rock and roll are going to rob me, but fuck it, you only live once, right? *You* pay attention, that's why I'll work with you, but half the humps working for this company wouldn't notice if their own dicks were on fire." He met Eddie's eyes in the rearview. "You know I ain't lyin'."

Chapter Ten

Dixon wasn't hurting for money, although he was very careful with how he spent the actual cash he had on hand. Even using cash to buy groceries and Starbucks and whatnot as often as possible, he still had a lot of that hidden away. Where no one would find it. While he'd paid for his flight and hotel with a credit card, he planned to pay for a lot of things in Las Vegas with cash, so his movements couldn't be tracked.

Detroit Metropolitan Airport, located twenty minutes southwest of the city, was a hub for Delta Airlines, as was Las Vegas (he was pretty sure Vegas was a hub for every airline), so getting a direct flight, even on short notice, was easy. He landed just after noon on Friday, collected his bag from the carousel, grabbed a taxi to the Planet Hollywood hotel and casino, and checked in. He would have preferred to stay at the Bellagio, but the room prices there were ridiculous. And then...he was supposed to wait. Wait for a call on the burner phone he'd brought along. That he made sure was fully charged. And that he'd triple-checked was getting a good signal inside the hotel.

But he didn't want to just sit in the hotel room. He was too nervous, too jumpy, and besides, he was in Vegas. He hadn't been to Las Vegas in…he thought back. Twelve years. With the now ex-wife. They'd done a little gambling, seen a show, done all the standard touristy things. Had good hotel sex. Quite unlike the reason for his current visit. Although he was not blind to the irony that he was, in effect, paying a bit of homage to Vegas' roots.

Walking the Strip he saw a lot of things had changed. Lots of new construction. He walked north on the sidewalk for a while, watching the passing people and cars. Twice he was passed by Ferraris colored brightly as parrots, the drivers loudly revving the engines in slow moving traffic, and he guessed they'd just rented the sports cars, likely for an hour, to cruise up and down the strip looking cool. But he was uneasy, and the passing scenery wasn't quite enough to distract him.

He'd been uneasy ever since that visit from Special Agent Gogolak of the FBI. Objectively, intellectually, there should be *less* reason for him to be nervous. The FBI had been after Pietro Bufonte since before Dixon had gone through the police academy. Probably since before he'd first gotten laid. Dixon had started doing favors for Bufonte, mostly providing information—for cash—not long after first meeting him, while investigating the death of his son. Bufonte had seen that Dixon was…agreeable. So their arrangement had gone on for years. But Bufonte was dead. As far as the FBI was concerned, Pietro Bufonte was a closed case. Sure, he was one of the ones "who got away", but all they could do now, all they were likely doing, was investigating the man's death, and cleaning up any potential loose ends—known associates, etc.—and figure out who was taking over his territory so they could go after that person. Dixon knew Bufonte hadn't hired the FBI to murder anyone, but no one else did, especially not the FBI, and it wouldn't surprise him if they were cleansing their files of anything that even hinted they might have been involved. So, he should have been breathing easier. But he wasn't, and not all of his nervousness came from thinking about what the FBI might be doing.

He drifted over to the huge pond in front of the Bellagio, but it was still daylight and the famous fountain, which sprayed brightly-lit water in time to classical music, wasn't running. He made a mental note to check back later—that final fountain scene at the end of *Ocean's Eleven* was great, and had been enough to get him and his wife to head out to Vegas that last time. His oldest might have been conceived in Las Vegas as well, the timing worked. Although the two of them had been staying at the Circus Circus, which was shabby even back then. Telling your tweenage daughter she was conceived during a romantic vacation sounded much better than admitting the condom broke while he was banging her mom, drunk on discount margaritas, in a rundown hotel on the cheap end of the Strip.

The sun was hot on his head and the back of his neck. He leaned on the fence and looked up and down the Strip at the tall hotels, the palm trees, and the passing pedestrians. Most of them were fat and looked stupid, but there was more than the average percentage of very interesting individuals. He heard a phone ringing, and it took him a second to realize it was the burner phone in his pocket. He never left the battery in it, and only used it to make outgoing calls, and had never heard the ring tone before. He didn't recognize the number, but that was as expected.

He cleared his throat, and licked his lips before answering. "Yeah."

"Phil's, inside TI. Seven o'clock."

"TI?"

The caller sighed. "Treasure Island." Then he was listening to a dead line.

Dixon checked his watch. He had over three hours to kill. He tried to ignore the fact that he'd broken out into an instant sweat during the call. He put the phone away, then looked up and down the Strip. Looking south he had to shield his eyes with his hand, as he was staring darn near directly at the sun. He looked north, and squinted. There, past the Caesar's Forum, past the Mirage, he could see TREASURE ISLAND written in red atop a hotel, maybe a mile away.

He had plenty of time to head back to his room, maybe watch TV, or take a shower, but he was far too nervous. He damn sure couldn't sit still, and needed to burn off some energy. He walked north on the west side of the Strip and entered the Caesar's Forum. There was a small shopping mall inside there, filled with shops displaying mostly high-end names. He wandered for an hour, going in and out of a few stores, not really paying attention to much, although he was repeatedly shocked at the prices of some of the items on display. Meant to suck the fresh cash out of the pocket of some fool who'd just won big at the slots. But, at some point, he started checking for a tail.

He was no spy, trained in tradecraft, but he knew a few tricks. Doubling back unexpectedly, especially on escalators. Doing slow circles on the mezzanine. Watching the reflections of passing people in storefront windows. He left the Forum, crossed the Strip on a pedestrian bridge, and entered the Venetian. He vaguely remembered indoor canals, and after wandering through a maze of a casino floor finally found the Grand Canal Shoppes. Another enclosed mall, meant to look like Venice, complete with an indoor canal with gondolas and a ceiling far above painted sky blue, with clouds. There were two floors of shops and restaurants and he wandered aimlessly once again, frequently checking to see if anyone was following him.

He wandered from the Venetian north to the adjacent Wynn, then back. With fifteen minutes to kill he headed back across the Strip on an elevated pedestrian walkway that deposited him in front of Treasure Island. There was a Starbucks there at the curb, and a daiquiri bar for passing pedestrians.

The casino floor began just inside the front door, stretching in front of him bright and loud. Slot machines and gaming tables. The hotels deliberately made their casinos difficult to navigate, so their guests spent more time, and likely more money, on the floor, but Dixon didn't want to spend any more time than absolutely necessary inside this place, the site of the meet. He found a big map of the casino on a floor display, and discovered what he was looking for was Phil's Steak House. And it was close.

Ignoring the crowds of people, and the noise of slot machines and people drinking, gambling, and having fun, he walked past a Vietnamese restaurant and just ahead he saw the sign for Phil's. Both cold and sweaty he walked forward on stiff legs.

The entrance to the restaurant was right off the main casino floor, and just one narrow doorway. A hostess in a simple black dress stood at a stand there. The menu was displayed behind glass on a wall nearby, and Dixon's eyes darted to it as he walked up—and widened at the few prices he saw. King Crab Legs $115. An 8-ounce filet was $62. They were charging twenty bucks just for a wedge salad.

"Hi, sir," the young hostess said brightly. "Do you have a reservation?"

"Um," Dixon said, frowning, then the man who'd been loitering nearby, who Dixon thought might be a waiter or a manager, stepped forward.

"He's with us," the man said, and jerked his head for Dixon to follow him.

He led Dixon through the restaurant, which was somewhat small, the walls painted a warm creamy yellow, with dark wood trim. Most of the small tables were full of diners. He could smell food, and undoubtedly the food smelled good, but his stomach was flip-flopping with nausea.

There was a private dining room in back. He brought Dixon in, then closed the door behind them for privacy. The room was full of people, a dozen of them sitting at a long table and half as many standing against the walls behind them. Not a single woman to be seen, which didn't surprise Dixon at all. There were appetizers on the table, crostini and oysters, and bottles of wine. Dixon was interested to see how many people looked at him curiously…and how many ignored his arrival. The man who'd led him back, who was in a dark suit and tie, held out a wooden bowl. "Phone, wallet, keys, everything into the bowl. Everything."

This was not unexpected, and Dixon emptied his pockets into the bowl. The man handed the bowl to another guy, who left the room, then had Dixon raise his arms and expertly patted him down. He produced a small electronic device and waved it over Dixon's entire body, head to toe. Then he turned and nodded, but Dixon wasn't sure who to. The man at the head of the table was still ignoring him. A balding man in his sixties looked at Dixon and pointed at an empty seat. "Detective," he said. The word got the attention of most everyone in the room, and the quiet talking ceased. Dixon took the seat, fighting the urge to clear his throat.

He'd done what research he could, homework, and due to the subject matter had even been able to use his work computer for some of it. As a result, he recognized a few of the faces around the table. The man who'd spoken to him was Carmine Vaccarelli, reputed head of the mafia in Chicago, currently under indictment by the FBI. Two seats down from him was Frank Licata, who the FBI said was the head of the mob in Los Angeles. Across from Licata was a younger guy, looking a bit uneasy. Dixon recognized him as Tony Iacobelli, who'd either been a competitor of Bufonte's in Detroit or someone Bufonte had been grooming to take over for him after he retired and/or died. The guy at the head of the table…Dixon didn't recognize, but could easily guess who he was. He'd heard a New York accent as the man was talking. He'd also heard one of the men speaking in a Boston accent, massacring his As.

Dixon's heart beat faster. He'd known he'd be meeting someone high up in the organization. Maybe a few important people. To give a report. But he hadn't been expecting a full meeting of the people running what was left of *La Cosa Nostra* inside the United States. What, back in the day, had been called The Commission. He had no idea if it still was.

"You're far from the only cop Pete had on his payroll, but they tell me you're deeper into this investigation than any of those others, and we need answers," Vaccarelli said. "We need to know who took him out." He moved his eyes to include everyone sitting at the table. "You've been talking to the FBI, right? Most of us here are betting that it was the

FBI what did it. Revenge for him turning one of their guys. And causing that big debacle."

Dixon blinked in surprise and sat up straighter. "No," he said shaking his head. "Didn't he tell you? I'm sure he probably told you. Mr. Bufonte did not order that FBI hit on the kid. Anderson. I know that's what everyone is saying. That's what the FBI is saying. Maybe you asked, and he denied it, and you didn't believe him. But he didn't do it. I know that for a fact. He wasn't behind that FBI agent shopping out that hit on Anderson."

That got their attention. Everyone was looking at him now. He tried not to swallow. The man at the head of the table leaned his big head forward. "This you know?"

"Yes. I don't know a lot about his business, but I know that. It wasn't him. Someone else was after Anderson. And that wasn't the first time somebody tried to kill Anderson that summer. There was another incident where some cops got killed. Somebody wanted Anderson dead, somebody either high up in the FBI or with their claws in them, but it wasn't Bufonte." Dixon blinked, then shrugged. "Well, not then. Later, of course, after he already had the blame, and his health was failing, he figured what the hell, and sent those guys to Arizona. And...the next day he was dead."

His news did not make any of them look happy. "You're sure," Vaccarelli said.

"One hundred percent."

"It's what I've been telling you," Iacobelli said, waving a hand.

The men around the table traded looks. Licata leaned forward, and jabbed a finger at Dixon. "Then our need to know who is responsible for Pete Bufonte's death is even more urgent." And he looked around. There were a lot of suspicious looks around the table. Dixon understood immediately what was going on. If it wasn't the FBI, then it was an inside job.

"I don't think it was anybody here," Dixon said. "And I'd bet money it wasn't the FBI. I talked with their lead agent on this recently, and have talked a lot with them over the past few years. They would manufacture evidence for an indictment, they wouldn't murder. This isn't them."

Every head there turned to look at him. "Who do you think did it, then?" the head man asked him.

"David Anderson."

"The kid?" one of the guys sitting at the table, who hadn't spoken before, said derisively. "That Pete thought took out Paulie?"

Yeah," Dixon said.

"Bullshit," one of the other men said, with a lot of force. "They was hit by pros. A team. We've read the police report on the incident, from Las Vegas Metro, before the FBI showed up and took over. This wasn't some kid."

Dixon shook his head. "Look, I know Anderson, better than anybody else does. I've been trying to nail him for Paulie. Since it happened. FBI can place Anderson in Las Vegas a few hours before the fire at Bufonte's house in Summerlin, but it sounds like that's all they've got. But this guy…he isn't just some kid. I thought he was, for a long time, but not any more. Look, he's in the middle of this because everyone, including me, thinks he ran over Paulie, because Paulie ran over his parents after a few too many, and got off, right? A simple revenge thing, and easy to understand. So that's one. But a few years before that, when he's still in college, he was doing a ride along with a local police department, and they get into a gunfight with some bank robbers. He killed at least two, I confirmed that. So that's three. So Paulie wouldn't have been his first." He looked around the table, holding up three fingers. "Then someone—not Bufonte—hired Detroit SWAT officers to take him out. And they damn well tried. That happened in front of witnesses, in front of a cop, and he killed three. Walked away without a scratch. Six. *Six*." He held up six fingers. "Those are just the ones I know about. He disappeared for a year, but I found him, because he was sitting next to a cop who was targeted by a Mexican cartel. He killed at least four of them, and they had fucking AKs. That was straight-up combat, some of it caught on camera." He looked around the table. "That's ten. So Bufonte finally had enough, the cancer was starting to eat him up, and sent four guys after him, down to Arizona. Anderson killed them all before they could get out of the fucking car. None of them even got a shot off. Which makes *fourteen*. Does that sound like just some regular kid to you? A kid that took out a SWAT team, in a stand-up gunfight, in the middle of a street. Shot it out with cartel maniacs at a goddamn Cracker Barrel. A kid that, near as I can tell, right before he dropped off the grid, and it's probably why he dropped off the grid, took out half a dozen special forces guys who came after him at his house in Arizona, and still no one knows who the fuck sent them. Or why. The FBI says Bufonte, but I absolutely know that's wrong. Which makes twenty."

He looked around the table. "How many people have you ever heard of who've killed twenty people, outside of war, who aren't behind bars? He's never even been *charged*. And why do you think that is? There's something going on with this kid, I have no idea what, but I think the cartel thing was a cover. Had to be, because what are the chances? Nobody's that unlucky, that would have to be coincidence on a Biblical level. This kid has a secret. A huge fucking secret. And he's killed twenty people, that I know about, to keep it. Or maybe other people are doing the killing for him, covering for him. It's so weird I don't know what to think. But whatever it is, this secret, I think it involves the US government, the FBI at a minimum, but probably something more. He's got no gaps in his personal history until he headed to Arizona, but I know there's something, somewhere. I think the thing with Paulie, with Mr. Bufonte, was just…" He waved a hand, trying to think of a way to describe it in a way they'd understand. "Side action for him."

"That's bullshit, there's no way that's not bullshit," one of the men standing against the wall said. Several of the older men sitting at the table glanced at him, and he lowered his eyes apologetically for speaking out of turn. But there were a lot of dubious looks around the table too.

Dixon shrugged. "There are police reports," he said. "Witnesses. Security video of some of it. There were six bodies—shot, burned, and *blown up*—found around his cabin out in the desert. He was shot and badly burned, and it's right after that incident that the recording of the FBI agent came out, arranging Anderson's murder with the Detroit SWAT team sergeant. Mr. Bufonte's name wasn't anywhere on that recording, it was the FBI who dragged him into it, within hours, to save their own ass, but maybe to stop people asking tough questions. I've got no way to prove it, but that FBI agent on the recording, he was the number two guy in the Detroit office, a big shot, and I'd bet money he was doing it for some other government agency. He would have the contacts. When this kid did surface, he had a driver license in a different name. A real driver's license, not a fake. And he was never charged with having a false identity, which means the government gave it to him. There's a whole web of secrets and lies around this kid."

"If all that's true, and I'm not saying it is, not saying it isn't," Vaccarelli said, "then what you're saying isn't just that he's not just some kid, he's working for somebody. Or was. Spook, spec ops, or a mechanic, some shit like that. So, to him, taking out Paulie would be easy, and then you not being able to pin it on him, with all this time and effort you've put into it, easier to understand. But that makes me more curious than ever. Can we get to him? Ask him a few questions? Nicely. Maybe not so nicely. Sounds like he might take a bit of not-so-nice to start talking."

Dixon shook his head. "There are too many eyes on him. He was in hiding, but with everything that's happened it seems he's decided he's safer hiding out in plain sight. After that cartel thing the local papers made him out to be a hero. He was photographed hanging out with the governor last month, and is friends with the sheriff, who is a big deal. He's not using the Anderson name, but there's no safe way to get to him. I could go down there as a police officer, a detective, and try to talk to him about one or all of the incidents, but he has a track record of refusing to talk to cops. He won't say shit, and he will lawyer up, so that's a nonstarter. The FBI likes him, a little bit, maybe more than a little bit, for Bufonte, but if they had anything he'd have been in cuffs. Word is they can place him in Vegas that night through traffic cameras, but if they haven't made an arrest then that's all they have. He won't even sit down for an interview with them to talk about Vegas, or Bufonte, or anything, with or without a lawyer. Or…" Dixon shrugged. "Maybe he's got some kind of secret deal with them. If he's working for the government, maybe the FBI has been told to bury whatever evidence they've got tying him to the crime."

Dixon leaned back and looked around. He didn't like

the looks he was getting from everyone around the table as they digested the information. And it was easy to figure out why. Bufonte was dead, and Dixon had never had an arrangement with Iacobelli, his presumed replacement. So if Anderson was untouchable, what use was Dixon to them? He cleared his throat. "But, I may have an angle," he said, trying hard not to sound as nervous as he felt. "I think I know someone that I can talk to. Someone who might know, who probably does know something. And there aren't any eyes on him. And whether or not he knows something...he might be the way to get to Anderson."

Vaccarelli looked at the man at the head of the table, who turned his watery eyes on Dixon. "Then do it," he was told. "Do whatever you need to do. Because we need answers. And just so's we're clear on motivation," he said. "Our contacts who got us the police report, also got us a few documents out of Pete's safe. Some stuff that might have caused troubles, if the police found it. Records of payouts to people. Pete was a very, what's the word, fastidious record keeper. Anybody he paid off, anybody who was useful, he kept a record. That information can always come out, if we're not careful with it," he said pointedly, staring at Dixon. And he nodded at the security man at the door. Dixon was dismissed. Apparently he wasn't invited to stay for dinner.

He stood up from the table, nodding at the few people who glanced his way, and stepped out of the private dining room. The man doing security came out with him, and held out the bowl for Dixon to grab his things, then went back inside the dining room. The wooden doors *thunked* as they closed.

"Excuse me," Dixon said to a passing waiter, as he

stuffed his wallet and phone into his pockets. "Is there a back way out of here?"

The waiter opened his mouth to say no, but then he saw where Dixon was standing. What room he just exited. "Of course. Follow me sir."

He led Dixon to the busy kitchen, and through it. On the far side he opened up a door. Dixon nodded at him distractedly and strode through. He found himself in a blank access corridor. He strode down it, steps echoing loudly, passing closed doors to either side, and pushed through double-doors at the end to find himself on a loading dock inside a parking garage. Presumably at the rear of Treasure Island, but he'd gotten turned around and had never had that good a sense of direction. At the moment he was alone, not a single person or vehicle in sight. Distantly he could hear traffic.

He turned, took a few steps, and vomited into the corner, falling to his knees, sweating and shaking.

PART II
TEMPEST

Chapter Eleven

It was a two-hour drive or more, depending on traffic, but Dave didn't think it was wasted time. The upscale Scottsdale Gun Club had a huge selection of what he was looking for. Plus, a few things he'd previously purchased there had saved his life, which tended to cement customer loyalty like nothing else.

The smell of good coffee was in the air as he pushed through the front door. The gun shop, which also had a small indoor public range and exclusive members-only private range, still looked brand new even though it had been in business for a dozen years. The décor had changed subtly since the last time he'd been in, but he couldn't put his finger on exactly how. The walls were painted almond with cherry wood trim and subdued chrome accents. The lighting was bright, but indirect.

He moved past illuminated displays of expensive pocket knives and flashlights to the counter running across the back. The wall behind the counter was filled with racks of rifles and shotguns, and rental guns—mostly full-auto weapons—were on pegs above the racks.

One of the polo-wearing employees behind the counter moved toward him. "Good morning. Can I help you with anything?"

"I'm looking for an AR," Dave told him, his eyes scanning the racks. There were dozens of them on display.

"Anything in particular?" the employee asked. His nametag read DOC. He had a pistol on his hip as did all the employees, and Dave casually glanced at it. A compact Staccato with a red dot optic on the slide. Expensive. He'd likely gotten an employee discount.

"Not exactly."

"Well, let's see if we can figure it out. Are you looking just for something to have a little fun with at the range? Something for home defense? Shooting competition, like 3-gun?"

"I used to shoot a bit of 3-gun," Dave told him. "I had a very nice rifle, a TTI, but then it…" *But then it was seized as evidence after I killed three cops with it.* "But then I had to sell it. So I know a few things. But I'm not looking for a competition rifle. Just something general purpose, for self-defense. Doesn't have to be sexy. Reliability is more important than anything else."

"It always is. Okay, how much were you looking to spend?"

"I don't know. Give me some options, from cheap to stupid expensive."

"Okay, well, first," Doc said, grabbing a rifle off the rack, "I've got some particular ideas that not everyone here shares." The rifle in his hand didn't have a magazine inserted, and he pulled back the charging handle, retracting the bolt, to show Dave that the chamber was empty, while keeping the black rifle pointed in a safe direction. "The main one being that if you're talking a serious gun, an AR-15, an AR meant for self-defense, it should have a pinned gas block." He pointed to the military-style front sight post of the gun in his hand, the base of which incorporated the gas block. There were two steel crosspins holding the front sight base to the barrel. "A lot of ARs these days have low profile gas blocks tucked under the handguards that are held in place with set screws. With a properly dimpled barrel and Loctited screws that gas block likely will never move. But a gas block that's pinned in place, according to military specs, won't move even if you drive over it, blow it up, or drop it out of an airplane. And that matters because this is a gas-operated gun. If for some reason your rifle doesn't run, the number one leading cause of that is issues with the gas not getting where it is supposed to go. Meaning the gas block. Follow me?"

"Absolutely. Pinned block good, screwed block bad."

Doc smiled. "Well, not quite, pinned block good, screwed block probably good. If you're buying it for just punching paper, it doesn't matter. If you're thinking of buying one gun to last you through the apocalypse, it had better damn well have a pinned gas block. At least to my way of thinking. After that, really, it's all about options. On the less expensive side we've got this right here," he hefted the rifle in his hands. "It's a Smith & Wesson. It's got everything you need, nothing you don't, and build quality is fair. But," he shrugged, "meh." He set it back in the rack, searched a bit, and came back with another black rifle that looked very similar. "Next up in price is the Springfield Armory Saint. Pinned gas block, but the furniture, the handguard, the pistol grip, the stock, are a little nicer, so you're going to pay a couple hundred bucks more. Okay, now, there are dozens of manufacturers, and I'm going to ignore the ones that are mostly show rather than go. And I'm going to skip over the middle-range for a second, and go to the top."

He put the Springfield Armory back in the rack, walked down the wall, and returned with a new rifle. It had a longer aluminum handguard with the gas block concealed beneath it. "This is a Knight's Armament SR-15. It's not the most expensive AR we have, but it's the most expensive combat-proven or combat-grade, shall we say, AR we've got in stock. Pinned gas block, all that. It's three times the cost of the Smith & Wesson. And I know we sell it, but I think it's hugely overpriced. For what you get, you're paying an extra grand at least just for the name on the side. But people still buy them, and will tell you they're the best. But if you ask them why they're better than a Geissele or whatever… crickets." Doc put the rifle back in its spot, then walked back empty-handed.

"Okay," he said, "now we come to the crowded middle-ground. There are a lot of companies that make good-to-great stuff that is priced in the middle of the pack. Bravo Company. Daniel Defense. A lot of people swear by Daniel Defense, and they've got a few military contracts, but in my opinion you're paying Cadillac prices for a Chevy. At the top end of that crowded middle is Geissele. In my opinion they're the best, period, regardless of cost, and they're still like seven hundred bucks cheaper than that Knight's. But that means they're still two grand or so. I paid that much for my first car."

"Yeah."

"If you don't want cheapest, but aren't willing to drop two to three grand, I've got just the thing. We just got in a shipment of these, and I think they're the best out there at this price." He walked over and came back with another AR-15 in his hands. To people unfamiliar with the design it would have looked identical to the other rifles, but Dave could pick out the minor differences. "You ever hear of Sons of Liberty Gun Works? No? Well, they stand by every single part in their rifles, and they publish the specs of every part in their guns as well. Type of steel, all that. This is their new model, designed to be everything you need and nothing you don't in a civilian fighting rifle. Pinned gas block with fixed front sight post as you see." He handed the rifle to Dave, who tried out the trigger and shouldered it a few times. "The barrel is as short as you can get before you have to file that pesky unconstitutional NFA paperwork, as that muzzle device is permanently attached. Comes with iron sights, as every serious rifle should have, great LaRue trigger, good stock and handguard, and an HRF enlarged magwell, which is overlooked by a lot of people but that I think is important." He gestured to the gun in Dave's hands. "Behold, the Simple Jack."

Dave blinked. "What?" He thought the man had said his name. "Jack?" he said, surprised. Then he blinked again. "Wait, like Simple Jack, from *Tropic Thunder*, the movie? The 'never go full retard' Simple Jack?"

"Well, I don't know, but you have to assume…"

Dave burst out laughing. "That's awesome."

"Seems deliberately designed to offend, but I'm okay with that. The very fact rifles like this exist offend some people. Are you local?"

Dave shook his head. "Prescott area."

"That's maybe even better. We've got a lot of two- and three-gun matches around here, if you wanted to get your game on, and this will work for that, absolutely, but that's not really what this is for. If you're looking for some tactical carbine training, Ravengard, the oldest and largest privately-run firearms training facility in the world, is half an hour north of Prescott."

"That's right, it is."

"Owning a piano does not make you a musician, as Jeff Cooper liked to say. They usually have a six- or nine-month waiting list, but there's a reason for that. Just a thought. So?" He gestured at the rifle in Dave's hands.

Dave nodded. "Yeah. But I'm going to need an Aimpoint, I see they're on sale. And half a dozen Magpul mags. Case of ammo." He pointed at the case between them. "And a Glock 19."

Doc had a big smile on his face. "It's days like these that make me wish I was on commission. You want coffee? Let me get you some coffee, while you fill out the paperwork, and I grab that other stuff."

Chapter Twelve

Arlene's ancient pink Geo Tracker—the BarbieMobile—had finally died. Aaron had done so much work on her Ford Taurus that he just adopted that as his. It had new tires, brakes, shocks, and exhaust, not to mention the replaced front bumper, and he'd done so much work to the transmission and engine that it was practically a SHO—it likely had three hundred horse under the hood now, although he hadn't had it tested, and didn't plan on racing it, he had his fastback Mustang for that. Arlene had bought a ten-year-old Honda CR-V for a steal, because it had fucked-up brakes. Well, fucked-up brakes and a weird fucked-up factory paint job, somewhere between gold and baby puke. Aaron had fixed the brakes. Arlene loved the color, once more proving that there was no accounting for taste.

He was cruising north on Telegraph, weaving in and out of traffic, just letting the engine breathe, hardly even speeding, when he saw the dark car in his rearview. He'd barely noticed it before the cop hit his lights. Lights in the grille and behind the windshield—an unmarked cop car, which should be against the law. Swearing, Aaron moved over into the right lane and turned into a parking lot. He was in uniform, heading to work, and visibly armed, which usually got him off with a warning.

He rolled down the window, pulled out his wallet, and put his hands on the steering wheel. He'd left early, he usually did, but probably this was going to make him late.

"Where are you going in such a hurry?"

"Heading to work," Aaron said. He turned his head, and blinked. The cop wasn't in a uniform, but rather a dark suit. Plainclothes? But the voice…. Aaron looked up as the guy stopped beside his door. He was familiar.

"You?" Aaron said. "The Bloomfield cop?"

"West Bloomfield," Dixon automatically corrected him.

"Whatever. The way-out-of-your-fucking-jurisdiction cop," Aaron said. Frowning, he leaned out his open window and looked at the car behind him, the hidden red and blue lights still flashing. "Unless you got fired and are working for Taylor P.D. now?"

"I can call them, if you want. I'm sure they can find something to ticket you for."

"What do you want?" Aaron said. "Are you still trying to find Dave? If so, you haven't been paying fucking attention to the news." While most of the news stories referred to him as Pima Jack, after that carload of mafia goons had shown up at his place and the dots didn't quite connect to the cartel, at least one Arizona news outlet had stumbled across the name Dave Anderson, and figured out he and Pima Jack were one and the same. Nobody seemed to care. At least, nobody in Arizona. But detective…Aaron searched for the man's name in his memory. Dixon, that was it. Detective Dixon had been trying to get Dave for years, to pin that hit-and-run death on him.

"Have *you* been paying attention to the news?" Dixon asked him. He was faking the confidence. Every time he'd confronted Abruzzo at his home the man had slammed the door in his face. He thought maybe surprising him away from home might shake something loose, but he was completely out of his jurisdiction, that was no lie, and would be hard-pressed to explain the stop to his boss. Hopefully he wouldn't have to. "Your friend Dave has bigger problems than just me. Pietro Bufonte's dead in Las Vegas."

"Yeah? So what. Good fucking riddance."

Dixon had seen something on Abruzzo's face. Just a hint of something, but. "So the FBI is after him for that."

"Bullshit," Aaron said. "That was mob-on-mob homo action."

"Was it? You don't seem too sure."

"There was like four guys killed, not just Bufonte. Four guys."

"Wouldn't be the first time for Anderson."

Aaron blinked. The man did have a point. "Yeah, well, you're not wrong there, Davey's got a helluva batting average, but what the fuck do you care? You're not FBI. Go talk to them, become a fed. What exactly do you want with me, Detective Dickbreath? It is Dickbreath, right? I think I lost your card." Aaron gave him a mean smile.

Dixon took a breath. Abruzzo always irritated the shit out of him, but now was not the time to let the man get under his skin. He was on a completely unofficial fishing expedition, and not for the West Bloomfield P.D., although he could explain away the stop to his chief, if he needed to. "I think you know exactly why I'm here. I have been working with the FBI. It's only a matter of time. And if you know anything, you're going down for conspiracy. Felony conspiracy. Federal time. The only way that doesn't happen is if you get out ahead of it. Cooperate. You're friends with Anderson. You've been out to Arizona how many times?" He decided to rattle the man with what he knew. "In fact, you flew out there that day. I don't think Anderson went up to Vegas by himself. I think he took you with him."

Aaron blinked in surprise. "You think I whacked a bunch of mob guys?" He laughed, and looked at the detective. Did the man really think that? He tried to gauge his expression. Probably not...but the man wasn't wrong about his out-of-state travel. Aaron had flown into Phoenix the day before the murders, and flown out the day after. But he'd stayed in Arizona the whole time. Doing other shit... that hopefully Dixon would remain clueless about. "You've got no proof, because it didn't happen."

Dixon stared down at Abruzzo. He hadn't told the FBI yet about the man's travel to and from Arizona at the time of the murders, which he'd just discovered. In part because he'd lied about his probable cause to get the warrant he'd needed to look at the man's bank account and credit card statements. But the FBI wasn't his problem, Bufonte's associates were his problem, and they didn't care about probable cause. If he told them about Abruzzo flying down there that exact day, perhaps being in on it but almost definitely knowing something about it, if Anderson really did do the hit on Bufonte—and Dixon now was convinced of it —he knew what they'd say. 'Get the truth out of Abruzzo.' "Circumstantial evidence has put a lot of people in prison," Dixon told him flatly.

"Well, seeing as you've just stated I'm a suspect in a quadruple homicide, I'm pretty sure we're done having this fucking conversation," Aaron said. "You going to ticket me, or arrest me? If not, I'm fucking leaving. And I'm tired of this bullshit harassment. It's been years. Fucking years."

"You should talk to me. Because next time, likely as not, it's going to be the FBI, and there's no wiggle room with them," Dixon tried, one last time.

"Is there a polite, legal term that means the same as 'fuck off'?" Aaron asked him. "Let's pretend I just said that."

"Last chance, Abruzzo. Talk to me, or it's going to be the FBI kicking down your door for four murders."

"Arrest me, or I'm leaving. I'm going to be late for work."

Dixon shrugged. "I gave you a chance." He took a step toward his unmarked car, then stopped and turned back. He looked at the dark green Taurus Abruzzo was driving. "How long have you had this car?"

"Like four months. Why?" It was the truth, Arlene had signed over the title to him earlier that year. But she'd owned it for a long time before that.

Frowning, Dixon shook his head. Abruzzo was dumb, but he wasn't that dumb, there's no way he'd be driving the car that was used to run over Big Paulie Bufonte years earlier, even if it did match the general description. There were a lot of dark-colored domestic sedans on the road. But, still, he'd check the registration. Just to make sure the man was telling the truth. Abruzzo flipped him the bird, then pulled out of the lot with a chirp of rubber.

"He flew down there the day before? And flew back the day after? Is that what you're telling me?" Dixon was sweating as he held the burner phone up to his ear. He was sitting in his car in a gas station on Telegraph Road in Southfield. He'd driven straight north up Telegraph after bracing

Abruzzo, but felt he'd needed to make this call before heading into the office.

"Yeah. Not Vegas, Phoenix, but close enough. Just a few hours away."

"And you didn't know this before why?"

"I had to pull his credit card receipts, and I needed to get a warrant for that. And I had to sling bullshit to get the warrant, in no way could he be considered a suspect."

"So he was in on the thing with our friend?"

"I don't know. He doesn't quite strike me as the type. But if he wasn't in on it, there's no way he doesn't know something about it. If Anderson did it."

"I don't knows and maybes aren't worth jack shit. We need to know for certain."

"I confronted him. I think he knows something, but I've got nothing I can use for leverage to pull him in on and sweat him. And he's likely to lawyer up."

The man on the other end of the line made a noise, somewhere between sad and disappointed. "You're thinking like a cop," he told Dixon. "That's a mistake. You should be thinking like a guy who's got everything to lose, he doesn't find out what we need to know. You understand?"

"Yeah."

"Really? 'Cause you seem like you're half-assin' it. We can send guys out to talk to this mook, but if we do that, what do we need you for?"

"I'll take care of it." Dixon was really sweating now. And cold, like he was sitting in a grave.

"You sure? 'Cause maybe you're confused here, about the situation. Tell me that you understand, that we're clear, about what you need to do. And not just about you finding out what needs to be found out, getting' answers. If after your talk you find out he was involved, you understand what needs to be done? Because if you make us send guys for him because you can't finish the job, they might as well come pay you a visit too. Close all the local accounts."

"I understand," Dixon said, his voice gray and dead, his eyes staring at nothing.

Chapter Thirteen

The man known as Pike woke up three minutes before his alarm was supposed to go off. He rolled out of bed, worked his neck, padded into the bathroom and used the toilet, then took a drink of water out of the faucet in the sink. Afterward he came back and stared out the window, through the horizontal blinds. Nothing was moving, and he remained still as well, his eyes darting over the scene. The music was there, faint, in the background, as it always was, and he let it in. *This Big Hush*, by Shriekback. An 80s band that almost nobody still remembered. The soft, haunting song was straight out of that decade. Bob had had the complete album, *Oil & Gold*, when he was in high school, thanks to director Michael Mann's great taste in music. *This Big Hush* was used in *Manhunter*, Michael Mann's excellent 1986 thriller starring a pre-CSI William Peterson and Brian Cox as the first, and best (in Pike's opinion), Hannibal Lecter.

The neighborhood was dark, but there were so many lights in the metropolitan D.C. area that few stars were visible due to the light pollution even if there weren't any clouds in the sky. Cities were like that. He'd spent a lot of time in very remote areas of the world, and enjoyed staring up at the heavens then, both with the naked eye and while wearing night vision goggles, which revealed an almost infinite number of stars. *There are more things in heaven and Earth, Horatio,/Than are dreamt of in your philosophy.* He smiled at the quote that popped into his head, and moved toward the small bookcase in his bedroom. His finger moved along the shelf, it was...there. *The Collected Works of William Shakespeare.* It had been a while since he'd read any of The Bard. The quote was from...*Hamlet*? Maybe. He put the thick hardcover on his bedside table next to the battered paperback copy of *Lucifer's Hammer*, which he was rereading for maybe the fifth time. With all the crap on TV, he was shocked that no one had ever turned the classic science fiction novel into a movie, or mini-series. It was the granddaddy of all disaster stories, and better than ninety-nine percent of all of them, although a lot of the cultural stuff, he had to admit, was a bit dated, as the book had come out in 1977. In the field he usually had an iPhone on him, and used the Kindle app, but when home he preferred actual books in his hands.

The alarm on his phone went off as the clock turned to four a.m., and he shut it off with his thumb. He slept in boxers, and he moved to the center of his bedroom, his feet silent on the laminate hardwood floor. He worked his neck again—it was still stiff from a minor grenade injury in Afghanistan eight years prior—worked his arms, then calmed himself. The music in his head—now *The Fire Inside*, by Bob Seger—faded to nothingness. When everything was calm and quiet, he spread his feet and started.

Some guys he knew did extensive stretching, or expensive stretching (Pilates), but he didn't think there was anything better for stretching, warming up, and working your core than tai chi—technically, *t'ai chi ch'uan*, but Americans shortened everything. He'd been doing it since he was a teenager and heavily involved in martial arts. To an observer it looked like he was doing karate, or maybe Jiu jitsu, only in slow motion. The flowing forms of tai chi were great for stretching, and balance, and focus, although he thought they resembled aikido *waza* more than karate.

He performed several *taolu* (solo forms), then paused, cleared his mind, and commenced the *42-form tai chi*, also known as the competition form or mixed form, a hybrid mix of many forms often performed in competition. When done correctly, at the proper speed, the 42-form takes just over six minutes. It had taken him some time to learn it, back when he was young, but now, after so many years, he flowed through it easily, never losing concentration, his knees bent deeply, his hands sleeping smoothly from *Grasp the Peacock's Tail* to *Single Whip*, then into *White Crane Spreads its Wings*.

His face was blank as the form took him back and forth across the room, his breath coming easily through his nostrils, his bare feet making barely any noise. The tai chi helped keep him very flexible, far more flexible than most men with his muscle were, and on *Lean with Body in Horse Stance* he got very low, his groin barely a foot off the floor. It helped with his balance, too, and it had been decades since he'd been unsteady while standing on one foot for *Turn the Body for a Lotus Kick*, swinging gracefully into *Draw the Bow to Shoot Tiger*. Then it was *Grasp the Peacock's Tail on the Left*, *Cross Hands*, and finally *Closing Position*.

He put on a t-shirt, shorts, and running shoes. He grabbed the GunPack off the nearby shelf—it was a fanny pack, but meant specifically for runners wanting to carry a pistol. The wide elastic straps kept it in place even with a loaded Glock 19 inside. At the front door he looked out the window. He didn't see any vehicles he didn't recognize in the parking spots out front of the row of townhouses, but that didn't necessarily mean anything. The professionals you'd never see coming, unless you got very lucky. But if you assumed they were out there, and looking for you, you paid proper attention. Even when back in the States. Which was why he'd replaced the front and rear doors of his townhouse with models that looked unremarkable but which were high-grade steel, and locked into steel frames that were bolted to the wood studs in the wall. Battering rams couldn't take down the doors, only explosives. But he had windows which were easily broken, so he had a secret exit as well— through the wall of his bedroom, into the master bedroom of the adjoining townhouse.

Ted O'Neill, who lived next door, didn't know about it, of course, but then again he was clueless about a lot of things. There was no sign of the work Pike'd done, but the 2 x 4 studs in the wall were sawn all the way through, and so was the drywall covering them, at least on this side, cut through and then spackled and painted over. He could bust through with a shoulder, and that might be just enough to live for another day.

McNair Farms was a planned community, 264 acres that used to be the McNair family dairy farm. Now it was houses, townhouses, and apartments, all the two thousand or so residents belonging to the McNair Farms Community Association. He'd bought his townhouse ten years prior with money he'd earned contracting with Blackwater and the various companies which had replaced it, doing work for the DOD, before going back to work directly for the government. Originally it had been simply an investment, a way to park a chunk of the money the government knew he had, and with Virginia real estate prices being what they were, it had been a big chunk. The three-story townhouse was just over two thousand square feet, with an attached one-car garage, and was now worth somewhere north of half a million bucks. Ridiculous, really, but Will Rogers had been right when he'd said "Buy land, they ain't making any more of the stuff." The townhouse was just one of the pieces of property he owned, but the only one in his name. He was two miles directly east of the Washington Dulles International Airport, and could occasionally see or hear those planes.

His route along the various sidewalks kept him inside McNair Farms, and even though there were a lot of driveways to cross, there weren't many cars to watch out for at that hour. He let the music play as he ran, and his subconscious, as usual, did a good job of picking out fast songs to help keep up his speed. His 5.8-mile circuit took him just a few seconds under forty minutes to do that day, going fast but not pushing himself, his subconscious choosing Jay-Z's *99 Problems* for him to listen to while he sprinted the last half mile. He tried not to frown as he cooled down—he remembered when the same amount of exertion put him over the finish line closer to thirty-five minutes than forty, but then again he was well into middle age. Almost forty-five years old, in a job where the physical toll usually caused guys to crash and burn by the time they were thirty-five. If they weren't flat-out killed on the job.

Back inside his townhouse he jumped on the exercise bike, and with the resistance set near the maximum he did two miles as fast and hard as he could. The bike was great for those rare days when ice or snow made running outside a no-go. He shut off the internal soundtrack specifically because that made it a little harder to keep up the speed. By the time he was done the sweat was dripping off him. But then he was done—today was only cardio.

He took a shower and dressed. He wasn't an office guy, he was a senior field guy who sometimes worked in the office, so while he didn't dress like a slob his outfits didn't usually meet the definition of "business casual". His thighs simply didn't fit into modern pants which mostly followed the styling of "skinny jeans", meant for guys who'd skipped leg day their entire lives. So he had to go with "tactical pants", or chinos or khakis made by tactical clothing companies, or alternatively clothing with an "athletic" cut, meaning made for dudes who actually had some muscle on them. Over a pair of loose green chinos—which weren't really loose around his thighs, but at least weren't tight as sausage casings, he didn't feel like he was reenacting *Robin Hood: Men in Tights*—he wore the home jersey of the New Zealand National Rugby team. And it wasn't a copy, it was an authentic team jersey, given to him by one of the players after he'd done a bit of executive protection in the UK back in his private contracting days. The team was commonly known as the All Blacks, and the black jersey featured a silver-fern frond in white over the left breast, and underneath that ALL BLACKS. He loved the doubletakes he got in the jersey, from people who didn't know it was the name of a sports team. Arguably the most successful sports team in the world. Which, traditionally, sported far more Maori and white players than blacks, as the nickname stemmed solely from the color of their uniforms, which had been all black since 1905.

He'd played some rugby when he was younger. The sport was amazing, a bizarre combination of soccer, wrestling, and MMA, played on a football field. Most of the pros playing it were built like MMA fighters, thick with muscle, and the black jersey—a collared shirt similar to a polo shirt—was loose enough on him to do a good job concealing the gun inside his waistband behind his right hip.

When he was in the field he always had a handgun, usually a sterile Glock 19—a soulless but efficient tool. When he had a choice he carried something with a little more style and grace—a customized Belgian-made Browning Hi-Power in a Kramer horsehide IWB holster. It wore Heinie sights, the front with a tritium insert, a Cylinder & Slide extended thumb safety, and slim checkered rosewood Navidrex grips. The magazine disconnect safety had been removed, and he'd beveled the magazine well opening in the frame himself. It was also fed not by an original 13-round magazine but a modern 15-rounder, with a spare in his left front pocket. Original Brownings were notoriously picky—eminently reliable, but only when fed with the round-nose ammunition it was designed for. His magazines were stuffed with Federal's famous 9BPLE load, a hollowpoint with a round-nose profile only sold to law enforcement (although available online in many places) because it was hot-rodded to a very high velocity.

It was sitting on his bedside table, although if something went bump in the night he'd likely roll right past it for the select-fire suppressed Mk 18 leaning in the corner. He unloaded the Browning, holstered it, then practiced drawing from concealment for fifteen minutes, until everything was smooth and the front sight settled nicely into the notch of the rear sight right as the trigger broke every time. Then he loaded the gun, stuck it back in the holster under his shirt, stuck the Mk 18 back in his gun safe, and headed downstairs for breakfast.

He was naturally thick, and the muscle made him even more so, so he tried to avoid carbs as often as he could. He made himself four scrambled eggs with a bit of shredded cheddar cheese and ate it at his small kitchen table while checking headlines on his tablet. Most American news outlets were worthless, distracting people with propaganda or gossip, and so while he did check the New York Times, Washington Post, CNN, and Fox News websites, he also checked the BBC, Sky News, RT (the Russian English-language news channel), and then moved on to the foreign language websites. He perused the websites of several Russian newspapers, Reference News out of China, Al Jazeera out of Egypt, and then The Yomiuri Shimbun, Japan's national newspaper, which had the largest circulation of any newspaper in the world. His Russian, Chinese, and Arabic were good, but his Japanese was rudimentary, so he read The Japan News in English. He'd had a week off from his day job, and hadn't been online at all, he'd been too busy, so he had a bit to catch up on. He didn't put his plate in the dishwasher and head out until after eight—when he worked in the office, he enjoyed the opportunity to work banker's hours.

Generally he did what he could to avoid drawing attention to himself, and so was driving a ten-year-old Subaru Outback that was practically invisible in suburban Virginia. With the addition of all-terrain tires the all-wheel-drive vehicle could get him anywhere he needed to go even with snow on the roads.

As he was backing out of his garage he saw Ted O'Neill walking across the lot. His wife parked her Acura in the garage, Ted parked his Chevy in their marked space in front of their townhouse. Ted waved to him and Pike gave him a friendly, noncommittal nod. Ted worked for the Department of Energy. A huge percentage of local residents worked for the federal government, and Ted was under the impression Pike worked for the World Bank. The cover explained his frequent absences, and was boring enough that nobody ever asked him more than a question or two about it. Not that 99% of all government jobs weren't boring.

The headquarters of the Defense Intelligence Agency was inside Joint Base Anacostia-Bolling (JBAB), a huge 900-acre government facility in southwest Washington D.C. The DIA's Defense Clandestine Service actually came into being in 2012, when the DIA consolidated several of its operational and military intelligence elements, including the Defense Human Intelligence and Counterterrorism Center, the Counterintelligence Field Activity, the Strategic Support Branch, and the Defense Attaché System. The end result was so big and powerful that some people referred to it as the second CIA. But all of those elements didn't quietly fold up shop and head under the same roof at JBAB—in fact, less than a third of the DIA's staff actually worked in the headquarters. The DIA-DCS still had a few "satellite offices", and quite often the most sensitive operations were planned there. There was a well-known DIA office in nearby Reston, Virginia. Pike, on the other hand, drove directly north five miles to the Atlantic Corporate Park in Dulles Town Center.

There were dozens of warehouses and office buildings inside a square mile, some unmarked, others with names mounted proudly on the outside, near the roof—DHL was a familiar name, but passing motorists could only guess what businesses Devrient, CyrusOne, and Cyxtera were engaged in. Rush-hour traffic was horrendous, as usual, which meant it took him close to half an hour to drive the five miles. Pike parked in the lot of a single-story office building. There was no sign out front, and there was no name on the doors or tinted windows. The building was wide enough that no one driving by could see the antenna array in the center of the roof.

The glass front door was locked, and he used his magnetic key card to get in. The small lobby was empty. There was a retinal scanner mounted on the far wall beside a door that would take explosives to breach. Pike bent down and placed his right thumb on the reader as the scanner checked his eye, then the door buzzed quietly.

Down a short hallway he entered an office space that, at first glance, would seem unremarkable for a small business, until you spotted the top-of-the-line computers, satellite phones, and encrypted communication terminals. The facility had a SCIF as well that saw regular use.

Pike nodded at a few people already working at their desks as he passed. He stopped in an open doorway and knocked on the frame. "I'm here," he announced to his section chief, the man who ran the shop. "What would you like me doing?"

Hansford Higgins looked up. He was ivy league, and while he'd never been in operations, he had done some work in the field when he was younger. Diplomatic Security Service or Department of State, something like that, working as a courier or an envoy, passing sensitive material outside of official channels. He was smart and—most importantly—usually knew what he didn't know, and was willing to listen to the people who did. He was maybe five years older than Pike but looked fifteen, due to a bad marriage, worse diet, and twenty years of sitting behind a desk. "Ah, there you are. Fresh as a daisy after a week off?"

"Don't I look it?"

Higgins snorted, the frowned. He gestured at Pike's big forearms, which showed a number of bruises. "Those from the op?"

"No, just having a little fun on my time off."

"Fighting?"

"Dating. It's a nightmare out there." In fact, Pike didn't really "date". He had regular relationships, but only with married women, simply because they had no expectations beyond the physical. If any of them started to get serious, he broke it off. Robin O'Neill, his next-door neighbor, was on the rotation. She and Ted seemed happy enough, but apparently Ted was a bit vanilla in bed. It was a total violation of Pike's usual "don't shit where you eat" philosophy, but Robin was gorgeous, and an absolute degenerate animal when her clothes were off. Who was he to say no?

Higgins barked out a laugh. "Okay, you got me. And if I didn't say it, and I don't think I did, good job on that thing last week."

Pike made a face. "The thing that wasn't what anybody thought it was going to be? The thing where Tommy likely got a career-ending injury? The thing where nobody is telling us shit? Although I should be used to that by now. Anyway, that's going to be it."

"Excuse me?"

"Maybe not today, or tomorrow, but next ten years, it's not going to be the Middle East, or Ukraine or Russia, it's going to be our southern border. And what comes across it. Or what and who have come across it, we have no idea who's in this country. The number of sleeper cells we probably already have in America..." He shook his head. "Although whether or not the politicians will ever admit that's where the problems are coming from..."

"Well, since you mentioned the Middle east, and you're

in-between missions..." Higgins looked around his desk, then peered at his computer screen. "The name Abu Ahmad al-Tunisi sound familiar?"

Pike leaned his shoulder against the door frame. "Da'ish? Sounds like Da'ish. But every other guy in their leadership is named Abu."

Higgins was nodding. "ISIL. Supposed to be the number three guy. Some intelligence has come in—we've got three potential rabbit holes for him, places he goes to lay low when the heat's on. I get the impression they're going to apply some heat, with the goal of forcing him to go to ground in one of these places. I don't know, but I suspect they do or will have the sites under surveillance—that's not us, that's being run out of JSOC."

"Boots on the ground?"

"Doubtful. Until they can put him there, I'm sure it's just satellites and drones, because those three sites, two are in Syria and one's in Iraq. I want you to give me a preliminary work-up of them. Just something bare bones initially, in case they want to send a team in to take care of business face-to-face, or to grab him, rather than send a cruise missile through his window. How hard of a target each site appears, how many men you'd want, with what gear. I'll get you all the satellite photos and video you need—you check the area for routes in and out by vehicles, any nearby landing zones if we go in by helicopter, the usual. You've got Arabic, right? Can you read it?"

"Passably."

"See if you can track down blueprints or the like for any of the addresses. Two of them are bigger than just simple houses, so there might be something to find."

"Syria and Iraq? Even if there are blueprints or architectural drawings in existence, the chances of them being digital, and available online freely or even to hackers, are slim to none."

Higgins shrugged. "Can't hurt to look. Do what you can, and get me something on all three locations by end of day, day after tomorrow. You don't need to work up a full assault plan, yet, just some…recommended avenues of approach, shall we say, for whoever might take their turn at the tip of the spear. And I truly don't know who that might be. SEALs, Delta, us, Ground Branch, maybe His Majesty's SAS." He licked his lips. "It still feels weird to say that. It's been the Queen forever. *Her* Majesty. Hell, that James Bond novel, then movie, *On Her Majesty's Secret Service*, when did that come out? And it's been longer than that."

"Longer than we've been alive," Pike agreed. "Book came out in the sixties. Pretty sure the movie did too."

"Back then your Russian would have come in handy. This may come to nothing, and may be a total waste of your time. How many missions have you prepped that never happened?"

"Far more than ever went off."

"Exactly. Okay, well, get to work, and let me know if you need anything."

"Are there K-cups for the Keurig?"

Higgins nodded once. "There are."

"Then I should be good."

Chapter Fourteen

Aaron picked up Arlene from work, as he had a buddy who owned a junkyard replacing her windshield, as hers had been trashed by a rock thrown up by a semi on I-75, and they drove toward home from Brinks. She was the vault manager, which didn't pay nearly as well as it sounded like it should, but they did okay. They were doing fine for money. His headaches didn't have anything to do with money, for once in his life. "You hungry? I'm hungry," he told her.

She shrugged. "I can eat." She had a big mop of blonde hair and was skinny as a rail, gifted with a metabolism that burned off a lot of calories even before she started slinging around boxes and bags of coin and cash at work.

They stopped at a National Coney Island close to their trailer park in Taylor. The chain had a dozen restaurants around the Detroit area, and was just one of many Coney islands in the area.

They walked past the SEAT YOURSELF sign and settled into their usual booth. Isetta saw them and danced over. She was nuts even by Aaron's standards, but she was a good waitress. She was a bit chunky, and almost always wore small cat ears in her hair. A little plastic tiara or whatever the hell they were called, like little girls wore, only instead of a crown hers almost always sported cats' ears. Today the ears were purple and sparkly.

"Hey you two," she said, bopping a bit from side to side. "The usual?" Most of the local restaurants had changed their menus and procedures thanks to the state government's insane overreaction to COVID, and the Coney island had moved to tablets for the waitresses to take the order and send it digitally and immediately to the kitchen, displayed on a screen for the cooks to see.

"Four Coneys with everything, no bun," Arlene said, nodding. "Diet Coke." It wasn't that she was off carbs, or allergic to wheat, it was that she was very picky about her carbs, and didn't think hot dog buns good enough bread to be worth the calories. 'Everything' meant the loose chili that Detroit Coneys were known for, chopped onions, and mustard. Aaron had been around the country a bit, and Detroit seemed to be the only place that knew how to make Coney dogs—chili dogs—right. Guys from Cincinnati would tell you that Skyline chili was great, but they'd be wrong.

Isetta was chewing on the inside of her cheek as she looked down at her tablet's display. "They moved things around on here. Where's 'No Bun'? I see 'Soggy Bun'…"

Aaron frowned. "Who the hell would want a soggy bun?"

Isetta shrugged. "You'd be surprised. I get one lady, comes in here, always wants her fries cooked 'light'."

"You guys barely fry your fries as it is," Aaron told her. He always ordered his extra well done, and still they were barely right.

"I know. I always order mine well done," Isetta agreed.

"How the hell would you even make a soggy bun?" Aaron said. "Spray it with water? Like a cat?"

"Steam it," Arlene suggested.

Aaron looked at their waitress. "Soggy Bunz was my stripper name. With a Z." She laughed so hard she snorted.

"No, it's soggy *bun*," Isetta corrected him.

"Maybe I've only got one. You don't know. Could be a birth defect."

"I saw a one-legged stripper once," Isetta said, out of the blue. "She might be only had one bun."

That made Aaron blink. "What?"

"Yeah, in Boomerang's, in Capac."

"There's a strip club in Capac?" Aaron said in disbelief. Capac was a tiny town in Michigan's "thumb" area, in the middle of nowhere, nothing but farmer's fields all around. Corn, soybeans, and sugar beets. The closest city was Port Huron, thirty miles away. "What, did she lose it in a tragic potato sack race accident?"

"Stop it," Arlene told him, but Isetta laughed and shrugged.

"I've heard of pregnant strippers, but one-legged, that's a new one," he said. "But I guess there's somebody into everything. What was her name, Eileen?"

"Oh, stop it, that's bad," Isetta said.

"Now I'm going to be thinking about one-legged strippers for the rest of the day," Aaron told her. "It's your fault."

She smiled. "I'm surprised with all the activism going on that they haven't started trying to shut down the strip clubs," their waitress said.

"The gays don't really care about straight strip clubs," Aaron told her.

"There's more going on with the LGBT movement than just gays," Isetta said.

Aaron shook his head. "No, there's not," he said. "Look. LGBTQ. L is lesbian. That's gay. G is gay. B for bisexual. Look, the whole bisexual thing is bullshit. If you're a dude who has sex with other dudes, that makes you gay, no matter who else you have sex with, so gay. T for tranny. If you're a dude pretending to be a chick and you want to have sex with a chick, that's pretend gay. If you're a dude pretending to be a chick and you want to have sex with a guy, that's real gay. Either way, it's gay. And Q is queer or questioning—which is gay. So, LGBTQ, gay gay gay gay gay." Arlene rolled her eyes. She'd heard this rant before.

"What about the plus they put at the end sometimes?" Isetta asked him.

"Pedophiles," Aaron said. The two women frowned at him, and he shrugged. "Hey, look, I don't make the rules. So…gay gay gay gay gay, wood chipper."

Isetta frowned. "I don't know about that."

"Maybe you don't want it to be true, but think about the customers who come in who are in that alphabet crowd. Any of 'em not gayer than Neil Patrick Harris giving Ru Paul a rub and tug?" Arlene's mouth opened in surprise, then she looked down at the table and shook her head.

"Well…"

"Yeah, exactly. The alphabet crowd is gay, and the pronoun crowd is crazy. It's a scientific fact." Aaron pointed at the tablet in Isetta's hand. "Diet Coke, baby Greek, and two Coneys with everything." She punched the order in, then twirled off, still frowning, but once again dancing to the tune inside her head. Aaron watched her go. "You think she's got like eighteen cats at home, place smelling like piss?

Or does she go the other way, have two grand worth of Bad Dragon dildos shaped like unicorn dongs and tentacles?"

Arlene looked around, making sure nobody was close enough to have heard him. "What is up with you?"

He shrugged. "I don't know. My tooth is still killing me." He reached a finger into his mouth and probed it. It was on the left side, about halfway back.

"Well, go to the fucking dentist."

"When am I going to go? I'm working all the fucking time. And you don't have a car right now. And whatever the dentist is going to cost, on top of what Billy's going to charge us for the windshield."

"You don't get to refuse to go to the dentist, then complain about how much your tooth hurts. That's a bitch move."

He opened his mouth to argue, then realized she was right. Which didn't put him in a better mood. Especially since it wasn't really the tooth that was bothering him. Or even trying to quit smoking. Or Peanut moping around. He hadn't told her about the West Bloomfield cop, Dixon, stopping him and accusing him of murder. Four murders. Which was ridiculous, Dave obviously didn't need his help killing people, dude had a fucking gift for that, but he couldn't exactly tell that to the cop. But complaining about your problems to people who couldn't help was a bitch move, and he knew better. "Sorry," he told Arlene, shrugging.

"You're having nightmares every night. Don't think I don't hear you getting up, you're not exactly quiet."

It wasn't just the nightmares, it was wondering, worrying every second, if that was the day they'd be kicking his door in, arresting him for murder. He wasn't quite convinced the FBI gave a shit about him, if they really thought he was involved in the Vegas thing, but he was a friend of Dave's. And had flown in to nearby Phoenix that day, almost like he was there for that reason. It looked bad, he had to admit. And either he was getting very paranoid or he was getting followed at work. Three times in the past two weeks he'd spotted what he was pretty sure was the same car behind them. The fact that it was a black Charger, looking exactly like an unmarked police car, like the kind feds would drive, made it worse than just some asshole looking for an opportunity to rob them. Unless it was Dixon again, but the cop didn't seem like the kind of cop who would just follow him, he'd confront Aaron, like he always did, if he had anything left to say.

"Why don't you call him," she said firmly. It wasn't a question. She thought it was worry over Dave. The FBI investigation. And he couldn't tell her she was wrong, not without making her an accessory to the crime he actually had committed.

"FBI's probably all over him."

"So what? If they are, they have to know you're his friend. Just a friend checking in." He frowned and made a sound. She rolled her eyes. "Why don't you just call her, then?"

"Her who?"

"His girlfriend. Lori."

"Pork Snorkle?" The nickname had been given to her by an adult film reviewer with *Hustler*. She hated it, even though it accurately described her most unique talent. No gag reflex, and the ability to shoot milk—or whatever—out her nose. "If they're watching him, they're onto her."

"And so what if they are?" Arlene said. She leaned back and crossed her lean arms. "It's not like you're the one who roadtripped to Vegas to shoot some assholes. Wait, do you think *they* think you're somehow involved in that, because you're Italian?"

Aaron opened his mouth in surprise. He leaned back in the booth and tilted his head until it was resting on the seat back and he was staring at the ceiling. Dixon had said the FBI was interested in him for Vegas, but it had never clicked in his head that maybe, partly, the reason why was because he was Italian. "Fuuuuck," he said with a sigh. Maybe it was better if he kept his distance from Dave. Didn't call him. Until this shit was sorted out, one way or another.

Chapter Fifteen

Dave walked into the lobby of the sheriff's department, waited a second for his eyes to adjust, then moved up to the front desk. The two deputies there were behind a thick layer of bullet-resistant Plexiglas.

"Can I help you sir?"

"Yeah, hi," he said, feeling a bit self-conscious. But he'd been in the area. "Is the sheriff in?"

"Do you have an appointment?"

"No, this was kinda spur of the moment."

The uniformed deputy frowned at him. Dave had a Detroit Tigers baseball cap pulled down low over his face. He wore a thin plaid shirt over a t-shirt, the plaid cover shirt unbuttoned in front for quicker access to the pistol on his hip. "The sheriff doesn't take walk-ins. You need to call his office, and make an appointment."

"Can you just call back there and check?"

The deputy narrowed his eyes. "I don't need to check," he said firmly.

"Yeah, okay, thanks." Dave sighed, then pulled out his

phone as he stepped away from the desk. He dialed a number. The call was answered after two rings and he said, "Hi. Sorry. Are you in your office? Do you have a minute? I'm in the lobby." He flicked his eyes over to the two deputies, who could hear him, and were looking at him, frowning. "Okay, great, I appreciate it."

He ended the call, stuck the phone back in his pocket, and waited, flashing a quick embarrassed smile at the deputies. They continued to stare at him until the phone on the desk rang. One of the deputies answered it. "Front desk, Eldon. Yes sir. Yes, he is. Yes sir, I can do that."

He hung up the phone, stood up, and moved out of sight. Then the door to one side, bearing the SHERIFF'S DEPARTMENT PERSONNEL ONLY sign, opened. "I guess he can see you now," the deputy said, frowning. "I'll take you back."

Dave took his hat off as he walked toward the man. It was bad manners to wear a hat indoors. "Thanks," he said.

The deputy stuck a hand out against his chest as Jack reached him, the man's eyes running all over his face. Tracing the scars. "Well shit, man, you could have said who you were," he said apologetically. "I didn't recognize you." The other deputy still behind the desk stood up and looked over at his partner's tone.

Dave shrugged. "I don't want to be that guy."

The deputy just looked at him. "Dude, you are that guy."

The sheriff's secretary just smiled at him and nodded her head at the open door. Osterman was sitting behind his desk. Dave sat down in the chair opposite him, hat in hand.

"To what do I owe the pleasure?" he asked Dave.

Dave frowned. "Lori tells me I am horrible at communicating. That the two of us together, me and you, are twice as bad."

Osterman shrugged. "Women generally will use twenty words when two will do. Or none at all."

"You're not wrong…but neither is she. So…now that I've decided to stick around for a while…" he paused, until he was sure Osterman knew he didn't mean Prescott but rather planet Earth, "I have been thinking about my future. I still haven't figured out what I want to do with my life, but I have figured out I'd like to be there for it. So to that end I bought a rifle."

Osterman blinked and frowned. He held up a finger, and leaned forward a few inches, the chair creaking. "I've never known you to be unarmed," he said slowly.

Dave took a deep breath. Baring his soul, even to someone he considered a friend, seemed a bit like therapy. And he hated it. He had to fight every word to get it past his lips. "But just with a pistol, since moving out here. Waiting for them to come for me. I couldn't not fight back, but…"

Osterman's thoughtful frown grew deeper. "You thought, without a rifle, it'd be more of a fair fight? But one you were sure to lose?"

Dave shrugged. "Last time I started a fight with a rifle in my hands, it was against four SWAT cops. And, well…"

Osterman nodded. "It ain't braggin' if you can do it. Right. But you are no longer in that…self-destructive frame of mind?"

"Correct. More proactive. I'm not expecting trouble, but I've learned that doesn't mean a damn thing. And I have pissed off a lot of people over the years. Anyway, I've got competition experience, know how to practice, and gotten lucky, but I realize I don't have any actual tactical training.

Especially with a rifle. I was reminded that just north of here is a facility…."

Osterman nodded again. "World-renowned. Trained everybody from the CIA to the King of Jordan to dentists from Des Moines."

"With a long waiting list for all of their classes, according to the website. I don't even know if they'd take me, given my history. But I thought maybe you might be able to write me a letter of recommendation or, I don't know…"

Osterman pursed his mouth, as if he was fighting back a smile. "I was around when it was founded, in fact. I'd been home from Vietnam for a bit. Still practically a newlywed, or so it seems now. Met the founder, who I have to say is a bit of a hero of mine. Have attended more than a few courses there over the intervening decades. I know the current owner, and the man who runs it, Cam Kendall." He looked around his desk and found his phone half-hidden under a sheet of paper. He pulled it toward him, flipped through the contacts list, and dialed a number. He hit the speaker button and they listened to the phone ring.

"Sheriff! How are you this fine afternoon?" The earnest, well-modulated tones of the man on the other end of the line made him sound somewhere between a politician and a high school football coach, eternally cheerful.

"Good, Cam, and yourself? I didn't catch you in the middle of anything, did I? Do you have a minute?"

"I'm just driving around, delivering popsicles to the students to help keep the heat stroke at bay. Let me pull over. What do you need?"

"I've got a young man here who would love to get into one of your carbine classes. I know how booked up you've been the last few years, but I was wondering if you've had any cancellations or the like where he could slip in."

"Well, as you said, we've been busier than a one-legged man in an ass-kicking contest, but when I get back up to the office I can check. Is this one of your men?"

Osterman traded a look with Dave. "No, more of a close personal friend. He was also wondering about your vetting process."

"Vetting? We do the standard background check. We'll need a driver's license, a few other things. Provided he's a U.S. citizen, as long as he doesn't have any felony convictions, we should be good."

Osterman looked at Dave and raised an eyebrow. "No, no convictions," Dave said, loud enough for the phone to pick it up. "I've never even been arrested." *Just detained a few times*, he added under his breath.

"I'll look at the class schedule when I get back in the office, then see if we've had any drop out," Kendall said. "Carbine, you said? What skill level class are you looking for? Beginner?"

Osterman had a twinkle in his eye as he said, "You might be in a better position to answer that than either of us."

"I'm sorry?"

"Well, Cam, I do believe you've seen him in action with a rifle. The bloody footage all over the news. And the footage that didn't make the news. During one conversation with me I believe you said, 'That young man's balls aren't steel, they're tungsten. I did not disagree.'" Dave made a face, and looked at the wall, embarrassed.

The silence on the line stretched out. Dave could hear wind blowing past the phone on the other end of the call.

Finally the man said, "I'll make it happen. Give me a couple of days."

Dave imagined that when the facility was new, it had been located in the middle of the middle of nowhere, as even fifty years later the high desert north of Prescott was somewhat thinly populated once you got away from the businesses and houses lining State Route 89 which ran north from Prescott to Paulden. The front gate of Ravengard was miles off 89. Once through the open front gate he had to drive a mile down the well-maintained gravel road to reach the cluster of tan buildings atop a low hill. There was a vehicle far ahead of him, and he could see one a few hundred yards behind, presumably other students arriving for class.

The sheriff had made the call to Kendall a week earlier, and two days later the sheriff had called Dave and told him an opportunity had arisen. Short notice, but considering Dave didn't have a job, that didn't really matter. He'd sighted in his new rifle, both with the iron sights and the Aimpoint Duty RDS red dot optic. He'd put a few hundred rounds through it at the range, mostly just reacquainting himself with the recoil and controls, and making sure his magazines functioned, but since getting the call he'd spent at least an hour every day inside his house practicing, snapping the rifle up to his shoulder and acquiring the dot, and trying to figure out how to quickly and efficiently maneuver it around corners and doors. He was still nervous; it was a bit like coming to Graceland to get singing lessons from Elvis.

The parking lot was square and gravel, surrounded on four sides by low buildings. In addition to the tall stone monument at the front with the giant black iron raven, topped by a tall flagpole flying a fresh flag flapping in the breeze, there were low evergreen bushes and trees dotted around, filling the crisp morning air with the fresh scent of high desert—juniper and sage. The sky was pale blue, dotted with just the hint of clouds.

He looked around, and saw signs for classrooms ahead. One long building had several doors. An older man, obviously an instructor, was leaning his shoulder against a post on the porch, thumbs tucked into his wide belt. He was maybe sixty, with a big tanned bald head, wearing khakis and a tan button-down shirt with a nametag over his breast. There was a big automatic proudly displayed on his hip, and the butt of a snubnose revolver peeked out above his belt. The man was big, and even a bit bent by age he was inches taller than Dave, and likely outweighed him by forty pounds. Dave figured that when he was in his prime the man had been a monster. He peered down at Dave placidly. He looked like someone who had been there, done that, and had nothing left to prove—exactly what Dave expected out of an instructor working at a world-famous shooting academy.

"Not sure where I'm supposed to go," Dave admitted. He glanced over his shoulder. Vehicles continued to pull into the lot. Students exited them, stretching and talking, but when they strode off they were heading in several directions.

"Just generally in life, or do you have more immediate concerns?" the man replied.

Dave smiled. "Right now, I'm just looking for my class." He checked his watch. He was fifteen minutes early.

"Which class? Got a few running today. Basic defensive pistol, advanced tactical shotgun. Mossberg's doing a media event as well."

"Carbine," Dave said. "Not sure what the official name is."

The man blinked his big eyes. "Well, we've only got one of those today," he said thoughtfully, squinting a bit as he looked down at Dave. He tilted his head. "Follow me."

Dave followed him through a nearby door. They found themselves in a small classroom, with three rows of short tables and folding chairs. Another instructor was inside, shorter and thicker and a bit younger than the first, with black hair and a dark green shirt over khakis.

"I'm Lou, this is Pete," the big man said, nodding to the second instructor. Dave smiled and shook Pete's hand, then Lou's. "We've got some paperwork for you to fill out before we get started. Standard boilerplate indemnifying us if there's an accident, but more importantly the lunch menu, as you'll be eating on site." Pete was studying Dave intently, his arms crossed. His nametag read LOPEZ.

Lou stuck his thumbs back in his belt. He said, "I figure brief introductions are in order. After spending about a dozen years with Uncle Sam's Misguided Children—" At Dave's confused look he said, "Marine Corps. After that, I spent most of a career working as a peace officer in southern California. Street, plainclothes, SWAT, and some competition shooting on the side." He looked at Pete.

"I spent thirty years in law enforcement and retired as a sergeant," Lopez said. "Everything from an FTO to a SWAT team leader. Overlapping with that was twenty years in the Army and Army Reserves." Dave nodded. As he expected, the place only hired people who had actually done what they were teaching.

"You've got three days with us," Lou told him. "We can look over your equipment, make recommendations, but in regards to training, we've got a standard curriculum for defensive and tactical carbine, but what are you hoping to get out of these three days? Anything specific?"

Dave blinked, and looked over his shoulder at the open door. "Are we going to wait for everyone else?"

The two men traded a look. "You're it, kid," Pete told him.

"Oh. Really? I didn't know." He looked back and forth between the men. "Well, I know how to run a gun, mechanically, but knowing how to work a rifle around cover, indoors or behind a car, I figure that might be helpful. Using a sling? Switching shoulders? I don't know if you teach that. Malfunction drills, I guess? You're the experts. I don't know if that's basic or advanced stuff, or what I qualify for. I know generally you have prerequisites for some of your courses, and I've never been here before."

The two men traded a look. "You want to know the difference between basic and advanced techniques?" Pete asked him. Dave nodded. "Advanced techniques are simply the basics, but successfully doing them while exhausted, injured, terrified, under fire, or some combination thereof. *If you can keep your head about you, while all others are losing theirs…*"

Lou kept his mild eyes trained on the young man. "Hmm. Well, I think we've all seen that video of you. Both of them, including the one inside the Cracker Barrel, which is by far the most…memorable. But a few seconds of his life doth not necessarily make the man, as they say. What kind of background do you have? Military or police training? Shooting experience?"

Dave shook his head. "No, no military or police training. Drove an armored car for a while. I did a decent amount of competition, and made it to Master Class in USPSA. I shot some 3-gun, but it's been a while since I did any of that." His eyes drifted up as he thought. Lou opened his mouth to say something, but Dave continued, talking to the wall. "Shooting experience? Umm…" He counted them up in his head. The ones he could admit to. "Five, I guess, although I'm not sure the last one counts as a gun*fight* since none of them got a shot off. They barely got out of the car, other than the one guy who stuck a gun in my face." He took a deep breath. "Twenty, twenty-one guys, total? I'm not really sure, at the Pima Motel there were three of us shooting, and the cartel guys were running all over, people screaming. It was kind of crazy, you can't really tell from the video. I'm not even sure who shot me when. And I was a little lightheaded from blood loss. Or maybe it was the concussion. The guy at the Cracker Barrel actually cracked my skull with that AK before I, um, bit his face off." He shrugged and frowned and gestured at his scars, then looked at Lou.

Lou didn't say anything for so long Dave wondered if there was a problem. The big man just stared at him, unblinking, then traded an indecipherable look with Pete. Finally, Lou said, "Good talk." He sighed, shook his big head, and rolled his eyes. "I think I'll go lie down," he said to Pete, seemingly ignoring Dave. "Maybe hug myself and have a good cry."

"Ummm…" Dave's eyes flicked back and forth between the two men.

Lou looked at Dave, nodded his head at the open door, and the bright parking lot beyond. "Go on, get your gear, and we'll look it over. Then we'll head down to the north range. Start with a simple twenty-five-yard zero." He looked at Pete and drily said, "I don't think we need to spend any time on the will to win and acquiring a proper fighting mindset, do we? I think we can skip right over that."

Chapter Sixteen

"You listen to country music?"

Aaron looked up from his phone as the armored truck bounced noisily down the road. "Country music?" he said disdainfully.

Eddie shrugged. "Man, I don't know what white people listen to. There's country music and, I don't know, Taylor Swift."

Aaron laughed. "Christ, you're killing me. That's like me saying that every black guy listens to rap."

Eddie shrugged again. "Well, I mean... I'm more into hip-hop than hardcore rap."

"If you don't like it, it all sounds the same," Aaron told him. "Shit." Aaron leaned forward in his seat. "You should listen to some actual music."

"What, like Kid Rock?" Aaron could hear the frown in his voice.

"Shit, no, I mean like actual music music, where they sang and played instruments. The kind of shit most kids these days have only heard of because they sample it on rap songs. Look at like a Billboard Top 40 from the seventies, that was actual music. Earth, Wind & Fire, Chicago, Stevie Wonder, Elvis Presley, Marvin Gaye. I'm more a classic rock guy, but I can sit down and listen to any of that stuff, because it's so good. Because it's actual fucking music. Anything where they're actually playing instruments and singing is morally superior to that other shit where they're just chanting to a beat."

"My moms listened to that stuff sometimes. My gramma too. There's good stuff coming out now too. Beyoncé can sing. Ariana Grande, Selena Gomez… mmm."

Aaron laughed. "We talking about singing or their tits and ass?"

"If you can get both, why not? Selena Gomez look fine now that she put on a little weight. Went to all the right places."

"And now we're back to black guys liking big asses. Talking in circles, just like we're driving in circles. But, you know…" Aaron looked off to the side, thinking.

"What?"

Aaron shrugged. "Just how most guys' tastes in women change as they get older."

Eddie snorted. "Shit, when I was a teenager, I didn't know anything about anything. It was all about a girl's looks. But the prettiest ones, all they's like to do is lie there and look pretty. They don't want to put in the work. Cuz they ain't never needed to. You get older, you learn bigger girls try harder. And appetites are appetites, she like to eat *this*, she prolly like to eat *that*, and ain't nuthin' sexier than a girl who likes to get down."

Aaron nodded in agreement. "Boys like Barbies, men like Arby's."

Eddie's eyes opened wide in the rearview mirror, and he laughed so hard he nearly drove off the road.

The Chase Bank branch was on Woodward Avenue in Detroit, at the corner of Englewood, roughly halfway between the famed 8 Mile Road to the north and the Detroit River to the south. Woodward Avenue there was three lanes in each direction separated by a center left turn lane, although the curb lanes to either side were filled with parked cars during the day.

Bordering the branch on the north side was the sad-looking Normandie Hotel, where you could rent rooms by the week, and probably by the hour. Across Woodward was a tire shop, and the barbed steel fence around the property was more impressive than what guarded most prisons.

Eddie turned onto Englewood, then turned into the bank lot. The lot was nearly full of cars, the spots angled for easy in/easy out. Behind the building there was a separate gated lot for the bank employees. It was the only way to prevent their cars from being stolen. The spots directly in front of the building entrance were handicap parking, and they were all occupied.

Eddie looked around. He wouldn't pull into a spot—if he did that, someone could park behind him, and block him in. "What do you want me to do? Park behind them?"

"Yeah. I shouldn't be long, but if you need to move back and forth a space or two to let assholes out, do it, we don't need them complaining to the company we're blocking in Special Olympians."

Eddie shook his head and turned around to look at Aaron. "Man, you cranky as fuck lately. And for you, that's saying something."

"Yeah, whatever." Aaron ducked his head and peered out the windows one at a time. "Why the fuck's it so crowded? Oh, never mind." He'd just remembered it was the last Friday of the month. Lot of people were cashing in their government checks, in addition to those working stiffs with their regular weekly checks. "You see anything?"

"Couple people sitting in cars, but they was here when we rolled up, *A-A-ron*."

Aaron barked out a laugh. "Man, that skit is the funniest fucking thing. I can watch it over and over. 'De-*nice*. Jayquellen? Where Jayquellen at?'" He sighed and looked around again. "Yeah, okay, pop the door. I've got a bag of cash and eight boxes of coin going in, so this is going to take a second."

Eddie hit a button and the electronic lock on the back door disengaged with a buzz. Aaron pushed it open, looked around, then jumped down. A car rolled past him, close, and Aaron eyefucked the driver, but it was just an old woman in a Buick the size of a Freightliner. As it passed by he heard something and looked up. Twenty feet away a guy was coming out from between two cars, moving toward Aaron. A Glock, its square snout unmistakable, stuck out at a forty-five-degree angle in one hand, extended magazine hanging far out the ass end of the gun, and as soon as the gun was up he pulled the trigger.

The roar was incredible, flame shooting from the muzzle, empty cases fountaining out the ejection port. The guy held the pistol half-sideways, the gun bucking in his hand like a wild animal, muzzle waving everywhere. Aaron saw it all in slow motion and he was falling backward, bouncing off the bumper, bullets spanging off steel and echoing hollowly as they ricocheted around the inside of the truck. Eddie gave a surprised, wounded yelp.

Aaron found himself on his back, head against a concrete curb stone as the gunman loomed over him, jabbing the Glock at Aaron's face. But the slide was locked back on an empty magazine. The armed robber stared in confusion at his gun, then Aaron's Colt was coming up. The first shot, fired from the hip, cracked right past the man's ear and he turned and literally dove for the nearby cars. Aaron came up shooting, pounding bullets into the hood past where the guy had disappeared, stalking forward as he fired, hoping his bonded-core ten-millimeters were punching through the bodywork into the bad guy, who had to be back there reloading.

The slide locked back on Aaron's Delta Elite after ten rounds and he ripped a fresh magazine from his belt, slammed it home, thumbed the slide release, then leaned around the front corner of the parked car, finger tight on the trigger—but there was no one there. His gun came up and followed his eyes as he scanned the parking lot, and out on Englewood a white minivan squealed into motion, rocketing down the side street.

Aaron tracked it with his sights, but he couldn't see who was in it—maybe it was just a terrified bystander. It kept on going out of sight, and Aaron swung back and checked around all the nearby cars, pistol leading the way. The man was gone.

Eddie came up panting, his old stainless S&W auto in his hand. He had a splash of blood on the white collar of his shirt from a ricocheting bullet jacket that had somehow snuck through the grated window into the cab. "You okay man? Fuck. You're bleeding."

"What?" Aaron reached a hand up and touched the back of his head. There was a deep gash there, where he'd smacked it against the curb.

"That's bleeding bad," Eddie said. "You want to sit down?"

"I'm fine," Aaron told him. He turned around, checking out the truck and the immediate area for threats once again, his heart pounding.

"Dude," Eddie said eyes wide, and nodded at Aaron's shirt.

Aaron looked down. It took him a second before he saw the small soot-edged holes in his white uniform shirt. "That's why I tell you to wear a vest!" he yelled at Eddie. "Ow." He felt them now, past the adrenaline high, two hits right in the ribs. Like getting popped by a Major League fast ball. Wincing, he sat roughly down on the sidewalk, then laid on his back, gun still in his hand. He heard voices, customers and employees coming out of the bank, talking loudly. "Ow. Call it in," he said, staring up at the sky. Blue, pale blue, with just a hint of clouds.

"John Phault."

"Yeah," Aaron said without introduction, "how many rounds do those big-stick Glock mags hold? Thirty-two? Thirty-three?"

"In nine-millimeter? At least thirty."

Aaron wanted to grumble and growl, but even breathing hurt. He looked around the exam room, which for the moment he had to himself. He was stripped to the waist after getting x-rayed, waiting to find out if any of his ribs were cracked. The ER doc had already sewed up the cut in the back of his head. Six stitches. The hits to his chest were swollen and red and the size of silver dollars, and the doc had assured him they'd turn dark purple and hurt even more before long.

"This asshole pops up from behind a car like a jack in

the box. He's got a Glock with one of those Wish-dot-com full-auto switches, and dumps an entire mag at me, gun held sideways like we're filming *New Jack City Two: Electric Boogaloo*. Hits the truck, hits the bank, probably hit the hotel in back. Maybe a passing plane. Only hit me twice, which honestly is a lot better than these assholes normally do."

"You don't sound too shot."

"Right in the vest. So this makes every sweaty day worth it. Although now I guess I need a new one."

"I know a guy can get you one at cost, when you're ready for a replacement. So what happened to him? You shoot him?"

"I don't think so. I killed the shit out of a parked car, though. I came up shooting, and he took off."

"Suppressive fire is a thing."

"I guess. But that's why I'm calling you. You still got that lawyer? The one who repped Dave when he shot those SWAT cops?" Phault was a private investigator whom Aaron had met a few times. Dave had been working for him when his troubles had started. Phault was older now, at least fifty, but he was solid, and Aaron knew he'd killed at least one guy, and the man gave off the vibe that he'd pulled the trigger on people more than a few times.

"I haven't had to use him in a while, but yeah, I've got his number."

"I don't know if I'll need him, but I might. Like I said, I didn't hit shit but Chevy."

"Maybe. You'd be surprised how far people can run after being shot, at least with pistols. That guy could turn up at an ER with a bullet in him still."

"Well, I'm already here, so that'll make things easy for round two. They didn't take my gun. I thought they took your gun."

"Where'd this happen, Detroit?"

"Yeah."

"Suburbs, maybe. Detroit, unless you left a body or a lot of blood on the ground, they're not taking a gun for evidence. You only take the gun when you need to compare the bullets out of it to ones they take out of dead bodies. Generally."

"Well, I put a lot of bullets into someone's car, you'd think an insurance company might care about that. If they were going to take it, I wish they'd do it now, and not show up next week, banging on my door at six a.m." He was pretty sure, no, positive, there was no way his gun could be tied to anything, but he was tired of fucking waiting. If they ran his ballistics through the system for this, at least he'd *know*.

"The cops giving you any grief?"

Aaron checked his watch. It had been almost four hours. The cops had shown up, but per company policy Aaron didn't say shit until one of his supervisors showed up. But Gary was cool, driving there in his personal car so fast you could smell his brake pads cooking when he rolled up. Detroit Fire Department showed up and looked at Aaron's head, and Eddie's ear. Then detectives, who took a bunch of photos and collected the empty brass. And a few bullets which had bounced around the inside of the truck. Then Arlene, who'd heard about the robbery attempt while working in the vault at Brinks, where her cell phone didn't have a signal. Aaron had left her two messages, to let her know he was okay. Whenever anyone took a run at an armored car the word went out among the companies, just in case the bad guys' plan was to hit several in a day. It was not uncommon. She'd rode to the hospital in the ambulance with him, and held his hand while he was getting stitches, now she was out trying to track down a vending machine that wasn't empty or vandalized. The shooting had happened late in the day, and after the tedious bullshit at the scene, and then the delays at the hospital, it was damn near getting to be his bed time. He was exhausted—while still full of nervous energy. Remnants of adrenaline, maybe. The gunfight kept flashing through his head. Major flashbacks, the whole thing and bits and pieces.

"Not really. Bank's cameras caught the whole thing is what I heard. They thought I was full of shit when I said he had a full-auto Glock, until they watched that video. He dumped that whole mag in less than two seconds. There was brass all over that parking lot. I'm surprised the FBI didn't show up."

"They didn't?"

"No. Aren't all banks federally insured?"

"Yeah. Did they get any money?"

"No."

Phault grunted. "No money stolen, nobody shot, maybe they've got better things to do. But they'll be reading the reports. You might get a call."

"Swell. Anyway. Um, hey, uh, you hear from our boy recently?"

"Not for…a few months. Are you…asking for a specific reason?"

"No." Aaron forced a laugh out. "But he might be mad, that there was a gunfight and he wasn't invited."

Phault laughed. "Weirdly enough, I know more than one guy like that. But just like Dave, he seems pretty good at making it happen just by showing up."

The door to the room slammed open with enough force that it bounced off the wall. Arlene was there, a candy bar in her hand and a mouth full of food. "Come here," she said, gesturing violently.

"What?" Aaron said, but she was gone.

Frowning, he moved to the door and stuck his head out. She was down the hallway, heading toward the small waiting room there. "Hello?" he heard in his ear.

"Yeah, hold on a sec," Aaron told Phault. He glanced back once at his uniform sitting on the chair in the exam room—his pistol was in Arlene's big purse, which was looped over her forearm—then he was after her, his paper gown rustling.

Arlene stomped into the middle of the waiting area, half the seats filled with people dozing or on their phones. She jabbed a bony finger at the TV mounted high up on the wall. "Is that what I fucking think it is?"

Aaron turned to look. The TV was turned to CNN, and it was a wide shot from a helicopter, looking down at a subdivision. There were cop cars everywhere, and flames shooting into the air. He frowned, and took a few steps closer to the screen. His eyes darted around, looking at the street, at the houses, and then finally reading the scrawl at the bottom of the screen. "Fuuuuck," he swore. "Turn on the TV," he said.

"What, me?" Phault said in his ear.

"Yeah."

"What channel?"

Aaron, staring at the mayhem on the screen, said, "I don't think it fucking matters."

Chapter Seventeen

MM wanted to make a name for himself with the cartel. To prove himself to Ybarra, in the face of Ramos' failure, and to show Ybarra he'd made the right decision in promoting him. Guns were easy to get on both sides of the border. And men, they had no shortage of men, but only a few were in the area. So they kept watch, while MM sent men across the border. Lots of men. Far more than they needed, even if half of them didn't make it across *la frontera*. But that was the point. To send a message.

Ramos had needed to wait until they could pinpoint the location of the witness against the cartel, which had taken a while. And then they'd needed to precisely coordinate their attacks, to better guarantee success. Not that that had worked out. MM didn't need to do any of that. He had the addresses he needed before he sent any men north. Only rough coordination was needed. And a bit of planning—it was probably better to do it later in the day, when the targets were more likely to be home. Other than that, it was just a matter of waiting for his men to get there, and arm them up in a way that was sure to send a message. Both proved to be easy.

But that wasn't enough. Not enough to make him confident. To that end, he went himself. He was no stranger to murder, and had been involved in several raids on rival cartel compounds and even a *federale* convoy. His English was good, although he had an accent—but he didn't figure that mattered. Not any more.

Once he assembled with his men north of the border, and saw that all of them—all of them but one—had made it across, he knew that success was guaranteed. They had overwhelming numbers. The only question was how many of them would make it back.

Well, there was a second question—exactly how to divide his forces. Because, despite the fact their targets weren't cops or judges, they were connected, and likely the local cops would make the connection pretty damn fast. This all had to happen roughly at the same time.

The two others, they'd done a lot of TV—maybe all the TV—but for all that, they weren't the one getting all the attention. The one who'd become a symbol. That made one of them far more important of a target than the others.

Everyone knew, in a war, destroying the symbols of your enemy was a necessary step on the road to victory. And once he'd succeeded, Ybarra would know he had chosen correctly, that MM was the right man for the job. Someone with intelligence, ruthlessness, and initiative.

Unlike Phoenix, or El Paso, they didn't have multiple safehouses set up in the area, but his senior man out of Phoenix had rented a local house for a week and they were using that as a base of operations. The first night MM arrived he looked at photos of the target houses. They were unremarkable American homes. None of them even had bars over their windows—this would be easy. They were all located inside *barrios*, so there were sure to be neighbors who came out to look, but…what was the American phrase? Ah, yes, "the more the merrier".

MM jumped into the passenger seat of one of their vehicles, an unremarkable sedan, and had the man most familiar with the area drive him past all the houses, which they'd had under intermittent surveillance for a few days. He didn't see anything troubling, and nothing to make him alter their plans. They would go in early evening, when the targets were most likely to be home, but it was still light out.

"Hey. Hey, asshole!"

Dave looked up, and looked around. He was still alone in his house, although it sure didn't sound like it. He walked into the spare bedroom and looked out the window, under the half-closed horizontal blinds. Lori was there, just a few feet away, standing in what had been her bedroom before her mother passed. "Me, I presume?"

She smiled. "Bring over some salad dressing," she told him. "And croutons. Do you have croutons?"

"You couldn't text me?"

"What would be the fun in that?" He heard a vehicle nearby, maybe pulling up outside.

"I'll check," he told her. "I don't think I have any croutons." She pouted. "Let me take a shower, and I'll be over in fifteen," he told her. She flashed a smile and walked away.

He turned and walked to the doorway. What was he…? Oh, yeah, the car pulling up. Maybe a couple of vehicles, actually, thinking back on it. They didn't get a lot of traffic on the street. It was a dead end, and his was the last house in the row. Which was one of the reasons he'd picked the house, back in the day, when he'd still been expecting to die in it—but not before putting up one hell of a fight.

Dave took one step toward his front window, to look out, when he heard a rush of steps and his front door flew open with a crack of shattered wood.

His hand had darted toward the pistol on his hip reflexively as he heard the running feet, and by the time his door was rebounding off the wall, a figure filling the bright doorway, pulling back the booted foot he'd used to kick the door open, Dave's G17 was coming out of the holster.

Dave's brain had time to register the silhouette of a rifle as his pistol came up, left hand joining his right around the grip, pushing the gun out, the first shot breaking just as his arms reached full extension. The pistol cycled in his hands as his finger tapped the trigger like a veteran telegraph operator sending Morse code, spent cases sailing lazily across the room, Dave only distantly hearing the gunshots. Dave rode the recoil up the man's chest into his neck and head, calling his shots, everything seemingly happening at half-speed. The intruder's finger tightened on the trigger as he went down, and Dave blinked in surprise as the rifle fired a huge, long, full-auto burst across the wall and into the floor, the muzzle flash bright in the dim room.

Another man was right behind the first, on Dave's porch, and he began firing before his partner was even all the way down. He had a pistol and his shots were wild, snapping through the doorway and the wall beside it. He wasn't sure where Dave was, but he moved forward as he continued to shoot.

Dave was off to the side, still in the doorway of the spare bedroom, and saw the man's moving shadow through the curtains covering his front window, but didn't immediately see the man. There was a two-foot-wide strip of wall between the front window and door and Dave began firing through it, toward where the man should be, working his rounds back and forth. His pistol was loaded with Federal 147-grain HSTs, chosen for two reasons—the HST was as well-respected as hollowpoints got, just as likely to expand as any other hollowpoint, and the heavy-for-caliber 147s were better suited to punch through barriers to reach the bad guys.

Dave saw a shoulder and head fall into view on his porch, hitting hard, the second man down, and then the front of Dave's house exploded. Wood splinters, drywall dust, and glass shards filled the air. He fell to the floor in surprise. The noise was incredible, pistols and rifles, the bullets flying through his front window, the open doorway, the walls of his house, smashing and bouncing through the house above and around him. He rolled behind the body of the first man he'd killed. Back to the floor, he could feel his house shudder from the rapid-fire impacts, see wild shots tearing holes in his ceiling. Felt the man's body twitch as it was hit by bullets.

Through his open front door Dave caught a glimpse of vehicles on the street and men in front of them, then something flew past his head to crash behind him. He heard a **FWOOMP!**, and felt a rush of heat, strange light flickering on the walls and ceiling. Another object came sailing in and he saw an orange glow before it landed at his feet. Then fire was everywhere—across the floor, crawling over the bodies like it was alive, and climbing up his pants.

He threw himself away from the open doorway and the bullets as the men outside continued firing. He kicked his legs, trying to put out the flames, but only fanned them. Dave looked over his shoulder to see his kitchen was a sea of fire, orange-red flames licking up the counters. His back door was there, now impossible to reach.

Bullets continued to fly over his head from multiple directions, splinters and glass zipping back and forth like raging hornets. He crawled across the floor as fast as he could, keeping as low as possible, feeling shards of glass cutting his palms and forearms, fire burning his legs.

Once through the doorway into his bedroom he grabbed the blanket off his bed and smothered the flames on his legs. Most of his jeans were gone below his knees, just black-edged ragged holes left, his skin underneath red and shiny. He was oddly calm—he'd been on fire before. Burned worse than this. He barely even felt the pain. And he'd been shot at how many times? Outside the bedroom the front room of his house was filled with fire—he couldn't get out that way...but that also meant nobody could get to him. The slide of his Glock was locked back. He reloaded it with the spare magazine off his belt, holstered the pistol, then lunged for his rifle where it was leaning in the corner, staying low. The Aimpoint atop it was turned on, the battery inside it good for five years. Its magazine well was stuffed with a thirty-round magazine, but the chamber of the rifle was empty. Dave worked the charging handle, then grabbed the wide nylon sling hanging off the corner of the bookcase nearby. At the end of it were three double magazine pouches filled with a total of five loaded thirty-round magazines. He threw it over his shoulder crossbody.

The wooden bookcases against three of his bedroom walls, stuffed with cracked paperbacks and flea market hardcovers and library sell-off lawbook collections, seemed to be, for the moment, stopping most of the incoming, which is exactly why he'd put them in place shortly after moving in, when he was simply treading water, waiting for someone to show up and kill him. But they were only three- and four-feet high, and the air above them, above his head, was alive with zips and snaps. Bits of drywall and insulation and wood splinters filled the room and rained down on him. The firing had slowed way down, now just occasional shots. He didn't know how many guns there were out there, but everyone had to've reloaded at least once, they'd already fired hundreds of rounds. He heard some shouting, the words indistinct. The heat inside his bedroom was getting bad, the smoke a foot thick below the ceiling.

Rifle tucked into his shoulder, Dave peeked over the sill of his window into the back yard. There was a man right there, thirty feet away, directly in front of Dave, an AR-15 in his hands. He was watching the back of Dave's house, most of his attention trained on the back door. Dave couldn't get to it, but the man didn't know that.

Dave reflexively shot him twice, the rifle blowing a fist-sized hole through his double-paned window, and the man fell over. Then the two other men in his back yard opened fire, and Dave dove behind his bed. He heard bullets thunking into his bookcases, and the books started to fly off the shelves. His bed shuddered.

He heard shooting and shouts all around—they had him surrounded. They were waiting for him to burn to death. If he tried to run out his front or back doors, or jump out a window, they'd gun him down. At the rate the flames were spreading, they'd only have to wait another two minutes before his entire house was engulfed in flames.

Dave wasn't panicked; it all seemed like a math problem he was trying to solve in his head. The solution was elusive, but he knew there had to be one. If there wasn't, well…no use focusing on that. Hopefully Lori was keeping her head down, but there was nothing he could do for her until he solved his own problems. He low-crawled to his doorway, then got up on one knee. The heat coming out of his front room was incredible, and he felt his eyeballs drying out. In front him was a forest of flame, licking up from the floor and crawling across the walls, nipping at his hands and arms. The ceiling was invisible past a thick layer of gray-black smoke which was quickly descending.

He stepped into the hallway, leaned out past the corner, and fired three quick shots out his open front door. Past the flames he couldn't really see much, but at his shots there was quick movement out there, shouts, and a sharp increase in incoming fire—which had been the point, to keep them focused on the interior of the house. But he was already moving, pulling open the closet door and dropping to a knee.

The hallway was dark and getting darker as the smoke obscured the windows. His hands searched for a second, then his fingers found the pull-ring for the trapdoor. Dave yanked it up, stuck his burned legs into the hole, then dropped down into the pitch-black crawl space.

Sue looked over as the board lit up. She listened to Holly talking to several callers, then she took a few steps and peered at Holly's computer screen, at the addresses displayed there. She practically shoved Holly to the side to reach the microphone. Holly was decent, but she'd only been on the job a month; she didn't *know*.

"Dispatch to all units; multiple nine-one-one calls, Glassford Meadows trailer park, Prescott Valley, fifty-three hundred block of Hydrangea Place," Sue said, her voice terse. "Shots fired, multiple shots fired, incident still ongoing. Sounds like a war, according to callers. Be advised, Pima Jack lives there. Repeat, Pima Jack lives on that block, responding officers highly cautioned. Unknown if he's involved. No further information at this time." She leaned back and let go of the transmit button. Sweating.

"Who should I dispatch?" Holly asked.

Sue shook her head. "You don't have to dispatch anyone."

"Why not?"

"They're all going."

"Who?"

"*Everyone.*" They heard shouting and running footsteps. They looked toward the door, and saw deputies running past. Heard shouting. Units started to call out on the radio that they were responding, the engines of their vehicles straining in the background.

Sue leaned back in. "Dispatch to all units, keep the air clear for the first unit on scene." She leaned her head toward Holly's headset, where the woman was listening in on several open 911 calls. Sue did her best to keep her voice even, and didn't quite succeed. "All units responding, be advised, we've got automatic weapons fire. I can hear it."

MM was standing behind the big old pickup, one of three vehicles they'd driven to the house of "Pima Jack". Two were parked on the dead-end street right in front of his house, and one was in the empty field off to one side. He had men on three sides of the house, which was so close to the adjacent house the flames shooting out one window were nearly reaching the neighbor's siding.

The small square house seemed half-engulfed in flames

now. He'd lost two men, somehow—they'd been gunned down almost before they'd gotten through the front door—but Pima Jack was still in there, and wasn't getting out. Not with twelve—ten, ten heavily-armed men waiting for him.

"Pay attention!" MM shouted to his men in Spanish, pointing at the front door. Through it he could see nothing but flame. "If he's going to try to escape, it will have to be soon." They kept randomly firing shots through the doors and windows and walls. Flames were shooting out of several windows now, thick smoke billowing out past the eaves.

"Jackie! Jackie!"

MM turned at the woman's voice and saw an elderly *gringa* standing on her porch in a faded housecoat, holding a strange creature that it took his eyes a few moments to identify as a hairless cat. The woman was staring out at the burning house across the street. Then her gaze dropped to MM. "What are you doing? What do you think you're doing?" she demanded.

Pumped full of adrenaline, MM laughed and fired a shot at her, which went over her head. She squawked comically and dropped the cat, which was hilarious to see, and scrambled back through her front door after her cat.

"You done fucked up!" he heard her shout back at him, her tremulous voice now strong and sure. "You'll see!"

A shot cracked by MM's head, and he ducked instinctively. He looked toward the house as another shot went by, but the shots weren't coming from there. A bullet hit the truck in front of him—on the side away from the house. MM looked down the street the way they'd driven in and saw movement at the end of the block, a man behind a truck. Popping up to shoot at them. "Marco!" MM shouted, and pointed. His man looked, nodded, and took a knee behind their other vehicle in the street, a big Chrysler sedan, and started firing his rifle at the distant bystander who'd decided to get involved. "Just keep his head down, we'll kill him on the way out," MM said dismissively. "*Gringos pendejos.*"

After the sunlight streaming through the windows and doors, and the bright flames everywhere, the crawlspace under his house was dark as a cave. Dave clicked on the flashlight clamped to the handguard of his rifle—just a simple handheld Surefire G2X in an inexpensive ring mount, as he'd already spent more money than he'd intended on the setup—but the 600 lumens lit up the space. He crawled through the dirt toward the back of the house, the light helping him avoid the support beams and keep his head low enough to avoid a scalp wound.

At the rear of the crawlspace he shut his light off, blinked at the sudden darkness, then looked for what he knew had to be there—gaps or holes in the skirt around the manufactured house. A few feet away there was a vertical gap about a quarter inch wide—probably unnoticeable from the outside, but from under the house the narrow stripe of light was like a beacon. Dave dragged himself close and put an eye to it. Swaying his head left and right he could see the two men in his back yard. They hadn't moved. One had a rifle in his hand, the other a pump shotgun. They were also inconveniently spread apart.

Dave backed off from the gap, shouldered his carbine, and braced his elbows in the dirt. Red dot of the Aimpoint optic hovering before his eye, he delicately crabwalked sideways, a quarter inch at a time, until the first gunman appeared through the gap. He was barely thirty feet away, but peering at him through a tiny gap made the distance seem greater. Dave centered the dot on the man's chest.

Taking a deep breath, Dave fired twice, then immediately rolled twice to the side. Out of the corner of his eye he'd seen the crawlspace skirt in front of him—a section of aluminum siding just nailed at the top—jerk violently at his muzzle blast. There was shouting, then firing, and bullet holes appeared in the skirt near where he'd fired the shot—and came his way, as the second man out there kept firing. Bright holes appeared in the aluminum, shafts of sunlight piercing the darkness, dirt kicking up as the bullets hit under the house.

Dave rolled again and again to avoid the gunfire, only stopping when he slammed his head into a wooden support beam. The bullets stopped just before they reached him. There was a tiny gap in the skirt a few feet off to one side. He scrambled over and put his eye to it. The second cartel gunman was directly in front of him, changing magazines and shouting for help. Dave jerked back to give himself room, shouldered his carbine, and fired blindly through the skirt, six rounds, the concussion incredible, the muzzle blast throwing up sand and dust in a cloud around him.

The lack of return fire was reassuring and, heart pounding, he moved up a bit to peer through the holes he'd just put in the aluminum. The second man was down in the dirt nearby, one foot twitching feebly.

Dave coughed and spit, blinking the dust out of his eyes, backing away from the holes he'd just made. Just in case. He could feel the heat above him, the entire house had to be on fire, but there was no smoke in the crawlspace. Not yet. Should he push his way out behind the house, now that it was, at least for the moment, clear? Or should he stay under the house? He didn't know what the right answer was. Maybe there was no right answer. He dug a fresh magazine out of the sling pouch and reloaded his AR-15 as he thought.

The door to dispatch was open, and everyone who'd been in the station who wasn't now screaming toward the incident at double the speed limit was there, and listening. Sue had the speakers on, so everyone could hear the radio and the callers they had on the line. At the moment, the radio was dead silent. The 911 callers—and there were a lot of them—were not. Holly was off to one side, talking quickly and quietly, frantically taking notes.

"How long before our guys get there?" somebody behind her asked.

"Thirty seconds," Sue said. It was a guess, but an educated one. The first 911 call had come in less than two minutes earlier. She bent to the microphone. "Units responding, be advised, address has been confirmed to be the residence of Pima Jack, and it is currently on fire. Multiple individuals with firearms reported in the street and around the residence, shooting into the house. Automatic weapons fire. Reports of armed civilians in the area responding. Fire and EMS have been dispatched, but will stand in reserve until the scene has been cleared safe. State police have been alerted." She paused. "Tohono One is inbound."

"Tohono One?" someone behind her asked.

"The sheriff. I only hope he doesn't kill himself trying to get there."

"Sue."

The veteran dispatcher looked over at the young trainee. "Yeah?"

Holly was frowning, and scratching her head with the end of her pen. "I've got more calls of shots fired. But it's the forty-seven-hundred block of North Morning Star in Prescott Valley. That's not in Glassford Meadows. Are they close enough to be calling in the gunfight at Pima Jack's house? Hearing that?"

Sue shook her head. "No."

Both women looked over as a unit called out on the radio. Sue bent to her microphone. "Unit calling in, repeat?"

"Twenty-two, ten seconds out," they heard. "Looks like I'm first up."

"Who's that?" someone asked.

"Toby Johnson," Sue said. She crossed herself.

He had his light on for the crawl, ducking under crossbeams. As he drew close to the skirt Dave cut his light and let his eyes adjust for a few seconds. The heat was worse under the front of the house. He could feel it in waves, like sticking his face into an oven. The fire hadn't fully burned through the floor above him, yet, but it was only a matter of time before the fire broke through, or the heat got too much to bear. A minute, maybe? He'd never been underneath a raging inferno before, and didn't know how quickly it was likely to burn downward. At least there was hardly any smoke.

The skirt on the front of the house faced the street, and it was in better shape. There were no gaps in it. No gaps but one, a seemingly big one from the amount of light it was throwing on a nearby support post. Dave crawled to it on knees and elbows. The opening was a vertical gap, over an inch wide, brightly lit with the thin light of early evening. And Dave saw the gap was between a piece of skirting and the side of his porch steps. His concrete porch steps.

Through the gap he saw two men in front of his house, and more in the street ducked down behind vehicles. All armed. Waiting.

Slowly, so as not to draw attention to it, Dave pushed the muzzle of his AR-15 through the gap. Even if it made him more exposed, he couldn't take any chances. Not with so many guys.

He took a deep breath, the air around him hot as a sauna, and started shooting. Closest guys first, dropping them with multiple hits each, seemed a good plan.

As soon as he started shooting everyone jumped and scattered. The second man, who'd been in his front yard, ran for the cover of the vehicles, and Dave shot him in the back. The other two there hid behind cars and fired at the house, not sure where he was. One man was crouched down behind a big pickup. Dave could see his feet and several inches of his legs above his ankles, and fired at them until the man fell down, screaming. Then he fired again as the man tried to crawl behind a wheel.

A man in the street spotted Dave's rifle finally and opened up on full auto with his AK-47. The bullets shot through the siding and ricocheted off the concrete, spraying Dave with chips. He rolled to the side, using the steps and his concrete porch for cover. There was shouting, and more men were shooting, bullets thudding into the dirt to either side of him. Dave pulled his arms and legs in and hugged the concrete. He looked up. There was a ragged line of bullet holes in the wooden floor, and the fire in his living room was quickly eating downward through them. Burning embers drifted down from the floor above his head like lazy orange fireflies, singeing his flesh where they touched, smoke curling around him now, the heat incredible. If he stayed there, he'd be dead. Cooked alive. If he stuck his head around the steps again he'd be dead—they kept shooting, pouring magazine after magazine under the house, keeping him pinned.

"Fuck," he swore, and began crawling backward, under the house, doing his best to keep the mass of concrete in front of him. Bullets thudded into the ground all around, spraying him with dirt.

"Twenty-two," Toby Johnson said into his handset, as the turn came up fast. Rocks spanged against the undercarriage of his Ford Explorer as he took the uneven gravel road at nearly twice the speed limit. "Ten seconds out. Looks like I'm first up." He stood on the brakes, feeling the pedal push back hard in pulses as the anti-lock brakes did their job, then he was skidding sideways through the entrance to Glassford Meadows. A few residents were on their porches, in their front yards, looking deeper into the neighborhood.

Poinsettia Boulevard was asphalt, with a narrow, raised median in the center. Toby pinned the accelerator and the turbocharged engine roared. Poinsettia wasn't quite straight, it had a few gentle curves to it, barely noticeable at the 25 MPH posted speed limit, but a technical challenge at 75. Hydrangea Place was a quarter mile up. He saw a column of smoke arcing into the sky—a house fire, and a bad one.

He was there in seconds, his plan to take the corner at Hydrangea, look down the street, and try to figure out what the hell was going on. But on the far side of the intersection he saw a man crouched down behind a pickup parked in a driveway. With a rifle in his hands, the distinctive profile of an AR-15.

Toby stomped on his brakes again and slid to a stop on the far side of Hydrangea Place across from the man crouched down behind the truck's rear wheel. The man was fat, white, and in his sixties—not exactly a high-crime demographic. He was also keeping the rifle pointed in a safe direction, and waving warningly at Toby. And shouting. Toby kicked his door open and shut off his siren.

"Watch out!" the man shouted, and pointed down the street. Just then several rifle rounds cracked by, and both of them flinched. Toby looked down Hydrangea Place, then grabbed his department-issued M4 and bailed out of the Explorer.

Toby crouched down behind the engine block of his vehicle and popped up briefly to look down the dead-end street, which was maybe a hundred yards long. There were more shots, fast and furious, but they weren't aimed in his direction. He saw a few men moving behind the vehicles at the end of the block. Reflexively he shouldered his carbine, put the glowing circle/dot reticle of his EOTech on one of the armed men he could see on the street, and fired several shots. The man fell over. Then Toby had to duck back behind his vehicle as return fire from several people chewed at his car, thonking into the bodywork and shattering his windows. He grabbed his PTT clipped to his shoulder.

"Dispatch, Twenty-Two. I've got vehicles, multiple bodies on the ground, and armed suspects down at Pima Jack's taking shots at me. I'm at the corner of Hydrangea and Poinsettia. I need a responding unit in the field next to the subdivision, covering that side. I've got at least one armed civilian in the fight, backing me up." He let go of the transmit button and looked across the street at the well-armed retiree. "Pima Jack?" he shouted.

"Fuck if I know, but if he went easy they wouldn't still be down there." There was a rush of shooting down near the burning house, rifle fire echoing off the buildings, and several people opened up on full auto. There were shouts and screams. "See?" the retiree said. He couldn't decide whether to smile or look sick. Toby risked a glance over the hood of his cruiser. He could see bodies and people moving around behind vehicles, but none of them were shooting at him at the moment. He shouldered his rifle, but he was afraid to shoot, worried about hitting Pima Jack or maybe another neighbor who'd joined the fight.

Dave peered out through the cluster of bullet holes he'd made in the skirting, a kinetic constellation, then kicked it off the back of the house and rolled out. He came up on one knee, but he was alone. His house was engulfed in flames—they were whipping out his windows like angry orange laundry in a stiff breeze, roiling over the eaves. The siding was buckling from the heat, the shingles curling.

Rifle up, he approached the corner of his house away from Lori's. Past his place was nothing but scrub field stretching for several miles, the property beside the subdivision still vacant after several development proposals had fallen through.

Instinct made him want to hug his house, but the flames and heat forced him to back off. He was fifteen feet from the corner of his house and still the heat was baking his face. He leaned out, saw nothing past his house, took a step, leaned out again—using the techniques he'd learned and practiced in the life-fire shoothouses at Ravengard—and past his Jeep parked in the carport next to the house saw a dusty compact SUV parked in the dirt past the end of the street. Two guys were crouched down behind it. One was watching the front of Dave's house, the other was reloading his AR-15 after just firing another full magazine into the side of the house. They spotted him just as Dave started firing, trying to bring their guns up and around, but his bullets found their marks, slamming into their bodies and knocking them to the ground. Dave fired again and again at the downed men, then fired half a dozen rounds through the windows of the SUV, just in case there was anyone in there behind the glare on the glass.

He pulled back behind his house, the flames roaring, things inside his house popping and snarling. He went to do a retention reload and saw his bolt was locked back. Had he fired that much? He didn't remember pulling the trigger so many times. He reloaded with a fresh magazine, then ran around the back of his house, around the back of Lori's house, and darted between Lori's house and the neighbor on the far side.

In shadow, he approached the corner of the house slowly, gun up. Peered back down the street. Twenty five-yards away two men were crouched behind a black Chrysler 300 in the middle of the street, halfway between his house and Lori's. They had rifles, and kept popping up to fire at his house. Dave leaned his left forearm against the corner of Lori's house, the siding digging into his flesh, and fired once. Then again. Both clean head shots, the men dropping instantly. He kept his rifle up, scanning the street. He couldn't see anyone moving, but he wasn't about to rush out there. Then he saw Mrs. Leslie on her porch, in one of her baggy housedresses. She came out on her porch, then walked straight down her steps and stomped right out into the middle of the street. And bent down and started yelling at someone? Dave frowned.

MM found he was wheezing as he crawled along the pavement. He was heading for the open field at the end of the street. The desert. He would find safety there. But the pain was incredible. Every muscle contracting made him want to scream.

"I told you," he heard.

MM turned his head and looked up. Standing over him was the old woman, no cat in her arms now, just a big kitchen knife in one hand. Her face looked triumphant. And furious. She bent down and stabbed him in the back with the knife. She hit his shoulder blade, so the knife only went in an inch, but the fresh pain got MM crawling faster. The woman easily kept pace with him in her pink fuzzy slippers. "I—" *stab* "—fucking—" *stab* "—told—" *stab* "—you!" she shouted. Her last stab at his back missed high and went through the side of his neck.

MM died in the middle of the street, his eyes open and staring at nothing.

"Lori! Lori!" Dave shouted. He jogged up onto her porch. By the time he got her front door open she was there, throwing herself into his arms. Then she recoiled. He smelled like smoke, was in fact wreathed in it, and covered in soot and dirt and blood head to toe. She didn't recognize him, only his voice, and his voice had that strangled, angry tone to it she'd only heard once before. His eyes were white circles in a face grimy black and bloody, patches of his hair burned off down to the shiny scalp.

"Are you okay?" she said, fighting back tears.

"I'm fine. Go, get out of here, let me make sure everything's safe," he told her. He looked down the street, and saw a cop car, and pointed at it. He heard a lot of sirens, very close, and rapidly drawing closer.

She ran up the street toward the police car. Dave shouldered his rifle and moved toward the carnage, checking behind vehicles for anyone hiding. He was surprised at how many bodies were in the street, he didn't remember shooting that many people. One of the men was wheezing and trying to crawl. Dave shot him in the side of the head. Shot two more men in their heads, just in case, as he didn't see any visible injuries on them. Then there was nobody left alive in front of his house. Nobody but Rose Leslie, who had a big bloody knife in one hand. She looked dazed as she stood in the street. But she wasn't injured, or in danger. Holding a hand up next to his face to block the heat he ran up his driveway. He couldn't move between his house and his Jeep, the heat was too intense, so he unlocked the passenger side door and crawled in that side. The windows seemed to help block at least some of the heat. Flames were shooting out, practically licking the glass. He started the Jeep and then backed down the driveway. He kept going until his back tires hit the curb on the far side, then he climbed out.

Rose Leslie blinked, and looked at him. Her eyes focused. "Jackie? Is that you? You look like a hot dog somebody forgot on the grill." She waved the knife vaguely. "I told them. I told them, but they didn't listen." She frowned.

"Why are you so dirty?" He could barely hear her over the sirens all around, and the roar of the fire at his back.

"Come on," he told her, tilting his head down the street. "Let's get you away from the fire." He reached down and carefully pulled the knife out of her hand and tossed it away. What he meant was, *Let's get you away from these bodies.*

"What about Mr. Bigglesworth?" She looked toward her house. The cat was nowhere to be seen.

"Mr. Bigglesworth will be just fine." Dave took her by the elbow and they walked up the street slowly. She was moving slowly, like her feet hurt, and before long he was limping too, as the adrenaline started to fade. His legs hurt. A lot of things hurt. Everything hurt. He took Rose Leslie's hand. It was warm and dry and small, thin skin stretched over bones. She didn't say anything, just patted him on the arm with her other hand a few times nervously, like she was calming a pet. He felt something on his legs and looked down to see his burned pantlegs were flapping around his knees, showing off his red, scorched shins. His knees looked like someone had gone after them with a cheese grater.

By the time they were halfway up the street toward the first police car, its lights spinning and flashing silently, other cars were behind it, the officers watching him approach. Dave had his rifle in his hand, carefully pointed down at the ground as he limped along. Lori was up there, next to a deputy who looked vaguely familiar. Three police cars swung around the first and raced down the street past him, the officers inside giving him looks he couldn't read. A lot of people were appearing from nearby houses, some of them holding guns. Others were holding phones, filming. All of them were silent and staring and wide-eyed as he limped up with Mrs. Leslie. He looked down again at himself. It wasn't just his pants, his shirt was burned in places, black-edged ragged holes showing bright red skin. He didn't remember getting burned anywhere but his legs, right at the start of the fight. Crawling over glass had cut his hands and forearms, and blood was caked on them. And over everything was a layer of dirt from moving around in the crawlspace.

As he neared the intersection another half dozen police cars roared into the neighborhood. They screeched to stops nearby. They weren't very loud for some reason; his ears didn't quite seem to be working right. The rifle inside the crawlspace had been loud as a bomb.

Dave looked at the deputy next to Lori, then at the others running up. "I think I got them all, but…" he said, shrugging. "I heard Spanish," he told them. "So, cartel, maybe."

Everyone was looking at him weirdly. He wasn't sure why. The deputy with Lori, eyes wide, told him, "Cujo, dude, you're on fire."

"What?" Dave said stupidly. He looked down at himself, then to either side. He saw the sleeve of his plaid flannel shirt, over his upper arm, was smoldering, small flames flaring into life and then dying into curling orange fibers, over and over, the smoke curling around his head. The hole in the shirt was slowly growing bigger. There were a lot of growing holes in his shirt from burning embers falling on him, the thin trails of smoke curling around his head. "Oh. Can you…?" He held his rifle out and the deputy took it reflexively with his free hand. Dave unslung the magazine pouches, dropped them to the pavement, then shrugged out of his shirt. When it dropped to the concrete at his feet it decided, at that moment, to burst into flame. Everyone stared at it.

Chapter Eighteen

"Two in the house, he says. Got 'em as they came in through the door. And ten more outside, in back, in the street…" Norm Hill shook his head. He was standing beside the sheriff, beside the sheriff's Tahoe, at the end of Hydrangea Place where it met Poinsettia Boulevard. At the opposite end of the street the fire department had put out the fire but was still dousing the hot spots just to make sure it stayed out. A dozen deputies were securing the scene, stringing yellow crime scene tape. The state police helicopter was circling far overhead. Two news helicopters were hovering nearby and occasionally orbiting the neighborhood.

The sheriff grunted. "Toby? He was first on scene, right?"

"Toby says he thinks he got one, but after that wasn't sure who was who down there, and nobody was shooting at him, so he held his fire. Then it was over and the porn star girlfriend came running up. The civilian Toby was with did some shooting, but doesn't know if he hit anything. A dozen guys, sheriff. A dozen fucking cartel guys, based on their tattoos. He says he heard them speaking Spanish."

The sheriff turned his head and raised his eyebrow. His detective was still shaking his head. "Forget for a moment the fucking insanity of this guy stacking more bodies in this town, that means the cartel sent eighteen, maybe twenty guys. Twenty soldiers. To deliver a message."

"That fact has not escaped me. Who's working this with you, Maria Flores?"

Norm Hill barked out a laugh. "We've got fifteen dead and three crime scenes, sheriff. We're all working this. Unless you're turning it all over to the feds, which I doubt. I imagine the FBI and DEA are already screaming up from Phoenix and El Paso, for what will become a 'multi-jurisdictional investigation'." He said the words with distaste. "Maria's over on Morning Star. Sam Wheaton's on site at the Grand Valley Pointe location." He paused. "You tell him yet?" By 'him' he did not mean Wheaton.

Osterman shook his head. "Not yet." Norm shook his head, frowning. Osterman told him, "I will."

"No, it's not that," the big pale detective said. He was staring across the street at Anderson, who was sitting in the back of an ambulance, his girlfriend next to him. The sheriff's men had set up a cordon of cars, and beyond them seemingly every resident of Glassford Meadows had showed up to observe. Every deputy in sight had an M4 slung or in his hands. Two of them stood by the ambulance, on guard. "Twelve men. Twelve men, some with automatic weapons. Surrounding his house. You see how many bullet holes are in the walls? Hundreds. The entire street is empty cases. Molotov cocktails. And he walked away. I mean, he looks like he was eaten and shit out by a grizzly, then set on fire, but he walked away. He was literally *on fucking fire* as he walked down the street with that old lady, the guys tell you that? That video's already been posted online. Walking a little old lady to safety, rifle in hand, covered in blood, half-black as charcoal, on Goddamned fire, the street behind him looking like Mogadishu. And he looks ready for round two. Sorry for swearing, but Jesus Christ, Sheriff."

Osterman looked up at him, the corner of his mouth twitching. "You believe in God, Norm?"

The question surprised him. "Can't say that I do, not with all I've seen."

Osterman nodded at the scene before them. "You've seen this," he said with a pointed look, then headed toward the ambulance.

Ernie met him halfway. Ernie had been a paramedic with the county for going on twenty years, and had seen it all. "How bad is he?" Osterman asked, trying to keep his voice level.

Ernie looked back over his shoulder, then shook his head. "First and second degree burns to a third of his body, at least. Dozens of cuts on his arms and legs, some of which are going to need stitches, after they've been cleaned out, because they're full of dirt. Minor smoke inhalation. Anybody else, they'd be screaming and crying, and I'd be rushing them to the ER. He doesn't seem to give a shit. I saw the video, I heard stories from the hospital, last time he was in there, but I didn't quite believe them. He got a problem with his nerve endings?"

"He feels the pain just as much as any man," the sheriff said. "It's just…he's figured out a way to not much mind." He walked toward the ambulance, nodding at his men on guard duty.

Dave was sitting in the back of the ambulance, Lori at his side. There were bandages over his legs and forearms and one on the side of his head, bright white against the soot and dirt. The smell of smoke was strong inside the vehicle.

"You're not special," the sheriff said.

Dave's head jerked up. "What?"

"Well, you're not *unique*," the sheriff told him, correcting himself. "You remember Larry Patros and Carl Nussbarger? The two men who came with you to the Pima Motel? Who fought with the cartel soldiers."

"Yeah, of course." He met with them every month or two with coffee. Less frequently, lately.

"Cartel sent men after them tonight too."

"Shit." Dave traded a look with Lori. "What happened?"

Frowning, the sheriff told him straight. "They're dead."

Chapter Nineteen

The incident was fifteen hours old when Osterman stepped up to the podium. None of the conference rooms inside the sheriff's department were large enough to hold all the members of the press who wanted to attend, so the press conference was being held inside one of the smaller auditoriums at the local community college.

Osterman looked out at all the faces, and the cameras, cleared his throat, and tapped at the microphone in front of him. That got everyone's attention, and they settled into their seats and got quiet. Some people, in a situation like this, would have their people lined up behind him like show ponies; Sam Wheaton was the only person from the Tohono County Sheriff's Department there, and he was only there to present a second familiar uniform and face. His people still had a lot of work to do, and so were out at the crime scenes doing it. None of the rest of the people lined up on the stage were his—there were two uniformed officers from the state police, and half a dozen men and women in conservative suits—federal agents from the FBI, DEA, and CBP.

"I have a statement to make," Osterman said. "Afterward I will stand here and answer any and all questions you might have, before turning it over to the state police and the various representatives from our federal agencies, but until then, let me speak." He treated all the reporters and journalists arrayed before him—very few of which had earned those titles, he believed—with a sharp look. "Arizona suffered a heinous attack yesterday. Three of our citizens lost their lives in brutal, barbaric attacks. One private residence was completely destroyed, and several others damaged. Several of the men responsible have been identified as Mexican nationals with ties to the *La Fuerza* cartel." He straightened just a bit, and glanced over his shoulder. The corners of his mouth dipped a tiny fraction. "While it is still early, and my brothers in federal law enforcement, as usual, caution everyone not to rush to judgement, not engage in irresponsible speculation about motive, at this point it seems clear this attack was in response to the incident last year. There is no mystery behind the motive, based on their targets. Larry Patros and Carl Nussbarger were two of the men who rushed to the aid of their fellow Arizonans last year, battling cartel assassins at the Pima Motel in Prescott Valley. I'm sad I have to announce that they were killed yesterday, in separate attacks on their homes. Mary Patros, Larry's wife, also died. Yesterday cartel soldiers also attempted to kill Jack Burton, the third man involved in the brave defensive action at the Pima Motel last year. This attack seems to be a retaliatory action against the brave men who dared stand up against the cartel. It was ugly, and brutal, the work of criminals and terrorists. Mr. and Mrs. Patros were slain at their kitchen table, just gunned down, like animals, by animals. Carl Nussbarger, it appears, was able to get to a gun and fire a few shots in self-defense, possibly wounding one or more of his attackers, but he was outnumbered and overwhelmed. If we could, I'd like to take a moment. A moment of silence, to pray for those we've lost."

He bent his head, closed his eyes, and said a prayer. Anyone who knew him knew it wasn't for the cameras—well, not *just* for the cameras. He meant it, and was truly praying. When he finished, he opened his eyes and raised his head. He leaned in toward the microphone.

"This isn't the Third World," he said slowly. "This isn't how we do things in this country. But we're sick, America. No, we're not sick, not *just* sick, we're at war, and nobody seems to want to talk about it. Admit it. Act like adults and address the problem, much less fix it. Nobody even wants to use the term 'illegal alien' anymore. We are being invaded. Thousands of people every day are illegally crossing our southern border—that's not migration, that's an invasion, and if they're just going to be allowed to walk across with no repercussions…that's the death of America. A nation cannot exist without borders. Without security. We would devolve into anarchy. Into Mexico. That seems to be the goal of these cartels, to turn us into them, and rule us with fear and violence as they do their citizens. Our leaders in Washington don't seem to want to do anything about it. Truly don't seem to care. At best, they're ambivalent. At worst…some of their policies seem designed to encourage this mass rush to and across our southern border. That cannot stand, or our nation will fall." He cleared his throat. "I have more to say on this, much more, but now is not the time. I promised to answer questions." He pointed. "Mindy."

He always went to her first, and everyone knew it. The two had known each other for nearly two decades, and while they hardly agreed on anything, they respected each other. She noticed the controlled rage behind his short rant had put some color in his cheeks, but he looked old and tired. He still hadn't fully recovered from being shot the last time the cartel had come to Prescott. Maybe he never would.

"Thank you, Sheriff. Mindy Tonaka, Fox News. Could you walk us through these attacks? Provide details?"

He nodded. "Of course, I'm limited in what I can say, as investigations are still ongoing, but around seven p.m. last night a carload of cartel—*suspected* cartel members pulled up in front of Larry Patros' house on the south side of Prescott. Three or four men forced entry and gunned down Mr. Patros and his wife in the kitchen of their house. At roughly the same time—so we believe it was a different group of men—a car pulled up in front of Carl Nussbarger's house in Prescott Valley. Again, three or four men forced their way into the house. Mr. Nussbarger had a dog, and perhaps it was the dog that warned him, because he was able to get to a handgun and fire several shots. From physical evidence at the scene," meaning blood spatter, "it appears he may have wounded one or more of his attackers. But he was outnumbered and outgunned, and he was found shot to death in his bedroom. They also killed his dog, whom I'm told was named Tinker, and was a three-legged fifteen-year-old Dachshund." He paused and let those words sink in, looking around the room. "Witnesses heard the shots and saw the men leaving. We are doing everything we can to identify these suspects, and CBP," he nodded toward the representative behind him, "is doing everything they can at the border, keeping an eye out for them. We believe at least some of them to be Mexican nationals." He smiled meanly.

Mindy's hand shot up again when it appeared he was done with his answer. "Yes, Mindy?"

"What about the third incident?"

Osterman smiled ruefully, but nodded. "Yes, that's the one that seems to have gotten everyone's attention. At roughly the same time as the other two attacks, a third attack was carried out at the residence of Jack Burton in Prescott Valley. Most everyone knows him as Pima Jack. That attack was not successful, although Mr. Burton's house was destroyed by fire. Molotov cocktails. Several other nearby homes were damaged as well. Fire and gunfire. Mr. Burton is currently in the hospital being treated for wounds suffered in the incident. Under protective guard. Between the three incidents, there were at least fifteen and upwards of twenty suspects involved."

She raised her hand again, but didn't wait for him to call on her. "We've heard there was quite a fight at Pima Jack's house. Amateur video is all over the internet, although you can't really see much. How many suspects were killed? I've heard as many as a dozen, but that seems…"

He smiled thinly at her, then nodded. "Yes, there are a dozen confirmed dead at that scene. We have already confirmed that many of them were known members of the *La Fuerza* cartel."

The man next to her shot his hand up, and Osterman pointed at him. "Doug Stimple, CBS. Were any of your deputies injured in the gunfight with the suspects?" With a dozen dead it only made sense that some cops had to've been injured, but there'd been no reports of cops going to the local hospitals.

The sheriff shook his head. "No, none of my officers were injured."

Mindy Tonaka perked up, and frowned. Just the way he'd said it...she knew him. Osterman was trying to hide something. But he wouldn't lie, the man was a Boy Scout in that respect. And she'd seen that video of Pima Jack walking away from the scene, dirty and limping, rifle in hand, house ablaze behind him—and what had to be bodies on the street. A lot of bodies. It almost looked like he was on fire in the video she'd seen, dust or perhaps even smoke coming off him. It had been quite...something. Something that Osterman had glossed right over. "Twelve cartel gunman dead, and none of your men injured? That's impressive. How many suspects did your men kill in the firefight?" she called out without raising her hand. Reports were that hundreds of shots had been fired in just a few minutes.

Osterman frowned at her. For not raising her hand...or for asking the question? Just from the way he was looking at her told Mindy that she'd hit paydirt. "One. Possibly," he admitted.

"Then who did?" one of the nearby reported asked, again not waiting to be called on.

Osterman took a breath. "A neighbor down the block, armed with a rifle, may have hit one or two of the men," he said. "We won't know for sure until the investigation is complete and we get back ballistics on any recovered spent projectiles."

"One or two out of twelve?" the reporter asked in follow-up. "So who shot the rest?"

Osterman peered at him, but the reporter wasn't going anywhere, and neither was the question. "Initial reports seem to indicate Mr. Burton," he announced. That got the reporters rustling.

"Wait a minute," Mindy said. She stood up. She was tall, and in her heels was an even more formidable figure. "Are you telling us the cartel sent a dozen guys with assault rifles after Pima Jack, and he killed at least *nine* of them by himself?"

"Well, they were armed with a variety of weapons, including some highly illegal machine guns, but...yes."

Doc Brennan and his senior nurse, Ginny, were standing at the end of Dave's bed and frowning at him. "What?" Dave said, looking back and forth between them. "You're acting like I did this to myself."

Ginny's scowl grew deeper. "Mm hmmph," she grunted.

Doc Brennan rolled his eyes and shook his head, then sighed. "Well, this is the least injured I've ever seen you, so I suppose there's that," he told Dave. "You were actually conscious when they brought you in. Has anyone talked to you about your injuries, or recovery time?"

"Not really. Mostly it was just diagnosing and treating. Burns and a few cuts. Really, I'm okay. I mean, it hurts, but..." He traded a look with Lori, who was sitting next to his hospital bed. She looked at him like he was stupid. She'd been doing that a lot.

Brennan had Dave's chart in his hands and flipped through it. "You've got first- and second-degree burns to your legs, your arms, head, and neck. Roughly thirty percent of your body. Minor abrasions to your arms and legs. A number of cuts to your arms and legs, requiring a total of..." He counted down the list. "Eight stitches, and five butterfly bandages. After extensive cleaning, as there'd been dirt ground into most of them."

"See?" Dave said helpfully. "Last time I was here it was sixty-something stitches."

"Sixty-seven," the doctor and nurse said in unison. Tandem disapproval.

"Right. And I was shot three times. This time I didn't get shot at all."

Brennan shook his head. "I don't..." he said. He looked for sympathy from his nurse, and she gave him a commiserating look. He took a deep breath. "Burns are nasty. I don't need to tell you that. Prone to infection, in addition to being very painful. And you ground your burns and cuts into the dirt, crawling around," he said disapprovingly.

Dave frowned at him. "I was kind of busy."

"Yes, well." Word was he'd killed ten men. Maybe a dozen. While on fire. *While on fire.* "I'd like to keep you here a few days, just to keep an eye on you. See how many more blisters develop. And don't pop those blisters, that's one sure way to get an infection. I'd really prefer you to be on an IV, burns are very dehydrating."

"I can drink. Bring me however much water or Gatorade or whatever you want me to drink, and I will. I don't mind, since I can get up and use the john myself, and don't have to use a bedpan."

"Not without assistance getting in and out of bed," Ginny told him. "You need to be careful with your legs."

"Absolutely. I'll be a model patient. But I don't want any morphine or other narcotics, I want my head on straight. Ibuprofen is fine. I can handle the pain."

"Right." Brennan handed his chart to his nurse. He told Dave, "I'll be back later this afternoon. Try not to go wandering around. There are deputies in the hall outside, armed for bear, just in case the bad guys want to finish the job. From the grumbling I'm hearing they actually seem a bit put out that it was pretty much over before they showed up. And there are news trucks all over the parking lot, cameras set up on tripods, so I wouldn't go sticking your nose against the window." He hadn't done a single interview with the media after the last incident. Even with most of his hair burnt off, and a few small burns to his face and ears, he looked much better than the last time, where his face had nearly been peeled off his skull.

"Quiet like a mouse in my house," Dave assured him. Then the corner of his mouth curled down, as he remembered that he didn't have a house. And Lori's house was damaged from the fire and stray bullets shooting through half the walls. He pointed at the side of his head. "Is there a way to tell if hearing loss is going to be permanent? Right now I can't really hear anything out of this ear, just ringing."

"And you're just now...?" Brennan sighed. "I'll schedule a specialist to take a look at you." With one last scowl at Dave he headed out the door.

The nurse, chart in her hands, frowned down at Dave. She looked from him, down to the paperwork in her hands, then back up. "If you had to describe the intensity of the pain you're experiencing," she asked him, the standard question long ago memorized, "on a scale from zero to ten, with zero being no pain whatsoever and ten being the worst pain you can imagine, how much does it hurt right now?" She glared at him, loose bandages covering half his head, both his arms, and his legs from the knees down, and pointed a finger. "If you say five, I'm going to punch you."

Dave frowned. "Three?"

Sam Wheaton stopped by a few hours later, chewing on his big cowboy moustache and looking ill at ease. It wasn't hard to figure out why, a cartel had seemingly declared war on his county.

"Been a little busy," Wheaton said apologetically, "but I wanted to offer my condolences. About Patros and Nussbarger."

"Larry and Carl? Yeah. We weren't exactly friends, but we kept in touch." Dave sighed. "Larry's wife hated me. Fucking hated me, for involving her husband. 'Dragging him into it'. And now they're both dead. So I guess she was right."

Wheaton shook his head. "You can't put that on you. He volunteered, didn't he? Jumped in the car with you, to race over to the Pima?"

"He's still dead."

"More people would have died, if you hadn't done what you did. I gave you a lot of shit at the time, called you the three stooges, but most people wouldn't have done what you did. It took guts. Well, for them. I know at the time you were half suicidal..." He gave Dave a look. Dave didn't argue, because the man wasn't completely wrong.

Dave cleared his throat. "Any luck finding the cartel guys who got away?"

Wheaton shook his head. "Crossing back into Mexico is always easier, we're not set up to look for that, and the Mexican authorities don't care too much, nobody's smuggling guns or drugs *into* Mexico. God knows how many tunnels there are. The feds are likely doing all they can, but with everything else they've got going on down at the border I doubt they've got many resources sitting idle." He rubbed his eyes. "Sheriff's been on a tear. First at his press conference, then an interview with Tucker Carlson that I think is going to get aired later this week. Already talked to a few senators and congressman, and he almost swore on one of those calls, which should tell you how worked up he was. He's like a dog with a bone, he's not going to let this go."

"He's not wrong, by any sane metric our border situation is..." Dave searched for the right word.

"Insane?" Wheaton finished for him. "Honestly, I'm surprised they went after Larry and Carl instead of him. Maybe they thought it would bring too much heat. Or he was too well-protected. Not an easy target...like you." He frowned at Dave and crossed his arms.

"Do I look like I got off easy?" Dave said, waving his arms covered in bandages. "Speaking of that...I owned a rifle and two pistols. You guys took the rifle and the pistol I had on me for evidence. My other Glock burned up in the fire. Along with everything else, including my clothes, my phone, everything. She can buy me some clothes," he said, nodding at Lori, "but.... I know you've got guys guarding me, but I still would feel a lot better if I had a gun of my own. And I'm going to be out of here in a day or two, I'm guessing, no longer under guard. Can you help with that? Getting me a gun. I can pay," he volunteered.

Wheaton blew a big breath of air out, ruffling his graying moustache. He frowned, then jerked his head toward the door. "I'll check with my guys, see if any of them has an extra gun they're interested in selling off. Considering half of them think the next thing you're going to do is walk on water, I don't think that'll be a problem. You got a problem with detectives coming by later, asking you a few questions?"

"Sure, but I don't know anything other than what I've

already said. They kicked in my door and then it was game on. I don't even remember half of it."

"Nevertheless. And if they haven't yet, I'm sure our federal brothers will want to talk to you as well."

"The FBI was caught on tape arranging my assassination," Dave reminded him. "And they're trying to pin Pietro Bufonte's murder in Vegas on me. They can go fuck themselves. I'm not going to jail for a process crime, saying orange in one conversation and red in another and thus 'lying' to federal agents. Seriously, please, let them know my exact response, word for word. Anybody else, sure, I'll talk to them. With my lawyer present."

Wheaton's moustache curved up as he smiled. "I presume he is expecting your call."

They all heard a ring, and Dave looked over at Lori. Wheaton gave a wave and headed out of the room, as Lori answered the call to her iPhone. "Hello?" She blinked twice, then a big smile spread across her face. She pulled the phone away from her mouth, and hit a button. "You're on speaker phone. Tell him yourself," she said.

"Asshole," Aaron announced loudly, and Dave burst into laughter, feeling some of the weight on his heart slide away.

Chapter Twenty

Victor Ybarra, head and founder of *La Fuerza* cartel, was conflicted. He liked for his men to use their heads, and show initiative. And MM had surely done that, with his attack in Arizona on the three men who'd thwarted the original operation to kill the witness against Roberto Muñiz, who had been an important man in *La Fuerza*. Except things had not gone well. Only two of the three targets were dead, and a dozen cartel soldiers, including MM himself, were dead in the third operation which had gone horribly, comically wrong. That saved Ybarra from having to kill the man himself for failing so miserably, so publicly. But the failure wasn't the worst part, it was that MM had executed the attack at all.

Hadn't Ybarra talked at length about symbols and martyrs? "This is what I was talking about!" he growled, jabbing a finger at the widescreen TV. On it was a clip of the American sheriff from when he testified in front of congress just a few days before. Talking about the disaster that was the border. Invited to speak because of the cartel attacks in his territory. And it was hard for anyone to argue with the points he was making, considering what had just happened.

All of MM's men—the surviving ones, that is—had made it safely back across the border. And that was another point the sheriff was making, that the border was so laughably worthless that even with every law enforcement agency on alert, they couldn't stop (what they'd guessed were eight) men crossing back over the border after committing murder.

Ybarra couldn't decide between cold fury and raging anger and bounced back and forth between the two, alternately shouting at his men and staring daggers at the TV, where the famous sheriff—who had as much influence, thanks to the second cartel attack in his territory, as ever—kept talking about border security, the wall, America's worthless 'catch-and-release' alien policies, on camera, broadcast to the nation. Kept talking to American senators, some of whom were coming up for reelection. And politicians who felt they had to do something were always dangerous.

"Do you want to go after the sheriff?" Miguel Aponte said dubiously. With MM dead he was unequivocal head of combat operations, in charge of hundreds of men and the military-grade weaponry to equip them. He would prefer to keep those—the men and weapons—south of the border, as he was infinitely more familiar with the social and political geography, but he'd do as he was commanded.

"No. Are you stupid? As much as an attack before would have made him a martyr, now it would be even worse." Ybarra gestured at the TV. "The man is in front of the American congress. He will be all over news shows for days."

"We killed two of the three. That's not exactly a failure," Iglesias said. He only dealt with drugs, and hadn't known anything about the attacks until they'd happened.

"That's how it's being portrayed in the media. And what *Los Zetas* and *Nueva Generacion* are saying. We look weak." They needed to do something—but something that would work, that would make them appear strong. "This sheriff looks strong. This *pendejo* Pima Jack looks strong." He chewed at his lip as he thought. "The sheriff, he is now too much of a figurehead. Pima Jack would be a good kill, a good message to send, but that can't happen now. He will have guards all around, I would guess, even if he is what they claim, which he is not."

His men frowned at him. "*¿Señor?*" Iglesias said.

"Twelve against one is not a fight anyone wins. They are lying about that and using him as a figurehead, a symbol, much like the sheriff. Americans love their heroes. He likely works for or with the American *federales*, the FBI or DEA, who likely learned of the plan and ambushed MM and his men. The American public doesn't know this, but still, it will be months before it would be safe to go after him." They didn't have months.

Nelson Santiago, standing in the corner quietly, cleared his throat. Ybarra looked over at him. "I don't want to do anything without permission," he said. "That seems a good way to get my head separated from my shoulders. But I may have a way to get at this Pima Jack."

"More gunfights in America involving the cartel we do not need," Timotéo Sandoval growled, throwing at glance at Ybarra.

Nelson shook his head. "I used to know some private contractors. Americans. Former customers, before I joined

La Fuerza. They'll do anything for money. If I can get in touch with them…?" He raised an eyebrow.

"More gunfights in America," Iglesias said dismissively.

"What if they can grab him? Bring him here?" He looked between their faces. Nobody was saying no. "I can't promise anything, but if they succeed, you could make quite a message out of him. And if they fail, they are Americans. Not cartel. The man has had problems with American criminals before. I looked into him. He has, or had, some sort of fight with an American mafia *jefe*. If we didn't use any of our men, even if they were seen, no one would tie it to us." He paused, and looked at everyone. "Unless someone else has another idea?" No one did.

Timotéo glanced over and traded a look with Miguel Aponte as the meeting broke up. Aponte's eyes darted over toward the head of the cartel, but Ybarra was already on the phone, growling at someone. The two men wandered out of the room and toward the rear of the building. The villa had a big pool back there, and there were always women lounging around. The women had learned to ignore the men, not approach them, especially if it looked like they were discussing business.

The two men moved away from the house, along the pool, stopping in the shade of a few palms. Away from all of the women. Both men were young. Aponte was a few years older than Timotéo, but smart, and ruthless; Timotéo trusted him. Timotéo frowned, looking back toward the house. "Since when does the bomb maker have American contacts?"

Aponte shrugged, keeping his expression neutral. "He knows more than bombs. He knows electronics, some computers. And as he said, former customers."

"He is a good bomb maker," Timoteo admitted. "He

knows wiring, explosives. Those cell phone spying gadgets. But he is the gear man. Who sits in the back room. I don't see him meeting with any of his customers. Knowing a group of American *mercenarios* well enough to hire them for a job?"

Aponte, it was clear, had decided to play devil's advocate. He had just a hint of a smile on his face as he said, "People surprise you."

"Ay, and that's what worries me. Could you have a man or two follow him, whenever he leaves the compound? I don't trust him. There's..." He shook his head. There was just something about the man. He couldn't put his finger on it, but he'd learned to trust his feelings. They'd kept him alive.

"Ybarra seems to trust him."

"Ybarra is a good businessman, but what we are in now is a war," Timotéo said. "A war we are losing. His focus is too narrow."

"He does seem...beset," Aponte agreed. They traded another look. Perhaps there was opportunity there. He nodded. "I will have a man or two follow Santiago. See where he goes. How is he contacting these Americans?"

"I don't know. Do we have someone who can check his phone, his computer?"

Aponte didn't answer directly. "I am more worried about Los Zetas than I am the Americans, whoever they are."

Timotéo shook his head more forcefully. "I know we have been killing each other, but Los Zetas are not our enemies. They are our competition. The government, the *federales* are our enemies." He gave Aponte a thoughtful look. "Cartels have joined together before."

Aponte glanced around. "Don't let Ybarra hear you say that. You know how he feels about them."

"Which makes me wonder," Timotéo said lightly. "He is more a businessman than a war leader, but mergers happen all the time with business. I do not think he has a plan to move forward."

Aponte's eyebrow rose. "And you do?"

Timotéo gave him a frank look. "I am sure I am not alone in planning for my future. For the future of *La Fuerza*."

Dave stood in the doorway and stared at the spare bedroom. That not even two weeks earlier he'd spent most of a day painting. The heat from the fire, just a few feet away, had buckled the siding on the outside of Lori's house, and discolored the paint on the inside wall. The smoke had poured in the open window, and turned the white ceiling gray. It had also made the entire room smell like smoke and ash, which is why they kept the door closed. He was glad the master bedroom was on the opposite side of the house. The fire department's high-pressure hoses had managed to get water inside the window, so it had run down the wall both on the inside and in-between the joists, causing a bit of warping and buckling. Lori hadn't had the insurance company out yet, but he knew the room would probably need to be completely redone—new drywall and everything —just to kill the smell of smoke. Compared to the fire damage on that side of the house, the dozen rifle bullets which had punched through the walls had done very little damage. Dave would have already spackled them over if he didn't need to leave them for the insurance company rep to eyeball. They were due out in a day. For her house. For his house…

He'd never gotten insurance. He'd figured if—when—someone finally came for him, he wouldn't be around afterward to care what happened to the place. It had been a bad assumption. But because he hadn't been emotionally tied to the house, its loss didn't bother him as much as it might have. He was glad he'd thought to save his Jeep. The plastic housing around the driver's side mirror was slightly melted, and the paint on that side very slightly discolored, but that was the only damage.

"I need to get out of here," he said, shutting the door on the damage. He could still smell the smoke; it was like he couldn't get it out of his nose. He smelled smoke throughout the day, and he wasn't sure if he was actually smelling it, or if it was some kind of post-traumatic odor flashback, if that was even a thing. He turned. Lori was sitting at the kitchen table in front of her laptop.

"Out to eat?" she asked. She glanced at her screen to check the time.

"Yeah. Somewhere with people." He walked over and stood next to her

That surprised her. "Yeah?" Her eyebrows went up. Normally he tried to avoid crowds, and he didn't like to be recognized.

"Yeah. It'll help distract me from…" he waved a hand vaguely toward the damaged bedroom and, beyond it, his house, which was a blackened shell.

"What are you in the mood for?"

"Steak," he said.

She rolled her eyes. "I don't even know why I asked. Where do you want to go?"

He considered. He couldn't wear a hat because of the

healing burns on his head. He looked more than a bit like a victim of nuclear fallout. "Dunphy's," he said, because it was dark. He'd be less likely to be recognized. She didn't seem to be surfing social media, he saw columns of figures on the screen in front of her. "What are you doing?"

"Just checking my investment account. The stock market has been so crazy lately I was curious. I try not to check it that often, my investments are meant to be long term, so I'm mostly invested in companies that are very conservative, economically. Like Toyota. But I'm invested in a lot of different things. Diversified. Just in case. High risk to no risk, including some CDs from the bank." He saw that she was on E*TRADE. His eyes scanned the columns and moved down to the bottom. To the totals.

"Holy shit," he blurted.

"I made a lot of money when I was working. You know women make all the money in porn."

"Yeah. But I thought you maybe had one, two hundred grand saved up."

"I was investing ten to fifty grand a year, every year I was working, never had a drug problem, and never bought stupid shit like a Mercedes G-wagon. And I had thirty thousand worth of T-bills mature right at the start of COVID, when the stock market was in the toilet. I invested it in Apple, Google, and Marathon Oil. Apple and Google have more than doubled, and Marathon is worth nearly ten times what I paid for it. I lucked out."

"You're paying for dinner," he told her firmly. "But I promise I'll put out afterward." She snorted. "Although my knees are still a bit raw…"

"I bet I can figure something out," she told him.

He'd had no clothes other than the ruined ones on his back and a pair of dirty underwear Lori found under her bed. So while he laid in bed waiting to be discharged from the hospital, she'd driven to the nearby Walmart and bought him underwear and socks and shirts and jeans and shorts—not a lot, but enough for a few days. Two days after getting released from the hospital he did some shopping of his own—a few more purchases at Walmart, but he'd also driven down to Phoenix and did a little shopping at the 5.11 Tactical store. He'd never been one to dress in "tactical" pants, but skinny jeans and burned legs were a bad combination. He bought several pairs of loose, baggy, tactical pants in gray and green. He'd had yet to wear them beyond trying them on in the store, as he stayed in shorts inside the house, but even though they didn't hurt nearly as much his legs looked worse. Like something out of a horror movie. He wouldn't go out in public in shorts, that would do nothing but draw attention. He'd driven back to Lori's house with his pants...and hadn't come out for days. Relaxing, and healing, and maybe mourning a bit over what had happened. Nightmares, of course—he was used to those, although now he had new material to terrify him. Sometimes he woke up with Lori hugging him—maybe he'd been thrashing, or shouting in his sleep. Thank God she never asked him if he wanted to talk—she knew he would, and did, but it had to be on his terms.

Dunphy's Steakhouse was in downtown Prescott, and housed in a former mercantile building that was built in the 1890s. The ceilings were hugely tall and covered with painted tin panels or something—Dave had never asked exactly what they were, but had seen them on the ceilings of several of the older buildings in town.

Lori parked her Toyota RAV4 at the curb in one of the angled spots and walked around. Dave was moving a little slower—he wasn't limping, but he was being careful. He had light, loose bandages around the burns on this legs and arms, just to protect them, and had on a loose long-sleeve plaid shirt over a t-shirt and the 5.11 pants. He also had a newly-purchased Gen 5 Glock 17 in the holster on his hip. He'd bought it from one of the Tohono County deputies. Technically it was used, but the man had told him he'd bought it but never fired it, and it was just sitting in his safe. He'd wanted to just give it to Dave, but Dave insisted on paying. He'd taken it to the range once and put a few hundred rounds through it, just to make sure it worked.

He followed Lori through the door to the hostess stand. The long bar was to the left, the main dining area to the right. Most of the tables were full, but the hostess led them to a round table near the back of the dining room. Like a lot of fancier restaurants, the lighting was turned down low inside Dunphy's, and there was a lot of dark wood, which Dave liked. But they'd only been seated a few minutes when Lori touched his hand. "I think those guys recognize you," she said, nodding toward the back of the room. There was a long table, with two women and eight men seated around it. They were all looking at him. Then one of the men was on his feet, and wending his way between the tables.

"I didn't want you to get up," Lou said to him. He smiled at Lori. "Ma'am." He tipped an imaginary hat in her direction, then looked back at Dave. "We'd be honored if you could join us, but would perfectly understand if you want to have a private dinner, just the two of you." He smiled and nodded and, without waiting for an answer, made his way back to his table.

"Those are all the instructors at the shooting school, Ravengard," Dave told her. "And the guy who runs the place, who's friends with the sheriff."

"So we should…"

"Probably." He wasn't sure how he felt about it. He wasn't in the mood to socialize, but the training they'd given him at Ravengard had definitely helped. Maybe saved his life.

They walked together to the table and took the two empty chairs. Cam Kendall got Lori's name and then formally introduced everyone to Dave and Lori, pointedly not introducing him to them. It appeared everyone there knew who he was. "Are you doing okay, young man?" Kendall asked him, looking concerned. "Physically," he quickly added. "Last I heard you were in the hospital."

Dave considered how to answer him. Finally he said, "Burns suck."

Kendall nodded once, sharply. "That they do," he pronounced, then launched into a story about someone trying to train a pig to square dance. He told it so intently Dave couldn't tell if it was supposed to be a joke or something that had actually happened.

There were appetizers already on the table, and when the waitress next appeared Dave and Lori ordered drinks—he got a Diet Coke. When she left, he looked down the table, and saw just how many of the people at it weren't drinking alcohol. He was pretty sure he knew what that meant.

During a lull in the conversation, which he wasn't participating in but rather just listening to, Dave asked, "We've got a dozen people, and I see just one glass of wine and one beer. Are you thinking the cartel might come back?" He'd been thinking about that. A lot. They'd returned to Prescott to kill three people, to send a message. They'd only killed two, and the message they'd meant to deliver had been seriously compromised by what had happened at his house. If they did come back, he would be the most likely target. The sheriff was a close second. There was a fully-marked squad car positioned at the entrance to Glassford Meadows most days. Dave was pretty sure it was there as deterrence and reassurance to the residents, most of whom, Dave was sure, would be happy if he moved elsewhere.

Most of the instructors sitting at the table traded looks, but left Kendall to answer. The man shrugged. "Likely somebody from the DEA or Border Patrol would be in a better position to answer that, but better safe than sorry." He flashed a smile at Dave and gestured at the men and women around him. "If they show up, we'd like to think we could give a good accounting of ourselves." He blinked as he had a thought, then did a quick, quiet census. The eight men and two women at the table were armed with a total thirteen handguns. The number put a proud smile on Kendall's face. He dipped his head toward Dave. "Plus whatever you might have on your person."

"Just a Glock 17 I bought off one of the sheriff's guys," Dave said. "Everything else I had was taken as evidence or destroyed in the fire." He frowned.

Kendall saw the frown, and smartly rapped the top of the table with his palm. "Enough talk about that." He turned his bright politician's smile on Lori. "Young lady, you look familiar to me. Where might we have met?" He cocked his head, and didn't notice three of his male instructors, including Lou, choking on their drinks.

Chapter Twenty-One

Winston Elliott, Director of the Defense Intelligence Agency, sat in one of the SCIFs inside the DIA headquarters in Washington D.C., waiting. He checked his watch, then went to grab for his phone, to check his messages, then made a rude sound and shook his head. The whole point of a SCIF—Sensitive Compartmented Information Facility—was that there were no airborne signals going in or out, and no cell phones or other electronic devices were allowed; he'd dumped his phone into a numbered tub outside the door. The room was secure from any and all kinds of eavesdropping, physically and electronically isolated from the building it was inside. One whole wall was screens, if he wanted to communicate with other SCIFs around the country or around the world, but those electronics were heavily encrypted.

There was a small red indicator light by the door, indicating that it wasn't closed, and that the room wasn't fully secure. Elliott checked his watch again, and was thinking about heading out to his phone, to make a call, when the door opened and the man he was waiting for appeared.

"Sorry about that," the slender blonde man said. He was bland and forgettable, in a gray suit that had nothing about it to catch the eye. From a distance he might have appeared in his twenties, but a closer look would show that under the longish hair and lean build he had some wrinkles around his eyes, and was in fact in his forties. He'd been using the work name Joe Clark for as long as he'd been with the DIA, twenty years, and was now one of the senior case officers in the agency. Not that they officially had case officers, but what intelligence agency wasn't engaged in secret activities? Dipping toes into ponds where they weren't supposed to be getting wet. Wasn't that the point of being in the game? It was always far better to beg forgiveness than ask permission...and put several layers of deniable assets between you and whatever was happening, in case you ever got called to testify before a Senate subcommittee.

Clark closed and secured the door, and the indicator light blinked from red to green. He shook Elliott's hand, then sat down.

"So what's so important you needed to meet in person?" Elliott asked the man. "In here?" He waved a hand around the room.

"Tentpole," Clark said, which was exactly what Elliott was expecting him to say.

"Things do seem to be a shitshow down there," Elliott agreed.

"And not in the right way. It's called Operation Tentpole for a reason. We're there to prop the weak ones up. And get them fighting amongst themselves."

"*Keep* them fighting."

"Same-same. So we didn't specifically choose La Fuerza,

but that's where our asset ended up, and that seemed perfect for what we wanted. Small, new cartel, looking to make a name for itself. So we get Weathervane embedded with them, helping them out, making himself valuable. And on this, they've fucked up. Twice, just recently, but three times. Four times, if you go back to the original incident in Arizona, and every time they try to make it better it makes it worse. It looks bad for them. The other cartels are circling."

"I presume you didn't come in just so you could vent." Weathervane was the codename for Martin Cabrera, undercover with the La Fuerza cartel as Nelson Santiago, electronics expert. It had taken him years to get in deep with them, but now he was rubbing shoulders with the decision-makers in the organization. Not management, but close to it, and able to affect decisions.

"Weathervane made contact via email. He's got an idea, a move he could make that would make him a golden boy with La Fuerza, and strengthen them down there. At least make them look stronger."

"Then why hasn't he already done it? Osterman's got the entire Congress riled up about the border, senators shouting at each other, governors mobilizing the National Guard to patrol the Rio Grande, the Attorney General talking about taking a trip down to eyeball the border crossings on a 'fact-finding mission'." He snorted derisively. Politicians, at best, were useful tools.

"Because he needs a little help from us to pull it off. And it's a little…well, I wanted to discuss it in here for a reason." He gestured at the SCIF around them. "But I think it's a solid plan, provided you're willing to sign off on it. Minimal risk, at least on this side of the border."

"Okay, color me intrigued."

"How close have you been following the incidents in Arizona involving the cartel? Have you heard the name Pima Jack?"

Winston Elliott frowned. "Pima Jack." Otherwise known as David Anderson. The man who likely had killed one of his most senior people, and so far gone unpunished for it. "Yeah. I know exactly who that is," he growled. "What about him?"

Chapter Twenty-Two

Pike closed the door to Higgins' office and sat down in front of his desk. He'd been summoned.

"Well, it looks like you were right," Higgins told him.

Pike nodded. "Of course I was. About what?"

Higgins snorted. "The border."

"Ah, yes." The cartel attack in Arizona, and the political fallout from it, had been maintaining a chokehold on the 24/7 news cycle for most of a week. Pike personally thought sleeper cell agents of nations hostile to the U.S., using the southern border to infiltrate the country, were a far more serious threat, but those cells might never be activated, depending on how well Washington D.C. was getting along with Beijing, Moscow, Riyadh, whoever. Cartels, on the other hand, couldn't seem to do anything quietly. The fact that they'd got their asses handed to them by armed Americans was especially delicious.

"And the squeaky wheel gets the oil."

Pike cocked his head at that, and sat up a little bit straighter. "Us being the oil?"

Higgins nodded. "I imagine everyone is lined up, FBI, CIA, you name it, especially if they start carving out big chunks of the federal budget to fund ops, but we've got a mission."

"Excellent. So what do you need?"

"I don't need a lot of bodies on this, and Gargoyle seemed to gel for you, so I'm keeping it together. I've got the rest of Gargoyle not on injured reserve planning a simple but sensitive snatch and grab," Higgins told him. "I want you on the transport side. Logistics. Lock in a private jet through one of our cutout companies, and arrange travel down to Mexico. If for some reason we don't have one available, maybe we can borrow one from one of the seven thousand shell companies Christians In Action operates. Now that they can't get any opium out of Afghanistan they've probably got nothing to do."

Pike smiled, then frowned. "Wait, we're grabbing someone in the States and flying them down to Mexico? Not the other way around?"

"Yeah. Live cargo drop. So you won't be landing at a regular airport." Which wasn't a big deal. Flying into the States was an ordeal, but Mexico simply didn't have the infrastructure to check on small planes that dropped off radar.

"Where are we going?"

"As yet to be determined. But we'll be flying out of Arizona, maybe Phoenix, so likely you'll be setting down in northern Mexico. Or they will."

"Not me?"

Higgins shook his head. "I know you've got fluent Spanish, but you look like a Viking. I only want to send guys down who look like they might be from the neighborhood, at least from a distance, just in case things go sideways.

Which is basically everybody on the team but you." Pike nodded. He had no problems blending in if he was anywhere between Ireland and Novosibirsk, but Latin America something else entirely. "You guys seemed to work well together, so I see no reason to split you up. Unless there's something I'm not aware of?"

Pike shook his head. "No, no personal drama. Everyone was solid."

"What about Fancy? He ready to go back in the field?"

Pike shook his head again. "He'll tell you he is, but he just got his stitches out. I'd give him another two weeks, at least."

Higgins nodded in agreement. "Three guys should be plenty on this. I'll send everything you need to a secure terminal, and you can start working on it. Line up the jet, the crew, you know, the usual, so when they roll up with the package all they have to do is jump onboard and the jet can take off."

"Do you care if I'm on site? You know I always prefer to be hands-on. I like to be able to look people in the face. Especially if we've got to borrow assets from the CIA." Seeing how squirrelly a co-pilot had once been before a flight had clued him in to something being wrong, and he'd been ready when the armed hostiles had shown up.

Higgins shook his head. "Do whatever you think you need to do. But there's a bit of a rush on this, they want this to happen by Friday."

"Four days? Four days to plan a snatch-and-grab of a high value target?" Something like that usually took four weeks.

"It's not as bad as it sounds. Minimal, maybe no security. High value doesn't mean high threat."

"I hope you're right."

"When are you going to get your own fucking phone?"

Aaron had never mastered the fine art of giving a fuck, and his voice tended to carry. Lori had handed her phone to Dave, but had no problems hearing the conversation, and she hid a smile.

"I don't know, I just haven't gotten around to it yet. Only like three, four people call me."

"That's just sad, man. Anyway, I gave Pork Snorkle's phone number to John Phault, for if and when he wants to call you. You talk to him lately?"

Dave thought for a bit before answering. There would be records of him calling his former boss, the Detroit-based PI. There shouldn't be any recording of those two most recent calls—one to Phault, and one return call the same day. Where he'd asked Phault for any Las Vegas addresses connected to Pietro Bufonte. And Phault had come through. And later that day, Bufonte had been killed in his Summerlin mansion. Phault had said there was no way the address search could be traced back to him. If anyone asked why Dave had called him, well, the two had history. "Month or two, I guess."

Aaron grunted. "Well, I've had a few calls with him recently. And his lawyer. Got into a shooting at work."

Dave sat up. "Yeah? You okay?"

"Dude, seriously? You burn down a baker's dozen of bad guys and you're asking about me?"

"Well…yeah."

Aaron sighed into his ear. "I'm fine. Took two in the vest. Emptied a mag at the dude, but I don't think I hit him. Scared the fuck out of him, though, he took off. Didn't get any cash."

"Then why are talking to a lawyer?"

"Just in case. And…something else. You know that fuckhead West Bloomfield detective, the one's been trying to pin the hit-and-run on you for years?"

Dave hadn't thought about the man in a long time. Maybe not since coming to Arizona. He'd had other issues to deal with. If there'd been any evidence tying him to that homicide, it would have come up by now. He had the vague recollection of a short guy with a lot of hair in a nice suit. "Yeah. I haven't talked to him in a long time."

"Well, he's been talking to me. A few times last year, looking for you. I didn't tell him shit, by the way."

"Of that I have no doubt."

"Yeah? Well, he came at me again a couple of weeks ago. I probably should have called you about it before this, but…it's not the kind of thing I want to talk about over the phone, but I can't afford to fly down there."

"Okay," Dave said slowly, curious. "About the hit-and-run?"

"No," Aaron told him. "Well, not just that. He said he's been in contact with the FBI. And that they think you had something to do with that fucker's murder in Vegas, him and his guys."

"Yeah, I'm aware. Bufonte sent guys to kidnap or kill me the day before. I was stressed out, needed to relax, and went for a drive. Drove around Vegas that night, looking at the lights on the Strip, trying to clear my head." He glanced at Lori, who was still listening. "I don't know anything about those murders, of course. Pietro Bufonte is a Detroit mob boss, so why would I even think he was in Vegas?" Lori nodded.

"Sounds legit," Aaron said. "But if the FBI is looking at you, they're probably listening to us right now. Even though one of their agents was already caught on tape trying to hire guys to kill you, so they should be the last agency going after you. Hi, FBI. Seems like you'd have grounds for one of those civil suits. For harassment, or whatever. Seriously, with their recent track record, the Famous But Incompetent should just disband. Morale has to be horrible over there. I mean, they haven't charged anybody who visited Epstein Island, but you can go online and find photos of their agents kneeling as BLM marches by. Embarrassment after embarrassment. I'm surprised more of their agents aren't retiring, or simply eating their guns. So many cops do. It's never too late to do the right thing." Lori opened her mouth in wonder. Dave just had to smile; Aaron was still Aaron.

"So far they seem to be keeping their distance. And why wouldn't they, I'm innocent. If they had any evidence, I'd have heard about it." He glanced at Lori, who was giving him a look and jabbing a finger at the phone in his hand. He knew why. "And speaking of murders, you know a guy was killed out here, maybe a mile down the road, the same night. Same night as what happened in Vegas."

Aaron didn't answer for a while. When he did, his voice was even. Measured. "Sorry, I don't follow the local Arizona news. One of Bufonte's guys? Cartel?"

Dave nodded at Lori. Just the way Aaron had answered, he knew. "No, it's the weirdest thing. When I was in the hospital down here—"

"Which fucking time? You're in the hospital more than Evel Knievel."

"The first time. When my cabin burned down, and my hands were injured. I was on sedatives, in my room, when a guy came to the hospital. A fed, I guess with a warrant? Maybe you remember. Tried to take me into custody. Osterman told me about it afterward."

"That maybe rings a bell," Aaron said slowly. "Brought a whole tac team with him. Osterman told him to pound sand, and if he tried to take you by force he'd kill him where he stood."

"He...what?" Dave hadn't heard that part of the story.

"You didn't hear about that? The sheriff didn't tell you? *Duuuuude*. There was a big face-off in the hospital hallway. This fed asshole in a suit said he was going to take you into custody, and if the sheriff got in his way he'd have him arrested. And the sheriff flicked off the safety on his shotgun and basically said 'You ready to meet Jesus? Cuz I got nothin' better to do.' And he fuckin' meant it, dude, you could see it in his eyes, and he was smiling when he said it, like he was hoping it would happen. Shotgun John, man, that fuckin' dude clanks when he walks." Lori's eyes were wide.

"I am somehow not surprised. Anyway, that's who was killed," Dave said. "About a mile from my place. They think. They're pretty sure it's the same guy, but his ID, name, prints, don't go anywhere. Like it's a cover identity."

"Like a spy?"

"Something like that. And he had a pistol, and suppressor, and night vision goggles on him. Serial numbers are untraceable."

"Really." Aaron definitely didn't sound surprised by the news. "Sounds like he might've been up to some shit."

"Yeah. That's what the sheriff seemed to think. Seems like they've got no suspects, no leads, the sheriff was even asking me if I knew anything. But, you know, I was in Vegas."

"Right. So...no suspects, no leads." Aaron didn't say anything for a long while. "Well, that sucks for them I guess," he finally said, his voice lighter. "So now all you've got to worry about is the fucking cartel, wanting payback for you fucking up their plans a second time. Maybe you should move back to Michigan. Or get a new identity, since Jack Burton is blown. Maybe Jack Bauer. Wait a minute. Wait a goddamned minute."

"What?"

"Jack Burton. Jack Bauer. Jason Bourne. James Bond. What the fuck is it with Js and Bs? How is it I'm just noticing this now?"

"You guys are like birds of a feather."

West Bloomfield Township Detective Billy Dixon had been heading toward his desk, having just returned to the station, when his chief of police spotted him. "Us guys who?" He looked around. West Bloomfield only had a couple of detectives, and he was the only one in the office at the moment.

"You and that FBI agent with the weird name."

Dixon set his files down on his desk and turned back to his chief. "Gogolak?"

"That's the one. Like a dog with a bone, both of you."

"About what?"

"The Bufonte hit-and-run homicide. He was back in here this afternoon."

"He was? In person? I thought he was based out of D.C."

The chief shrugged. "Couldn't tell you. It's probably on his card, which is sitting on my desk, you need it."

"No, I've got one. What did he want?" Dixon hadn't heard from the FBI Special Agent since the sit-down meeting they'd had weeks earlier. Before Dixon had even gone to Vegas. The man hadn't called…but he'd shown up at the station? Had he not gone back to D.C.? Or was he back in town? If so, for this or something else?

"Just wondering if he'd seen everything in our files. I told you to cooperate fully with them." There was an unspoken question in the statement.

"I did. I showed him everything I had. Which is everything we have. Gave him copies of anything he wanted."

"He thought maybe you were only showing him the stuff you thought was pertinent, so as not to waste his time. I get the feeling he's one of those guys who would sift through fifty Dumpsters full of diapers looking for a McDonald's receipt to nail a suspect."

Dixon shook his head. "I met him in the conference room. Brought in literally every piece of paper I have on this homicide. Was he looking for something in particular?"

The chief shrugged. "Couldn't tell you. Spent a few hours at the spare desk, looking through what we had. If he found something new he didn't say boo."

Dixon frowned. "And then he took off? Back to D.C.?"

His chief shrugged again. "Don't have a clue, I've got enough to do around here."

Dixon checked his desk. Gogolak hadn't left his card or a note to indicate he'd been back. "He didn't leave me a card," he said distractedly.

"Like I said, I've got one on the desk." The chief stuck a thumb over his shoulder.

Dixon dug out his phone, and checked for any missed calls or texts from the FBI Special Agent. Nothing. He looked up at his chief and forced a smile. "Nah. He probably figured out it was a waste of time. If there was anything there, I would have nailed Anderson with it by now." He had run the plate on Aaron Abruzzo's dark green

Ford Taurus, seeing as it matched the general description of the vehicle used in the hit-and-run, but like the asshole had said, he'd just bought it a few months earlier.

"Oh, I know it," the chief said. "Like I said, a dog with a bone." He gave a wave as he turned to go. "I'm heading home early. I'll be back in a few hours, for the township board meeting."

"Better you than me."

Dixon went and sat behind his desk, thinking. Thinking and sweating. It had felt like he was running out of time, and that was before he'd heard Gogolak was back, sniffing around. Bufonte was dead, but undoubtedly they were looking into known associates. Trying to figure out who would fill the vacuum. Gogolak didn't have anything on him, because there was nothing to be had—Dixon had always used a burner, and always called one of the burners that Bufonte or his guys carried. And he'd always been paid in cash, so there was no paper trail. No paper trail…except the records Bufonte had kept, apparently.

That was his problem. Not the FBI. The group of older Italian gentlemen who wanted answers. And who were seemingly growing tired of waiting for them.

Chapter Twenty-Three

There were complications, but only minor ones. His address was a clear no-go, simply because it didn't exist anymore. But they found the only vehicle registered to him nearby, so he had to be close. Direct surveillance of the vehicle from the ground was high risk—it was in a somewhat isolated spot, there was a heavy local law enforcement presence in the area, and most of the residents displayed an increased awareness of their surroundings. They did a few drive-bys, just to see what the location looked like from the street, but then backed off. Especially when they saw how many eyes were on them. The locals were on high alert.

While the mission wasn't being directly video monitored —in real time or otherwise—by headquarters, due to its ultra-sensitive nature, the remaining members of Gargoyle had access to their usual toys. They had a drone on station, orbiting a thousand feet above the target's vehicle, the second day after they'd been given the mission. As lightly loaded as it was, with just a high-resolution camera, the FULMAR X drone could stay on station nearly twelve hours. They confirmed the target was at the location, with his vehicle, the next day.

There was open country adjacent to the target's residence, so they had options. The third night, Dog and Boot came in cross-country just before 3 a.m. and checked out the residence from close-up. Dog had a hand-held thermal scope, and the drone was equipped with one as well—between the two they were able to determine the target was inside the house with another person, the two of them sleeping together in a room against the side of the house. Just feet away from a neighboring house, which was also occupied. Stealth would be a necessity, because it seemed clear if they were spotted by anyone, things could go very bad very quickly. Luckily, the houses were very lightly constructed—no brick, no stone, just siding over wood and drywall.

Dog was team lead, but he listened to everyone's ideas, and studied the live feed from the drone, before deciding on a plan. There was a police vehicle positioned on the only road in or out of the neighborhood, and its occupant was sure to take note of any cars going past in the middle of the night. Maybe the cop would just let them drive in and out, or maybe he'd follow them. Stop them. Ask questions. Want to search the vehicle. It wasn't a chance they were willing to take. Which meant more work for them, but a drastically reduced chance of having to kill cops, so they were okay with it.

The FULMAR drone had a 3.1-meter wingspan, but the wings detached for transport and it weighed barely twenty kilos, so it was easy to hide in a regular civilian vehicle. It was launched by the high-tech equivalent of a slingshot (technically referred to as a catapult), off a narrow aluminum ramp aimed up into the night sky, just like jets off aircraft carriers. Cherry stayed with the vehicle, a pickup truck registered to a nonexistent address in Phoenix, studying the feed from the drone. He had the drone's thermal camera set to white-hot, and the figures of his two teammates making their way on foot across the high desert plain blazed like lit candle flames against the cool night air.

There were only a few wispy clouds in the sky, but luckily the waning moon was only a quarter full, a sharp-pointed crescent low on the horizon as the two men made their way steadily across the uneven ground. They were wearing panoramic night vision goggles—"quad NODs"—and between the moon and the stars the scrubby, shrubby fields they walked through were bright as day. Still, they moved carefully, with a purpose, nobody wanting to twist an ankle on an unexpected hole.

As they drew close to the row of houses the light grew brighter, the exterior lights blazing like fires in their goggles. Still, it wasn't bright enough to flip up their goggles, especially since they deliberately made their approach down a corridor of shadow where they avoided any direct light. Dog lifted a fist and sank to a knee in the dirt one hundred meters out from the target house.

"Cherry, talk to me. You got anything?" His voice as he spoke was barely above a murmur, but their comms were state of the art.

"Stand by." There was nothing moving around the target house other than an animal Cherry had ID'ed as a cat. Anything warm enough to be alive would be bright white against the shades of charcoal that was the desert at night. He worked the joystick. The drone banked and described a wider circle, far enough overhead that even in the quiet evening air the low hum of its propellers was completely inaudible. They only had thirty seconds to wait.

"Police vehicle has not moved from the front of the complex. Nothing else moving near you. You're clear." The thermal sensor inside the drone was good enough to see the outline of the officer inside the car, and from the heat bloom under the hood and the waves of faint white coming out the exhaust in back it was clear the car was running.

"Copy. Heading in."

They moved a little faster to cover the last hundred meters, still doing everything to not make noise, and were happy to slide into the deep shadows between the two houses. Then they slowed to a crawl. Dog stepped carefully up to the window, but couldn't see anything through the NODs—the focus was all wrong. He flipped them up, and waited a few minutes for his eyes to adjust to the darkness around him. Then he put his eye to the window, and moved it all around. There were narrow blinds on the inside of the window, but there were enough tiny gaps between them that he could get a rough idea of the shape of the bedroom on the far side. More importantly, he could see the door was open between the bedroom and the rest of the house.

Dog backed carefully away from the window and slowly shrugged out of his backpack. He crouched on the ground beside Boot and with deliberation opened the zipper, moving with a speed so glacial the zipper never made a sound. Boot pointed, and moved past Dog to the far side of the house where he posted up, keeping an eye on the street from the shadows.

The drill Dog pulled out was a special one, with options no commercial customer would be interested in. The motor was encased in an insulated cover, so you practically had to put your ear to it to hear it when it was running. And it could run at a very slow speed.

Dog had inserted the bit before they'd started on their

cross-country hike, so after getting the thumbs-up from Boot he took another peek through the window, moved over a foot, and put the tip of the bit up against the siding. There was more than a bit of guesswork involved, he couldn't quite tell where the furniture was in the room, if there was anything up against the interior wall. He pressed the trigger, and the bit began to chew through the siding almost soundlessly. The bit was making more noise than the motor, and after he got through the siding he paused, and listened. There was no sound from inside the house.

The bit was a long one; long enough to get through siding and an exterior wall. They weren't pressed for time; being quiet was far more important than anything else. Stopping periodically to listen, barely putting any pressure on the drill as it hummed away, after eight minutes Dog felt the tip of the drill bit pop through the wall on the far side. He immediately shut off the drill, and carefully pulled the bit back. He put his eye to the hole, but couldn't see anything, not that he expected to. He put his ear to it next, and listened intently. After quite a long time, he heard light snoring.

Dog replaced the drill in his backpack, closed it up, then moved to Boot's backpack, which he'd set down next to the other. Inside it was the tank of gas. There was a long coil of rubber tubing attached to the tank, tipped with a narrow, foot-long aluminum rod. Dog moved the tank into place beneath the hole he'd drilled, then grabbed the rod and slid it carefully into the fresh hole. It hung up briefly, then pushed all the way through. Just from how much of the rod was protruding from the siding on the outside told him that at least an inch of rod was through the wall on the inside of the bedroom.

Dog moved to the window again and chanced another

look. There wasn't much to see, but he was trying to guess the volume of the room. The door being open was the issue. But the gas was very slightly heavier than air, so it should remain close. He moved back to the tank, did the calculations in his head, then checked his watch. "Gas going in," he murmured into his mic, then turned the knob atop the tank and opened the valve. The hiss was faint and only lasted for a second, until the valve inside was all the way open. Then he waited, arm up, the luminous hands of his watch bright in the dark.

Back in the day, the Russians, when trying to rescue some hostages taken by Chechen terrorists, had used far too much gas—believed to have been a fentanyl derivative—and instead of simply knocking out the terrorists and their hostages inside the Moscow theater killed over a hundred hostages through unintentional overdose. Dog wasn't using fentanyl or any kind of opiate, but an overdose of the gas he was using could be fatal, so he kept a close watch on the time, and promptly shut off the gas when his rough calculations told him that the occupants inside should be unconscious. He stuffed the tank back inside the backpack.

"Cherry?" he asked.

"Still clear," he heard in his ear. Boot turned toward him and gave him a thumbs up—he'd seen nothing moving.

"Going in."

Boot followed him to the back of the house. There were windows all around the house, mechanically easy points of entry, but if you forced something just the wrong way with a window the glass could break, and cracking glass was shockingly loud. Instead, they moved to the rear door. Peering through it, Dog could see it led into a kitchen. He worked the lock with a pick gun as it was quicker and easier in the near dark. The lock on the door handle only took him ten seconds. But above the knob was a deadbolt, and it proved resistant to the pick gun. Dog tried for a few minutes, then put the pick gun away and pulled out his small case, and knelt before the door. He could see just well enough to choose a tension wrench and a short hook. Lock picking was all done by feel, so the darkness wasn't a handicap once he got the tools inserted. He worked his way front to back and back to front, working the pins while he kept a steady pressure on the wrench, and in less than thirty seconds he felt the lock give and turn. The deadbolt retracted with a soft clack.

He put his tools away and traded a look with Boot. They pulled on their gas masks, tightened them down, and went in. They found the target in bed with a woman. Dog approached carefully, and clamped a hand over the man's mouth just in case, but he didn't so much as twitch. He and the woman were unconscious. Dog pressed his fingers to the man's neck, just to make sure, and found his pulse—slow, but steady.

If they could guarantee being safely able to drive in and out of the neighborhood without drawing the attention of the police he would have had Cherry pull up outside on the street, but Higgins had made it clear this snatch needed to be clean and quiet. Dog planted his feet and hoisted the man up, over his shoulder, and headed out.

Boot closed the back door behind him, then jogged around to the side of the house to retrieve the backpacks as Dog marched cross-country with the man over his shoulder. SEALs went more for running than rucking, but more than a few times he'd done five-mile marches wearing backpacks that weighed in excess of a hundred pounds. Of course, that had been when he was much younger. Still, he only had to carry the man a quarter mile. His main worry wasn't the weight, it was turning his ankle on an uneven spot of ground.

A quarter mile from the house, across the field, was a slight rise, and Dog laid the man down there. They were hidden from view. They only had to wait a few minutes, then heard the pickup creaking as it bounced across the ground. By the time Cherry pulled up Dog had the man hogtied. Boot and Cherry lifted the man into the back seat of the pickup. Cherry had recovered the drone, and it and the catapult were in the bed of the truck, disassembled and under a tarp.

"Do we stick him?" Cherry asked.

Dog shook his head. "Don't want him to overdose. No way to be sure exactly how much of the gas he breathed in. We'll wait til we get him to the plane, jab him there."

"And where exactly is there?"

"A semi-abandoned airport about an hour and a half south of Phoenix. So we've got a three hour drive."

"It's going to be dawn before we get there," Boot said, looking at the unconscious man.

Dog shrugged. "We've got a blanket to throw over him."

The Eric Marcus Municipal Airport, outside of Ajo, Arizona, situated in the thinly-populated Sonoran Desert region, was publicly-owned by Pima County. It had two 3800-foot runways, perfect for small, single-engine planes. Officially a Gulfstream G550 jet needed 5900 feet of runway, but that was fully loaded with 1800 pounds worth of passengers and full tanks of gas, which could take it from New York to Bahrain. As lightly loaded as it would be, the short runways of the municipal airport were more than long enough. Pike had triple-checked that fact.

There was no tower at the airfield—incoming aircraft were handled by Albuquerque Center ATC (over 400 miles away), with some FSS flight information coming from the Prescott Airport (over 100 miles away). The ATC at Phoenix Sky Harbor International Airport was too busy with commercial jets to bother itself with a tiny regional airport that barely saw thirty aircraft a week. If you shut off your transponder going in or out of Marcus, and kept below a certain altitude, you'd be invisible to any radar installations in the area. And the airport was just thirty miles north of the border.

The dusty pickup truck rolled onto the airport property just before seven a.m. The Gulfstream had landed just half an hour before, and Pike had spoken to the crew, a pilot and co-pilot. Officially they worked for Ballard Transport, a private company, but Ballard was a shell of a shell of a shell run by the CIA, and they did work for the CIA, DIA, NSA, whoever needed their services.

Pike looked around, then stepped up to the truck as Dog climbed out. "No problems?" He glanced into the back seat. There was something there beside Cherry, covered by a ratty blanket.

"No, we're professionals, not cartel fucktards. Day I can't do a simple creep and sleep is the day I need to retire." The two men looked around. There was nothing to be seen—the airport was in the middle of nowhere, a few miles from Ajo, Arizona, which held barely three thousand people.

"Looks clear. Let's get him in," Pike said. He stood watch, looking around, as Dog and Cherry pulled the hogtied man from the back seat of the truck and carried him up the stairs into the plane. They kept him wrapped in the blanket, and from a distance it didn't look like a body. Boot drove the truck away from the plane, and Pike headed up into the jet.

"He still out?" Pike asked.

Dog pulled the blanket off the man and tossed it aside. He was lying on his side in the middle of the cabin, between the well-appointed leather seats, wearing nothing but boxers. Dog nudged him with the toe of his boot. "Looks like it. Guess I got the dosage right." Dog produced a hypodermic and stuck the man in the arm.

Pike blinked twice, and kept the expression on his face neutral. He squatted down next to the unconscious captive and looked at his face. His eyes ran down and back up his body, landing once again on his features.

Boot came jogging up the stairs into the plane. "You're taking care of the truck, right?" he asked Pike.

Pike looked over at him. "Yeah."

"Keys are in it."

"You got a target package on this guy?" Pike asked, gesturing at the body at his feet.

"On an encrypted flash drive in the truck, along with a laptop and all the drone hardware. Can you make sure that gets back where it's supposed to be?" Cherry said. "I don't want anybody coming after me about that, I know how much those things cost."

"Of course." Pike stood up. "Password for the flash drive?"

"DonkeyBalls," Cherry told him. "All one word, the D and B capitalized."

Dog snorted and shook his head. "I presume you picked that." He looked at Pike. "We good?"

"Yeah. Plan is to head more or less straight south across

the border through a gap in their radar coverage, then turn southeast. Then I guess you're landing at an airport somewhere in the mountains?"

"Handing this guy off to someone who is very squirrelly, so we aren't landing anywhere close to where he is. Once we get there we wait to be contacted, then we'll drive and meet up somewhere. May have to sit and wait for a day or three, depending, is what I was told."

Pike looked around at the interior of the executive jet. "You heavy?"

Dog shook his head. "Not crossing the border. Just in case. But there's a locker at the airport should have everything we need."

"Because a body swap in the middle of nowhere Mexico seems like a great place to get shot in the back of the head."

"Especially when you're dealing with cartel assholes." He saw the surprise on Pike's face. "Oh, you didn't hear that part? Yeah, I guess that's why they didn't want your white face down there, we're handing him off to a cartel, not the *federales*, and everyone's already going to be twitchy as shit. So yeah, we're definitely going to roll up heavy, just so nobody gets any stupid ideas."

Pike frowned. "You should have more than three guys."

Dog shrugged. "Less exposure, I guess."

"Going in sterile?"

Dog nodded and traded a look with Boot and Cherry. "No IDs, no gear, completely deniable assets."

"Then I guess I don't need to tell you to watch your asses."

"Couldn't hurt," Cherry said.

"How are they contacting you?"

"We've got a satphone." Dog checked his watch. "We've got to go."

"Right." With one more glance at their cargo Pike moved toward the door. By the time he got to the pickup the co-pilot was pulling up the stairs and the engines were warming up. He watched the jet taxi to the end of the runway, turn around, and then take off. He looked around, but there still was no one to be seen.

His rental car was parked off to one side. He left it there, and instead climbed into the cab of the pickup. The small laptop was in a case on the front seat. The unmarked flash drive was in a pocket inside.

The white face on the floor of the Gulfstream had surprised him.

He'd assumed, as this op was "cartel related", that they'd be grabbing a cartel member hiding inside the U.S., possibly someone high-ranking, and renditioning him to the appropriate Mexican authorities for incarceration, torture, or execution. But the guy they'd grabbed, even though he had a tan, was definitely white. And was being handed off to one of the cartels?

Someone in bed with the cartel, then? A high-ranking informant, government or maybe involved in law enforcement, feeding the cartel valuable intelligence, who'd outlived his usefulness? But this guy had not been any pasty, doughy desk jockey. Which had Pike very curious. More than curious—he had a feeling. A bad feeling. And he'd learned to trust his feelings. Which is why he turned on the laptop, and when it was booted up stuck the flash drive in the USB port.

The information on this mission, like most of them, was compartmentalized. There could be some argument that if Higgins wanted him to know the details of the target he would have been briefed. But Pike, technically, was still team lead on Gargoyle, and had every right to know the details of the mission his men were on. Or so, at least, he could claim.

The target workup was pretty thorough. Name, age, address. Several photos, although the guy had seen some rough miles since the last one was taken.

Target has multiple confirmed kills and is likely to be armed. Not surprising. Which is why they'd gone in soft and quiet.

Under local law enforcement protection. Which was interesting.

Possibly under FBI surveillance. Proceed with extreme caution to avoid being compromised. Separate target from any electronics to avoid remote tracking. Which was fascinating. Why the hell was the FBI looking at this guy? Because of cartel ties? It sure seemed like he had to be a bad guy, the file included two names for him, an original and an alias. But…the FBI was after him, while local cops were protecting him? Maybe the local cops were bent, in the pocket of the cartels. It was all too common. However, there was no information about that in the package. None at all.

There was something twisted going on. Par for the course when dealing with intelligence agencies, but still. Maybe the DIA or CIA was working with one of the cartels to bring down another. Maybe the man was some sort of bait. It could have been any one of a hundred scenarios, but no matter what, it meant that guy they'd just grabbed was dead.

Pike sat in the cab of the pickup, frowning. He still had that feeling. A weird feeling. A weird, bad feeling. He pulled out his work phone, and checked the signal. It was weak, but there. He started Googling the man they'd just grabbed. Both his provided names. Wondering if he'd find anything. Anything at all.

He found everything. Thousands of search results.

Ghosts and Madmen

Dozens of news stories. This was not a nobody. Pike knew him—not his name, but his work. He'd seen it on fucking CNN. The burning house. The bodies in the street. And then the video from the motel, from the year earlier. This was *that* guy?

Pike frowned at the search results. He'd known the man had to have messed with the cartel at some point, otherwise they wouldn't want him dead. And he was under no illusions, that's what they planned to do to him, kill him, the only question was how much pain he'd suffer first. Probably a lot. So the fact that there were results didn't surprise him, but...this guy sure didn't seem like he was bent, or a bad guy, which begged the question—why was he being delivered to the cartel? That's a question which likely would never be answered. Secrets were part of the intelligence business, after all. And it was an ugly business.

He kept scrolling. It was the news stories from another incident, involving the same man, that gave Pike pause. One not directly related to the cartel...but the details of which made Pike physically jerk.

"What the...?" His head came up. He didn't see the airport around him, because he was thinking. Then he tossed the laptop to the side and jumped out of the truck. He jogged over to his rental. He tossed his work phone into the cup holder of the rental, and grabbed his backpack from the back seat. Then he jogged back to the truck.

The burner was in an EM-protected bag inside the backpack which blocked all signals like a Faraday cage. Pike stuck the battery back in the phone, and powered it up. He dialed a number as he walked away from the truck, away from any possible electronic devices with microphones. Listened to it ring as he stood in the middle of the runway, desert all around. Checked his watch.

"John Phault."

"John. It's Bob Grinnand. You remember calling me up, earlier this year, asking me to run down some addresses in Las Vegas linked to a name? Off the books, so it couldn't be traced back in any way to you?"

There was a brief pause as his old friend took a second to think back. "Yeah, absolutely."

Bob leaned forward. He spoke slowly and clearly. "Who was that search for, and why?"

PART III
BROTHERS IN ARMS

Chapter Twenty-Four

Lori was doing her best to not cry, to not hyperventilate, to not scream, and it wasn't working. She felt herself spiraling out of control. "I slept way late," she said. "And when I woke up I felt slow. Stupid. Like I was drunk or high or something. Dave wasn't here, but I thought he must have let me sleep long, and was out running. But he never came back. Not for an hour. Then two. And his car's out there. His phone's right there." She pointed. "I almost called nine-one-one. Then I remembered the security system I helped my mom install. She was always worried about break-ins, not that it was really a worry, but sometimes the brain cancer made her really paranoid, you know. It records on a twenty-four-hour loop or something like that. So I went into her account, rewound it, to see where he went, and saw…" She pointed at the screen of her laptop, then hiccupped and fought the fresh tears.

Sheriff John Osterman put a calming hand on her shoulder and leaned over and peered at the image, which was in high definition and full color—not that that the color helped when the only illumination was a few feeble night-lights, everything was shades of gray. The video was frozen right at the moment the two men made entry through the back door. Wearing what appeared to be gas masks, their hands covered by gloves. White or Hispanic males, he could see that, from the skin around their eyes, and muscular, but that was about it. They were wearing nondescript long-sleeve shirts and dark pants. He hit the button to let the video play once again. Less than a minute later the men reappeared, and one of them had Pima Jack, apparently unconscious, slung over his shoulder. Not struggling with the weight.

"Should I have called you?" Lori said. She'd called him from Dave's phone, as she didn't have the sheriff's personal number. "I wasn't sure what else to do."

"No, you did good," Osterman told her. He pulled out his phone and called Maria Flores, his senior detective working the cartel attacks.

"Maria Flores."

"Detective, grab Norm Hill and an evidence team and meet me at the next-door house to Pima Jack's former residence."

"Yes, sir. Why?"

"He was kidnapped this morning. Two men, at least. It appears they gassed him and his girlfriend, as they went in wearing gas masks and gloves, and she never heard a thing and felt stoned when she woke up. These were not amateurs. I don't know, of course, but I have to assume the men are affiliated with a cartel."

"Oh my God."

"Keep this off the air. Use your phones."

"You're not going to…why would you keep this quiet?"

"They may be trying to make a run for the border. If

they are pros, they'll be monitoring our radio chatter. They've got a few hour head start, but maybe they've had some bad luck. I'm hoping we can make our own luck. Snag them before they know we know. Because if they panic, they may decide killing him is easier."

"Jesus, sir. You know—I mean, I don't have to tell you. He's killed how many of their men? They get him across the border, into cartel territory, they're going to make an example out of him. And they use chainsaws and pit bulls for that."

"I'm aware. Get a move on. I've got Border Patrol and a few federal contacts to alert." He hung up, dialed a number, and while it rang looked at Lori. "Show me where you were sleeping."

Dave didn't "wake up". He floated up from nothingness, gradually becoming aware of various things. Heat. Pinching, aching discomfort. Faint nausea. A serious need to urinate. After a while he understood he was hearing things, sounds, around but mostly in front of him. And he was lying on his side. In a moving vehicle, he eventually realized. One that creaked and swayed.

He tried opening his eyes. That made things less dark, but no clearer. His vision was blurry. He blinked and tried to focus. It didn't take him long to understand that his eyes weren't the problem, there was a mask over them. No, not a mask—masks were tight. This was something else, an inch or two away from his eyes. Dark, but with small enough gaps that he could see pinpricks of light. A hood or a bag, he ultimately understood. There was a bag over his head. Not burlap, but some kind of cloth. It smelled dusty.

The sunlight was warm and bright past it, he could sense that.

Past the noise of the truck—because it felt like a truck to him—he heard something. Someone breathing, maybe? Then a man spoke, quietly, and another answered. Dave wasn't able to catch the words.

Focusing on the unseen men helped, because the movement of the truck was making him sick—up and down hills, and swaying around curves. To distract himself from the nausea he flexed his arms, and hands. The sensations there were a conflicting nightmare. He finally realized his wrists were tightly bound, his circulation restricted enough that his hands were half-numb, and half in shrieking agony. His hands were bound together, behind his back. Not just that, but they seemed to be connected to his feet. And there were bindings around his ankles as well. Which meant he was hogtied.

Kidnapped, he had to presume. And hogtied. Taken from his bed, while he slept? He should have been terrified. Panicked. Instead, he felt a weird calm as he evaluated his situation. Maybe he was in shock? Either way, it allowed him to think clearly. Ask the right questions. Had they killed Lori? The question held terror for him, so he tried to look at it rationally. They'd knocked him out somehow, there was no other explanation for how he could have gone to sleep in his bed and woken up here. Did that mean they'd drugged Lori too? Maybe. Probably. He doubted they could have taken him out of bed without waking her up unless she was drugged too. Which made him feel better, but only a little.

He presumed he was dead. That these men who'd grabbed him were taking him somewhere to be interrogated, and then executed. There was no shortage of people who wished him ill. Three groups of people, in fact. The cartel would have no qualms about grabbing Lori. Hell, they'd kill her in front of him. Torture her. That was kind of their thing.

But the guys with him were speaking English, not Spanish, so he didn't think they were cartel. And with their poor track record against him, it seemed doubtful the cartel would try a technical kidnapping instead of a flat-out execution. And the professionalism they'd shown getting him from bed to the truck seemed to indicate they weren't affiliated with Pietro Bufonte. The performance of members of American organized crime had always struck him as unimpressive.

Which meant these guys were feds. CIA, or maybe FBI guys from one of their black bag departments. Here because of his fingerprints? No, they'd had plenty of time to examine his hands. They could easily see he no longer hand any usable fingerprints, so he was no danger to the status quo. So…why? To punish him? For killing their guys? Maybe they thought he'd killed Colman, or whatever his name was. The guy Aaron had shot. That had to be it. It had to be.

He couldn't help but laugh out loud. He got a light punch in the side, enough to get an "Oof" out of him and make him tense up.

One of the men said, "Shut the fuck up or we'll gag you."

Inside the hood, Dave was biting his lip, trying hard to keep from laughing. All the things he'd done, all the people he'd killed, and now he'd been kidnapped and was being taken to what undoubtedly would be a very ugly death…for a murder he'd had nothing to do with. Amazing. Ridiculous. Ironic.

Perfect.

At least that meant Aaron was out of danger.

Chapter Twenty-Five

"*Who* is here?" DIA Director Winston Elliott frowned at the phone on his desk. His secretary repeated the name. Elliott frowned, then nodded. "Sure, send him in."

"Sergeant, how can I help you?" Elliott asked the man.

"I haven't been a sergeant in a long time," Bob Grinnand said. And he felt conflicted about that. Things had been simpler when he was younger, and still in the military. Not easier, necessarily, but... He looked around the office, eyes running over the window and the bookcase. Mostly filled with books that looked like they'd never been opened. "Are you confident your office is secure? Perhaps we should talk in a SCIF."

Elliott blinked and leaned forward. Anyone else he would have brushed aside the remark, but from this man it wasn't an idle suggestion. He had a lot of people working for him, and under normal circumstances would likely not know the name of anybody on the operations side. But Grinnand had quite a resume before coming to work for the DIA—U.S. Army Special Forces, then ultimately he'd joined

SFOD-D, "Delta Force", and spent nearly a decade with them, and as more than a simple trigger puller, although he'd excelled at that as well. He'd worked on three continents, mostly in places where U.S. troops had never officially had boots on the ground. And he'd seen combat everywhere he'd gone. Since most of the operations he'd been involved in were secret he could never get the recognition he deserved for his actions, but still he'd managed to be awarded a Silver Star and two Purple Hearts. There were several blank spots in his work history that even Elliott, as director of the second most powerful intelligence agency in the United States, didn't have the default clearance for, which he found fascinating. TS-SCI level compartmentalization was a given, but this was something…else. After leaving the army Grinnand had hired on with Blackwater and a few other DOD contractors for a few years, then joined the DIA DCS and gone back into government service. His performance with the DIA had been exemplary. Unlike most operators he showed an equal aptitude for the intelligence side of things, but then again the man had a 150 IQ, if Elliott remembered correctly. Spoke several languages.

"Sure, let's take a walk."

The nearest SCIF was very close, and that wasn't an accident. The two men left their phones outside the door, then sat down at the conference table.

"Pike", as usual, was hard to read, but he didn't look happy. "How up to speed are you on current field operations?" he asked Elliott.

"That depends. Which operation are we talking about?" Elliott cocked his head, studying the man.

"The one my team is on. Right now. In Mexico."

Elliott nodded. "I'm…aware of the details."

Bob frowned. "I apologize for not using the chain of command, and skipping right to the top like this, to you, but what the hell are we doing turning over an American citizen to a Mexican drug cartel?"

Elliott frowned. "I met with you out of respect for you, but apologizing doesn't mean it is acceptable for you to step out of bounds like this."

Bob nodded once. "Yes sir, but this man isn't a criminal. It would be one thing if he was a member of a rival cartel, but in this case he seems to be the opposite."

"You are completely out of pocket. This is an ongoing operation and not something we should be discussing. At all. You should have raised your concerns with Higgins. He would have told you you weren't cleared for any further information, and that should have been it. But instead, here we are. Here I am." He looked like he'd eaten something sour.

"I know sir. This is far from my first rodeo. I am not some dewy-eyed virgin. I have done more than my share of shady shit. But this is…I was worried about the company. I just wanted to make sure the orders didn't get wildly fucked up somewhere. That things were unfolding as planned. Because if this ever came back on us…"

Elliott leaned forward. "Why would it?"

Bob grimaced. "That's one reason why I wanted to talk to you, sir. The snatch was clean. Gassed him and his girlfriend. Went in through the back door. Which is always a good idea, these days everyone's got those Ring video doorbells, recording everything. But apparently the place had one of those do-it-yourself home security systems, with cameras. Got my guys going in and out."

"What?" Elliott's eyes were wide.

Bob held up a hand. "They were wearing gloves and gas masks, so there's no way they can be identified."

"We didn't check for that?"

"It was a rush op, sir. But from the video it's apparent that it was a professional job. Local cops saw the gas masks on the surveillance video, and it didn't take them long to discover how the gas was introduced. They're getting impressions of boot treads and the like. It won't lead anywhere, but…"

"I haven't heard about this."

Bob shook his head. "The news hasn't been made public. But I have contacts."

"I…see."

"Local law enforcement isn't quite sure how to address the situation, but they're scrambling. Have contacted Border Patrol and other federal agencies in the area. They've put out a net, hoping they can catch them before they reach the border. Nobody knows for sure who grabbed him, but they can guess, given his track record with the cartel. And this guy…the cartel is not going to just yell at him. In fact, whatever they do, they might make it public. Release an ISIS-style beheading video or somesuch, so it will be very clear who kidnapped him. Which is even more heat and attention. So you see why I wanted to speak with you. For confirmation that this was the plan."

Elliott just regarded him evenly. Deliberately not saying anything. Which meant Bob wasn't telling him anything he didn't already know. Bob thought about that. Elliott watched the wheels turning in the man's head.

"My team is supposed to meet a contact, and deliver the package to him. He's quite a valuable package, to the right people. Which would make that contact very popular, with those right people. So we're giving them Anderson…

but why? What are we getting in return?" Bob thought. "Good will? No, we'd only do a move like this for something tangible. He can't know anything, so his value is who he is." Bob thought some more, and it hit him. He blinked and leaned back. "We've got somebody inside a cartel? Maybe inside La Fuerza? They've been fucking things up, whoever brought in Anderson would be a rock star in their organization. A golden boy. We're doing this to help him out?"

Elliott leaned back. Didn't say anything. Bob nodded. "Right. Okay. So, just to be clear, you're aware of the details on…Operation Golden Boy, let's call it, everything's going to plan, apart from the video hiccup which shouldn't lead anywhere, and I shouldn't worry."

Winston Elliott stood up and smoothed his tie. "I'm glad we had this talk. I appreciate your concern. I like your initiative, and that you've got some valuable contacts. But I assume this is the last time you're going to ignore the chain of command and go off on your own?"

Bob stood up and shook the Director's hand. "Yes, sir. Thank you, sir."

Bob waited until he was ten minutes away from the DCI HQ and Joint Base Anacostia-Bolling before pulling into the parking lot of a strip mall. He left his work phone in the car and walked away from it as he put the battery into his burner phone and turned it on. He watched traffic roll by as he listened to it ring.

"Yeah."

"Okay, so, he's fucked," Bob told John Phault. "The plan is to turn him over to the cartel. For leverage, or to get an in with them. I suspect we've got an inside man. And bringing this guy in will make him a hero."

"He's killed a bunch of their guys. Embarrassed them. They're going to torture him, or worse."

Bob nodded. "And let everybody know about it, otherwise what's the point. Maybe do it on camera, carve him up like a Christmas turkey, release the video."

"Bob, I know him. I know his friends. He worked for me for a few years, he's a good kid. I killed someone who was trying to kill him, for fuck's sake. We've got history. Sound familiar?"

Bob just grunted, chewing on his lip.

"Are you okay with this?" Phault demanded.

"I am very much not okay with this," Bob said.

"Then can you help me?"

Bob frowned. "Help you do what?"

"I don't know. I've got an obligation. I have to do… something."

Bob made a sound. "I need to put somebody under surveillance, get them followed in Detroit traffic, you're my guy. I would go through a door with you any time. But this is a little outside your wheelhouse."

"Are you forgetting a little Christmas vacation we had?"

Bob shook his head. "That was twenty years ago. Shit, that was a lifetime ago. And getting into a few gunfights with some rogue CIA assholes doesn't make you an operator. Even if you've killed more guys than some operators I know."

"I have to do something," Phault repeated.

Bob nodded. "You did. You called me."

"No, you called me, remember? So you know this is wrong. What are you going to do?"

Bob sighed deeply. "My guys have him in Mexico.

They're supposed to turn him over to the contact. Tomorrow, unless that changes again."

"Tomorrow?" Phault's voice went up an octave. "Shit."

"They've got a satphone on them. I can trace that, get their exact location."

"Okay. And?"

Bob stared out at the desert. "Fuck. Fuckfuckfuck."

Phault made a sound in his ear. "You don't know him, Bob. But I do. He's only in this mess because he killed too many of the wrong people. Or, really, the right people. He's one of us. I don't know how much 'gray area' spook shit you've been doing, but you are not one of those soulless amoral fucks who does whatever he's told because the government says so. Those are the people we fought. Together. And it cost us. We both lost people. And if I had to do it all over again, I would. You can't be so fucked up you think this is okay. Do you?"

Bob shook his head. "Dude, you have no idea." He sighed. Staring out at the heat mirage starting to shimmer over the landscape, Bob said, "I should be able to hook up with them before they meet this cartel contact."

"Okay. And then what?"

Bob was staring off at the horizon, not seeing anything. "Fuck if I know. I'm making this up as I go along. I haven't caused an international incident in a while, so I suppose it's time."

"Try not to behead anyone. But then again, it is Mexico."

Chapter Twenty-Six

"Are you fucking kidding me?" Aaron raged into his phone.

"What?" Arlene said. She was sitting at the other end of the couch. He'd muted the TV when he answered the call, but she didn't know who it was from.

Aaron jumped to his feet. "Are you fucking kidding me?" he shouted into his phone.

"WHAT?" Arlene yelled at him, now somewhere between irritated and pissed off, but not as much as he was.

He stomped around in a circle, waving his free hand. "How the fuck? I mean—the guy can't go two fucking days—yeah, okay. Yeah. I'm coming down there. I don't care," he growled. "Yeah. Fine. Fuck!" He jabbed the CALL END button with his thumb.

"What the fuck is going on?" Arlene demanded.

"Dave got kidnapped by the fucking cartel."

"What? He what?" She found herself on her feet. "Where is he?"

"I don't know. Nobody knows. That was Pork Snorkle. They fucking drugged the two of them, and grabbed him in the middle of the night. Came in wearing goddamn gas masks."

"When?" Arlene asked, bewildered.

"Last night. Osterman's got everybody working it, I guess, Border Patrol and all that bullshit, but they're keeping it quiet. Off the news. I've got to go down there." He checked his watch, then looked out the window. It was already dark. She'd waited all day to call him. Just one more thing which pissed him off.

"What are you going to do?"

He threw his hands up. "I don't know, but I've got to fucking go," he shouted at her.

They stood facing each other. She opened and closed her mouth twice, then said, her voice calmer, "I think I've got enough left on the Visa for a plane ticket. Detroit to Phoenix, right?"

"Yeah." He took a couple deep breaths. "You want to book that? I can take care of the rental car."

She nodded. "Go pack."

Twenty minutes later they had a flight booked and a rental car reserved. Aaron checked his watch again. The flight was a redeye, and leaving in two hours. It was maybe a half hour drive to the airport, including parking his car, and he had to check a pistol—already locked in the case, inside the bag he was going to check—so it would be close. "I gotta go," he told Arlene, kissing her.

She followed him to the door. "You be careful," she called out, as he jogged to the Taurus.

"Yeah," he muttered, thinking that was very fucking unlikely. He tossed the bag into the back of his car, got behind the wheel, and took off.

He had no idea how fast he was going, but he was sure as fuck weaving in and out of the traffic on Telegraph when he saw the flashing red and blues in his rearview mirror. He swore, and just for half a scond considered making a run for it. He figured he had a fifty percent chance of getting away—the Taurus was as fast as any cruiser, and he could drive. But that meant an even chance of getting arrested, or wrecking. And if that happened, he wouldn't be there for Dave.

Aaron pulled into a parking lot, and the cruiser pulled in behind him. He couldn't see shit past the flashing cop lights, other than it was a sedan, not one of the SUVs all the departments were going to, because none of the new sedans were big enough to transport people in the back seat.

"Get out of the car."

"What?" Aaron said. It had been shouted, and not said over a PA. He rolled his window down and stuck his head out. "What?"

"Get out of the car and walk back to my cruiser." The voice was muffled, the cop a silhouette, still in his seat, behind his open door.

"Son of a bitch," Aaron grumbled, but climbed out of the car.

"Back up toward me."

Back up? Were they doing a felony stop on him? He hadn't been going that fast. Biting back some choice profanity he kept his hands away from his sides and backed up half a dozen steps toward the cop car, then paused.

"Keep coming."

Aaron went to take a step, then hesitated. Cocked his head. Did he…?

"Keep coming."

Aaron kept his hands halfway up, but he looked over his shoulder. He couldn't see shit past the flashing red and blues, but he tried anyway, squinting. "Dixon?" he said suspiciously. The Taser's barbs hit him in the middle of the back and he froze up, vibrating in place for a few seconds before falling over.

Dixon held the trigger down as he quickly moved out and around his open door. He rolled Abruzzo over onto his stomach and quickly cuffed him. He'd wanted him as close to his cruiser as possible, so he'd have less distance to move him. Abruzzo'd smacked his head into the concrete when he'd fallen, and the cut was bleeding. The sight of it made Dixon smile.

Traffic on Telegraph was slowing down, gawkers staring at the police lights as usual, but he'd angled his car so they couldn't see the driver's side of it until they were past. Between that, the flashing lights, and the darkness, he was probably good. He opened the rear door of his unmarked Charger, then rolled Abruzzo over, grabbed him under the arms, then half-dragged, half-carried him to the rear of the cruiser. For once the man wasn't wearing a gun. He was panting and saying half words as he recovered from the Taser.

Dixon got him into the back seat, face down. "The fuck—? The fuck are you...?" Abruzzo said groggily, trying to sit up. With a smile on his face Dixon punched him in the side of the head, following an urge he'd had for years, ever since first talking to the man. Abruzzo's head bounced off the seat cushion. Dixon almost punched him again, but instead grabbed the roll of duct tape and wrapped it around Abruzzo's mouth—twice, the guy had a big fucking mouth—then several lengths around his ankles. Then, just to be sure, he ran tape between his cuffs and the tape around his ankles. He wasn't going anywhere.

Dixon closed the back door, jumped behind the wheel, shut off his lights, drove around Abruzzo's car, circled through the parking lot, and pulled out onto Telegraph. Just as Abruzzo started to make noise from the back seat and thrash around. Dixon was covered in a cold sweat. Scared, in fact. But that wouldn't stop him from doing what he had to do. The throbbing in his knuckles seemed a harbinger of things to come.

Dixon had been part of a multi-jurisdictional task force that had arrested over thirty people as part of an organized shoplifting ring—labeled "retail fraud" in Michigan. They'd recovered millions in stolen property. Almost all of the suspects had plead out in the case, although a few—the ringleaders—had refused to plea bargain and were awaiting trial. The recovered stolen property was in various police evidence rooms throughout the metro Detroit area. The property had been kept in several small warehouses, which remained empty and in legal limbo as the criminal cases progressed.

Dixon headed north up Telegraph to one of the vacant warehouses. It was on the south side of Pontiac, a struggling ghost town of a city. The space wasn't meant as a warehouse, it was just an empty unit in a small business park that was almost all empty units. Dixon parked the Charger around back and used a crowbar on the lock.

There wasn't much left inside but a few boxes, a broken desk, and several chairs. Dixon set one of the chairs in the center of the space, then went back out to the car and dragged Abruzzo in. The man struggled as much as he was able, which wasn't much. With some difficulty Dixon got him in the chair. He duct-taped his ankles to the legs of the chair, and taped his cuffed hands behind the chair. Then he closed the back door and took a second, behind Abruzzo, where the man couldn't see him. He took a deep breath, and worked his neck. This was…he wasn't comfortable doing this. But he had no choice. *Man the fuck up*, he mouthed silently at himself. Then he stomped around in front of Abruzzo and ripped off the tape covering his mouth. It ripped off some of Abruzzo's moustache and a bit of skin off his upper lip, and the wound started bleeding. There was already dried blood all over his face from the superficial scalp wound.

"I knew you were gay, but I didn't figure you were into the kinky shit," Aaron said, then his head rocked back as Dixon punched him.

Dixon held the fist up in front of Aaron's face as his eyes refocused. "I am," Dixon said, "I am going to enjoy this, you white trash motherfucker. All the shit you've given me over the years, I am going to take my time beating the ever-lovin' shit out of you. I'm not sure if I'll even get around to asking you any questions."

"Help!" Aaron shouted. He paused, and looked at Dixon.

Dixon held out a hand. "Go ahead. Knock yourself out. Nobody to hear you. That's why we're here."

Just because somebody says something doesn't make it so, Aaron had learned that long ago. "Help!" he shouted. "Help! Help!" He got as loud as he could. Bellowing. "Rape!" He paused, listening, then gave Dixon a smirk.

"Really? You're still making jokes?" Dixon punched him

in the stomach and Aaron wheezed, bent over until his forehead nearly touched his knees.

When he was able to catch his breath Aaron straightened up, glaring at Dixon. He yanked and flailed at his bonds, but there were too many layers of duct tape, he couldn't get free. All he managed to do was tip his chair over, and he landed hard enough on the cement floor to smack the side of his head. Dixon grunted lifting him back up, setting the chair back on its legs.

"Help!" Aaron tried again. It couldn't hurt. Beyond the bare walls of the space they were in, he could hear…nothing. Fuck. He stared daggers at Dixon. "So is this some petty revenge bullshit, because you're short and undoubtedly have a tiny dick?"

Dixon stepped in and punched him square in the face. Aaron heard and felt the crunch as his nose broke. Blood started running across his mouth and down his chin. It hurt, but for some reason Aaron didn't care about the pain. The pain was just more bullshit he had to deal with, and he was done with the bullshit.

"Fuck you," Aaron spat. "You thinking punching someone cuffed to a chair makes you a big man? A tough guy? Let me up, we'll see how tough you are. I'm tougher than you just sitting here and bleeding, fucker." He gathered up a mouthful of blood and snot and spit it at the cop. Dixon dodged it and stepped in again with a hard right jab. Aaron saw stars as his head popped back. He yanked at his bonds again and roared in frustration.

Dixon shook his hand, and massaged it. Abruzzo had a hard head. His knuckles were already throbbing. He pulled out his Taser, and replaced the cartridge, while Abruzzo watched. He didn't have many spare cartridges for the thing, but Abruzzo didn't need to know that.

"Did you enjoy it the last time?" Dixon asked, raising the Taser. Abruzzo's eyes followed it, like he was tracking a dangerous predator. "We don't have the death penalty in Michigan, no electric chair, but maybe I can give you the next best thing." And he shot Abruzzo again, center chest, the gun going off with a sharp pop/snap. He could hear the hum of the electricity as Abruzzo danced in the chair, blood drops flying off him, the gun snap-snap-snapping as Dixon kept the juice on. Abruzzo would have fallen over if he wasn't tied to the chair. Dixon's only real worry was that the guy would have a heart attack. Although that maybe would be a way through some of his problems.

"You're an asshole," Aaron said, when he recovered. He was panting. He glared up at the cop. "Never been Tazed before. Check that off the bucket list, I guess. Not as fun as your mom giving me a knobber, but then again what is?" He worked his neck and spit blood onto the floor. "So what the fuck is this about? Wait, didn't you say you had some questions, Detective Tiny Hands?"

Dixon smiled meanly. "I did."

The blood was still dripping off Aaron's chin. It was all over his shirt and pants. He ignored it as he thought, squinting up at Dixon. "For you? No, West Bloomfield doesn't give a shit about me. So who are you working for?"

Dixon rolled his eyes. "You're not that dumb, are you? I think you can probably figure it out."

"Absolutely. I'm sorry I banged your mom. But she was begging me for it."

Dixon wasn't that good with his left hand, but the knuckles on his right hand were already throbbing. The short left jabs hit Abruzzo in the cheek, rocking his head back three times.

Aaron spit at him. "Fuck you, princess. My girlfriend

slaps me harder when we're fucking." He had more than a good idea why the cop had grabbed him. He wasn't surprised somebody had grabbed him—he'd earned it—he was just surprised it was this asshole. He whoofed as Dixon punched him in the stomach again, and he puked a little. The stomach acid burned his mouth and nose and made his eyes water. He shook his head to clear his eyes, and spit out the bile. Aaron didn't think he was a tough guy, necessarily. He knew a tough guy—Dave had been shot and burned and had his face turned inside-out by the side of an AK, and didn't seem to give two shits about it—but Aaron was stubborn. He'd be goddamned if he'd ever give this asshole cop answers.

"We've got all night," Dixon told him. "I've got nowhere else I'd rather be," he said warningly. "Why don't you tell me what I want to know. Then you can get the fuck out of here."

"You must think I'm as stupid as you look," Aaron said, through bloody lips. "Which is really insulting."

Dixon punched him in the chest, left-right-left-right, and finished with another jab to his already broken nose. Aaron yelped, then wheezed and coughed. He hawked up some bloody phlegm and spit in to the floor. "You suck at this," he told Dixon. He looked up at the man. "I mean, I've never been tortured before, but still, you kinda suck."

"You want me to do this again?" Dixon said, pulling out the Taser.

"*Ride the Lightning*," Aaron croaked. "Metallica. Eighty… four, maybe?" He squinted at Dixon. "Fuck you. You're short even when I'm sitting down." He made a sound and he bit his tongue a little, and his teeth clacked together, as Dixon shot him with the Taser again.

As Abruzzo jumped in the chair Dixon fumed and

sweated. This was not going the way he'd expected. He'd thought a little pain, one, maybe two punches, the terror of being kidnapped and tied to a chair, and Abruzzo would start crying, one of those fake tough guys. Begging to do whatever he could to be let go. But instead…this.

That was his last cartridge. He set the Taser aside. Moved close to Abruzzo as the man slumped in the chair, bloody and sweaty and panting. Squatted beside him. Tried to sound friendly. "Tell me who did it. I know you know. I just want you to tell me. Admit it. You're friends with Anderson. You're maybe his only friend."

Aaron turned his head. His face was swollen and bloody from his hairline to his jawline. He looked rough. He smiled, a horrible smile, showing blood-stained teeth, and asked Dixon, "Does your husband know why you're out this late?" And he laughed at the look of fury on Dixon's face, and took the punch in the side of his head. Then Dixon reached behind him, grabbed one of Aaron's fingers, and snapped it. His scream was both satisfying and terrifying. Things were escalating into a realm Dixon had refused to even consider, but knew was a possibility.

Dixon walked back around in front of him, and waited for the man to come down from the pain. Focus. "You've got a lot more fingers," Dixon told him. "You ever want to be able to do anything again, you better start talking to me."

Wincing, Aaron gritted his teeth. He moved his tongue around inside his mouth—he'd bitten a chunk out of it when getting Tazed, but that pain was nothing compared to his finger. Still, if there was one thing he knew how to do, it was say no. "Now you're in trouble," he panted. "That was your mom's favorite finger." Okay, two things—say no, and be an asshole. He was fucking world class at that shit.

Dixon lunged in and hammered him with a right hook.

Aaron's head snapped back and the lights fluttered. He almost passed out. He groaned, and slumped over in the chair.

"We're just getting started," Dixon told him. "We've barely been doing this twenty minutes. We've got all night. All day tomorrow. Forever. We're here until you start talking. Tell me about Bufonte."

Aaron spit out a bloody tooth, and stared at it on the floor. Explored the new hole in his gumline with the tip of his tongue. Then he looked up at Dixon as the man's words registered. "Wait, you're here about Bufonte? That thing?"

"Why did you think I wanted to talk to you?"

Aaron laughed, drops of blood flying from his open mouth. Laughed loud and long. "Holy shit, I thought you were here about Arizona."

"Las Vegas is in Nevada, idiot."

That just got Aaron laughing louder, almost maniacally. It took him a while to stop. "So, wait, that means you're just working for Bufonte?"

"Yeah, and I want to know everything you know. About Anderson. Not just the hit-and-run, but about Las Vegas. I know he did it, you know he did it, but I want to hear it from you."

"So you're not moonlighting for the spooks, you're just a dirty fucking cop?" Aaron barked out a laugh and shook his head. "Short, and bent. Motherfucker. I'm the Italian, but *you're* working for the mob? Isn't that cultural appropriation or some shit? *Vaffanculo*."

Dixon stomped around behind him, and broke another of his fingers. Aaron's scream was short and high-pitched. "Not so funny now, is it?" Dixon spat.

"Fuck you," Aaron shot back at him.

Dixon was getting tired of his shit, and losing his

temper. It felt like he'd lost control of his life. He took it out on Aaron, punching him in the face. "Tell me!" he shouted.

"Fuck you!" Aaron shouted back.

"Tell me, you motherfucker," Dixon growled, and punched him again, blood flying.

"Fuck you, I won't do what you tell me!" Aaron shouted, his voice almost sing-song.

Dixon hit him with a left. Aaron's head rocked back. "You talk to me, and this stops."

"Fuck you, I won't do what you tell me!" Aaron yelled, his eyes wild. A fresh split between his eyebrows was pouring blood down his shattered nose.

"Tell me!" Dixon shouted into his face.

"Fuck you, I won't do what you tell me!" Aaron screamed. He leaned forward, into Dixon's face, screaming louder and louder. "Fuck you, I won't do what you tell me! Fuck you, I won't do what you tell me!" The veins were bulging in his neck and forehead. Dixon started hitting him, over and over again, hard and harder, but he wouldn't shut up, wouldn't stop shouting his defiance, blood flying with every blow, his nose totally flattened, another tooth flying out of his mouth, eyebrow splitting. Dixon's fist pounding down like a sledgehammer, and then both the front and back door burst open and men were running in, yelling, pointing guns.

Dixon found himself face down on the cold cement, Abruzzo's bloody tooth on the floor right in front of his nose. Someone yanked the pistol out of Dixon's holster. He looked up to see FBI Special Agent Gogolak standing over him.

"You're full of surprises," Gogolak said.

"Jesus Christ," one of the other agents said, looking at Aaron. "He killed him."

"Fuck you," Aaron croaked. "I look great."

"Somebody call an ambulance."

"Are these Taser cartridges?"

"Cut him loose," Gogolak said. He looked down at Dixon. "Somebody's been a very bad boy."

"You were following me?" Dixon said, still stunned by how quickly the situation had changed.

"Tracker on your car. Driving around late at night was a bit suspicious. Had no idea what you were doing here, but it seemed promising, so we set up on you. We were just going to wait, but the screaming sort of forced our hand." He glanced over at Aaron, as one of the other FBI agents used a pocket knife to cut through the duct tape. "Who's this?"

Dixon groaned, and laid his head back down on the cold floor. Abruzzo's tooth seemed even bigger. Mocking him.

"Give me five minutes with him, I'll get you whatever you want to know," Aaron croaked. Two men helped him up out of the chair, hands still cuffed as they didn't know who he was. He almost fell down twice until his legs took the weight. He had a man to either side of him, holding his arms, but with all the blood he was able to jerk out of their grasp, take two quick steps, and kick Dixon in the chest hard enough to rock him. Then a second time. Then they were pulling him backward, toward the door.

"Fuck you!" Aaron shouted at the figure on the floor. "Fuck you!" The two FBI agents dragged him outside and leaned him up against one of their vehicles.

"Relax," one of them yelled at him. He looked at Aaron. "Christ, he really did a number on you. You need to lie down until the ambulance gets here?"

Aaron spit a wad of blood on the ground. He looked between the two agents who'd pulled him outside, and the other agents busily going back and forth. He smiled, showing off his missing teeth, one eye so swollen he couldn't see out of it. Just the sight of him made them wince. "Who are you? Why'd he grab you?" one of them asked him.

"That's my question as well," Special Agent Gogolak said, striding into view.

"I'm friends with Dave Anderson," Aaron told him. "He grabbed me because he wanted to know whether Dave was involved in that bullshit in Vegas."

"And was he?"

Aaron spit another wad of bloody snot on the ground in front of the man's wingtips and peered at him with his one good eye. "I'll tell you what I told him," Aaron said, and then didn't say anything. For ten long seconds, while they glared at them. Then he told them, "Good to see the False Flag Bureau of Investigation still remembers how to investigate actual bad guys."

The agent beside him shoved Aaron angrily, and he almost fell down. Aaron gave him a dirty look and pronounced, "Shit, I forgot, it's Forever Bothering Italians. Listen, every minute I stand here, bleeding, cuffed, with broken fingers, strengthens my civil suit. I'm a millionaire already, my bank account just doesn't know it yet. You want to get in on that action? No?" He looked around. "Anybody got a cigarette? Shit." He was in a huge amount of pain. Probably wouldn't be able to walk tomorrow. But he hadn't said shit. Not a fucking word.

Chapter Twenty-Seven

Bob thought long and hard about the best way to do what needed to be done. The Director of the Defense Intelligence Agency himself had told him everything was proceeding according to plan, so heading south of the border using his own name might raise some flags.

Control what you can control.

So he broke out one of the sets of IDs he hoped the government knew nothing about, drove to a nearby Starbucks, used a sterile tablet connected to their wifi to book a flight, and drove to the Philadelphia airport.

It wasn't enough to just use a name that wasn't on anybody's radar. The airports were filled with cameras running facial recognition software, and every government intelligence agency had real-time access to them. He put on a snap-brim hat, glasses, and stuffed small sponges in his cheeks to change the shape of his face. Combined with the baggy pants and shirt he put on, slouching his big shoulders, walking like he was tired and his feet hurt, he looked somewhere between pudgy and fat and very little like himself. It wasn't perfect, but it was good enough.

He flew from Philly to Albuquerque, arriving so late he almost couldn't get a rental car. He grabbed a Jeep Grand Cherokee—a little flashier than he would have liked, but he wanted the ground clearance and four-wheel-drive capability, just in case. The drive from Albuquerque to the border, straight south on I-25, took about four hours. Ten miles before the Mexico border, I-25 cut through the westernmost corner of Texas. There were several border crossings in El Paso, and he diverted over to I-110 and the Bridge of the Americas International Bridge. Even in the middle of the night there were cars lined up, but there wasn't much delay, at least on the American side. Border Patrol didn't give much of a shit about people going into Mexico. Especially not a middle-aged white guy. He was just waved through.

On the Mexican side the guard at least asked for his ID, and why he was coming into the country. Bob handed him the passport he had for Robert Anderson of Houston, Texas —backed up by a driver license, two credit cards, and other supporting documentation in his wallet and on the web— and told him simply "Business," acting bored and sleepy at the same time. Two minutes later he was through and into Ciudad Juarez. Only then did he take off the hat and glasses and pull the sponges out of his mouth.

Even if they'd disassembled the car down to the frame, and given him a body cavity search (or an MRI), they would have found nothing, because there was nothing to find, other than the small folding knife in his pocket, which was completely legal. It was quicker and safer that way. He drove south through the city on Mexico state highway 45.

The south end of the Nuevo Hipodromo neighborhood,

on the far side of Juarez, was a commercial area, filled with business parks and warehouses for various businesses including trucking companies. Pepsi had a big distribution center there. Mexico being Mexico, most of the area—the *Zona Industria Panamerica*—was secured behind gates and metal fencing. Or an eight-foot concrete wall, which ran along Avenida Tecnologico. Bob punched in the code to get in the gate at the north end of the complex, drove past Z Gas, took the third left, and then turned in at a row of low buildings. The first one was a towing company. The second building was roughly the size of a double-wide trailer, white to shake off the baking heat of the sun. At three in the morning the air was downright chilly.

Bob parked in the lot and punched the code into the mechanical keypad on the door. Inside, the interior was stuffy and still warm, as the air conditioning was almost never turned on. Inside he was greeted by bare walls and floor. There was one stained, disgusting mattress in a corner, and a desk and a few chairs. He kept the space dark, working in the gloom.

He pulled the mattress to the side, revealing bare floor... and a tiny steel ring that might go unnoticed. He grabbed the ring and pulled. The trap door swung up, revealing a set of steep wooden stairs leading down into inky blackness. He didn't bring a gun with him across the border, but he did bring a flashlight, a little inoffensive Surefire Aviator. He clicked on the tailcap and started down the stairs.

The space was somewhere between a cave and a basement. He stepped to the side and flipped the switch, and two bare bulbs hanging from the ceiling blazed to life. Against the far wall were two large trunks. The same code that got him through the gate, and into the building, opened the locks on the trunks, each of which was large enough to hold two bodies. There were no bodies inside, just guns and ammunition and assorted gear operators in-country might find useful. He had a pretty good idea of what was inside them, because he'd helped set up this cache. He'd set up caches all through northern Mexico in the past few years, and in fact around the world. Most of them, including this one, belonged to his current employer.

There were a dozen pistols inside one case, all identical Austrian-made Glock 17s that were sterile. He had no idea what result any government agent would get if he tried to trace one of their serial numbers, he just knew it wouldn't come back to any individual person or U.S. government agency. Beside the guns in the trunk was a cardboard box full of factory-fresh magazines. And beside that was a stack of 9mm ammo boxes. 124-grain JHPs from Sellier & Bellot, made in the Czech Republic. He eyed the Safariland holsters and magazine pouches in two big Ziplocs but left them alone for the moment.

Bob pulled two purple nitrile gloves from the box sitting right there and proceeded to load up three Glock magazines. He grabbed one of the pistols at random and worked the slide, checked the trigger, and looked it over. It looked like it had never been fired. Unfamiliar, untested guns were not what you wanted to take into combat, but beggars couldn't be choosers. He loaded the Glock and stuck it on his hip in a Safariland paddle holster, two spare magazines on his other side. Then he moved to the other trunk.

He had a choice of rifles. Half the long guns in the second trunk were battered HK G3s that more than likely had come from the stores of the Mexican Army. They'd carried G3s forever, and many of their units still did, having not yet switched over to the FX-05 *Xiuhcoatl* FireSnakes, which superficially resembled HK G36s. It was a reliable, hard-hitting rifle, but big and heavy. If he grabbed one he'd be relegated to iron sights. The other guns in the trunk were all Colts—three were M4A1s, and three were Model 733 Commandos, shorter guns with 11.5-inch barrels and collapsible stocks.

All the Colts were old enough they had carrying handles, and mounted atop each one was an Aimpoint red dot—old school, but still very effective. Bob grabbed a Commando, surprised at how short and light it was—when you weren't slapping PEQ-15s, quad rails, white lights, and all the other shit onto an AR, they stayed very light.

"We're not here for your money, we're here for the bank's money," he growled, tucking the butt of the short-barreled rifle into his armpit and waving the muzzle around in brief imitation of his favorite scene in any movie ever. The best gunfight to ever come out of Hollywood. Then he got back to work.

He spent ten minutes checking out the rifle—powering up the optic, working the charging handle, trying the trigger in both semi- and full-auto. He broke it down and checked out the internals. The gas rings on the bolt seemed to be good. Firing pin moved freely, and protruded the right distance from the bolt face when all the way forward. The bore was clear, with good rifling.

Some things he had to trust, others he could verify. He kept the bolt carrier group out of the upper receiver and headed upstairs with it. Walked out to his rental, which sat, the engine ticking and cooling, in the night air. Bob set the upper receiver assembly on the roof of his Cherokee and aimed it at a warehouse across the street, across an empty parking lot. The exterior of the building was lit up by security lights. Bob looked through the upper receiver and down the barrel of the upper and tapped it a little, until he could see the sign on the distant building, underneath one of the lights, through the narrow bore. Then he let go of the upper, and rose onto his tiptoes to look through the optic. The red dot was glowing brightly. Too brightly. He turned it down without disturbing the upper, then moved back and forth a few times, looking between the barrel and the optic. The sign on the warehouse was roughly fifty yards away, and if the optic wasn't exactly zeroed, it was within a couple inches. Bore sighting: complete.

The bolt carrier was properly lubed. Back inside, Bob reassembled the short carbine, worked the charging handle a few times, then looked at the trunk which contained the Glocks. Stacks and stacks of aluminum GI magazines for the Colts, all loaded with military green tip light armor piercing ammunition, stared up at him. Not his first choice, but it would work. He grabbed ten at random, tested their springs with his thumb, also checking that they were fully loaded. They all had Colt or NHMTG floorplates. He unloaded one and saw it had a Magpul anti-tilt follower.

There were empty duffel bags and backpacks beside the trunk, and he grabbed one and started stuffing gear into it, checking his watch. He had at least a four-hour drive ahead of him, and wanted to be in position long before he needed to be.

Chapter Twenty-Eight

Timotéo Sandoval frowned as his phone rang. Simply because it was so early in the morning. But he saw it was Miguel Aponte, so he assumed the man had a good reason for calling. "I have only had one sip of coffee," Timotéo said. "The sun is barely peeking over the hills. Is someone dying? I hope so."

"Before the day is out, perhaps," Aponte said. "You wanted me keeping an eye on Santiago."

"I did."

"It is not as easy as you would think. The man deals with electronics. Hardware. Security systems. Not bombs, so much, but he spends a lot of time by himself. Moves around between our safe houses, warehouses."

"And? I know you didn't call me to tell me you had nothing."

"And he has sent and received several encrypted emails. To an anonymous Gmail account."

"Don't we all do that? We are involved in, what is the American phrase, a 'criminal enterprise'." Not that things weren't different in Mexico. Half of the government was on the payroll of one cartel or the other. In American, the government was the cartel.

"I suppose. And he has a new satellite phone. Or it seems new, my men haven't seen it before, but for the last two days he has been taking it with him wherever he goes. A top of the line Iridium, or so it appears."

"Hmm."

"We captured the number. He's only made two calls in those two days. Well, he called out once, and received one call."

Timotéo rolled his eyes. "This is like listening to a story from my niece. Having to pull out every detail. Who did he call?"

"I don't know. We couldn't hear the audio. But the call he placed, it was to another satphone. That was located in Kansas City at the time."

"Kansas City, Kansas? In the United States?"

"Is there another? Yes."

"Who was he talking to?"

"*No se*. I have no way of knowing that."

"I thought this man of yours was good," Timotéo demanded.

"He is. That's how we know where the call landed. And that Santiago is sending encrypted emails. We put a GPS tracker on his car. It was the easiest way to keep track of him, as he moves between the various properties, as I said. That's why I called. Half an hour ago he left from his home. When it was still dark. Alone. Heading up 49. Still going."

"Up," Timotéo repeated. "North?"

"*Si*. My men are following him, at a distance, out of sight."

Timotéo frowned. Leaving before dawn was unusual.

Most of the men he worked with stayed up until dawn, and then slept until noon. Three hours north of Torreón was Ciudad Jimenez. Three hours past that was Chihuahua. They had men and operations all through the area…but nothing Santiago was involved with. And past Chihuahua…. "He calls *Los Estados Unidos*, and then the next day gets up and leaves before dawn, driving north? I don't like that. I don't like that at all."

"Didn't he say he had American contacts? To go after the *puta* in Arizona who killed our men?"

"I still don't like it. By himself? *¿Solo?* How many men are following him?"

"Three men, in two cars. He is not driving fast."

Timotéo was running toward his bedroom, to put on pants. "Send me their phone number. I am going to try to catch up." He had a Range Rover with over five hundred horsepower. And there were more men he trusted in Ciudad Jimenez he could call. "Don't lose him!"

The rendezvous point was roughly twenty miles, thirty kilometers, directly north of Chihuahua. It was in the middle of nowhere, in the foothills of the Sierra Madre Occidental mountains, a bit northwest of Cerros El Contrabando, a nearby peak with a 1500-meter elevation. Bob had been able to figure that much out, but any satellite images he pulled up of the GPS coordinates didn't show him anything other than brown-green slopes and unmarked dirt roads. Some of which ran arrow-straight for twenty or more miles, which made him suspect they weren't roads at all but rather access trails following overhead power cables or underground gas lines.

He drove south on Mexico 45 for hours. After three hours the sun came up, and he saw he was driving down the middle of a wide, flat valley, with mountain ranges to either side of him, far in the distance. There was more green than he was expecting, irrigated fields and even orchards, although he didn't know what kind of trees he was looking at. He didn't see any fruit, but maybe it was the wrong time of year.

Following the prompts on the Garmin GPS unit he turned off 45 next to a restaurant and drove straight east on a well-maintained dirt road. There were ordered fields to either side, and he passed a plant nursery. A mile on he crossed over railroad tracks, passed an agricultural wholesaler, a field of sunflowers, and then the road became a trail, and wound up into low hills, which were green and brown. Beyond the hills was a low mountain range. From what he'd been able to determine from satellite imagery, there was no human habitation east of the railroad tracks until you crossed that mountain range. Twenty miles of open country. A perfect spot for a covert rendezvous.

The rental SUV was great for dirt roads, but not set up for off road; it simply didn't have the proper tires. But Bob knew what he was doing, and two miles out he turned off the road, which had become an ill-used two-track, and slowly wound his way southeast across uneven ground, low bushes occasionally scraping the undercarriage. He chose his way carefully, avoiding gulleys and rocks big enough to cause damage, the tires rolling over bare dirt and thick patches of short grass. After ten minutes he found a perfect spot between two low hills. The Jeep was hidden from view from anyone unless they found the little valley, or they had a drone up. Which was always a possibility.

He pulled off his plaid flannel shirt, which was getting a

bit hot anyway. Underneath he wore a tan t-shirt, which he figured was good enough of a match to his surroundings. From the duffel bag he retrieved one of the chest rigs he'd grabbed at the cache. It was a custom piece made by Tactical Tailor in coyote tan. No armor plates, it was just a low-profile gear-carrier, with three pockets for six rifle magazines across the front and a few small pouches for other items. He stuffed the pouches with loaded magazines.

He'd grabbed a Gerber LMF II knife from the gear box at the cache—a simple no-frills utility/combat piece with a half-serrated blade just under five inches long—and duct-taped its sheath upside down over the thick strap running over his left shoulder. Then he pulled the knife from the polymer sheath and went to work, cutting off branches of nearby bushes and tossing them onto the hood and roof of the Cherokee. It took him about ten minutes. The end result wasn't perfect, but now the vehicle didn't stand out, and the foliage cut any reflection from the glass and steel.

Bob hadn't wanted to cross the border with any gear that would draw attention to him, and that included clothing. No boots, but the waterproof trail-running shoes on his feet had nubby soles that were just as aggressive. He had on khakis, and now over the chest rig he threw a cotton canvas long sleeve button-down shirt. It was thin cotton, and an odd gray-green in color, not "tactical" at all...and yet perfect camouflage in the half-green hills of northern Mexico. Much better camouflage than his pale arms. He pulled a faded and stained khaki Green Bay Packers baseball cap out of his carry-on and tugged it down over his blonde hair. He checked his watch. The rendezvous was in two hours, and according to his GPS unit he was 1784 meters from the spot it was to occur, just over a mile, across hilly terrain. Which should be plenty of time for him to scope it out and get into position.

He heard birds and insects and the low rush of wind through the bushes and over the grass, but otherwise the hills were quiet. He slung the Colt Commando across his chest, grabbed the duffel bag containing the remaining rifle magazines, bottles of water, and a few energy bars, gently pressed the car door closed until it clicked, and headed north.

The mountain range angled northwest, so as he headed north he gained elevation, going up and down gentle hills covered with scrub bushes and low trees. He was careful as he crested each hill and ridge, peering around to make sure there was nothing and no one nearby before quickly going over.

The land around him browned a bit after half a mile of hiking. He found a dried stream bed to follow. It led him northwest for over a quarter mile, the walking easy as striding down a sidewalk, then when it turned east he climbed the rocky bank and stuck his head over the top. In front of him the ground was brown and uneven, dotted with dark green bushes and tufts of light green grass. Crouched low, he moved slowly forward a hundred yards, then went prone in a patch of half-dried grass. He slithered to the top of a slope, underneath one of the thick bushes, and peered down. There, maybe eighty yards ahead and a bit below him, was the site of the meet.

There were no whole structures at the location, just the ruins of several small buildings at the junction of one rutted two-track, a narrow gravel road running arrow-straight north and south—perhaps an access road for an underground pipeline?—and one dirt road coming in from the west. The road coming in from the west was the road Bob had turned off, and the most likely avenue of approach. The site was in a bit of a shallow bowl.

There was one wooden structure, listing badly to the side, little more than a shack. Across the road the foundation of a larger building squatted like a tooth with a bad cavity, the jagged cinderblock walls less than two feet tall. And between the two were some blocky metal boxes sprouting up from the ground that were dusty but seemed well-maintained, likely belonging to a utility company.

Binoculars would have been good, but he didn't have any, and somehow—good genetics from his mother's side— he still had 20/15 eyesight. Keeping motionless in the shadows under the bush he scanned the area all around. It wasn't color that stood out to the human eye as much as movement, but he didn't see anything, color or movement, other than a few small birds that darted in-between bushes. The skittering of what was probably small lizards. It was quiet. Moving slowly, he checked his watch. Eighty minutes until noon, the scheduled time of the meet. Reaching back carefully he extracted a bottle of water and an energy bar from the bag and settled in.

Fifteen minutes before noon he saw a faint dust plume from the north, and a minute after that a truck appeared, bouncing down the access road. It was a battered old Ford, dusty from the trail, the occupants invisible behind the glare off the glass. The truck paused at the top of the last hill. Presumably the person or persons inside were checking out the area. After several minutes the truck rolled down the slope and stopped beside the ramshackle shed. A man hopped out and checked inside, while another jumped out the opposite side of the truck and stared at the mountain slopes to the east, then turned and looked at the rolling hills to the south. Straight at Bob. Bob was a shadow in a shadow, kept still, and went unnoticed.

A third man climbed out of the driver's door and looked all around. Dog. And Bob recognized the other two as Cherry and Boot. Dog pointed, and Cherry, carrying a rifle, jogged to the top of a small hill to Bob's right and laid down behind an offroad tire-sized boulder. Overwatch. Dog and Boot moved to the back door of the truck and lifted out a hooded figure and set him down in the shade of the shack. Then waited.

Bob had never, officially, been a 'sniper', although he'd gone through Army sniper school and done the job more than a few times. And he had the patience. Once his team arrived, he didn't move a muscle other than to pull his Colt a little closer and set his chin down on the side of the receiver, to save his neck muscles.

At noon, Dog checked his watch. At ten past, he pulled out a satphone and looked at the display. Perhaps to check that it was on. The air wasn't too hot, yet, but the sun was, and Bob was getting a bit of mirage as he stared down at the scene before him. He could feel the sun beating on his legs, but under the bush his head and upper body were comfortable in the shade.

At twenty-two minutes past the hour he heard a sound. He moved his eyes more than his head. The sound grew louder, and resolved into the low murmur of a vehicle engine right before a compact SUV crested a nearby rise. It was driving in from the west, on the main access road. It slowed down, then stopped, a hundred yards out. Paused ten seconds. Then the SUV started moving forward again, heading toward the truck, the shack, and the captive.

"Keep your head on a swivel," Dog told Boot.

"Absolutely," Boot said. He'd been standing beside the truck with nothing in his hands, the pistol at his waist mostly hidden from view, but as the vehicle rolled toward them he pulled his rifle out of the back seat and held it down along his leg. They'd visited a cache in Santa Ana, about fifty miles south of Nogales, and geared up before heading south to Hermosillo and then east across the mountains. Dog had grabbed an HK G3, because he loved the old-school big bore battle rifles, and Cherry and Boot had both grabbed old Colt M4s topped with new Aimpoints. He held the rifle loosely and scanned the surrounding countryside, but nothing else was moving.

The Hyundai SUV stopped fifty feet away. The driver waited until the dust cloud blew past, then got out. He was of average height and unremarkable in appearance, and looked like a local. "You speak English?" Dog asked him.

"Yeah, I speak English," Marty Cabrera, otherwise known as Nelson Santiago, told him with a flat midwestern accent.

"Well then." Dog took a step and pointed at their prisoner. He was on his side, still bagged and tied, lying in the dirt in the shade thrown by the shed.

The man undercover in the cartel frowned at the figure. He was frowning because he was not happy. Turning "Pima Jack" over to the cartel had been his idea, sure, but he still wasn't blind to what that meant. An ugly death for a guy who just happened to be in the right place at the wrong time.

"Just you?" Dog asked. "He should be good, but we can strap him down in the back seat or whatever, so he's no trouble." Then their heads jerked up as the whistle echoed off the hills.

Bob pulled his fingers out of his mouth. He saw Cherry out of the corner of his eye, looking for the source of the whistle. "I'm coming in!" he shouted, loud enough for everyone to hear. Then he looked to the side. "Cherry, don't you fucking shoot me."

Cherry, prone behind the rock, jerked at hearing his name. "What?" he said reflexively.

Moving slowly, Bob slid back out from underneath the bush and stood up. He pulled his ball cap off and turned his head left and right, so they could see who he was, then put the cap back on, grabbed his rifle and the bag, and walked toward the rendezvous. "Cherry, you stay there," he called out.

"Copy that." Cherry had no idea what the hell was going on, but in that case, prone behind a boulder with a rifle in his hand wasn't a bad position to be in. He checked behind him, just in case.

"Who the fuck is this?" Marty asked. He had his hands on his hips. He had a pistol stuck in his waistband, but had only brought it in case he needed to threaten the captive.

"Our team leader," Dog said.

"What's he doing?"

Dog shrugged and traded a look with Boot. "Fuck if I know. I didn't know he'd be out here." When Bob was twenty yards away Dog said, "You don't trust us to do a simple hand-off?"

"Undercover Boss, Cartel Edition?" Boot added.

Bob stopped in front of them and shook his head. He looked from Dog to the man he didn't know—presumably the inside man—and back. "Things have changed," Bob told them. He peered over at the captive, still lying in the dirt, wearing nothing but boxers and a canvas bag over his head. "We're not handing him over."

"What?" Marty said. "What do you mean you're not handing him over?"

Dog sighed. "Bullshit politics, or bullshit spook shit?" he asked Bob. It wasn't the first time he'd been out on an op and had the ROE change, or been given a new objective that was completely opposite of why they'd gone into the field in the first place.

"Does it matter?" Bob said.

Boot made a sound. "Fucking mushrooms again, man, they keep us in the dark and shovel shit on us."

"Wait, what do you mean you're not handing him over?" Marty demanded. "Says who? Why?"

"You tell people you were coming out here to pick him up?" Dog asked the man.

"What? No, why?"

"Because then nobody will know you didn't," Dog said with a shrug. His team leader had told him the handoff was cancelled, so it was cancelled. It was that simple.

"What? No. That—hold on," Marty said, flustered. He pulled out his satphone and dialed a number.

"Who are you calling?" Bob asked him.

"My contact," Marty told him. He was only supposed to call Joe Clark in an emergency, but this seemed to qualify. These guys were supposed to be turning Pima Jack over to him. And now they were refusing? "What's my codename?" he demanded of Bob, suspicious.

"I don't know," Bob said. "I don't give a fuck." As the man wandered a few steps away, listening to the phone ring, Bob looked at his guys. "I don't care if he's calling the President."

"You're the boss," Boot said in agreement. "But if we're

not going to do this, we should clear the fuck out of here. We just have to figure out what to do with—" he glanced over at their captive, but then the satphone call connected.

"What's going on? Are you in trouble?" Joe Clark said in Marty's ear.

"No. Well, I don't know. I'm at the handoff, and they're not handing him off."

"I told you to only use this number in an emergency," Clark said. He sighed. "What, do they want money or something?"

"Heads up!" Cherry shouted from behind his elevated position fifty yards away. "I've got somebody inbound." They looked over, and saw a dust cloud. A big dust cloud, coming in from the west.

"I thought you didn't tell anybody about this meeting," Dog said.

"I didn't," Marty said, confused, as several vehicles crested the distant hill. Two, three, four vehicles.

"What's going on?" Clark said in his ear.

Timotéo stomped on his brakes and his Range Rover slid just a little bit on the gravel. He stared down at the scene before him as the other vehicles pulled up to either side of him. There, there was Nelson Santiago. With three other men, one of whom clearly was a gringo. Was it a hostage tradeoff, the American Ybarra wanted so much, the *pendejo* Pima Jack? Or was it something else? He couldn't tell. If it was something else, some betrayal of La Fuerza, Santiago needed to die. If the men were delivering Pima Jack to Santiago…Timotéo's mind raced through the possibilities. *Mierda*, killing Santiago and taking credit for the capture of the American would be the smart move. *Un movimiento brillante*, especially in the cartel's cutthroat world where you usually moved up in the ranks through attrition.

Timotéo rolled down the windows to either side of him and looked at the men. Eight men, eight veteran killers in three vehicles, not including him in his white Range Rover. All armed with automatic weapons. Against but three armed men, and Santiago, who Timotéo had never even seen shoot a gun. "*Matarlos*," Timotéo said loudly, with a smile. "*Matarlos a todos.*" Kill them. Kill them all.

His men shouted, and two of their vehicles tore off down the hill toward the men, bouncing wildly. Timotéo opened his door and climbed out to stand behind it. All he had was a pistol, and wasn't about to go charging down the hill, but he knew how to look the part of a combat commander. The two men in the truck beside his Range Rover jumped out and started shooting over the hood and around their doors at the gringos in the valley, as two carloads of cartel soldiers roared toward them.

"Contact!" Bob shouted, as the vehicles raced down the hill toward them. A man hung out an open window and fired an entire magazine full-auto at them. The bullets thudded into the ground and flew over their heads. Two hit the Hyundai. As Dog grabbed Marty and pulled him to cover behind the pickup Bob planted his feet, shouldered the Colt while flipping down the selector, and calmly began shooting, tracking the closest vehicle, a black Cadillac Escalade. The driver was coming straight at them, thinking his passenger, the one shooting, would force them to keep their heads down.

Bob fired half a dozen times at the man hanging out of the open window, until he slumped and dropped his rifle, then began pouring rounds through the windshield glass, at the driver. The big Cadillac suddenly lost acceleration and veered to the side, smacking into the other vehicle, an older Mitsubishi SUV. The two vehicles ground sideways to a stop in a cloud of dust. While the driver of the Mitsubushi tried to extricate his vehicle the remaining men still alive in the two vehicles bailed out of them and used them for cover as Dog and Boot poured fire at them.

Cherry couldn't see those cartel men, but he could the two at the top of the hill, by a truck parked next to a Range Rover. They were shooting wildly down into the valley and had no idea he was there, off to the side. He braced against the boulder for the sixty-yard shot. The man on the passenger side of the truck stepped back, out from the cover of his open door, as he reloaded his rifle. Cherry shot him twice and watched him fall. The other man was in-between the two vehicles. Not much more than the top of his head was visible, and it was moving.

The rear tire of the Ford truck blew out as it took a hit, and it dropped several inches. Marty shouted in surprise. "There's not enough room behind here for all of us," Dog said, looking at Marty, Boot, and Bob, who'd pulled back behind the pickup after taking out the Cadillac. Dog fired four times at the crashed vehicles, his G3 rocking him back, then shouted "Cover!" and took off, running across the road. Boot and Bob fired at the cartel soldiers. Bullets kicked up dirt behind Dog, but none connected. He dove behind the broken cinderblock walls on the far side of the road.

Boot moved to the back end of the pickup and Bob leaned around the hood, using the engine block for cover. The cartel soldiers were popping up behind their vehicles to fire at them. Usually short, full-auto bursts. But half of them weren't even aiming, they were just pointing their rifles in Bob's general direction. Bob heard bullets hitting around him, thunking into the truck, and zipping by over head, but if they actually hit him, it would be by accident.

Thank God for amateurs, he thought, as he laid his rifle down atop the hood and crouched behind it. The rifle would work just fine lying on its left side, ejection port aimed at the sky, and only the very top of his head was visible behind it. He just had to be aware of the offset, using the optic sideways. But there wasn't much at forty yards or so.

With Boot firing rapidly, and Dog laying down heavy-caliber suppressive fire, chewing up the cars, the cartel soldiers' aim wasn't getting any better. They were popping up like gophers. Bob prepped the trigger, waiting, then fired. Prepped the trigger again, fired again. Another was poised to jump up, visible through fractured auto glass, not realizing he wasn't behind cover, and Bob fired four times until he disappeared. A man appeared, sprinting away from the cars, away from them, heading up the slope toward the two vehicles parked in the distance. Bob, Boot, and Dog fired simultaneously, and he dropped.

Timotéo watched the two vehicles roar toward the gringos with laughter and bloodlust, then everything seemed to go wrong in just seconds. The gringos avoided the incoming fire and shot at his men, and the big Escalade crashed into the other vehicle. The Americans were devastatingly accurate, and he watched one man after another go down, even if only half their head was visible for a second.

He turned to the men beside him, firing around their truck. He only saw one man, in-between the two vehicles, ducking down and popping up to fire downhill. "Get down there!" Timotéo shouted, pointing. "They need your help."

The man looked at Timotéo, then downslope at the two tangled vehicles, and then a piece of his head flew off and he dropped from view so fast his expression didn't even have time to change. Timotéo's eyes widened. He was all alone atop the hill. He looked at the other two cartel vehicles. He could see behind them, and mostly what he could see were bodies. Maybe one or two of the men was moving, but that was it. The fight was over. The fight was lost.

Swearing, he ducked back inside his vehicle. It was still running. He kept his head below the dash, threw it into reverse, and hit the gas. The Range Rover surged backward. A bullet cracked the glass above his head, but he didn't raise his head. The SUV bounced wildly as it blindly rolled backwards. Only when he was sure he was out of sight, behind the hill, did Timotéo risk a glance through the windshield. He was safe for the moment, out of view of the Americans. His Range Rover had left the road and slammed into a big thorny bush, hanging up. He shifted into drive, turned the wheel, and hit the accelerator. The tires spun for a few seconds, a few seconds when he was terrified he'd be stuck there, then they bit and the vehicle rocketed onto the roadway.

Fishtailing, Timotéo headed back toward the main road as fast as he could, crouched down in the seat until he was sure he was out of firing range. Then, swearing, he pulled out his phone as the SUV flew down the road. He swore again, louder, as he saw it was searching for a signal.

Cherry fired at the Range Rover disappearing over the hill. He looked at the two-car pileup, then down at his teammates, hunkered behind cover. "Moving!" he shouted. He pulled back from the boulder, scooted down the back side of the hill, then ran off to the side, keeping a slope between him and the action, although he was only hearing a few occasional shots.

He came up a slope, rifle up. The enemy pickup was there at the top of a low rise, two bodies next to it. He used it for cover, and glanced to the west—all he could see of the Range Rover was a plume of dust as it raced away. He backed up, circled around as fast as he could, then came up behind the two crashed vehicles.

They were thirty yards from him as he popped up. He only saw one man moving behind the Mitsubishi and shot him, then put bullets into all the other bodies as well, just in case. Then he waved at Boot, who could see him, and approached the bodies. Two men dead in the vehicles, and three dead behind them. He looked around, and slowly straightened up. "I think we're clear," he called out.

"Jesus Christ!" Marty said, crouched down behind a tire. He was shaking. He had his pistol in his hand, but he'd never fired a shot.

Boot laughed as he stood up. "That was fun," he said with a mean smile. He was almost vibrating with adrenaline.

"Anybody hit?" Bob called out. "Check your shit." He

glanced down at himself, then over at Dog who was stepping out from behind the cinderblock wall, which had quite a few fresh holes in it. "Well, that went about as well as you could hope for," he said. He looked around, then walked over to where the captive was on the ground. Dusty, but not sporting any new holes. He nudged the man with his toe. "You still with us?"

"Are you fucking kidding me?" the man shouted, his voice only slightly muffled by the bag around his head, jerking against his restraints. "Are you fucking serious right now?" Bob laughed.

"Who the fuck were those guys?" Dog asked. He addressed the question to the man he didn't know.

"I don't know." Marty was shivering.

"Well, let's go look," Bob told him. "C'mon."

He walked with Marty over to the two vehicles. Dog followed. Bob pushed two of the men over onto their backs with his foot, so Marty could see their faces. "Shit. Yeah, I know this guy. This guy too. These are our guys."

"Our guys?" Dog asked.

"Our cartel. La Fuerza. Where I was embedded." He looked up toward the top of the hill. "What was that? The white car that drove off."

"Range Rover," Bob said.

"Shit. I think I know who that was." A sudden thought hit him and he turned to Bob. "Was that why you weren't turning over the guy to me? Because you knew I was burned? My cover was blown?"

Bob almost smiled at the opportunity he'd been given. "I didn't know they'd be showing up here. Who got away?"

"Timotéo Sandoval. One of Ybarra's lieutenants. An up-and-comer. Shit. I guess I'm fucking burned." They walked back toward the buildings.

"Yeah, it's time for all of us to *di di mau* before your guy comes back with reinforcements," Dog told him. He looked at the truck they'd taken to the meet. It was badly shot up, with two flat tires. Marty's Hyundai wasn't in much better shape.

"Cherry!" Bob shouted. Cherry was positioned halfway up the slope, providing overwatch. Bob pointed at the truck atop the hill. "See if that's good to go." Cherry gave him a thumbs-up and jogged toward the Toyota. "I've got a Cherokee staged about a mile from here, so we've got that as a minimum," Bob said.

"Yeah, great, but what do we do about this guy?" Dog said, nodding at the underwear-clad body lying on the ground in front of them. He pulled his pistol from its holster and looked at Bob expectantly.

Chapter Twenty-Nine

It was surreal. Dave had been in half a dozen gunfights, and after the first one he'd never been scared. But lying there, on the ground, in his underwear, helpless, as a war raged above and around him, he'd felt paralyzing fear. He couldn't see, couldn't move more than to wiggle, and he was afraid to do that. He was in shade, and assumed, hoped he was behind cover, and thrashing might put him into the line of fire. He had no way to know.

The people who'd kidnapped him seemed to have won the fight. He was disappointed by that, but then again he didn't know who they were fighting. Cops? Soldiers? Maybe even cartel? It felt like desert, what they'd been driving through, and he wondered if they'd somehow crossed into Mexico while he was drugged. He'd heard some Mexican music, and people speaking Spanish, in passing, as they drove along, but that didn't mean anything—you could hear that anywhere in the American southwest. Sometimes it seemed like there were as many Spanish-language radio stations in Phoenix as English.

The guys around him were talking, but they kept walking away, out of earshot, and he couldn't follow the conversation. Until several of them walked close to him. "Yeah, great, but what do we do about this guy?" one of them said, and Dave knew they were talking about him.

There was no answer, just steps coming closer. He had no idea what was going on, and was pretty sure he was going to get a bullet in the back of his head. He had the sudden urge to ask them if Lori was okay, but bit it back. No matter what they told him, it could be a lie. Better to die not knowing. He couldn't do anything about it anyway. He'd rubbed his skin raw trying to get free of the duct tape, with zero success.

He was pushed over, half onto his face, and he closed his eyes. He couldn't see anything anyway, but it seemed more appropriate—when you were getting executed, shot in the back of the head, shouldn't you have your eyes closed? Not that he'd given up, but hours and hours of struggling with his bonds had done nothing.

Instead of a sharp pain, then nothing, he felt tugging. Then the length of tape securing his wrists to his ankles was cut. He blinked in surprise. Then the knife came in again, and began sawing between his wrists. The tape parted, and he was rolled back over. Onto his ass, sitting up.

As he peeled the tape from around his wrists, someone unwound the tape that was loosely around his neck, holding the bag on his head. His wrists were raw, but the pain seemed distant. Inconsequential. When his wrists were free he slowly raised his hands, then tugged at the bag. It came off his head without resistance.

Dave blinked, blinded for a few seconds by the bright sunlight. When his eyes focused he saw four men staring at him with various expressions on their faces. At least two of the four were white guys. So, not cartel? He had no idea who they were. They looked serious. Like professionals. Heavily armed.

"I think this is a really fucking bad idea," one of the two closest said, frowning. He held a huge rifle in his hands. Dave recognized his voice as one of the men who'd kidnapped him. "Dragging a civilian across the border? Who's likely to slot us if we give him half a chance?"

The other man, standing closest to Dave, held up a finger. He was thick, with a close-cropped beard and blonde hair. Older. He wore his gear like he'd been born in it. He pulled out a satphone and dialed a number. Listened to it ring. Then it was answered.

"Yeah," he said. "I've got him. Yeah. Pissed, what do you think? Do you think you could say a few words to him, so he doesn't try to kill my guys anytime they look away, for the, uh, misunderstanding? Right. Here he is."

While the three other men looked on, the fourth man handed Dave the satphone. Dave licked his dry lips, cleared his throat, and said, "Hello?"

"Dave, it's John Phault. That guy standing in front of you? That's Bob, a friend of mine. Trust him with your life."

Dave blinked a few times. Just a few seconds earlier he'd been waiting to be executed, and now…this? His brain was taking a bit to catch up to his changing circumstances. "What?"

"I've known him for over twenty years. Those addresses in Vegas you wanted? He got them for me, although he didn't know it was for you. Listen, do you remember that day we were in the strip club, doing a surveillance, and I got a little drunk and maybe mentioned I signed an NDA, in relation to an incident where a lot of people died? Where I killed a lot of people. Bob was there. He signed it too. I'm not even sure who he works for now, whether it's Delta Force or the CIA or some agency I've never heard of, but he risked his life to come get you. Because of me. Because it was the right thing to do. That's who he is. So if you could not kill his guys while he tries to get you back home, that'd be great."

Dave licked his dry lips again. Peered up at the man standing in front of him. Who seemed supremely confident. Even amused by the situation. "Sure."

"Excellent. Put him back on."

Dave held the satphone out, and Bob took it. He said a few curt words, then hung up. "You know this guy?" Dog said, frowning, looking between the two of them.

Bob shook his head. "Never met him. But I know a guy who knows a guy. It's a small world."

"What is?"

Bob looked at Dog. "D'you do any research on him other than reading what was in the packet?"

"No, the packet was a full workup. Had everything we needed."

"Yeah, on who, and how, but no why. If you'd bothered to Google him at all you'd know the cartel wanted him because he killed a bunch of their guys. Embarrassed them."

"Like that Pima Jack guy?" Boot said.

Bob rolled his eyes, and jabbed a finger at Dave. "He is that Pima Jack guy."

"That wasn't in the workup," Boot said defensively.

"*Jack* was. Jack Burton."

"Oh. Shit. That's who we grabbed?" Boot looked at Dave, sitting in the dirt.

"And that's why you don't do any Googling," Dog told him. "Better to not know."

Cherry pulled up in the dead men's Toyota Tundra and stuck his head out. "Busted glass and a couple bullet holes, but it runs fine," he announced.

"We need to fucking move," Dog said. "Ten minutes ago."

Bob held out a hand to Dave. "Come with me if you want to live."

Dave frowned, and cocked his head at him. "Really? *Really?* How about we get me some pants. And a fucking gun."

Dog snorted. Like that was going to happen.

It was a risk, but one Timotéo was willing to take. The Range Rover was out of sight, parked behind the combination restaurant/grocery store, between two other white vehicles. On the far side of the building from the access road. He stood in the front of the store, ignoring the staff and the few customers, staring out the windows. There were a number of routes the Americans could take, but this was the quickest to get them out onto pavement. Onto Mexico 45, which headed almost straight north, to the border, and the United States. After what had just happened, they'd be in a hurry to get back across *la frontera*.

He had a signal there, and had already called Aponte. "Twenty, thirty minutes," the man told him. The closest reinforcements he could send.

"They'll be gone. If they're not gone already."

"Well, while you were busy being shot at, we've been tearing apart Santiago's apartment. We found an old laptop, maybe he forgot he had it. There were encrypted emails in it as well, but they'd been opened, and my man was able to access them. Do you remember the revenge killing in Arizona, perhaps two years ago? Los Zetas had just taken out one of our shipments, and we had an opportunity to get back at them. Killed two of their men."

"Of course I remember it. That really escalated things. And got Muñiz arrested."

"Well, it looks like Santiago orchestrated the whole thing. Framed Los Zetas."

"I told you when it happened there was something off about it. Los Zetas were denying everything. And they never do that, they always take credit. Even for things they don't do."

"Looks like you were right. I'm going to keep looking, see what else I can find. Figure out how else he fucked us. Who do you think he was? An American? That's what Ybarra thinks. But doing what?"

Timotéo had a lot of suspicions, but no way to know which of them, if any, were accurate. He hung up and called the head of the cartel. He'd already talked to the man once. Keeping secrets from the man was far more dangerous than admitting you made a mistake, but Ybarra hadn't put any of the blame on Timotéo. At least, not yet.

"I told you!" Ybarra shouted in his ear.

"Um, *señor*?"

"That this Pima Jack was more than he appeared. That there was something else going on. And now we see he is special forces."

Timotéo frowned. "I don't think that's what—"

Ybarra interrupted him with a rude noise. "What else could it be? Working with Nelson, *ese pinche pendejo. Coño traidor*." He spat. "Do you think he was a gringo, all along?"

He didn't wait for Timotéo to answer. "You and Aponte. You take care of this." Then he hung up.

Timotéo sighed and waited, impatiently. Ten minutes later his eyes darted over. A red Toyota pickup, the same truck that had been next to him during the fighting, and a silver Jeep Grand Cherokee, sped down the dirt road past the business. Both were full of men. The Americans and Santiago. They turned north and accelerated. They were out of sight in just a few seconds.

Timotéo called Aponte back as he strode out the front door and walked around to his Range Rover. "They are in two vehicles," he told the man, and described them. "You know where I am. If they continue straight north, they'll be in Juarez in four hours. Less, if they speed."

"I have men I trust in Juarez. I'm not sure who I have in-between. Maybe they won't go for the border, maybe they'll hide out. Maybe they'll turn off. Cross at Agua Prieta. Nogales."

Timotéo shook his head as he climbed behind the wheel. "That doubles their journey. Get who you can. Get them into position. We have American spies, or Special Forces, with a traitor. They must be punished. I will make some calls as well."

"You?" While he'd been with La Fuerza almost since its inception, Timotéo was still a young man, barely past twenty.

"I may have some contacts that you don't," Timotéo told the older man, with a wicked smile.

"Holy shit. Holy shit," Marty said, shaking. The shock of the gunfight was hitting him all over again as he sat in the back of the Cherokee. Dog was driving, Boot in the front passenger seat. "How did you guys…?"

"What?" Dog asked.

"There were all these guys. And then they were all… dead."

Boot rolled his eyes. "That's the difference between amateurs and professionals. Between guys who know what the fuck they're doing, and assholes with guns. Between the four of us we've got, what, close to eighty years' experience doing this shit, and twenty combat deployments?"

"Plus a whole lot of missions like this, that never officially happened, and don't count as combat," Dog pointed out.

"I'm Marty," he told them.

"I don't give a fuck," Boot said.

Dog glanced at him, then said, "We're not here. We're deniable assets." He was a car length behind the Toyota, fighting the urge to speed as they headed north. They didn't need to get pulled over.

"What?"

"Which means we've got no support structure. No emergency extraction plan in place. How about you get back on your satphone and call your guardian angel."

"For what?"

Dog and Boot traded a look. "Helicopter," Dog said. "A helicopter would be good. Any kind of extraction. Plane. Hot air balloon. Zeppelin. The Red Baron's fucking biplane."

"Funicular," Boot said with a smile.

"What the fuck is that?" Dog asked.

"Cable car that goes up and down a mountain."

Dog rolled his eyes and looked back at Marty. "Otherwise we've got to drive all the way to the border, and across it. After pissing off the biggest bullies in the neighborhood. Who have military-grade weapons."

"Oh, right, yeah." Marty dialed the number.

Clark answered on the second ring. "What the hell is going on down there? Was that gunfire?"

"Yeah. Cartel tried to take me out at the prisoner exchange. Timotéo Sandoval, with a bunch of *Las Fuerzan*. I don't know what did it, how they found out, but I'm done down here."

"Shit."

"I'm driving north with the special forces team. They're hoping you can send a helicopter or something, to pick us up. So we don't have to drive the whole way. Sandoval got away, and is probably sending guys after us."

"Something big enough for six guys," Dog said from the front seat.

"You hear that?" Marty asked his handler.

"Yeah. Where are you now? How far are you from the border?"

Marty repeated the question. Dog told him, "Half an hour north of Chihuahua, so at least three hours from the border."

"Right," Clark told him. "I'll get back to you."

"Hola, dead man."

Timotéo bit back the retort on his lips. Now was not, so much, the time for ego or pride. Not when he needed something. And, as it turned out, when the man he was talking to on the phone had been right all along.

"I owe you an apology," Timotéo said.

That momentarily struck Ruben Flores silent, as

Timotéo thought it might. As Timotéo's opposite number with Los Zetas the two men were officially mortal enemies, but the men had known of each other before joining their respective cartels, and viewed their jobs with a more impartial, business-oriented eye than many of the cartel soldiers. So they occasionally traded intelligence, and engaged in back-channel communication, if the result was mutually beneficial. Although that relationship had definitely grown more than rocky as La Fuerza had decided to pick a fight with Los Zetas for money, power, and territory.

Flores' silence continued. Timotéo cleared his throat. "You claimed you were not involved in that incident which led to the thing in Arizona."

"The 'thing'," Flores said mockingly, "where you tortured and killed two of our men for something they didn't do?"

"Yes, that," Timotéo said with a sigh. "It turns out one of our men lied about that. Framed Los Zetas."

Flores digested that information. "And why are you telling me this now?"

He was taking a risk, but Timotéo thought it could work to his advantage. To La Fuerza's advantage. "The man was working for the Americans. An informer, or maybe some sort of spy. An undercover agent."

"Again, I ask, why are you telling me now? What do you want?"

"This man, who betrayed us, and through his betrayal caused your men to die, is now racing toward *la frontera* with a group of Americans, trying to escape. I don't know who they are, CIA, or probably military Delta Force or Navy SEALs."

Flores barked out a laugh. "La Fuerza just cannot do anything right, can it?"

Timotéo muscled down his pride. "I am not telling you this just so you can laugh."

Flores laughed again, just to rub it in. Then he got serious. "So you want *us* to kill them? And then what? Become America's number one most wanted?"

Timotéo had thought very carefully about the situation. "If they were supposed to be here, they would be flying home on one of those Black Hawk helicopters. Not driving a stolen pickup. Whoever they are, whatever they're doing, they're keeping it secret from the American people too. And the American people do not want to hear about American soldiers being killed anywhere, but especially not in Mexico. If they got captured, killed, it would be an embarrassment for them. They would keep it secret, and deny everything. But everyone in Mexico would know. Every cartel would know. It would be a huge victory."

Flores didn't say anything for a while. "Thinking of changing teams?" he finally asked.

"Everyone wants to be on the winning side," Timotéo said truthfully.

Flores pondered the situation for a few long seconds. Eventually he said, "Give me what information you have."

Dave was in the back seat. He moved over behind the passenger, and stared at Bob. Glared at Bob. Bob ignored him as long as he could, then glanced back at him. "Are we going to have a talk?" Dave demanded. The best he could say about his situation was that he was no longer hooded and in his underwear—but the clothes they'd found for him they'd pulled off a dead man. There was a little blood on the collar of the shirt, but what bothered him more was the stink. The clothes smelled like the man hadn't bathed in a week.

"Maybe later," Bob told him. He flicked his eyes at Cherry, who didn't catch the signal. Dave understood the man didn't want to talk in front of his companion, but it still pissed him off. Now that he wasn't hogtied, hooded, and waiting for death, he was a little less accepting of his situation. He looked back and forth between the two men, huffed a sigh, then sat back.

"So we're in Mexico? How far from the border?"

"Three, four hours."

"If we go straight there," Boot said, glancing at Bob.

"What do you mean?" Dave asked.

"They'll likely be looking for us," Bob admitted. "We've got a safehouse in Juarez, but I don't know if hanging there for a few days will be any safer than us just making a run for the border, crossing before the cartel can get shit set up. They can set up on the border crossings and wait forever, if they want. There is a right choice, but there's no way to know what it is."

"We can cross anywhere we want," Cherry told him. "We could drive to fucking Tijuana if we wanted."

"Yeah, but that's more time. You know how many eyes they've got in this country. I think the safest bet is to cross as fast as possible."

"I guess we'll find out."

Dave waited a while, then leaned forward. He looked back and forth between the two men. "Not one?" he said. "Not one apology for kidnapping me?"

"I had a job to do," Cherry said. "Nothing personal." He shrugged.

Frowning, Dave looked at Bob. Bob didn't even glance

his way. "Assholes," Dave told them, his hands clenching. The urge to start punching had him white-knuckled.

"And this is why you're not getting a gun," Cherry told him.

His secretary announced the man, but still Winston Elliott was surprised to see Joe Clark in his office. "I thought you were doing fieldwork."

"Yesterday, and tomorrow, but today I was local. And it's a good thing. We need to talk. Not here."

"You know, this office is in as secure a building as you're likely to find," Elliott pointed out. "I make sure my office is swept once a month."

Clark shrugged. "I'm protecting you as much as I am me."

Elliott sighed. "Fine." He followed the intelligence operative to the SCIF. Then the two men sat down.

"Weathervane is blown," Clark told him, without preamble. He paused a few seconds, waiting for the Director of the DIA to remember who Weathervane was.

"You're sure?"

Clark nodded. "Totally. Delivery team got into a full-blown firefight with cartel troops at the handoff. His cartel. His people."

"Shit." Elliott thought for a while. "How much time have we spent on this?"

"Years. Two, over two years to get him here. There. So close. And now this." Clark shook his head. "We haven't spent much money or resources, but having a guy that high up was going to be so much more valuable than simple signal intercepts. He was going to be able to influence cartel strategy. Anyway. He's on the move right now, calling for an extraction."

Elliott was chewing on his lip as he thought. "The whole point of Operation Tentpole was to pick a weak cartel and prop them up, get them to start fights. Keep them focused on each other, so they kept their shit south of the border. And he ended up in La Fuerza, which was small and struggling. Now not so small, but still struggling. Worse than ever, if I hear it right."

"You do."

"Hmm. Okay, so let's big picture it. Weathervane is blown. He's no longer a functioning asset. What happens if we extract him?"

Clark made a face. "If they know we got him out of the country, that's a failure on their part. Another failure. If they never see him again, can never confirm he got out, they'll still assume. And they'll look weaker than ever, because word is going to get out. Word always gets out."

Elliott nodded. "Which will compound the problem. Right? Weathervane is out, done, but maybe we can salvage Tentpole. The mission objective is still the mission objective. If La Fuerza is going to survive, and keep causing problems, they need to get a win here. Maybe we can find an angle. Get something out of this years-long attempt to strengthen them."

"Don't extract him? Let it play out?" Elliott gave him a thoughtful shrug. Clark frowned. He'd been Martin Cabrera's handler the entire time he was undercover with La Fuerza. He hated to throw away an asset, even an arguably ineffective one like Cabrera. "Even if we do that, there's no guarantee La Fuerza will have any luck. Our teams are pretty damn good, everybody's got high-level background and years of combat experience. And Mexico isn't a hostile state, not like Syria or Somalia."

"How many operators are down there?"

"Three. Half a team, since it was just a snatch and grab. Plus Weathervane."

"Who has no field combat experience, if I remember correctly. Let it play out," the director told Clark. "If he makes it home, good for him. If he doesn't make it home, good for the mission objective. La Fuerza finally looks like it grew a pair and did something right."

"Okay," Clark said slowly, still thinking. "Or," he said slowly, "instead of leaving things completely up to chance, we could give the situation a nudge."

"What did you have in mind?"

"I've got several contacts with the federales. Half of whom are bent, and working for the cartels. Bent or not, they'd all be interested to hear about international fugitives in their country. Perhaps arms smugglers, considering they will almost definitely be armed. Weathervane's got a satphone. We can track him in real time using that. Forward that information."

"That doesn't help move the mission forward, if it's the federales who take him out. Unless I'm missing something?"

Clark shrugged. "Just trying to look at it from every angle. Weathervane surviving, and making it out of the country, back home, doesn't advance our mission, our agenda at all. But his death in Mexico might be leverageable. Depending."

Elliott thought about the situation for a long minute. Then nodded. "Do it," he said.

Chapter Thirty

"It's been an hour," Dog said. "Call your guy." He looked at Marty in the rearview mirror.

Marty nodded, and placed a call on the satphone. He was worried, but it only rang twice before Clark answered. "Joe. Where are we on that helicopter? Or whatever."

"It doesn't look like it's going to happen," Clark told him. "Sorry."

"I don't have my passport. None of these guys have ID, and we can't just drive through one of the checkpoints without them." He looked at Dog for confirmation, and the man shook his head.

"I'm sure you can figure something out. Those guys are pros, and that border's not exactly tough to cross, women and children are doing it every day. Call me once you're across." And he hung up.

Marty frowned at the phone in his hand, then at Dog. Dog sighed, and pulled out the burner he had. Called the number for the fresh burner Pike'd brought with him across the border, while staring out the windshield at the Toyota in front of them. "Okay," he said, "do you want the good news or the bad news?"

In the Toyota, Bob listened silently as the information was delivered. "Getting across the border isn't an issue," he told Dog. "There's plenty of ways across. It's getting to it. Cartels run the city, and if our boy's friends have contacts there, we could be on their radar."

Dog turned on the phone's speaker. "Who runs Juarez?" Dog asked Marty. "What cartel?"

"Juarez Cartel, although we've been pushing into their territory. As have Los Zetas. There's been a lot of fighting in the city."

"So three cartels?" Boot said. "Plus increased military and police presence." He worked his neck. "This should be fun." He looked at Bob. "Drive casual."

Bob snorted. "They don't know where we are. They shouldn't know what we're driving. If we can make it into Juarez, we're golden. Over a million people there, we can disappear in the noise." He checked the clock on the dash. "Two hours, maybe less. Keep your eyes open."

Half an hour south of Ciudad Juarez, Mexico 45, the Chihuahua-Miguel Ahumada Highway, rolled through a barren landscape. The land to either side of the highway was nearly flat, empty grass-filled sandy fields that ran away to isolated brown peaks in the distance, wavering in the mirage. The road was in surprisingly good condition, two lanes in each direction separated by a grassy median.

They passed an Oxxo gas station on the south-bound side, the building painted in bright red and blood-orange colors. There were a few semis parked beside the building, and half a dozen cars in the parking lot. As they passed, two cars pulled out of the lot and headed northbound several hundred yards behind them.

The Toyota and the Jeep were in the right lane, and not going especially fast. The cars behind them kept their distance. Bob pulled out his phone and called Dog in the Jeep behind them. "You spot those vehicles pull out?"

"Yeah," Dog said. "Probably nothing to worry about. Just paranoia. Coincidence. So…you want to speed up or slow down to find out for sure?"

"Um…." Bob said, thinking, then he saw the sign on the side of the road. "Hey, look at that, a scenic pulloff, to look at the…" He squinted at the sign. "Parador Dunas de Salamayuca."

Dog looked left and right. "They are pretty dunes." Boot snorted.

The scenic turnoff was on the far side of the highway. Bob slowed down, pulled onto the gravel crossover, then across the southbound lanes into the gravel parking lot, which was empty. Dog drove the Cherokee to the far end of the lot. Everyone in the two vehicles watched the cars—an old BMW and a newer Chevy—seemingly slow down a bit, but then keep going, disappearing over a rise.

There was a covered bench in the center of the parking area, sturdily built out of aluminum. It made Bob wonder if this was a bus stop, or the local authorities had thought some shade might be a good idea for any visiting tourists. The low dunes stretching away on either side of the highway were pale, the sand nearly white.

Dog caught Boot's eye and nodded at the bench. Boot hopped out of the Jeep and sauntered over to the bench. He stood behind one of the thick upright supports, in the shade, M4 held casually down along his leg. And they waited.

Cherry noticed Bob was bobbing his head, just a little bit, and tapping his thumb on the steering wheel as he stared out at the highway, waiting to see if the vehicles would return. Cars and the occasional commercial truck passed regularly, heading in both directions. "What's playing on the radio?" Cherry asked.

"Stones," Bob said, without looking at him. "*Gimme Shelter*."

"Seriously?" Cherry sat up in his seat a little bit.

"Yeah. Why?"

"Your subconscious isn't exactly subtle." Bob just shrugged, never taking his eyes from the road. Cherry snorted. "Well, let me know if *When the Levee Breaks* or the *Free Bird* guitar solo comes on."

Dave had no idea what they were talking about, but he was sweating, staring out the windshield, waiting to see if carloads of cartel soldiers were going to come pouring into the scenic turnout. "Seriously, do you not have a spare gun?" he asked again. He'd looked through the bag in the back seat—there was gear, and loaded AR magazines, but no guns. Neither of the men in the front seat answered him. "Assholes." He'd already asked if he could call Lori, to let her know he was alive, and okay. He'd been told to wait until they made it across the border. Which—he grudgingly admitted—made sense.

After five minutes it was clear the two cars weren't coming back. Bob rolled down his window and waved at Dog. Dog whistled, and Boot jogged back to the Jeep. They drove out of the lot with a fantail of sand and headed north once again, a little bit faster. Half a mile up the highway bent northeast to avoid a small rocky mountain straight ahead, and on the right was a several hundred meter-tall radio/cell phone tower painted red and white. Around the base of the big tower was a makeshift parking lot for service vehicles, surrounded by scraggly bushes. Three car lengths behind the Toyota, Dog glanced over as they drove by, and hit redial on his phone.

"Tell me you saw that," he said to Bob.

"Oh yeah," Bob replied, looking in his passenger side mirror. At which point the three vehicles parked beneath the radio tower—the BMW, the Chevy, and a KIA SUV, pulled out behind them. "Contact rear, three vehicles. The question is…what are we going to do about it?"

"Looks like they're going to make that decision for us," Dog said, as the three vehicles behind them accelerated, and started quickly closing the gap. Boot swore and hit the button to roll down his window.

"Move!" Cherry shouted at Dave as he launched himself into the back seat. He grabbed the sliding window and opened it, then shoved the muzzle of his M4 through.

The three pursuing vehicles were one hundred yards back. Then fifty. "What's the ROE?" Cherry shouted. Bob opened his mouth, but before he could say anything the decision was made for them. A man leaned out from the passenger side window of the BMW, which was in the lead. There was something in his hand. To other eyes its identity might have been unclear, but they easily saw it was a machine pistol.

The cartel soldier with the machine pistol let loose a burst, but the BMW was still forty yards away and none of the bullets found their mark. A man stuck his upper body out of the KIA SUV and began firing bursts from an AK-47.

There were many different schools of thought—strategies and techniques—when it came to fighting from moving vehicles, but they were all, to a point, situationally dependent. The truth was it was hard as hell for anyone to hit anything from inside a vehicle that was wildly veering back and forth. When dealing with bad guys who were more likely to hit what they were aiming at through luck, rather than skill, it made more sense to provide a stable platform for your team, so they could quickly take care of business.

Bob abruptly swung over into the left lane, so Cherry would have a clear field of fire past the Jeep, and kept the Toyota steady. Cherry, and Boot from the Jeep, began firing, rapid, aimed, supported shots at the pursuing vehicles thirty yards distant and closing. The guy dropped the machine pistol, and Cherry began firing at the driver's side of the BMW's windshield. The BMW veered to the side and sailed off the road in cloud of dust. The cartel soldier with the AK-47 emptied it without hitting anything and ducked back inside the KIA to reload. Cherry dumped half a magazine into the windshield of the wildly swerving KIA, and whether the driver was hit or just panicked, the end result was the same—he jerked the steering wheel, and suddenly the SUV was rolling, bouncing across the gravel shoulder and into the dunes. Together, Cherry and Boot concentrated their fire on the remaining vehicle. The driver of the Chevy sedan stomped on the brakes, but was too slow— they saw the Chevy begin weaving, then it drifted toward the median, the windshield cratered and smoke seeping from under the hood.

Bob watched the rearview mirror for thirty seconds as he drove steady in the left lane, Cherry reloading in the back seat, then moved the Toyota back into the right lane.

"There's no way those fuckers didn't call someone," Cherry said. "There's going to be more assholes."

"And apparently they know what we're driving," Dave said from the back seat. Bob threw him a dirty look, but the man was right.

"Carjack some fresh rides?" Cherry said.

"Lot of shit that can go wrong with that," Bob said. "And we're almost there." He frowned, weighing their options, then stomped the accelerator. The truck surged forward. The needle crept up toward 100 MPH, and stayed there. Dog kept the Cherokee right on their tail.

Fifteen minutes later they reached the south end of Ciudad Juarez and had to slow down to the speed limit. Businesses lined both sides of Mexico 45, and the traffic was growing heavier. Cherry leaned forward and squinted. There were flashing lights in the street maybe half a mile ahead, some sort of police activity. "What's going on there?" he asked.

"Doesn't matter," Bob said. He turned into the entrance drive and rolled up to the familiar keypad. Two minutes after that both vehicles were parked in front of the small commercial building housing the cache he'd visited less than twelve hours earlier.

"Any of you ever use this? No?" They followed him in. Bob yanked the mattress out of the way, flipped up the trapdoor, and headed down the stairs. At the bottom he flicked on the lights. "There's water, but no food. Grab whatever gear you need," he told the team, as they headed for the trunks. "Hopefully we're done with the excitement and whatever you grab we're just going to dump before we cross over, but…" He shrugged. He moved to the far wall where there were some cubbies. He pulled out a stack of maps and went through them on the floor. He found the page he was looking for.

"In case we get separated," he said, jerking his head. He pulled out his Surefire, as the basement was dim, and used it to light up the map. He put a finger on the map of Ciudad Juarez. "This is our exfil point. It's eight, maybe ten miles from here." They came close and studied the map over his shoulder, then moved to the trunks, opened them, and started grabbing what they thought they might need.

"Ten minutes," Bob told them, checking his watch. Then he heard a ringing. He looked around, then pulled the satphone out of a pouch on his vest. He looked at the number on the display. "Oh, this can't be good," he said, moving closer to the stairs for a better signal. He answered the call. "Hey, Steve, what's up?"

"This number?" the voice on the other end of the line said, and read off a ten-digit phone number. "Is this you?"

"Hold on." Bob put the device on speaker. "Repeat that." Steve did.

Marty blinked. "That's my phone number," he said from across the room.

"Yeah, well your phone number is fucked," Steve announced. "You wanted me to keep an eye on any increased communications traffic. And right now I've got people being fed the real-time GPS location of that satphone. They're being vectored toward it as we speak." His voice echoed hollowly around the small basement. Everyone stopped what they were doing and listened.

"What people?" Bob said, his voice flat.

"Two units of *Policia Federal*, the Mexican federales, to start with," the mysterious Steve said. "They've been told the coordinates track to the location of dangerous, heavily-armed foreign terrorists. But there's so much phone and radio traffic I can't even keep track of it all. Your location information has also gone out to several cell phones affiliated with at least one, maybe two different Mexican drug cartels. Who also, like the federales, seem to be on the move. To you."

"How much time do we have?" Bob asked him.

"A minute, maybe two," Steve said.

Boot looked at Bob. "Those flashing lights we saw? For us?" Bob shrugged. There was no way to know. Boot told him, "Half the federales are corrupt as fuck."

Dog was frowning. "I thought we were off book," he said, nodding at the phone in Bob's hand with some confusion.

"We are," Bob said. "He's my guardian angel. Time to go!" he shouted. "Everybody grab your shit, we're out the door in ten seconds. Talk to you on the other side," he said into the phone in his hand, and disconnected the call.

"Who the fuck was that guy? Dog asked, gesturing at Bob's satphone.

"One of my OG teammates from back in the day," Bob said, as everyone started clambering up the nearly vertical stairs. "Go, you fatasses, get up there. We've got assholes inbound, probably the only reason they're not on us already is the gate at the entrance." He started up after Dog.

Dave looked at the line of guys going up the stairs, then back at the trunks which they'd left open. And made a decision. He darted to the trunks, his eyes taking in the contents. Then he grabbed a tactical vest and threw it over his head. He grabbed two handfuls of loaded AR-15 magazines and tossed them into one of the backpacks sitting beside the trunk, and then snagged the last Colt Commando in the trunk before running to the stairs.

Outside, everyone was climbing into the vehicles. Marty

took his satphone and threw it toward the distant warehouse, shouting obscenities, too busy now to wonder exactly who'd betrayed him.

"Anybody not in uniform comes at us, you dump 'em," Bob announced loudly. "In uniform...fuck. Just...try not to shoot first. Maybe we can still get out of this quietly."

If anyone in their rush to get into the vehicles noticed he'd grabbed a rifle they didn't say anything as Dave climbed into the back seat. But once he was in, Cherry turned around and glared at him. "Secure your shit, I don't want to get shot in the back," he growled as Bob threw the truck into reverse. But he didn't try to take the gun away.

The two vehicles rocketed away from the building. Bob reached the first intersection and turned left, heading away from the only entrance to the industrial complex. "Where the fuck are we going?" Cherry said.

"Hold on," Bob told him, as the engine roared. In the back seat, Dave fastened the vest around his chest, then started stuffing the pouches with magazines. When they were full he slammed a magazine home into his rifle and chambered a round. He felt better with a loaded gun in his hands. Much better. The Colt functioned exactly the same as his rifle, except it had a shorter barrel, and was presumably full auto. He turned the rifle in his hands and looked at the side of the receiver. There was a third pin, right above the selector. Yep, full-auto, if he needed it.

The street ended. The Toyota hopped the curb and bounced across an uneven, undeveloped lot straight toward the eight-foot cinderblock wall bordering the property. Bob skidded the truck to a stop and swung it around. "Hold on," he said warningly, then threw it into reverse.

The rear tailgate hit the wall square on, in-between two concrete supports, at twenty miles an hour. Everyone inside the truck was thrown around, and the tailgate and rear of the bed crumpled. They looked through the rear window. The wall appeared undamaged for several long seconds, then the entire section of wall toppled over in one piece.

The tires spun dirt up as Bob drove in a tight circle and straight out through the opening he'd made, the Cherokee right behind him. They found themselves on a street paralleling the wall, running north and south. At the moment it was empty of traffic. Bob turned north and punched it.

Chapter Thirty-One

The two vehicles roared up the street, soon overtaking traffic. When he couldn't get around the cars to the right Bob raced past them in the center left turn lane, Dog on his tail in the Cherokee. Then traffic got too thick to weave through, and a median appeared between the north- and southbound lanes. "Fuck!" Bob cursed. He glanced in his rearview mirror. "See anything?"

"Not yet," Dave said, looking out the rear window.

The traffic grew thicker, moving along at a sedate speed, and businesses appeared to either side—they were entering a thriving commercial area. A mile after crashing out onto the roadway they drove between a Walmart on one side and a Soriana grocery store on the other. There were hundreds of vehicles in the lots, buses, and taxis, and moving cars everywhere. "Keep your head on a swivel," Bob warned them. "Windows going down, guns coming up, whatever."

They found themselves in a knot of traffic, and it slowed as it neared the next intersection with Bulevar Zaragoza. Bob found himself behind a red Nissan stopped at the red light, and he looked everywhere. There was a Wendy's and a Little Caesar's in the strip mall on the far side of the crossstreet. To the right the four divided lanes of Zaragoza angled slightly uphill before curving out of sight. To the left, the west, Zaragoza rolled down a gentle slope, and half the city seemed laid out before them, stretching out for miles to a row of rocky brown peaks in the distance. And a quarter mile away down the road, two dark blue pickups bounced crazily onto the street, then accelerated toward them. It took Bob only half a second to identify the markings along the sides of the trucks—POLICIA FEDERAL.

"Shit!" Cherry said. He'd spotted them as well.

Bob's eyes flicked to the traffic light, but it was still red. He stomped on the gas, and the Tundra's bumper crashed into the rear of the small Nissan, shoving it out of the way. Horns blared as the cross-traffic veered around the surging Toyota or slammed on their brakes. Bob kept the accelerator pegged as the truck juked around the other cars like a pinball in play, Dog right on his ass.

The two vehicles raced north once again, the street, for the moment, clear of other vehicles. Just past the strip mall Bob turned onto a side street, the truck's tires howling. They shot down a narrow street, low one-story houses to either side, most of their windows and doors barricaded with wrought iron or barbed wire, or both.

"Do you think they saw us?" Dave asked, trying to peer past the Cherokee.

The first intersection was a quarter mile ahead, and they'd almost reached it when the police pickups appeared behind them. They skidded to a stop, backed up, and then turned down the sidestreet in pursuit.

Bob took the turn in a power slide, the Toyota spraying dirt and gravel as he headed north on a narrow avenue that looked more like an alley than an actual street. They got airborne as they flew over a cross street, sparks flying. Three blocks up the street was blocked by derelict vehicles. Bob took a hard right, the Toyota nearly going up on two wheels.

They seemed to be deep in a neighborhood, and Bob kept taking turns, left and right, always heading northeast. Then they came to a major street heading almost straight north—Mexico 45 once again. Bob sent the Toyota through a break in traffic, across the southbound lanes, the truck bouncing over the low gravel median, and into the northbound lanes, where passing traffic slammed on their brakes and honked at him. Dog was just a few seconds behind them in the Cherokee.

"I think we're clear," Cherry said, looking around wildly.

"Yeah?" Bob said, and pointed out the windshield. Off in the distance they could see a helicopter, low over the city, banking toward them.

"You think that's for us?"

Bob squinted. It was a dark blue helicopter. A Eurocopter EC 120B Colibri, he was pretty sure, and while it was too far away for him to read the writing on the side, it sure looked like the right size and length to be "POLICIA FEDERAL". Better that than one of the many Black Hawks the *federales* had, but still....

There were cars everywhere, traffic in front and behind, plus the helicopter. "Damn, I think I see the *federale* pickups way back there," Cherry said, leaning out the open window. He pulled back inside. Dave was sweating from the stress. He rolled down his window the rest of the way as the Toyota swerved around traffic, Bob honking and lightly tapping a few bumpers. A gray Ford Escape pulled out in front of them from a sidestreet, and Bob had to swerve wildly to avoid a collision with the little SUV. The back window on the driver's side started rolling down, right in front of Dave, and he looked over to see a pair of eyes looking at him. And in the man's hands, a submachinegun.

Dave swore soundlessly, shoved the muzzle of his Colt Commando out the window, and opened up on full-auto from six feet away. The noise was incredible. Fire flew from his muzzle, and ejecting cases bounced around the cab. His burst blew through the window still going down, into the gunman in the back seat—and the man beside him, armed with an AK-47. The driver of the Escape weaved wildly. Dave fired three bursts at him before connecting with the man's head, and the Escape smashed weakly into the side of their truck before angling off and colliding at full speed with a parked car, the three men inside dead.

Before Bob or Cherry had a chance to say a word more gunfire erupted, and they could hear bullets whipping past. They ducked instinctively. Boot opened up from the Cherokee at a minivan on their tail—a man was hanging out the open sliding door, firing a big Galil. Boot hit him and the man fell out of the minivan and was run over by another vehicle racing after them.

"No, a red Toyota pickup, and a silver Jeep Cherokee!" Timotéo shouted into his phone. "Travelling together, heading toward *la frontera! ¡Lleno de Americanos!*"

"Where are they?"

Timotéo rolled his eyes. "I don't know. You're supposed to be looking for them, *idiota!* They were heading north up 45."

"Oh, *si*. We are in the city now, we will find them and kill them."

Timotéo stabbed the disconnect button on his phone angrily. "Fah!" He knew La Fuerza already had half a dozen teams in the city looking for the Americans, with as many more just a few minutes away. He hoped that the ones he wasn't hearing from understood the assignment, and were busy doing their jobs. In addition to—maybe—Los Zetas. He was in his Range Rover in the parking lot of a small restaurant, three miles from the border in the center of Ciudad Juarez. He'd been five minutes behind the Americans travelling north on 45, and rolled up on the carloads of men they'd killed within a minute or two of it happening. He assumed they'd continued north into the city, and maybe had already made it to and across the border. But none of the men in the city, monitoring the border crossings, had spotted their vehicles. Maybe the Americans had stopped somewhere.

His phone rang again. He checked the display, and saw it was Aponte. "*¿Que?*"

"Everyone we have in the area is already in the city, looking for them, or on their way as fast as possible. At least thirty men. Most of them have radios. Cheap Chinese ones, but they should be good enough inside the city."

"Good. They should be positioned on the main highways heading to the border crossings."

"*Si, eso se ha hecho*. We have a drone up, near *la frontera*. And one of the teams is monitoring the police radio channels. Who did you call?"

"What?"

"Did you call *La Policia Federal?*"

"No," Timotéo said, mystified by the question.

"*Los federales* are after them as well," Aponte told him.

"They are?" Timotéo said in surprise.

"*Si*. American terrorists, they are calling them. Dangerous. That was not you?"

"No." He had contacts with the *federales*, but hadn't called them as he assumed they would not get involved if the operation involved Americans.

"Interesting. They have many units looking for the gringos."

"The corrupt ones, in our pocket?"

"No. Well, some. This order came down from their headquarters. I am listening to them, one of my men in Juarez has a phone next to the radio." Timotéo realized he could hear it in the background. "Hold on." The noise increased, radio calls going back and forth, but he couldn't make out the words. Aponte came back on. "It sounds like they are chasing them."

"The Americans? Where?"

"Somewhere in the city. I do not know the streets."

Timotéo threw up in hands in frustration. But just then a blue police helicopter thundered overhead, low in the sky, curving to the east. He only paused a second before he threw his idling SUV into gear and raced after it.

His phone rang again as he slalomed around slower-moving cars. He hit the speaker button without looking at the display. "*¿Si?*"

"You must have some very interesting friends," Ruben Flores said. The Los Zetas lieutenant sounded amused. And maybe something else.

"I am an interesting man," Timotéo said. "But what do you mean?" He didn't have time for games.

"Several of my men got phone calls from a strange number. And the man gave them GPS coordinates of your

Americans. Who would have GPS coordinates of an American special forces team?"

"Maybe one day we can share secrets," Timotéo said. "Did your men kill them?"

"They escaped the compound before we could move in, but it sounds like we've spotted them. On 45, heading toward *la frontera*. It should only be another few minutes."

Timotéo glanced out his windshield at the helicopter in the distance, banking hard. Was Mexico 45 in that direction? He wasn't sure, but probably. "You may have some competition from *los federales*."

Flores snorted. "*Los federales no son competencia*," he said, and disconnected the call.

Timotéo could barely focus on driving, his mind was racing so. *La Policia Federal* was being mobilized against the Americans? Someone was feeding real-time GPS coordinates of the Americans to Los Zetas?

What the hell was going on?

"Reloading!" Cherry called out, ducking in the back seat next to Dave. A bullet shattered what was left of the back window and spat shards all over both of them. Dave saw a low-slung purple Honda coupe racing up, a pistol sticking out a window. He aimed at the car, but before he could fire Boot lit the man up from the Cherokee, killing both the passenger and driver, and the Honda veered into oncoming traffic. There was a huge crunch.

Bob slammed on the brakes and swerved around a slow-moving old VW van. Dog passed them in the Cherokee, slipping through a momentary gap in traffic. A burgundy Mitsubishi came zipping up behind them, the engine revving. There was a loud boom and a thunk as something hit the back of the truck. Dave spotted the muzzle of a shotgun above the passenger side mirror of the car. He fired at the wildly swerving car, even as he bounced around from Bob juking left and right. It took him half a dozen shots before he connected, then he fired three rounds through the windshield at the driver. Then his Commando was empty.

"Empty! Reloading," he said, ducking down low. Cherry was already up, covering out the back, and saw the Mitsubishi drifting aimlessly across the traffic lanes, bouncing across the median, sending up dust.

Dave grabbed a fresh magazine from his vest. What was this, his third magazine already? And weren't they still miles from the border? That wasn't good. The floor by his feet was littered with spent cases. Then he remembered the backpack in the back seat with them, and looked around for it. He found it on the floor, and pulled loaded magazines out of it to refill his chest rig. Then he sat back up and looked around. They were following the Cherokee, forcing themselves through thin traffic. There didn't seem to be any immediate threat from cartel vehicles, but blue police pickups were closing on them quickly, less than a quarter mile away. And the helicopter, which had roared by overhead once at speed, was now circling around, moving slower.

"We need to get the fuck out of here," Cherry growled.

"That's what I'm trying to do," Bob said, as he slammed the Toyota's bumper against the corner of a small sedan. It bounced out of the way and he stomped the gas, chasing after the Cherokee.

Dave watched the police vehicles closing the distance. "Are we shooting at cops?" he asked.

"That's up to them," Bob said flatly. "Shit!" The traffic

in front of them cleared just in time for them to see why—the federales had a roadblock up, four trucks across the lanes, with armed men standing in the beds of the trucks. Dog took an immediate right onto a sidestreet, and Bob followed in the Toyota.

"Where does this go?" Cherry said, looking out the windshield.

"I don't know, but we're still heading in the right direction."

The police helicopter returned, and hovered almost directly above their two vehicles as they sped along. Bob swore, glancing up at the aircraft. You couldn't outrun a helicopter. But that didn't mean they were without options.

Dog locked his brakes up ahead of them, then took a sliding turn left onto another major street. Bob was a heartbeat behind him in the Toyota. There were no cars immediately around them at that second, and Dave looked out the back window—only to see half a dozen assorted vehicles packed with armed men racing toward them. Definitely not cops, but behind those cartel vehicles, federale pickups. Dave spun around and looked out the windshield. Right in front of them the federale roadblock vehicles raced out of an alley, bouncing wildly, and spread across the street, blocking it. Dog slammed on his brakes and jerked the steering wheel, the Jeep going airborne over the low median, but the low bush that didn't look like anything at all in fact concealed a water main which raked across the Jeep's undercarriage, gutting it like a fish. The Cherokee flipped over onto its passenger side and slid across the oncoming lanes. Bob stomped the brakes of the Toyota and it shimmied side-to-side before the back end broke loose. It spun around and slammed into the side of a federale pickup.

The Mexican Federal Police wore dark blue uniforms

and black body armor. Some of them wore black helmets and balaclavas. Dave stared at them, frozen, and the police officers, just a few feet away, stared back. Then the pursuing cartel soldiers screeched up and started firing, and all hell broke loose.

Bob ducked down below the dash and shoved the gas pedal, but a minivan stuffed with cartel men slammed into the rear of a small car and drove it into the Toyota's grille, and that pinned them in place. The Toyota's rear tires spun and smoked but it couldn't move. The federales opened up, shooting at everything, killing three of the cartel men before they could even clear the minivan. The surviving man retreated into the middle of the street, firing wildly, hiding behind another vehicle.

Every window of the Toyota exploded, raining glass down on Dave and Cherry in the back seat. Bullets thunked into the Toyota's bodywork from every direction.

"Truck's fucked!" Bob shouted. They needed to clear the kill zone. He risked a glance out his window—there were guys with guns everywhere, shooting, running in-between the cars filling the street. Another car screamed straight at them, windows pockmarked with bullet holes, the driver already dead behind the wheel—it hit the rear of an ancient Chevy at speed, went airborne, and came crashing down on its side just in front of their truck.

Bob twisted and looked the other direction, in time to see one of the federales standing in the bed of the pickup look down toward him, and take aim with his rifle. Bob bailed out of the truck, the officer's bullets punching through his door, and ducked down between the truck and the steaming car still rocking back and forth on its side. For the moment he was hidden from the federales manning the roadblock. He fired quick aimed shots around either side of the car, through gaps in the traffic, but didn't dare pop up to look around. He was pinned down. Cherry fired from the back seat, exposed, armed men everywhere, suppressive fire, working the trigger as fast as he could. It was a madhouse, fifty men with guns, more, in and around a sea of cars, everyone shooting and running, bullets flying in every direction, with dozens more federales racing up, seconds away.

Incoming fire blasted through the cab of the pickup, making Dave duck. Cherry, crouched on the seat beside him, firing madly, jerked, and then was falling back against Dave, half his head gone. Dave twisted out from under him, shaking the blood out of his eyes. The police in the bed of the pickup were right there, firing in every direction. One of them saw Dave, and dropped the muzzle of his rifle.

Time slowed down.

Dave was simply quicker. He brought his Commando up and fired a burst. As the man crumpled Dave fired at the other officers filling the bed of the police pickup, working the muzzle of his short rifle back and forth, emptying the magazine.

His door was jammed, and he couldn't get over Cherry to use his door, so he crawled through the missing back window into the bed of the Toyota as bullets whipped by. He laid in the bed of the truck and reloaded, then sat up. The cartel members were trying to rush forward in-between the cars. There were so many of them, with federales in front and behind, shooting at everything—Dave had been in fights before, but never anything like this, it was like a tornado in Times Square. Bob was right there in front of him, taking snap shots around either side of the crashed car, with no way to move from his spot without dying. Dave caught a glimpse of Dog on the far side of the street, ducked down between the upended Cherokee and a smoking Ford Mustang, firing his G3. He was covered in a lot of bright red blood.

Dave flipped his selector to semi-auto and fired at everyone he saw in the street. The noise of his singular rifle was lost in the sound of battle. Then he was empty again, and still there were guys everywhere, shooting at him, at the guys who'd both kidnapped and rescued him. If something didn't change, and soon, they'd be overwhelmed.

Dave dove from the bed of the Toyota to the bed of the federale pickup. He peeked over the far side. Past it the street was clear. He could take off running that way. Maybe make it to the border. The thought was there, in his head, but he shook it away as he lay on his back in the bed of the pickup, on the bodies of the men he'd killed, reloading his Colt. And as he lay on his back, looking up at the sky, he saw something.

"Who gave you this mission?" Timotéo demanded. He was standing beside his Range Rover in the parking lot of a tire store. He could hear the shooting just on the other side of the building, on the next street over—dozens of people shooting, so loud he could barely think. Like a war. It couldn't last for long, the Americans were surely done for. But he needed answers, and the sergeant with *La Policia Federal* had been in La Fuerza's pocket for a year.

The man sat behind the wheel of one of their pickups. He shrugged. "It came down from *El Comandante*. Strict orders. And he has not been bought, unless you consider him being in the pocket of the government, and the Americans, bought." It was clear he did. So did Timotéo, but they didn't have time to talk about the politics of the imperialists.

"And they gave you GPS coordinates? Any other information?"

"Just that they were heavily armed American terrorists, who should be shot on sight."

Timotéo frowned. That didn't make sense to him, and he didn't like things he couldn't understand. Just then a white pickup came racing up and stopped beside him in a cloud of dust. The sergeant's eyes went wide and he grabbed his rifle when he saw the truck was filled with armed cartel soldiers. They saw that and went for their guns.

"*¡Calmate!*" Timotéo shouted, stepping between the two trucks, holding up his hands. "We are on the same side."

The La Fuerza thug behind the wheel sneered at the cop. There was no love lost between the cartel members and the federales, even if they were on the take. To most men in the cartel the only good cop was a dead one. The man then looked at Timotéo. "We're here, where do you want us?"

"You can't hear that?" the federale sergeant said insultingly, jabbing a thumb toward the sound of the battle.

"*Pinche cerdo*," the cartel man spat at him. "*Escucharé el sonido de tu madre mientras me la follo por el culo.*"

"*¡Cierra el pico!*" Timoteo shouted at the thug. "The Americans are pinned down. Trapped. I think it will be over soon. You can go around the back of this building, and check, but—" his head snapped up at the new sound. "What is that?"

"Trouble," the federale sergeant said. He threw his truck into gear and took off toward the sounds of conflict. The cartel men stared after him, then looked at Timotéo.

"Well? Go after him!" Timotéo shouted. "Make yourselves useful!"

Bob fired at a man running between two parked cars, an MP5 in his hands, then he was empty again. He ducked back behind cover. He couldn't see the Cherokee from where he was crouched, and when he glanced back at the Toyota pickup it looked empty. There was so much ordnance flying over his head, smacking into the cab of the truck, he couldn't even step over to check inside the Toyota. Were both Cherry and Anderson dead? Shit. That left Dog and the crew in the Cherokee.

Bob got a fresh mag into his Commando, thumbed the bolt release, then watched a grenade—minus the pin and lever, always an important detail—roll across the pavement to him. He casually scooped it up and whipped it underhand as he moved from his position, taking three quick steps then ducking down behind a bumper. The grenade went off a second and a half later, still in the air, the shrapnel peppering several men hiding behind cars. They screamed.

Bob scooted along a Subaru, shot a cartel solder in the face as he peeked out, then hopped the man's falling body as he darted between two vehicles. A man came out of nowhere, in Bob's face, the Beretta M12 submachinegun in his hands coming up. Bob grabbed the man's wrists to control the Beretta's muzzle, spun him to the side, kicked his feet out from under him, and drove the man's head into the concrete with an elbow. He shot him in the back of the head to make sure he stayed down.

Bob edged out past a Ford Explorer and looked down between two rows of cars. Half a dozen cartel soldiers were visible before him, ducked down behind bumpers, jumping up to shoot crazily at the federales in front and back, having seemingly forgotten about Bob and his people. Bob gunned four of them down before they saw him, then the survivors dove for cover. Bob darted across the opening before they could return fire. When they did, they were shooting where he used to be, not where he was.

Bob was in the traffic lane next to the median. The Cherokee was just on the other side of it, half-hidden by a smoking flatbed truck. Even so, there was a lot of open ground in front of him. He looked around for inspiration. Or help. Then he saw Anderson, his face covered in blood, climb to his feet in the bed of a federale pickup, visible to God and the world, ignoring the bullets zipping all around him like he was immortal, or bulletproof. He grabbed the pistol grip of the M60 machinegun mounted on the metal frame behind the cab, settled the butt into his shoulder, pulled the trigger, and didn't let go.

The thundering sound of the heavy-caliber belt-fed machinegun rocked the street. Anderson swung the muzzle left and right, shooting anything and everything that moved, hardly getting off the trigger, a two-foot tongue of flame licking from the barrel. The bullets cracked above Bob's head. Anderson got the attention of every single person across the field of battle. Bob took the opportunity and ran across the median, bent double, to the Cherokee. Dog was there with a bad leg wound, Marty too, cowering. Behind him, the M60 continued its thunderous rain of destruction.

Boot was still inside the Cherokee, his foot trapped under a seat. Bob crawled inside and yanked and pulled and finally Boot's boot was free. They clambered out of the Jeep just as Anderson burned through the last of the 200-round belt.

"Let's go!" Bob said, and ran for the line of federale pickups on the north side of the blockade.

As soon as Dave started shooting, the big mounted belt-fed thumping back into this shoulder at 600 RPM, every eye turned in his direction. The cops hiding behind the adjacent pickup looked up and over at him, did a doubletake, then turned their guns on him. Dave twisted, firing over the hood of the pickup, raking the row of federales with a long burst, watching them fall like dominos. Then he turned back toward the street, the gun thundering, spitting out cases and flame and disintegrating links, the big bullets dropping running men, blowing out windshields, and punching through auto bodies to reach the men hiding behind them.

Everyone seemed to be shooting at him, and he could hear and feel the bullets whipping all around, teasing the air and spanging off the steel supports of the gun and thudding into the pickup's body, the very air around him filled with hot angry metal, but once again he wasn't afraid. He was too busy. He felt distant pains but he ignored the distractions, focusing only on the sights of the gun and the threats in front of him.

The federales on the far side of the blockade, a hundred yards away across a sea of violence, were confused—between his tactical vest and the fact he was on a belt-fed in the bed of a marked pickup, more than a few thought maybe he might be another federale, and instead only fired at the cartel men in the street.

Dave didn't see Bob—Bob was gone. Maybe he was dead. Maybe they were all dead. Maybe he was the only one left. "Come on!" he screamed in frustration. "Come on!" Dave poured fire down the lanes of traffic, putting long bursts into anyone left, right, and center, the belt of ammo whipping out of the metal box beside the gun like the teeth of a chainsaw, and then the smoking machinegun fell silent. He'd burned through an entire 200-round belt.

Dave left the smoking M60 and jumped down on the north side of the vehicle barricade. Then Bob and the remaining others were there, Dog limping badly. "We need a vehicle!" Marty shouted.

Dave was so happy to see them alive he froze for a second, then looked at the federale pickup they were crouched behind, surrounded by the bodies of officers he'd killed. Its windows were blown out, but other than that it seemed to be in okay shape. And it was running. "Why don't we take this?" he asked.

Bob blinked...and then they were all piling into the four-door pickup, a Ford F-150. Dave rolled over the side into the bed and lay there as Bob twisted the wheel and took off with a squeal of rubber, bouncing over bodies.

The gunfire and police presence had cleared most of the traffic from the area, and Bob pinned the pedal as he raced north. Dave lay on his back in the pickup bed, stretching out his arms and legs to keep from sliding back and forth as the truck danced from lane to lane, the tires howling and chittering as Bob took corners at speed.

The helicopter roared overhead, so close the rotor wash blew grit into their eyes. The noise was incredible. On his back in the bed, Dave watched the helicopter bank in a hard turn and then come after them. It was right behind them at first, then angled over. And the side door of the helicopter slid open.

"Guys!" Dave shouted from the bed.

"What?"

"Helicopter!"

"No shit," one of them shouted back.

"No, I mean—" Dave said, as the helicopter came up,

pacing them, the door open, and a federale was there, leaning out into the wind, a big rifle in his hands. And he fired at them, long bursts. The bullets raked the driver's side of the F-150. Someone inside the cab shouted in pain. Bob slammed on the brakes to change their speed and the helicopter soared by, then it slowed as well. The door gunner in the helicopter fired again and the truck lurched as a tire blew. Bob gunned the engine and the truck surged forward, but more slowly than before as it fought the flat tire.

Boot swore and pointed. "Federales up ahead!"

"I see them," Bob shouted. More blue trucks, filling the road, screaming into the intersection just ahead. He looked for a way out, and didn't see one.

The abrupt changes in speed bounced Dave around the bed of the truck. He threw out a hand for support and fought his way to his knees just as the helicopter slid sideways, closer to them, the door gunner reloading his G3, ready to finish them off. Dave raised his Commando, flipped the selector all the way forward, and dumped his entire magazine into the side of the helicopter barely fifty feet away, fighting the recoil. The door gunner fell back, cockpit glass shattered, and the pilot jerked wildly.

The helicopter rose up, banking hard, the rotors clawing at the air, a vertical blurred line for just a moment, the bird sideways, hanging motionless right above them. The illusion only lasted a second, then the aircraft turned over, went nose down, and gained speed as it plowed into a gas station at the intersection ahead. The big initial explosion was followed half a second later by a huge fireball that spread across the intersection, a bright billowing curtain of death, engulfing the federale pickups. A dozen men in uniform were suddenly human torches, falling out of pickup beds, dropping their guns, running blindly with their hair on fire, screaming. The orange-red flames shot one hundred feet in the air, and then a second set of pumps exploded. Burning fuel and red-hot shrapnel sprayed in every direction.

Bob ducked down behind the wheel and kept the accelerator pinned. Their stolen pickup soared blindly through a wall of orange flame and black smoke, smashed into the rear of a burning truck and knocked it out of the way. Then they were through the blockade and racing north once again, flat tire screeching louder as the rubber was worn down to the rim. Dave reached a hand up and felt his head —most of his hair was burned off. The column of smoke and fire, fifty feet wide, rapidly receded behind them. But three federale pickups burst out of the inferno in pursuit. Dave fired a few bursts at them, but Bob had the truck dancing around slower-moving traffic and he fell to all fours, then again. The second time, a wooden box slid across the bed of the truck and slammed into his leg. It was very heavy. Dave grabbed it to toss it over the side, then he saw what was stenciled across the top. He flipped open the lid to see that it did, in fact, contain grenades. M67 fragmentation grenades, to be precise.

He grabbed one. It was heavier than he was expecting. And the pin was much tougher to pull out than he would have thought, but that only made sense. As soon as it was out he tossed the grenade at the federale vehicles chasing them. He saw it bouncing along the concrete, a rapidly disappearing black spec. It blew up well behind the pursuing vehicles. He grabbed another grenade, and when he had the pin out he just dropped it over the side.

"What the fuck are you doing?" Dog shouted, looking at him through the back window. Dave held up another grenade in explanation, pulled the pin, and dropped it over the side as well. He looked back and saw the second grenade explode with a flash just behind a federale Ford Explorer, shredding its back tires. It swerved wildly, and crashed into the F-150 next to it. The third grenade exploded right beside the F-150, and it and the Explorer drifted off to the side, spraying steam and smoke.

The third federale raced up, closer, too close for a dropped grenade to explode anywhere close to it. It was a Charger, the windshield stitched with a line of bullet holes. It raced up nearly beside their truck. The passenger window came down and an officer stuck his head out, aiming his rifle at them. Dave's throw was horrible—he wasn't used to the weight at all, and it threw his aim off badly. He was aiming at the gap between the federale and the Charger's A-pillar, and instead the grenade slammed dead center into the Charger's damaged windshield—and stuck there, sunk half into the safety glass. The car swerved wildly and then decelerated suddenly as the driver slammed on the brakes, and the passenger climbed half out of the window, trying to reach the grenade. "Fuck you!" Dave shouted, then the roof blew off the car, the windshield disintegrating in a crystalline spray. The passenger flew from the cruiser, tumbling across the pavement, legs severed at the knees. Dave was peppered with bits of angry heat. The driver was gone, the passenger compartment nothing but a hollow smoking cavity open to the sky. For the moment they had no pursuers

"The fuck are we?" gasped Dog from the back seat. He finished tying off a tourniquet above the wound on his leg —the bullet had gone in one side and out the other, and had been bleeding badly.

"I don't know," Bob admitted. "But we're still heading in the right direction." He took a turn off the main road and they found themselves in another residential area—a neighborhood, and a nice one, although every house squatted behind fences and bars. The posted speed limit was 40 KPH—25 MPH—and Bob raced the smoking pickup down the street at sixty miles an hour, the flat tire now a bare rim, hissing and shrieking against the pavement, throwing sparks.

"Marty's hit!" Boot shouted. The covert agent was slumped against his door, his side wet with blood.

"Do what you can," Bob called out. At the end of the street he stood on the brakes and took a right. There was a church to one side, and the fenced lot of a country club on the left—definitely a better neighborhood. The narrow street curved back and forth, heading east. C. Senecu became Baudelio Pelayo, and they passed high-walled compounds, perhaps belonging to some of the very people trying to have them killed.

Bob got the truck up to 70 MPH and fought it through the gentle curves for a minute, then stomped on the brakes as the street ended at a major thoroughfare. There were two streets just before them, angling together in a narrow X, and past those the area was all commercial, warehouses and light industrial buildings.

The truck raced across one street, barely missing the honking, dodging traffic, crashed awkwardly over a set of curb stones, then bounced onto a wide street, heading roughly north. They had thirty seconds of relative peace, then three vehicles came racing out of sidestreets after them.

Dave was sitting up in the bed of the truck, back against the cab, and saw them first. "Bob!" he shouted. The shrieking of the sparking rim across the pavement almost drowned him out. He fired bursts through the windshield of a Mazda and it jerked to the side and smashed into the Chevy Malibu beside it, both vehicles filled with cartel soldiers. The two vehicles spun into a parking lot in a dust cloud. Then a white Ford pickup came out of nowhere and slammed into the side of their vehicle so violently Dave was almost thrown out of the bed. The federale pickup spun sideways, the bare rim skipping across the pavement. Both pickups stalled.

Boot dumped half a magazine from his M4 into the windshield of the white pickup, killing everyone inside. Bob tried restarting the federale pickup, but it was dead. "Everyone out!" he shouted. Several more vehicles were approaching, their engines racing.

Dave rolled over the side of the bed and landed on his feet. He had a bad cut across his forehead, and the blood running from it joined Cherry's blood on his face. "Covering fire!" Bob shouted at him. He and Dave posted at either end of the pickup and fired at the approaching cartel vehicles as Boot pulled Marty out of the truck and slung him over his shoulder. Dog's leg was both stiff and numb, but he could walk. "Go!" Bob told them, pointing north, between some commercial buildings. He fired at an ancient gold Camaro. The driver panicked and collided with a light pole. Dave had three cartel vehicles racing toward him. He fired at them as Bob grabbed him by the back of his vest and pulled him after the rest of their team.

"I'm out!" Dave shouted, as his bolt locked back. Bob stopped and let Dave keep moving past him, then he started firing as he backpedaled. The vehicles skidded to a halt in the middle of the street and the men inside bailed out and started shooting back with pistols and rifles. Bullets whipped all around them as Bob and Dave reached the corner of the building, and temporary safety. Dave reloaded with blood-spattered hands.

"Leapfrog," Bob shouted at Dave, hoping he'd understand, and waited half a second to make sure he did. Then Bob ran past him, past Dog with his bad limp and Boot carrying Marty, to the end of the small office building. That corner was clear.

Dave fired, quick single shots. Dog and Boot passed Bob, then Dave stopped shooting and ran past Bob. Bob set up at the corner of the building. A guy popped out at the far end and Bob dropped him with a clean headshot. Fired again and again, suppressive fire to keep their attackers from advancing. Then he heard Dave shout "Go!", and Bob took off and ran, overtaking Dog and Boot as Dave fired past him at the pursuing cartel men.

They reached the end of the second building and then gunfire erupted—some of the cartel men had circled around the far side of the buildings. Bob ran up to find two cartel men dead, and Boot on the ground with a fresh wound to one arm. Beside him Marty was on his back, shirt soaked in blood, eyes open and unblinking.

Bob yanked Boot to his feet. "Leave him, he's dead," he told Boot, nodding at Marty. "Run. Go!"

It was a tactical retreat through a light industrial area. The cartel men would break from cover to run after them, and each time Bob or Dave or Boot would drop one or two. They'd retreat to the next building, bullets hitting wildly all around them, and then the same thing would repeat. They were trying to break contact, but they couldn't move fast enough, and there were too many cartel men.

Past the last building was a cross-street, and incredibly there were cars driving on it, the drivers deaf or maybe just inured to the sound of gunfire. Bob ran out into the middle of the street and pointed his Commando at the first vehicle he saw, and the driver stomped on the brakes. "*¡Sal de pinche auto!*" Bob roared, a blood-spattered Viking, and the driver did just that, diving out of his door almost before the vehicle had stopped moving. He took off running and never looked back.

Dog, Boot, and Dave came running up. Bob fired a burst past Dog's head, dropping a cartel soldier in midstride. Dog stared at the vehicle. It was a white Ford Transit van. It looked like one of the stupid ugly Johnny Cabs from the original *Total Recall* movie. Ridiculous. "What, they didn't have any golf carts?" he growled as he wrestled open the door. They heard engines and everyone looked over. Big engines, getting louder. Closer. And then they saw federale vehicles, pickups and Chargers. Over a dozen of them. Seemingly pursued by just as many cartel vehicles, pickups and SUVs and sedans. The entire city, coming for them, or so it appeared. "Fucking go!" Dog shouted, as Bob jumped behind the wheel. Dave dove into the back of the minivan, landing half-atop Dog, as it slowly accelerated away.

There were shelves on either side of the cargo area, and Dave looked at them. They'd stolen a van belonging to a cleaning service—he saw mop buckets and sponges and jugs of foaming cleanser. Boxes of rubber gloves. Rolls of toilet paper.

"How far are we from the border?" Boot gasped from the front seat. He was examining the wound in his arm. There was raw meat showing, and blood was running freely and dripping off his elbow.

"Maybe a mile," Bob said through clenched teeth.

"Fuck." A mile was forever. Especially when there were too many cars to count chasing you. Half of them police vehicles. The small engine of the minivan strained as Bob pressed the accelerator to the floor. They flew up a narrow street, Bob passing the slower-moving traffic on the right and left, sometimes swerving into oncoming traffic.

"What song you got in your fucking head now?" Boot spat at Bob. He'd ripped off his sleeve and was tying it around his arm.

"*Free Bird*," Bob said. Boot wasn't sure if he was joking.

Their pursuers drew rapidly closer—the two lead vehicles were a dusty federale Charger and a new pearl-white Cadillac Escalade, clearly a cartel vehicle. Dave stood inside the back of the minivan, braced against the racks, and watched out the back windows, tinted against the desert sun. He saw windows roll down on the passenger side of the Cadillac, guns come out—and then they were firing at the police car beside them. The Charger skidded off to the side, the dying officer bouncing bonelessly behind the wheel. The Escalade surged forward. Dave fired three shots, dead center on the driver's side of the windshield, and the Escalade lost speed and drifted off to the side. But behind it, a tide of vehicles surged forward, growing ever closer.

"You need to go faster," Dave said warningly. It was like that scene in Jurassic Park, the T. rex in the Jeep's side mirror, running up, mouth opening, its teeth huge, **OBJECTS ARE CLOSER THAN THEY APPEAR.**

"I'm working on it!" Bob shouted back, slewing the underpowered minivan around the other cars, using the entire road. But an overloaded four cylinder wasn't nearly enough.

Dog stood beside Dave in the back, feet braced against the opposite shelves to keep from being thrown around, and opened up through the back windows of the Transit minivan. Every trigger pull of Dog's big HK G3 in the back of the tiny van was like a grenade going off. It made Dave's Commando sound dainty.

Police and cartel vehicles raced up, uniformed cops in the beds of pickups, cartel soldiers hanging out of windows, police and cartel shooting at each other and at the fleeing minivan, vehicles violently ramming. Dave and Dog poured fire out the back of the minivan at any vehicle that drew close, blowing out the back windows. Even with the police and cartel fighting amongst themselves there were too many of them. For every vehicle that dropped out of the pursuit another one, or two, appeared. The only reason they weren't already dead was the street—it was only two lanes wide, so only two and sometimes three vehicles could approach at a time.

Dave emptied the last of a magazine into the windshield of a rusty Oldsmobile. It spun off to the side and went airborne. And was immediately replaced by a federale Charger. He reached down to his vest to reload. He only had two magazines left. Then he saw Dog was on the floor, covered in blood. "Dog's down!" he shouted.

Boot turned in his seat, saw Dog, and cursed. He undid his seatbelt and moved to the man's side.

"Fuck it," Dave said, grabbed one of the grenades he'd stuffed into his empty magazine pouches, yanked the pin, and tossed it through the empty window frame. It rolled along the pavement, disappeared under the pursuing vehicles, and then suddenly a Hyundai was three feet airborne, sideways and smoking. The vehicles to either side drove around it, one slowing down as the grenade had shredded two of its tires.

"You've got nades? Don't fucking save them!" Bob shouted from the front seat, looking at him in the rearview mirror. Dave nodded, and let another grenade fly through the window. He didn't have a chance to see what damage it did.

"Okay!" Bob called out. "Here we go. Hold on!" And then the minivan hopped a curb and bounced wildly across a vacant lot, nothing under their tires but dirt and dry grass. A plume of dust sprang up behind them, slowing their pursuers for a second, then they jumped the curb as well and spread out across the lot. One federale pickup raced ahead of the other vehicles, the driver perhaps an aspiring Baja racer. The two uniformed officers standing in the bed hung on for dear life.

"Brace!" Bob shouted, and a second later the minivan was airborne. Boot and Dog came up off the floor, then they all slammed into the back of the front seats as the minivan crashed into and through a half-open aluminum-roll up door, landing at an angle.

Bob was out of the minivan before the federale pickup came crashing through the other door, landing on its side and spilling the officers in back across the oil-stained concrete floor. Bob shot them on the move, then fired bursts through the top of the cab into the men inside as he stalked forward. He dropped his rifle and scooped another up off the floor—an M4 like his, but with an underbarrel grenade launcher. He cracked the M203 open and saw there was a 40mm grenade already loaded into it, spun toward the sunlight, and fired.

The HE grenade hit a cartel Suburban which exploded in a ball of flame. The other vehicles racing up immediately slammed on their brakes. Bob pulled back from the door, dumped the empty 40mm case, then moved to one of the dead federales. The man had a bandolier across his chest. Bob flipped him over and pulled out a fresh 40mm grenade. He loaded and fired it at the vehicles lined up across the vacant lot fifty yards distant. A police Crown Victoria peeled open explosively in a spray of glass and steel. Bob reloaded the 203, then tossed it to Boot as the man staggered up.

"Dog's gone," Boot said, as Bob wrestled the bandolier of grenades off the dead cop and handed it to him.

Bob nodded. "Cover the front!" he said. He picked his Commando up off the concrete. "I need a minute."

Boot nodded and jogged off. Dave was there, using the cinderblock wall for cover, staring out at the sea of faces and guns. Incoming fire began, ragged at first but rapidly increasing in volume.

"I'm almost out of ammo!" Dave shouted. They were in a small garage, with oil stains on the floor and auto parts piled against one wall. Boot had run through a door into the front of the building.

Bob pulled two magazines out of his vest and threw them across the concrete floor to Dave like he was skipping stones across a pond. He pointed toward the forces arrayed outside. "Keep them pinned. I need a minute!"

"There's too many," Dave said, feeling like he wanted to cry. The cars—police and cartel—stretched from one end of the dusty field to the other, as far as he could see. Half-encircling the building Bob had chosen for their last stand. Dozens, maybe as many as a hundred people—fighting each other, sure, but also pouring fire at the garage doors. Dave kept popping out to shoot, then ducking down to avoid the incoming, and every time he looked out it seemed like there were ten more people out there trying to kill them. Three of the cars were on fire, but nobody seemed to care. Dave fired and fired, then ducked down behind the wall and grabbed a loaded magazine off the floor. The concrete around him was already littered with spent cases. They could hear Boot firing bursts from the other side of the building. The muffled *CRUMP* of a grenade, then bursts of automatic fire. Then another grenade explosion.

Bob frowned. Dave was a bit outnumbered. He backed

up around the far side of the overturned federale pickup. He was in shadow, and the engine compartment provided good cover. Meanwhile, through a gap between the pickup and the concrete wall, he could see a fifty-foot stretch of cars, cops, and cartel assholes.

He planted his feet, tucked the Commando's stock into the pocket of his big shoulder, braced his left elbow against the pickup's fender, and started firing. Whether they were standing or running, fully exposed or showing just half a head, nearly every shot he fired found its mark. He ignored the bullets flying his way, shattering the cinderblock behind him, thunking into the overturned truck, and spanging off the metal shelving. Thirty seconds, thirty rounds, and twenty people were down, some of them dead, the rest screaming for help, but the incoming fire dropped off considerably. While he'd been shooting he'd heard Boot fire two grenades—the man was burning through them fast. The building had to be completely surrounded.

"That should buy us some time," he said, running past Dave. "Keep their fucking heads down while I look for this thing."

Dave had no idea what he was talking about, but he kept firing. He burned through another magazine, and reloaded using the second magazine Bob had tossed to him. More federale vehicles were pulling up outside, and the volume of fire increased, but barely half of it seemed to be directed at the garage. There was a war going on out there between the cartel and the police. And between the cartel… and the cartel? It looked like some of the cartel soldiers were shooting at each other. A federale pickup rolled up in a cloud of dust, and the man standing in the bed, behind the machinegun mounted behind the cab, opened up with long bursts. Dave threw himself to the floor as the heavy bullets pounded against the cinderblock wall, and started punching holes through it. Dave scrambled out of the way and rolled behind the Transit van, hoping the engine block would provide enough cover. Bullets hit all around him.

"I've got it!" he heard Bob shout. "Boot! Come on!"

Dave looked around. He didn't see Bob. Boot appeared in the doorway leading to the front of what Dave realized was a gas station with a service garage. The incoming fire from the belt-fed drove him to his belly. He looked around, as confused as Dave felt. "Where are you?"

"Storage room!" The shout came from an open doorway.

Boot caught Dave's eye. "Come on." He got to his feet and darted toward the doorway, only to stagger and fall. Dave ran to his side and dragged the man through the doorway.

"I'm hit! I'm hit!" Boot gasped. He pulled a hand out from under his vest and it was bright red with blood.

Dave looked at it, then past the man. Past him was... nothing. The storage room was empty. And the door they'd come through was the only way in—or out. Maybe it had been a trick of sound, but Bob wasn't there. Dave stepped up to the doorway. Random bullets slammed into the open door and the shelves. He leaned out and fired several bursts. Maybe he could drag Boot out of there...but go where? The field behind the gas station was filled with armed men, and they were now running fast and driving slow across the field, toward the gas station garage, firing constantly. They were getting confident; tasting victory. He caught a glimpse of something flying through the air, a blur, slower than a bullet, right toward the upended minivan, and then it exploded. The 40mm grenade ignited the Transit van's gas tank, and the blast threw Dave back into the room. He bounced off the shelves and landed on all fours, fresh sharp pains all over his body. It felt like he'd been stabbed by a handful of knives all at once.

"What are you doing? Come on!" Dave looked over, and saw Bob's head and shoulders sticking out of the floor. Dave's brain couldn't process the image for a second, and he thought the man's body had been severed in some sort of horrible industrial garage accident. Then he saw the hole.

Boot was close enough, Bob grabbed him by the straps of his vest and pulled him into the hole. Dave crawled up and looked down. The square opening was dark, but he saw a ladder leading to a dirt floor maybe ten feet below. He grabbed the trap door and pulled it over his head as he climbed down the stairs. When the door was snug above his head he dropped to the ground and looked around. He was surprised to find himself at one end of a tunnel with a bare dirt floor. It was dimly lit and led off into the distance. Bob was dragging Boot down the tunnel. Dave moved after them, grabbed Boot's other shoulder strap, and together they dragged the gasping man down the tunnel.

They'd made it thirty yards when Boot swore. They turned and saw the ladder lit up—someone had opened the trap door. Dave and Bob tightened their grips and sped up, doing their best to run down the tunnel dragging Boot. Boot started firing, his muzzle flash lighting up the tunnel and sending clouds of dust flying off the walls and drifting down from the rough plank ceiling. Bullets whizzed around them. Dave felt a burning pain in his thigh and he went down with a gasp, then was back up. Bob smashed a lightbulb as they passed, hoping the dark would help conceal them.

Boot ran dry and reloaded. Dave risked a glance behind him and saw muzzle flashes. At least one person was down there, crouched or prone, and someone else had stuck their hand through the trapdoor, holding a rifle, and was firing blindly. Another dark figure jumped down into the tunnel and began firing. Boot gasped and flailed as he was hit again and Bob and Dave went down.

Dave rolled over and fired between his feet at the distant figures, pulling the trigger as fast as he could. Bob added his fire, short, controlled bursts. It seemed to work—the gunfire from the end of the tunnel stopped. Bob reloaded quickly, then grabbed Boot and resumed dragging him. Dave, moving slower, was at his side a second later.

"Last mag," Dave gasped. Bob nodded. They dragged Boot along as fast as they could, Bob smashing the lightbulbs as they went. Boot's breathing was harsh and ragged. Dave's eyes were growing adjusted to the dim light. The tunnel stretched straight as an arrow before him. They'd gone so far he couldn't see the sliver of the trapdoor anymore, but he also couldn't see the end of the tunnel in front of them. It seemed to stretch into infinity. How long was the goddamn tunnel?

More gunfire erupted, and bullets hit the walls and floor around them. Boot fired at the muzzle flashes, and then his gun fell silent. Dave looked and saw the man's head slumped over on his chest. The incoming fire increased. Dave let go of Boot, turned, and fired toward the muzzle flashes, which seemed closer than the end of the tunnel. They were advancing. Bob kept dragging Boot, and Dave backed up, firing. Then his gun was empty.

"I'm out," he shouted at Bob, his hearing wrecked from firing in yet another enclosed space. He took a deep breath. "Fuck it," he said, pulling the pin on the last grenade and sidearming it as hard as he could down the tunnel.

"The fuck did you—down!" Bob said, and tackled him. They'd just hit the tunnel floor when the grenade went off.

The noise was incredible. Rocks and dirt and shrapnel flew above their heads. The blast killed several lights, and the tunnel in front of them filled with dust, thick as a Middle East sandstorm.

Bob fought to his feet. "Take him!" he shouted. Dave grabbed Boot's vest straps and dragged him backward while Bob fired controlled shots down the tunnel. There was some return fire, but it was sporadic. Nobody could see through the dust filling the air.

Bob's Commando ran dry, his last magazine, and he dropped it. Drew his Glock from his holster and continued firing. Bullets hit all around them. Something tugged at Dave's side and he fell down, then was up again, ignoring the pain, dragging Boot. He didn't know where they were going, but the tunnel couldn't go on forever.

Then he slammed into something. He turned, ready to fight, and saw wood slats. A ladder. "Bob!"

Bob glanced over his shoulder as he reloaded the Glock. "Go!" he told Dave, then resumed firing.

Dave climbed the ladder awkwardly, his body responding oddly and throwing out warning signals. He came up against the wooden trap door and put his shoulder against it and shoved it open. He crawled up and found himself in a small room.

"Grab him!"

Kneeling beside the open trapdoor Dave reached down and grabbed Boot. With him pulling and Bob pushing they got him up the ladder. Bob shoved Boot to one side and rolled the other direction, gasping for air. He reloaded the Glock again, shoved his hand down through the trapdoor, and blindly fired half a dozen shots. Then he risked a look, sticking his head down through the hole. He jerked it back, and bullets peppered the ladder, spraying wood and dirt.

"When you switch to a pistol, they figure you're just about out of ammo," Bob said.

Dave was fighting for air, covered in blood and sweat. He looked at Boot, but the man was dead, eyes staring blankly at the wall. "Let's…go…" Dave panted, and tried to get up. His leg went out from underneath him. And his arms didn't seem to be working all that well either.

"Hold on," Bob said calmly. He stuck his Glock back in its holster, and then reached down, into the shadows between the flooring and the dirt wall of the tunnel. He produced a small mechanical device, a short cylinder with a T-handle. Then he reached back in, and pulled out the ends of two wires

"Bob," Dave croaked. The guys in the tunnel were still shooting, but they were close enough he could hear them shouting. He rolled over and searched Boot's magazine pouches. They were all empty.

"In a minute," Bob said, seemingly relaxed. The ends of the two wires had been stripped of plastic insulation, but they were a bit dirty. Bob blew on them, then wiped them clean with his fingers. He inserted one into the little device, clamped it down with a thumbscrew, then did the same with the other.

"Bob!" Dave could hear their fucking footsteps. The entire tunnel had to be filled with guys coming after them, and they were seconds away.

"Let's hope this works," Bob said cheerfully. He laid down on his back away from the trapdoor, gave Dave a wink, and said, "Fire in the hole." He twisted the short handle at the top of the device in his hands.

Dave bounced three feet into the air, and a gout of dust blew out of the hole and filled the room. The concussion cracked the drywall around them. Dave landed on his back, stunned. He couldn't hear anything, just a giant ringing in his ears.

Bob slowly sat up. Blood was running from his nose. He looked down into the hole. Three rungs of the ladder were visible, then it disappeared into loose dirt. The tunnel was gone. Filled in. However many men had been inside when the charges had blown—he'd planted one at each end of the tunnel and one in the center, all those weeks earlier—were now buried alive. Well, technically, pulped by the pressure wave of the C4, then buried. He worked his neck, shook the dirt out of his hair, and looked at Dave. "You're a goddamn madman," he said admiringly.

Bob worked his jaw a few times. He dragged Boot over and put the detonator in his hand, then knelt over Dave. He checked him over for wounds with one hand while he pulled out his satphone and made a call. "Oh, that's not good," he said to Dave, as he listened to the phone ringing in his ear. "I didn't think most of this was your blood. Ooh, that's worse. Shit." He hit the speaker, and set the phone down on the floor next to him.

Dave could see his lips moving, but heard nothing beyond the ringing hum. "I can't hear anything," Dave said loudly. It felt good to be lying down. Not moving. Behind the adrenaline coursing through his veins was a wall of pain waiting to sink its teeth into him.

Bob patted him reassuringly on the shoulder, and gave him a thumbs up, even as he pulled a package of QuickClot combat gauze out of a pouch on his vest.

"Glad you're still with us," Bob heard from the phone. "From orbit it looks like half of Juarez is on fire."

"Only half? Hmm. I need a sterile vehicle," Bob said into the phone. "And a medic."

"You're injured?"

"Just the usual bumps and bruises from a bit of the ol' slap and tickle, as those fairies in the SAS like to say. But I've got a plus one, and he's in rough shape. What do we have in El Paso?" And as he waited for a reply he bobbed his head to music only he could hear.

Chapter Thirty-Two

Osterman was standing behind his desk. He wasn't sure when he'd stood up, but he'd been on his feet now for maybe an hour, taking and making calls. Thinking and worrying and doing anything and everything he could to uncover exactly who had taken Anderson. Where the boy might be. Unfortunately, none of his efforts seemed to amount to much. After a full day he still knew nothing new. No additional evidence had been found at the scene of the abduction. No one—anywhere—had spotted the men or Anderson. And his federal contacts had come up dry. No news was—maybe—good news, but the longer the boy was missing, the worse his odds got, and it had been over thirty-six hours. There'd been no sign of him anywhere along the border. Osterman's one slim realistic hope had been that whoever the people were who'd grabbed him, they'd get nabbed trying to spirit him across the border. But…nothing. No calls from CBP. No calls from anyone.

His desk phone rang and he grabbed the handset. "Osterman."

"Sheriff, it's Charles at the front desk. I've got a reporter out here asking for you." His deputy could probably hear Osterman's scowl over the phone line. He quickly added, "Um, I know what we're supposed to say to the media, but she says she knows you?"

In the background, Osterman heard a faint voice. "Tell him it's Mindy Tonaka."

"Sir, she says—"

"Yes, I heard her. Send her on back."

Osterman had his cell phone in his other hand. He took a breath, set his cell down, then sat himself down behind his desk. A few seconds later Mindy Tonaka appeared in his doorway. She was, as usual, stunning, dressed for the camera in a tailored dress and heels. Tall and slender, with jet black hair. Physically, the exact opposite of his wife, but still, he appreciated the view. "Sorry to just drop in, Sheriff, but I can't get anybody on the phone. Not even you."

Osterman frowned, but didn't deny it. She'd called his cell phone at least twice, and he'd sent her to voicemail. "No rudeness intended, Mindy, I'm just in the middle of something, and—"

"Pima Jack's kidnapping?" she said, one eyebrow raised. That caught the sheriff by surprise. He looked up at her, mouth open. It made her smirk. "I do have sources, you know," she told him. She held up a hand. "Not your men, they won't speak out of turn, and God knows I've tried to get them to, over the years. But apparently you've reached out to a number of federal contacts. And they do love to talk. Pima Jack was kidnapped this morning by the cartel?"

Osterman made a face. "I can't talk about any active investigations, Mindy, you know that." Which was a confirmation, without him confirming it. She blinked at the news, and moved close to his desk.

"Oh my God. That's—why aren't you putting that out? We could help! His name, his face, get everyone looking for him."

"I had a strategy. Which does not seem to have worked. He was gone for hours before we even knew, so it was a thin chance to begin with."

A shadow filled the doorway and they both looked up to see Norm Hill. He was taller than Mindy in her heels and twice as wide. He looked from the sheriff to the reporter—who he recognized—and back. "Sorry," the detective said. "I can come back."

Osterman held up a finger to stop the man. "Anything new?" he asked hopefully, but the expression on his detective's face told him the answer.

Norm shook his head, once again glancing at the reporter. "Not really. Footprints. Tire tracks. We've taken casts, for comparison. Nothing…actionable."

As Osterman frowned his desk phone beeped. "Sheriff, I've got Special Agent-in-Charge Harlin of the DEA on the line for you," Sally, his secretary, said over the intercom. Norm's eyebrows went up at that. So did Mindy's.

"I'll just—" she said, motioning toward the door.

Osterman held up a finger again, and gave a tiny shake of his head. "Put him through," he said. When the light lit up he punched it with a finger, and put the call on speaker. He pointed a finger at Mindy, and gave her a stern look. She ran a finger across her lips. "Osterman."

"Sheriff, Doug Harlin." Harlin ran the DEA's Phoenix division.

"Doug, normally it's good to hear your voice, but today has been a bit of a weight on me. Are you calling with news about our boy?"

"No," Harlin said, and Osterman's shoulders dropped.

"Well…I don't know. By any chance have you been following the news out of Mexico today?"

Osterman shook his head. "No, I've been a little bit busy. Why?"

Harlin clucked his tongue. "Well, there was a massive dust up in Juarez earlier this afternoon. It's all over the Mexican news channels. Big battle between the federales and, from what it sounds like, at least two cartels. La Fuerza and Los Zetas. And La Fuerza was involved in your abduction, or so you suspect."

"Yes. Aren't the cartels always at war with each other, and the police down there?"

"Yes, but not like this. Let me see…" And he read to them. "'*Today's violence has carved a miles-long path of death and destruction across the city.*' A bit poetic for my taste, but not wrong. Biggest battle they've ever had in Ciudad Juarez, and that's saying something. Footage from news helicopters is incredible, couple city blocks on fire, bodies in the street, crashed cars, burning cars, more bodies…looks like they were filming a *Mad Max* movie. Initial reports are upwards of a hundred people injured or dead. I know Juarez is eight hours from you, but considering how your troubles seem to be cartel-related, I thought I might pass on the news."

"Thank you," Osterman said. "I appreciate it. Can you keep me updated if you get any further details?"

"Absolutely."

When Osterman ended the call Norm Hill was shaking his big head. He almost looked like he wanted to laugh. "What's so funny?" Osterman asked him.

"Are you kidding me?" the detective said.

"What, you think Pima Jack was involved?" Mindy said. "You know how many big gun battles there are in Mexico between the federales and cartels? Between the cartels?"

Norm was still shaking his head. "Every time this guy gets into trouble he drops multiple bodies. They grab him, we think drag him down to Mexico, and now just over the border they've got the biggest gunfight in cartel history? What are the chances?"

"There's no way," Mindy said. "Mexico has been a war zone for years. Decades. Maybe you're hoping he's still alive, I know we're all hoping that, but…"

Norm looked at the sheriff, but Osterman's expression was unreadable. He leaned a shoulder against the door frame and crossed his arms. "Fifty bucks," Norm told her flatly. "Fifty bucks says that was him."

Chapter Thirty-Three

With his seniority, Dr. Ethan Brennan didn't do that many surgeries anymore, but he was always doing consults, and there seemed to be no shortage of patients in the Prescott area. The average age in Arizona had to be edging up with all the retirees moving to the southwest, and if there was one thing senior citizens had a lot of, it was health problems. Job security, he supposed.

Part of his job was doing rounds, talking to patients. Making sure their treatments were working. That their recovery was going as planned. Listening to their complaints. And he was a good listener. A great listener. It was what made him so great at diagnoses. But, as a result, he always worked late. It was part of what made him a good doctor—he went home when the job was done. If it took a long conversation with a patient to determine exactly what the problem was, to spot an issue, he was willing to do it. His wife understood. She didn't necessarily like it, but she understood. But his inability to get out of the office, to get out of the hospital on time, had caused her to put her foot down—on the days when he was off, he was off. No answering phone calls. He was off. Unavailable. It had been that way since he'd had a pager instead of a cell phone.

He'd just had two glorious days off. He and Deborah had slept in both days, just a little, played nine holes of golf the first day, ate a delicious brunch the second day, and for the rest of the time did...nothing. Puttered around the house. Watched Netflix. Flipped through stupid videos on his phone while avoiding anything that could be serious news or politics. He'd even picked up a book and read fifty pages. It had been wonderful. On his days off the world could be on fire, and he wouldn't know. Which was always a bit scary, driving in to work after a day off. He had no way of knowing if the hospital was full of cholera victims, or kids burned in a horrible bus accident.

He filled up his Thermos with fresh-brewed coffee in the kitchen and headed out in his BMW. He knew it was clichéd for a doctor to drive a BMW, but he didn't care—he loved his X6. Technically an X6 M60i, in Tanzanite Blue II Metallic. And there weren't that many of them, so he was pretty sure the distinctive lines of the coupe-style SUV, plus the exclusive paint job which had cost him an additional two grand, had gotten him out of some speeding tickets from the Sheriff's men. The damn car had 523 horses, how were you supposed to keep it even near the speed limit with that kind of power under the hood?

He was early, the sun was still barely over the horizon, when he parked in the gated doctor's lot. He grabbed his Thermos and walked through the lot around to the front of the hospital. Not the main entrance—there was never anything happening there, that was just where family members came to check in, prior to visiting patients. No, he walked to the emergency entrance. That was the heart of the hospital. You wanted to know how things were, stick your head in the emergency room. Was it filled with bloody, unhappy people? Was it empty and quiet? Were there ambulances stacked up three deep outside?

He stopped on the curb, took a sip of his coffee, and looked around. Everything seemed quiet. There was one ambulance parked a good distance away from the ER doors, but it looked like it had been there all night. That was a good sign.

Doc Brennan started walking toward the ER doors. He heard a car coming up behind him. It slowed and rolled up next to him just as he neared the building. He looked over to see a silver sedan, the passenger window sliding down. "Hey, you a doc?" the driver said pleasantly, almost cheerfully. "You look like a doctor."

"Yeah, can I help you?"

"Yeah, you can help me with him," the man said. He threw the car into park and jumped out. Brennan had the impression of a thick man with a beard, a ball cap pulled down low over his face. He jogged around the car to the rear passenger door and pulled it open. Then he lifted out a man and laid him gently on the sidewalk. The man groaned. His clothes were bloodstained and cut open. Brennan saw compresses and expertly applied bandages. Most of the blood was dried to a near brown—they weren't fresh wounds.

"He's stable, but you're talking multiple gunshot wounds and more than a bit of frag, so I wouldn't leave him lying there for too long or your premiums are likely to go up," the man said. "He was given one unit of plasma, but he's still probably a quart low. Given a total of sixty milligrams of ketamine, last was twenty milligrams intramuscular administered four hours ago. There's QuickClot on those bandages. Hmm. I think that's all." Then he jogged back around to his open door, jumped behind the wheel, and drove off with a chirp of rubber. And a wave. A fucking wave of his hand.

Brennan stood there with his mouth open, then knelt down next to the body on the sidewalk. The man was on his side. Brennan touched his shoulder and rolled him a bit, just so he could check his head and neck, see if he was conscious. The man turned his head and looked at him, squinting against the glare of the bright morning sun.

"Hey, doc," David Anderson said through teeth clenched in pain.

"Are you shitting me?" Brennan said, loud enough for his voice to echo off the front of the hospital.

Chapter Thirty-Four

Bob stopped in Higgins' open door. "Sarah said you wanted to see me?"

His section chief was digging around in a desk drawer, and sat up. Bob was in a long-sleeve plaid flannel shirt over jeans. "Yeah. You enjoy your personal day?"

Bob shrugged. "Better than some, worse than others."

"Yeah, well. Anyway—uh, what the hell happened to your hands?"

Bob looked at them. His hands were liberally covered with scrapes and abrasions. There would be bruises, but they hadn't shown up yet, or were too deep. And he was wearing a long-sleeve shirt and moving slowly for a lot of very good reasons. "Gardening."

Higgins laughed. "You fucking guys. All of you, adrenaline junkies. You know, I know you're in great shape, but you're not twenty-five anymore. You go fighting in amateur MMA tournaments, freeclimbing, or whatever, I don't want you out for six weeks with a broken leg you're claiming happened on the job."

"Understood. Low-impact gardening from now on."

Higgins shook his head. "Yeah. Anyway. When was the last time you spoke with anybody on Gargoyle?"

"When we met at the airport in Arizona. I handed over the package. Then they took off southbound. Why?"

Higgins shook his head. "They're late checking in."

Bob shrugged, seemingly unconcerned. "Shit happens. They have a clean satphone. Did you ping it?"

Higgins nodded. "We tracked its movements. It's not active now, but last coordinates were in Juarez."

Bob nodded. "So they were on their way out. Maybe they're having some trouble getting back across the border. Didn't I hear the cartels were acting up in Juarez? That'll lock down the border tight, both the official crossings and whatever channels the cartels have operating."

Higgins nodded. "Hopefully we'll hear back by tomorrow. If not…they were down there as deniable assets, no IDs, sterile gear, but you know how to look around, get some answers, without involving us officially. I don't want to send up a flare until I've got something concrete. Upstairs doesn't want to be bothered with 'what-ifs'."

"Absolutely, sir."

Dave opened his eyes. He blinked them a few times to focus them, and saw a very pretty, glamorous, middle-aged Asian woman standing at the foot of his hospital bed. She looked familiar, but his brain was moving a bit slow from the painkillers.

"You cost me fifty bucks," she told him.

Dave knew he was a bit under the influence, but still he thought he would have remembered some sort of financial arrangement with this woman. "Sorry?" Was she one of Lori's former co-workers? She looked good enough, but he didn't think that was it. So where had he seen her? She was really familiar. He glanced around. Lori had been sitting with him, but she wasn't there now.

"Detective Hill, Norm Hill—the big guy?—with Tohono County, was sure that trouble down in Juarez involved you. I figured there was no way, with how bad things are down there. But here you are." Her mouth twisted up in a rueful smile.

Dave waited a bit for his brain to catch up. He licked his lips. "Juarez. Mexico? I never left the country. I was in Detroit visiting friends."

She snorted. "While I admit you do look like you spent some time in Detroit, I think we both know that's not true. You were shot fifteen times."

Dave reached out for the cup by his bedside. He sipped at the straw. "I was only shot twice," he told her. "And neither of those were life-threatening." One in his side, just above his hipbone, tearing out a nasty big chunk of flesh, or so Doc Brennan had told him, the other through his right thigh, just missing his femur and femoral artery. "The rest of the wounds were…other stuff." It wasn't like he could lie about his injuries.

She threw her hands up and gave him a dirty look. "Like that's any better?"

Dave frowned. He finally recognized her. "You're a reporter, right? Friend of the sheriff."

Mindy nodded. "He was in here earlier, but I guess you were sleeping. I know they've got you on some painkillers. To be fair, you've looked worse."

"I've looked better."

She smiled ruefully and shook her head. "You think Pima Jack had a fan club here before…"

"What do you mean?"

She crossed her arms and cocked her hip. "Mexican drug cartel—presumably—kidnaps you out of your bed in the middle of the night. Forty-eight hours later you're dropped off by a mystery man in front of the ER. With gunshot wounds, what they tell me was enough grenade shrapnel in your body to make a grenade, and half your hair burned off. Smelling like gunpowder, according to Ethan Brennan. I don't even know how much shooting you have to do to actually smell like gunpowder. I didn't know that was even a thing. Anyway, meanwhile, between point A and point B, one of the biggest battles in the history of the Mexican drug cartels happened just over the border. Current body count is nearly fifty dead and twice that many wounded, and it keeps going up. I mean, they never announced anything, so the public didn't know that you're gone, or that you're back, but even the dumbest cop on this department can see two plus two equals four." And she pointed a slender finger at him.

Dave shifted in the bed, and winced a bit in pain. "Detroit is lovely this time of year."

She rolled her eyes. "Detroit isn't lovely any time of year. The sheriff has some deputies stationed in the hall outside for security, as apparently you haven't told him anything either, and he doesn't know exactly how pissed off the cartel still is at you. You should hear what they're saying in the halls, the rumors flying around, which I would say are crazy and nuts, but here you are. There's cell phone footage of somebody shooting down a helicopter, and the deputies out there are convinced it's you, even though I've seen that footage, and you can't tell who it is. Whoever it was has to be dead, they rode that truck into a wall of flame that was fifty feet high. But, still, they'll probably ask you to autograph their guns before you go." She gave him a smile.

Dave coughed a bit and sat up. "How clear is that video?" he asked quietly.

That stopped her. She opened and closed her mouth, then blinked twice. She looked toward the closed door. Thought of her job, thought of her love of reporting—and of her respect for the sheriff. And the sheriff loved the man in front of her. "Not very," she said finally. "It's very shaky. It would be incredible footage if it wasn't so shaky. And the truck—you—the person in the truck is far away and moving fast. And mostly looking away from the camera." She shook her head. "Even after they stabilize that video, no way to definitively ID the person in it. Not even their race." She gave him a long look. He stared back, then gave a very small nod.

Jesus. It was worth the fifty bucks to find that out, even if she never could tell anyone. But if that had been him in the back of the pickup…who had been driving? She took a deep breath. "Lillian Osterman sends her love; I ran into her at the station earlier. Anyway, I *am* happy that I lost that bet. They tell me none of your injuries are immediately life-threatening, there's just a lot of them. Maybe when you get out of here, and have had some time to recover, I can take you out for a nice dinner. You and your girlfriend. Ask a few questions."

"No comment," he croaked.

She smirked. "Yeah, well, you can't blame a girl for trying."

Five minutes after Mindy left Lori came through the door. She was in fresh clothes, which explained where she'd gone. "I saw Mindy Tonaka in the lobby," she said, as she plopped into her chair beside his bed. "She seemed...I don't know. Excited? We talked for a little bit. She's just as nice as I hoped she'd be. And she's just as pretty as she looks on TV."

"She was up here for a while."

"Did you tell her that I think she's hot?" Lori asked him.

Dave smiled. "The topic of a threesome did not come up."

Lori pouted. He couldn't tell if it was real. He smiled, and drifted off for a while. When he looked back over at her he saw she was quietly crying. "What's the matter?"

"Can you at least try not to get hurt anymore?" she said, fighting back sobs. "I can't tell you how many days I've spent sitting beside your bed in this hospital."

Dave did feel bad about that. "I always *try*," he said. She glared daggers at him. "I'll try harder," he said quickly. "I don't know if I'm done with all this bullshit," he said, gesturing at himself and the hospital room, meaning, more than anything else, the cartel business. "It feels like I am, but..." and he shrugged, then winced, because shrugging hurt. "I can..." He was going to say move out, but he didn't really have any stuff at her place. Just a few clothes, most of which were brand new. "Find an apartment, I guess? Maybe stay at the Pima. I bet they'd give me a good rate," he muttered.

"What?" she said, her voice cracking. "I'm not kicking you out. Don't be an idiot. You're not getting rid of me that easy. I love you!" Tears were running down her cheeks. "I just wish you weren't so..." She searched for the words, couldn't find them, and just sighed, long and loud. He nodded. She wiped at the tears. "Now all we need to do is get you a job," she told him. "Maybe crash test dummy, that seems safer that what you've been doing." And she frowned at him, eyes narrowed. He knew better than to say a word.

They were in the SCIF, phones left outside. Clark had brought in two big cups of coffee from a Starbucks he passed on the way in to headquarters.

He took a sip, and nodded at the DIA Director. "You were right, no matter what happened, it would probably work out in our favor, and it did. Federales look pathetic, weaker than ever, and all the cartels look strong. Or, at least La Fuerza doesn't look weak. Lot of turmoil. And it's all south of the border."

"Our asset?" Elliot asked.

Clark shrugged. "No word, so have to assume he was one of the fatalities. Lot of bodies down there. A lot. This was huge. So the Mexican government won't be surprised if representatives of the US government come down to look at things. DEA. FBI Counter-Intel. See if any faces were on the watch list and so on. I'll be going down with ICE credentials. I'm sure I'll recognize some of the faces. If I see even one belonging to the team that was with him, you can assume they all bought it down there. But…"

"But what? Aren't all the loose ends cleaned up?"

Clark shook his head. "Weathervane might have bought it, but the package the team took down to Mexico is back at home. Not saying anything. In fact, he's denying he ever left the state. Even though he's pretty banged up. It was never publicly announced that he was taken, or missing."

Elliott frowned. "Is he an operator? Specialized training?"

"No, but he does seem to have more than his share of luck. Good and bad."

Elliott grunted. "Well, maybe they just cut him loose down there, when they found out Weathervane was blown. And he made it back on his own. Mexico's not Syria, so that makes more sense than anything else."

Clark dipped his head in acknowledgement. "I don't know what he could say about what happened, about the team, that anyone would believe, or that he could prove, but we'll monitor him, just in case." He sighed. "But…"

"Another but."

Clark shook his head, and frowned. "When I spoke to Weathervane. Right after he found out he was blown. He was with the team, and wanted me to arrange a helicopter. Big enough for six guys."

Elliott blinked twice. "Six?"

"Yeah. Delivery team was three guys. Plus Weathervane. Even if you add the package that's just five. So who the fuck is the sixth guy?"

"Maybe he just can't count. Or was counting the pilot."

"Maybe. But I'm going to look into it. This thing in Juarez is an opportunity, and I think we'll be able to leverage quite a few things out of it. I'll likely be down there for days, maybe a week."

Elliott nodded. "Keep me posted."

Chapter Thirty-Five

"Dude, really, it's great to see you," Aaron said, as Dave settled down in a chair at his kitchen table. "How long's it been since you've been here?"

"Years," Dave admitted.

"Ma was here, right?"

Dave smiled. "Yep. Smoking her cigarettes, trying to give her cancer cancer." He reached down and patted Peanut. "Glad to see Peanut, but somebody's not moving so fast."

"Yeah. Recovering from a little surgery, which makes three of us. Intestinal blockage. And she's got some arthritis, but she's taking pills for that now. I didn't even know dogs could get arthritis, thought it was just a people thing. Arlene should be home before too long. I will make you the famous Abruzzo family spaghetti for dinner." As Aaron spoke, he was pulling fresh vegetables out of the refrigerator. He made his sauce fresh, and it would need to simmer on the stove for a few hours. "Peanut's not the only one moving a bit slow."

"Give me a break. I'm not sure if I was even cleared to fly. I got hit by shrapnel from like three grenades. And shot twice."

"In Detroit." Aaron snorted. "You really told them you were vacationing in Detroit? Dude, that's classic. So what did happen? I mean, I saw the news. Well, the clips on YouTube from the Mexican news, giant cartel battle with the cops, somebody shooting down a police chopper, and you must have been in there somewhere, but give me the details."

Dave shook his head. Didn't say anything for a while, until Aaron looked up from the tomatoes he was dicing. "What?"

"I can't."

"Dude, you know I can keep a secret. You *know*." He looked hurt.

"Oh, I know. But it's not my secret to tell. And that's all I can say."

Aaron frowned. "I don't know what the fuck that's supposed to mean, but okay." He sounded hurt too.

Dave decided to change the subject. "I thought you got beat up or something. You look fine. I mean, just the regular amount of ugly."

"It's been over a month. Stitches out, swelling's gone. But look." He stepped away from the counter, hooked a finger in the corner of his mouth, and pulled his mouth open wide. Showed Dave the damage. "He knocked out two of my teeth. One was fucked up anyway, needed to be pulled, but they don't need to know that. Going to get some of those dental implants."

"Aren't those expensive?"

"Expensive as shit. But I'm not paying for it. You're

looking at a millionaire." He held his hands up like a victorious prize fighter.

"A millionaire can't afford a nicer trailer?"

"Fuck you, at least I've still got a house." He looked at Dave for a reaction.

"Wow. Ow." They traded grins. "So tell me, what the hell's going on with all that?"

Aaron whistled, long and low. "As the bruthas would say, I about to be gettin' paid. Oh, wait, here, look at these." He dug in a nearby drawer, pulled out some photos, and tossed them on the table next to Dave.

Dave winced just staring at the pictures. He looked from them, up at Aaron, and back down. "Jesus."

"Evidentiary photographs documenting my wounds suffered at the hands of Detective William 'I'm So Fucked' Dixon," Aaron said, paraphrasing his lawyer. Taken after he'd been driven to the hospital, before any treatment. Before and after the wounds had been cleaned. After the stitches, and his fingers splinted. There was so much blood across his face in the 'before' photos you couldn't see the extent of his wounds. "Twelve stitches. Broken nose." Aaron held up his hand. "Broke two of my fingers too. Still not completely healed, but as long as I don't lift anything heavy… And I didn't say a fucking word. About anything."

Dave met his gaze and nodded. "So, lawsuit? How do you think that's going to go?"

Aaron laughed and started throwing vegetables in the pot. "Are you kidding me? Soon as it hit the news, I had lawyers calling me up before I was out of the hospital. All the Detroit A-list ambulance chasers, Bernstein, Fieger, that blonde A-rab chick looks like a retired porn star…. This would be bad anywhere, but in that country club zip code? A senior detective, under investigation by the FBI for ties to organized crime, abducting and torturing someone? They can't make this go away fast enough."

"The department's not directly liable, is it? I mean, he was off duty. Or, at least, not acting in his official capacity."

Aaron barked out a laugh, and counted his points out on his fingers. "Using a department vehicle, department handcuffs, department fucking Taser, a long history of harassing the victim—that would be me—and he was asking me questions about one of his cases. The completely illegal racial profiling, because I'm Italian. They're liable as shit. And that's without the FBI arrest and criminal conspiracy charges against him. He was on the take from the mob for years, while working as a cop. The question isn't if they're going to pay to make this go away quick and quiet, but how much. My lawyer is thinking at least three million, maybe ten, but more likely five if I want to settle out of court quick. We're waiting for their first offer."

"Five million bucks?"

Aaron pointed at the photos on the table. "You were on a jury, and a cop did that to someone, because those photos are sure as shit going to be introduced as evidence and shown to the jury, how much money would you give the plaintiff? And it's not just me coming out of nowhere filing an excessive force complaint, we go to trial we're calling FBI Special Agents to the stand to testify I was tied to a chair, covered in blood, my teeth on the fucking floor next to all the spent Taser cartridges. Photos of it all, including Dixon's bloody knuckles. If we have to go to trial, we're asking for fifty million in damages plus medical expenses, and they know it. And they know we're likely to get it. Police chief has already been forced into retirement. They're panicking. So, five million, maybe more. My lawyer and I have a bet on their initial offer, which will be a lowball—I say eight, he thinks four. And we'll come back with a counteroffer that's at least double that. Either way my lawyer's going to take his chunk, and then there's taxes, but I should be set."

"Provided you invest it, and don't do something stupid like buy a Lamborghini."

"Fuck you. Live fast, die young. Arlene's already out shopping for tits, although I didn't tell you that. You hear from the FBI?"

"About you getting your ass beat? They did reach out to my lawyer, wanting to talk to me about Vegas, and Dixon asking you questions about me, but my default response to them is 'fuck off'. Unless they arrest me or serve me with a subpoena, I won't even meet with them. But they only called once. Which surprises me. Usually they're more… persistent."

"Well, duh." Aaron snorted.

"What does that mean?"

"I'm guessing they're under orders to stay the hell away from you. First they had one of their extra special agents on tape arranging your murder, and now there's a detective torturing your very best friend in an attempt to leverage information about you, or maybe even from you. Talk about being the victim of criminal behavior on the part of law enforcement. Sounds like a civil rights violation to me. Grounds for another lawsuit. Somebody says your name, the FBI runs the other direction."

"Well, let's hope so."

"You're bunking here tonight, right?"

"Yeah, if that's okay. For the duration." He was in Detroit for three days, and Aaron had taken some time off. "I've got a meeting tomorrow, but other than that we can just hang out or whatever." He reached down and scratched behind Peanut's ears.

Aaron popped the caps off two bottles of beer, handed one to Dave, and then clinked them. They smiled, and drank.

He hurt all over, but only a little. The ibuprofen took the edge off, and made him not quite so stiff, which he felt was more important. He had the Glock in an appendix holster, down the front of his pants just to the right of his belly button, because the wound on his hip prevented him from carrying there as he usually did.

The restaurant was big, but had a number of oddly shaped smaller rooms, so he had to wander a bit to find Bob. The man was sitting at a round table, facing the entrance. In a baggy shirt, with his wide jaw, he almost looked chubby. There were two men with him, and they watched Dave approach. One had fine blonde hair starting to recede, cut short. His arms showed low body fat and more than a bit of muscle; he looked like a combat Marine nearing retirement age. The other man had brown hair and was closer to slender. For three random guys in their mid-forties they looked to be in very good shape. None of them were drinking alcohol. Dave would have bet any amount of money they were all armed.

There was already a big antipasto salad on the table and they'd all been eating. "Am I late?" Dave asked. He knew he wasn't. In fact, he was five minutes early.

"Just catching up," Bob said. "Haven't been together back home in a while." He watched Dave take a seat. "You look like you're healing nicely."

Dave shrugged. "None of them were really serious wounds."

Bob snorted. "You're about the only guy I know who's taken close to as much incoming I have and is still with us. The thing with throwing frags is you're supposed to duck afterward."

"Well, it was my first time."

Bob was smiling. "You ever been here before?" 'Here' was the Alibi restaurant, on Rochester Road in Troy. Dave shook his head. "Great pizza. We already ordered. If you're not hungry you won't hurt my feelings by not eating. You're not here for the food."

"Why am I here?" Dave asked.

"You been following the news out of Mexico?" Bob asked him.

"Yeah. Mostly just to try and get a feel for whether they might be interested in taking another run at me. You're not, are you?"

That got another smile out of Bob. "Officially, it was a battle between the Mexican Federal Police and several cartel factions. The biggest battle in history, with at least sixty dead and more than a hundred and twenty injured. Numbers vary, depending who you ask. No mention of Americans involved at all. The federales came out as the big losers in all this. They look like an absolute clown show, taking it from both sides and the middle. I don't know if that's actually fair or accurate, but that's the impression everybody has. The cartels look much more powerful, and there's now talk that a merger might be in the works. Cartel consolidation. You seem to have been forgotten. They've moved on."

"Well, good."

"As for your other outstanding issue…I met him, you know. Twenty…shit, twenty-five years ago. Man, how time flies." He looked at his two companions, and they nodded.

Mostly they were watching Dave. Studying him. It felt like a job interview, which was weird.

"Who?"

"Pietro Bufonte. Sat down with him in his restaurant. Me and John. John Phault. We thought maybe he was the cause of some of our problems. Turned out he wasn't. Just his people. Small world. Weird. But I am convinced things happen for a reason. You needed addresses for your road trip to Vegas. And if it wasn't for that..." He shrugged. "Anyway, the FBI is keeping that case open. After all, it is a quadruple homicide. But they've got nothing. No evidence, no witnesses, just a lot of people with motive, none of whom—including you—are going to tell them shit. Which brings us to today. I appreciate you keeping your mouth shut about *our* little road trip. But it seems you're good at that. Not the covert stuff, but rather keeping secrets."

Dave frowned. It didn't seem like he was talking about Vegas. "What do you mean?"

Bob leaned forward, and put his elbows on the table. "I've been doing this a long time. Some things about your situation just didn't add up. Even though it has individual outliers, the FBI as an organization is a huge bureaucracy, and does things in a predictable way. The way they were acting towards you was an outlier. Uncharacteristic. Which meant I didn't have the whole picture, just a piece of it."

Dave didn't say anything. He just sat there. He'd sat through all sorts of police interrogations and never said a word. The only thing different about this was he didn't have a lawyer by his side. And didn't quite know who Bob worked for. Or even why he'd wanted to meet. And he'd told Dave to leave his phone and any other electronics at home. Not in the car, home, so his phone was on Aaron's kitchen table. Bob just sat there, calm, comfortable, in no hurry. The two men with him did the same. Dave just as placidly returned their gazes. He was prepared to sit there forever.

Bob, studying him, gave a little nod. He continued. "So, I looked into it. It seems that you are quite close with our larger-than-life sheriff down there. I thought if anybody might know the true story of what's going on, it would be him." Bob nodded. "The matching fingerprint thing makes complete sense. I could totally see how the FBI would go balls to the wall to try and take you out to keep that from becoming public knowledge."

Dave opened and closed his mouth several times. "Fingerprints?" he finally said, doing his best to look confused.

Bob smiled. "Man, and I thought I knew how to keep my mouth shut." He glanced at his companions and they grudgingly nodded.

Dave couldn't just leave it, but he thought a bit about how to proceed. "Do you know the sheriff?" Dave asked, picking his words carefully.

Bob shook his head. "No, but I know someone who's friends with him. And he called the sheriff up, and we got the true story behind the feebies' white hot hate for you."

Dave frowned. "Bullshit," he said. He couldn't believe the sheriff would tell anyone his secret, and that was plain on his face.

Bob nodded. He gestured at the skinnier of his two companions. "This is Jerry. This is Ron," he said, indicating the one who looked like a Marine. "I've known them since we were teenagers. We're trying to decide if we want to offer you a job. Well, I've pretty much made up my mind, your bona fides are pretty goddamn solid, but I don't have the only vote."

Dave hadn't stopped frowning. "What kind of a job?"

"First," Bob said, "assuming I'm not lying, who can you think of that is personal friends with the sheriff, who also, let's say, has the power to create a completely secret off-the-books intelligence organization inside the U.S. government? Or, at least did."

Dave didn't have to think about it for very long. "Him?"

"Just trying to give you a feel for the kind of league you'd be playing in. You want to call Osterman when you get back to your phone, go right ahead, but who else knew about your little secret, who would tell it to me? That sneaky fucker Colman? Dead. I never liked him anyway. Mickey? Dead. Just about everybody at the FBI who knew why they wanted you dead has now died, most of them under mysterious circumstances. Government cleaning up after itself. I suspect your buddy Aaron might know, but from what I hear he took a world-class beating and didn't say shit, so you know he didn't tell me anything. And, let me tell you something, the courage and character of your friends says a lot about you."

Jerry looked at Bob. "Did you just compliment yourself?"

Bob flipped him off. Meanwhile, Dave sat there, stunned. There were only three people whom he'd told about his fingerprint problem, and only two of them knew about Mickey by name—Lori and Osterman. Osterman had recovered his burned body from inside Dave's cabin. Dave had only told Lori because he kept shouting Mickey's name in his sleep. The nightmares had been bad for a while.

Bob smiled and went on. "You've had both the FBI and DIA try to kill you multiple times. After having done nothing wrong. And the mob, but I suspect you earned that. Back in our youth," he nodded at his companions, "we had a significant percentage of the CIA's State-side operators try to kill us. After having done nothing wrong."

"The thing with John?"

The three of them nodded. Bob confirmed, "The thing with John. It was...commensurate in scale with our little Juarez jaunt, shall we say. These two idiots might have been there as well." He tilted his head left and right, indicating his companions. "And it too got hushed up, at the very highest level. We all signed an NDA, so I can't, I *won't* say much, but I will say that's the first time I met a President. We made a lot of very high-ranking contacts because of how that all played out. And it gave us a very jaundiced view toward our government."

"Love the country, hate the government, just like those rebellious Founders intended," Jerry said with a rueful smile.

"We've been working to do the right thing, from the inside, ever since, but for quite some time ours was an... informal operation, shall we say. Just a few like-minded true believers, taking opportunities when they arose. But that powerful friend of the sheriff...after seeing just how broken our intelligence and federal law enforcement agencies were, how corrupt, fighting against the will of the people rather than for the country...well. You can talk about draining the swamp all you want, but dismantling, disbanding sizable chunks of the government just isn't possible, it's simply not going to happen short of the entire government collapsing. But he's not the kind of guy to let something like this go, especially considering how they went after him personally— for things he didn't do. And for everything you know that made the news, there are ten things even worse behind the scenes. So. You don't think somebody with that kind of business experience would know how to siphon off one ten-thousandth of one percent of the government budget every year, for this secret organization he dreamed up? Hardwired permanent funding, in ways no one would ever notice, using programs no politician would ever think to touch, like Social Security. Making it immune from the results of elections, considering how he's lost all faith in those."

"One ten-thousandth of a percent? How much money is that?"

"Not much, in the grand scheme of things. Sixty million bucks a year, that's our operating budget. Our budget is less than a rounding error for the government, and it's more than enough, considering most of us work inside the government, utilizing its resources and intelligence right under its nose. You'd be one of the few exceptions. But it would be nice having someone with no formal affiliation, who doesn't have to explain why he missed work for three days."

"I'm just a guy. With no training," Dave said.

Bob nodded. "We'd fix that. Send you a few places. The most important part is your motivation. Pretty sure, based on your colored history with them, you'd have no moral quandaries about watching the watchers. And not just watching. Stepping in, from time to time, to correct a few things. Do the right thing. I've seen you in action, so I have no doubts about your performance in adverse environs, shall we say. Physical bravery. What's far more important to us is your motivation. That you'd want to do this, because it's the right thing to do, because it needs to be done. That you don't care about the money."

"Money?"

Bob shrugged. "Well, it would be a job. The name on your paycheck would be some bland corporation no one has ever heard of. And your job title would be something equally bland and boring. Enough money so that, after taxes, cash flow wouldn't be one of your headaches. But if you were thinking of going into this for the money, you're not our guy. But you don't seem especially wealth driven."

"Names," Ron said, speaking for the first time.

"Right," Bob said with a nod. "Everything we do is behind the scenes, lowest of low profiles. So we couldn't have David Anderson on the payroll, even though it's a pretty common name. Jack Burton is compromised too. We'd have to set you up with a different name on the books. Then again, you decide to do this, you'll have all sorts of IDs in different names. The advantage of having jobs inside government, inside the intelligence apparatus, is getting to use all their toys behind their back. The driver licenses, passports you'd be supplied with, they'd actually all be real. Government issued. Most of the people doing work for us, in every agency you can think of, don't know it's for us. We're in the walls."

"The ghosts in the machine," Ron added.

"That's not what that means," Jerry told him.

"What's it mean?"

"It means souls."

"You sure about that? Anyway, it's still pretty accurate." Ron looked at Dave. "We're an invisible watchdog agency nobody knows exists. No official oversight, although Bob does meet with our, uh, founder about once a year and give him a progress report. But we've got official authority. In fact, a signed letter of creation and authorization from, well, the President." There was no reason to be cute about it. "But as soon as we come out into the light, we're done for. So we stay ghosts. But we've got teeth, and the will to do what needs to be done. Following...this country's foundational principles, we'll call them, and one of those is that government itself is a necessary evil, both necessary and inherently evil. We can't fix everything, the problem is far too big, and we're small, but we do what we can. Doing what's right, but not necessarily what's legal. Just to be clear. I'm confident you know the distinction. You've lived it. And this problem exists across party lines, the entire government has been weaponized against the American people. We've shut a lot of shady shit down. Put a lot of bodies in the ground. Leaked some important things to the media… although half the media, more, is in bed with government, so that doesn't have the same impact it used to. And so far, nobody's noticed any pattern to the random acts of rebellion."

Dave frowned. "Steve?" he said, having a thought. "The guy on the radio."

Ron and Jerry looked at Bob. Bob nodded. "High up in the NSA. One of our founding members. Also on that road trip we can't really talk about. I'm currently with the DIA, the Defense Intelligence Agency, but I've been around, and have contacts all through JSOC. Jerry's with the DEA. Currently doing a stint at their headquarters—which he doesn't much like, but it's very useful for our purposes."

"D.C. sucks ass," Jerry agreed. "Best thing to do would be to back off and nuke the site from orbit. It's the only way to be sure. But seeing as that's not an option…"

"Ron's a senior investigator for the IRS," Bob said.

"IRS?" Dave said in surprise.

"Arguably the most powerful government agency," Ron said.

Dave thought about that. The man wasn't wrong.

Bob asked him, "You still with the same girlfriend? How stable is that?"

"Good," Dave said. "Solid."

"Really? Hmm." Bob looked at Ron. "Goat, you'd want me to hire him just based on who his girlfriend is."

"Who is she?"

"I'll tell you later," Jerry said. "You'll embarrass yourself."

"Again, I have no training for any of this," Dave said.

Jerry snorted. "Dude. You've seen combat. A lot of it. Lived under an alias. Proven you know how to keep one hell of a secret. Hell, a lot of secrets. Had your own government try to kill you multiple times, and lived to, well to *not* tell the tale. You're platinum pre-qualified, and nobody can teach that. The shit you don't know, electronic countermeasures, disguises, improvised explosives, that's easy in comparison."

Dave sat and thought for quite a while. They didn't pressure him; they just waited. Two pizzas arrived, and they dug in. Bob was bobbing his head. Ron looked at him. "What's the radio station playing now?"

"*Everything in its Right Place*," Bob told him around a mouthful of pizza.

Ron frowned. "Who the hell sings that?"

"Radiohead."

"Radiohead? Ugh. Your brain has the worst taste in music."

Jerry shook his head. "This coming from a guy who thinks Jon Bon Jovi is a musical genius."

"Who the fuck likes Radiohead?" Ron said.

Jerry gaped at him. "Douchebag, *OK Computer* is considered one of the greatest albums of all time."

Dave watched them going back and forth. It was clear they were all old friends. He sat and ate for ten minutes. Eventually he spoke. "I'm not saying yes, I'm not saying no, but…" He sighed. "You want to get me IDs in different names?" He gestured at his face. "I don't exactly blend in with the crowd. Not sure what you envision me doing, but…"

Bob leaned forward and peered at his face critically. "Nobody knows your face outside of Arizona. And I think a good cosmetic surgeon would be able to reduce those scars to where they're hardly even noticeable, especially under a beard. They're not bad now, but you're right, the less memorable you are the better. We've all got scars from fighting this fight. Unlike yours, most of them don't show."

"Ron's ear," Jerry said. "Steve's finger." Dave looked over and saw one of Ron's ears was mangled. "Everything else is covered by clothes. Or time."

Bob told Dave, "You're a bit beat up right now, but you're younger than us. You'd be fresh blood."

"Fresh and motivated," Jerry said.

"I'm not saying it'll be easy," Bob told him. "There's a very good chance we'll end up in federal prison. Or dead, depending. We've lost people. But we can sleep at night. We're doing the right thing. *'They fought here alone, and gave up their lives, so that this nation should not perish from the earth.'* What kind of price can you put on your soul?"

Osterman had kept asking him what he wanted to do with the rest of his life. This seemed like fate, or something. It didn't even look like he had a choice, the universe had conspired to put him in this position. "This is good pizza," Dave said.

"It is," Ron agreed. They waited.

"Okay," Dave told them.

Next in the James Tarr Conspiracy Thriller Series

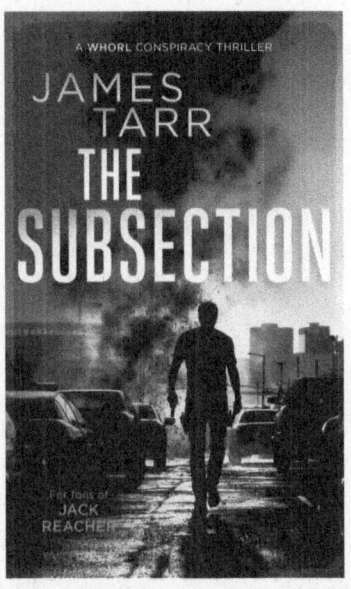

vinci-books.com/subsection

In a world of secrets, Dave Anderson faces enemies on all sides—even within his own government.

Recruited by *The Subsection*, a covert team dedicated to protecting America, Dave uncovers a chilling conspiracy: the CIA is funding terrorist groups to manipulate global events.

Turn the page for a free preview….

The Subsection: Chapter One

PART I: STOMACH AND TEETH

Playhouse Square

James Blinkenschaal yawned, took a long draw of coffee out of his flip-top insulated mug, and blinked with exaggerated care several times, trying to wake up. It had rained a little in the late morning hours, and the streets of downtown Cleveland were wet, reflecting the reds and greens of the traffic lights. It was peaceful, and he had the radio off. There wasn't much traffic—yet—and he enjoyed the hiss of the Durango's tires on the wet pavement, loud enough to be heard over the low rumble of the hemi. As he rolled into the downtown area the buildings around him grew taller. Depending on the district the towers were older and historic, with a lot of brick and stone, or more modern with steel and glass. Lights were starting to come on in some of the windows, but for the most part the towers were as dark and quiet as the streets.

But the wet traffic lanes and the smeared reflections of the lights triggered a memory. He'd landed an insurance case, years earlier, for a nationwide carrier he did a lot of work for, and their client was one of the big Hollywood movie studios. Someone had stolen some expensive electronic equipment from a location shoot, and the studio wanted it handled quietly, preferably without involving the police. Because the facts of the theft strongly indicated it was an employee, someone on the film crew. He'd figured out who was responsible pretty quickly, and turned his evidence over to the adjuster, but for a somewhat simple case it had been fascinating. He'd learned so much, talking to the movie industry people. Studios at the time were occasionally filming street scenes in Cleveland for big productions, having the modern downtown areas fill in for New York or other generic urban locales, just because it was so prohibitively expensive to film in NYC—in addition (apparently) to it being a giant pain in the ass due to all the permits and union bribes required to grease the wheels.

One assistant still photographer he'd interviewed had talked about "the water truck", and Blink—almost everybody called him Blink, Blinken, or Blinky—had thought he'd meant a truck that delivered drinking water. The guy—who'd gone on to some success on his own with his photographic "urban landscapes"—had shaken his head. "No, look at any TV show or any movie filmed outside on the street," he'd said. "Even ones that are filming under an overhang. The pavement—concrete, asphalt, whatever—has always been wet down. Almost always, ninety-eight times out of a hundred. Sometimes if it's a small space it's just a PA with a hose, but for a big area it's easier to use a water truck, especially if you're doing take after take. It drives down the street and sprays water. Enough to get it wet, but not to leave much standing water, maybe just a puddle or two out of the way."

"Why?" Blink had asked.

"Because it looks better, man," the skinny photog had told him. "It looks *so* much better. Dry pavement is just flat. Doesn't give you anything. Might as well be standing on sand. *Ugly* sand. Wet, you get more saturated colors, blacker blacks, richer tans, but mostly it's due to the reflections. Wet pavement reflects lights, the reflections of your actors, clouds, movement, everything."

And damned if the guy hadn't been right. Blink couldn't watch a movie or TV show now without noticing the wet pavement under the feet of every single actor, even if there wasn't a cloud in the sky. Even if they were filming inside a damn parking garage with a roof over their heads.

Cleveland's Theater District was considered part of the city's downtown, but was on the south side of it, just over a mile southeast from the Rock & Roll Hall of Fame perched on the shore of Lake Erie. His destination was Playhouse Square, the beating heart of the theater district. It was the largest theater district in the US outside of New York City, not that anybody outside of Cleveland really knew that. But in-between the theaters and the businesses servicing those patrons of the arts—restaurants and hotels—were all sorts of mundane businesses.

He took several turns on streets that felt narrow from the buildings towering overhead, then pulled to the curb on 14th Street south of Euclid. The US Bank Centre was one of the largest buildings in Cleveland—not the tallest, but it spread over most of a block, a modern mirrored monstrosity in an area filled with old, beautiful, historic buildings.

Blink's focus was on the physical therapy center on the south side of the US Bank Centre building. It was part of the building, inside it on the ground floor, but it had a separate entrance. Mirrored glass double doors which could be opened with the push of a button, at the top of a long concrete handicap ramp. The ramp went up one direction, then turned and went the other before reaching the level of the door, the angle so gentle even someone rolling themselves up in a wheelchair would have no problem. There was a second door barely ten feet to the side, at the top of five steps. It fed into the US Bank Centre, although there was a door just inside which led into the therapy center's lobby.

Directly facing the south side of the building and the two entrances was a parking garage, and in-between the two was a small courtyard with a few steel tables and some decorative planters with low groundcover and small trees trimmed to provide the most shade.

Blink had scoped out the location the day before. There was no way to park a vehicle on the street long enough to do the job for which he'd been hired—the spots were metered. The first floor of the parking garage, directly across from the small courtyard, had no windows, and from the second floor (and up) the trees blocked the view of the entrances. So there was no way to park a vehicle with a stationary camera inside it where it would do the job. But those planters bordering the courtyard...they were perfect.

He looked around once more. There was very little traffic, foot or vehicle, at six in the morning. Humming to himself, he grabbed what looked like a big rock off the front passenger seat and climbed out.

His knee was a little stiff from just half an hour in the car, which told him there was likely a storm brewing. He stepped in front of his Dodge, walked across the sidewalk, and into the courtyard. It was empty, and badly lit by a few exterior lights. There were security cameras galore inside the US Bank Centre, but none covering the courtyard—at least that he'd been able to tell. So he was relaxed as he looked around.

Blink stepped into one of the planters, his shoes sinking slightly into the decomposing wood chips. The ground cover was bright green (more gray than anything in the cool pre-dawn light) and no more than ankle-high, which was perfect. He set the rock down into a small gap, then moved to stand behind it, looking back and forth between the rock and the two doors on the side of the building. He bent down and readjusted the rock, rotating it very slightly left. Then, satisfied, he strode back to his SUV, climbed in, and drove off.

The Subsection: Chapter Two

Murph Takes A Trip

Murph squinted, and groaned. Something really, really bright was shining in his eyes. So bright he thought his eyes were open for a second. Until he cracked his eyelids, and took the full glare of the morning sun right in the retinas, like a razor sharp dagger.

He grimaced, clamped his eyelids shut again, and took inventory. It was not a quick process, but he wasn't in a hurry. Eventually he realized that unless gravity had reversed, he was lying on his back. The sun was warming his face and chest. He could smell dirt and water. Hear water, in fact, somewhere nearby. The rushing sound of it seemed all around him, burbling, swirling…

Abruptly he turned on his side, away from the glaring sun, and vomited. Just three heaves, his whole body jackknifing. Not much came up, although the stomach acid burned his lips and tongue. He knew not to eat much before taking peyote, as he almost always vomited after. Sometimes during. So he'd begun fasting beforehand, and hadn't actually eaten anything for a few days. The hallucinations from the mescaline were wild, and he felt bad for a few hours afterward, but the clarity that filled his mind for the next week was incredible. He'd done some of his best work during that post-peyote clarity. But the first few hours afterward...ugh.

This trip had been...he didn't even know how to describe it. Transcendent? Illuminating? He couldn't remember most of it, but the impact it had on his brain, on his subconscious thought processes, couldn't be understated. He had several new ideas, revolutionary avenues to explore to help solve his superconduction and scaling issues.

With his face shielded from the sun he opened his eyes again. His view was entirely Mother Earth—dirt and sand and a small tuft of slender, pale green grass. It was beautiful. He could feel the sun on his back. It was hot, but because the air around him was cool he could tell it still must be early in the morning.

Murph rolled onto his knees, then climbed to his feet, dizzy only for a second. He put his back to the sun, blinked his eyes a few times, and saw he was a dozen steps from the river. It was wide and placid here, and the riverbank sloped gradually down to the water, which was equal parts green and blue, with currently only a hint of mud clouding up the eddies and swirls. He looked down and saw he was dirty, caked with dust and grime like he'd been rolling around for hours. Mind still getting up to speed, it took him a few more seconds to realize he was naked under all the dirt.

His tongue felt swollen and dry, his lips hard and ready to crack. He swallowed a few times, licked his lips, then said, "Hunh." He heard a few birds, the clicks of something that could have been a lizard, a hard-shelled insect, or small rocks tumbling somewhere nearby, and over it all the soothing rush of the river. But no yells or screaming, which was good. Not that he looked that bad, clothed or naked, but people were weird when it came to nudity. Completely irrational. But then, people were irrational about almost everything. It was what made humanity both great and terrifying.

He looked left and right, but he was all alone. He headed into the river and spent a minute scrubbing off, dunking himself in the cold water. That woke him up the rest of the way, and when he popped his head up and swept his hair back he looked around carefully. He spotted the notch in the canyon wall he was looking for, maybe half a mile away across the valley floor, up a short gentle slope covered with grass and cacti. There was still nobody in sight either up- or downriver (which is why he'd chosen this part of the canyon), so he strode out of the water and slowly walked across the rocky, dusty ground, picking his steps carefully. There were low bushes to either side, sage and juniper and some small cottonwood trees. The banks to either side of the river were uniformly green with life, but get just a short distance away and the land became little more than dry earth and bare rock baking under an intense sun.

Ten minutes later he reached his tent, which was still in shadow. The cliff face rose steeply to either side—the spot he'd chosen was a narrow notch that was easy to miss unless you were walking right along the rock wall. The layers upon layers of rock had been laid down during the two billion years of the Proterozoic eon and Paleozoic era and eroded by the Colorado River over an estimated five million years —although there currently was a heated debate between geologists about that, some of which said the canyon had been formed over seventy million years. The steep rock walls stretched up to either side, stripes of orange and tan and brown and red in a dozen different hues. Sometimes—okay, usually—he went wandering when he took peyote, and so chose isolated campsites, nowhere near any of the usual tourist areas, but usually he never walked or crawled more than fifty feet during the night. Half a mile was a record, and he could feel it in his feet. In his knees. His soles were sore, and there were minor cuts and scratches on both his shins and abrasions on his knees.

He hooted and stomped his feet just to scare away any critters that might be nearby—rattlesnakes were the main worry—then crawled into his tent and pulled out his backpack. He had one one-liter bottle of distilled water remaining, and cracked the top on that and drank it down. It was still cold from the night before and tasted incredible, and seemed to fill dry cracks all through his body. That was it for the water he'd brought with him, but he had a water purifier. These weren't store-bought bottles but rather collapsible ones he brought with him whenever he went camping. He'd refill them before heading back out. The Colorado River water was full of minerals and didn't taste good, but he wasn't so much of a masochist that he'd backpack in days' worth of water when there was a river literally *right there*. The fifth longest river in the country.

Murph pulled a spare pair of boxers out of his backpack, tugged them on, then went looking for the clothes he'd been wearing the night before. He found his shirt twenty feet from the tent, draped over a small spiny bush. Fifty feet past that, out away from the cliffs, he found his left shoe atop a flat rock, a low-topped Merrell hiker that was light, comfortable, and had very aggressive tread. But that was it. He started a spiral search pattern, and after ten minutes had found his pants, socks, and underwear. But he couldn't find his damn right shoe. He couldn't hike out of the canyon with just one shoe. Well, he could, but it would be brutal.

He went back to where he'd found his left hiker, figuring he wouldn't have gone far before taking off his other shoe. He finally found it, well-hidden in the deep shade under a crucifixion thorn bush wrapped around a small cactus as if they were in a life-or-death struggle.

Immediate problem solved, he straightened and looked around him. As usual, the landscape was incredible, unbelievable. The peyote cleanse had sharpened his senses. His eyesight was clear, and he could hear the rustle and burble of the river as if it was just a few feet away, not half a mile.

He got his peyote from the locals, Hualapai indians, and it was the good stuff. He'd met a few of the younger braves during one of his first trips to the canyon, and they'd introduced him to a few of their friends in the Havasupai tribe, where he'd done a bit of business—some of it peyote-related, some of it computer/internet-related, for them and tribe. He often parked on reservation land if he wanted to hike in places he wasn't likely to meet another human soul. It depended on just how alone he needed to get with his thoughts. But he always got their permission first, the white man had already fucked them over enough. Then again, that was all of human history, a story of victors and the vanquished.

People sucked. That was why he preferred nature. Nature was bloodthirsty—'red in tooth and claw'—but not evil. Mother Nature might be trying to kill you, but it was nothing personal.

The canyon walls to either side were so tall that if the valley hadn't been so wide, the Arizona sun so high in the sky, it would have been dark and oppressive. Instead, but for the south rim wall still in shadow, the canyon floor was bright and warm. Not hot, not yet, but it was liable to get there long before noon.

He appreciated that the National Park Service didn't try to sugarcoat it. It was a mile in elevation down to the river and another mile back up, which meant miles on switchback trails, and even the easiest trail wasn't so easy with that kind of elevation change. Most people simply couldn't make it down to the Colorado River and back in one day. The NPS's 'Introduction to Backcountry Hiking' brochure had warnings in red all over it, including "Know how to rescue yourself". And it was always ten or twenty degrees hotter down at the river than up at the rim, which mattered in the summer when it was in the eighties up top. Seven thousand feet of elevation along the South Rim, eight thousand at the North Rim, while the river flowed roughly two thousand feet above sea level. You'd see snow up on the rim through April while people down along the river were sweating and getting sunburned. All of which meant the people you were likely to meet at the bottom of the canyon were a different breed than those fat lazy NPCs lining the rims, looking down. Younger, in shape, more independent. Still, on average, over ten people a year died in the canyon. He didn't know the details, but he guessed most of them were from falls or heart attacks. But what a way to go. What *a place* to go.

At that thought Murph looked around again. It was gorgeous. Life—existence itself, just the fact of *being*—was wonderful, but there was something to be said for the natural wonders of the world still unfucked by humanity. For all of its tourists—and he doubted more than five percent of them ventured beyond the south rim between

Grand Canyon Village and the Desert View Watchtower, a mere thirty-mile stretch in a park larger than the entire freaking state of Delaware—the Grand Canyon was definitely at the top of the list of nature's home runs. Unspoiled. He wouldn't have minded dying there. The Grand Canyon was one of the most beautiful places on earth, and maybe his favorite. His plan was to never die, and he was actually making some substantive progress on that front, but just in case that didn't work out he was compiling a list of places where he'd like his ashes to be scattered. Most of them were in the Grand Canyon. The Park Service, of course, would never allow it, but what they didn't know....

Humming to himself he walked back to his tent, broke it down, and strapped it to the outside of his pack. He policed his campsite, making sure he hadn't left any garbage, then walked down to the river and used his purifier to fill up three liter bottles of river water. It took a while, but he was in no hurry. He didn't have anywhere to be...well, ever, technically, but that's not to say he didn't have work to get back to. Responsibilities he'd taken on. Promises he'd made. And for that he needed a signal. He'd been out of contact, off the grid, for over three days, since he'd started the climb down from the south rim. No radio, and no cell phone—not that they really worked anywhere inside the canyon, or once you got more than a few miles away from the heavily-trafficked tourist areas. A satphone would have worked down in the canyon, most of the time, but the point was to be out of contact with everyone and everything but Mother Nature. He drank most of a liter as he stood beside the river, having learned long ago that the best place to store water in a desert was inside your own body, and then refilled the bottle and stuck it in his pack. Then he shouldered his pack and headed out.

The vast majority of tourists to the Grand Canyon only visited a few spots that were easy access and provided great views. Ninety-five percent of them hung out at the southeast corner of the park, travelling along the South Rim between Hermit's Rest and the Desert View Watchtower which were just twenty miles apart in a straight line. Thick crowds of people, many with dogs, many of them not speaking English. When he did venture among the crowds he wished more of them didn't speak English, so he couldn't hear how stupid their comments were. Some did nothing but drive up to the visitor complex on the south rim, walk up to Mather Point a hundred yards past the idling tour buses, and jostle for space so they could take a selfie without anyone else in the picture. Then head toward the gift shop to buy some of the touristy memorabilia made in China. Which was a shame, because the park was huge. HUGE. The Grand Canyon was up to a mile deep in most places, often eighteen miles wide, and 277 miles long. 1900 square miles!

His first trip to the park he'd been standing at the Mather Point overlook, looking out at the enormity of the canyon, trying to spot the helicopter he could very faintly hear. And he finally did, off to the northwest, a dual-rotor machine tracing the course of the Colorado River—far, far below him. He'd never looked *down* on a helicopter before. At least one company did helicopter tours of the canyon.

Looking at the map they'd given him at the entrance he'd figured out the helicopter had been three miles away, and nearly three-quarters of a mile below him—and compared to the expanse of the canyon stretching in every direction, the helicopter had seemed close. Close enough to touch, like a green and white insect buzzing lazily along. It was that experience which had convinced him to get away from the tourists and do some real exploring. And he'd never regretted it.

There were well-known hiking trails, and of course you could book a horse-riding trip in the canyon, even mules, but if you weren't a big fat slob with a jiggling body full of preservatives and micro plastics and were willing to put in the work and maybe even sweat a little, and had some time, it was easy to hike through areas of the national park where you wouldn't see another person for hours or days at a time. Half the time he didn't even follow established trails, he just let his soul guide him. Although, over the years, he had hiked most of the well-known trails—Bright Angel, the North and South Kaibab Trails, and visited the Phantom Ranch. The Hermit and Grandview Trails. He'd skinny-dipped at Havasu Falls, ascended Mt. Trumbull, and walked across the Uinkaret volcanic field.

He checked his watch—just before eight a.m. Knowing the time he broke camp would tell him when he was getting close to his destination. He had a compass, but he wouldn't need it. The Colorado River was a known entity, running east to west through the canyon, although it did wind back and forth like a huge, sinuous snake. In a lot of places you couldn't walk close to the river, as it was rushing through deep rocky ravines, but you always knew where it was. He had about six hours of easy hiking east before it would be time to turn south and work his way up a trail the Hualapai had shown him. It was so narrow, and steep in some places, he wasn't sure it hadn't originally been a game trail—quite different from the maintained trails most of the tourists used that, while dirt, were nearly wide enough for a Jeep.

It was almost impossible to spot the end of his trail as it neared the river, but he knew to look for a promontory of rock in the distance shaped like a crooked nose. When he drew opposite that, it would be time to head away from the river, and he'd find the trail winding through the scrub on the narrow valley floor. Between where he was and the switchback trail up the rocks he expected to see very few people. Maybe none on land. Likely there'd be people floating down the river in kayaks or canoes, but that would be it. Whitewater rafting was a popular pastime, but not in this area of the Colorado.

Five hours later he stopped to refill his water bottles. He'd been stopping every hour for five minutes, to rest a bit and drink water, but was getting near to the point where he'd leave the river, and wanted a full complement of water, just in case. He'd been following one of the narrow trails that wound along the valley floor and stuck close to the river. They'd started out as game trails, but had been widened a bit over the years by human feet. He'd seen two people two hours into his journey, hikers, but they'd been on the opposite side of the river, which was fifty yards wide at that point. They'd exchanged waves, but that was it.

He drank half a liter, relieved himself in a bush, then set about using the purifier to refill the plastic bottles. The sun was bright and hot, the air dry. He hadn't seen anybody on the river all morning.

"Hello? Hey!" After so much quiet the human voices were strange. He looked up. Staggering around a rocky outcrop a hundred feet away were a handful of people who looked like they'd been dragged behind a car. Two girls and two guys who looked to be in their early twenties. "Can you help us?"

"With what?"

One of the guys was chubby and pale, the other was skinny. One young woman was a thick, pretty brunette, the other was a skinny blonde who seemed to have a great body but with a mannish, horsey face. They were all sweating and sunburned and covered in dust. And seemingly exhausted. They walked up.

"We're lost."

"You're in the Grand Canyon," Murph said. He jerked his thumb over his shoulder. "That's the Colorado River."

"Very funny, smartass," the skinny guy said. "We know we're in the fucking Grand Canyon." They crowded around him and looked up. Murph was tall and skinny, with a big mop of sun-bleached hair atop his head making him seem even taller.

"No, I mean," Murph said, "the river goes through the park from one end to the other. It's very tough to try to swim across it unless you're in one of the wide, slow moving areas, so most people stay on one side or the other unless you're rafting or kayaking. And there's cliffs all around. So how can you be lost? Follow the slope down until you find the water, then go upriver or down and go back out the canyon the way you came in."

"We got high last night, and couldn't find the trail," the blonde told him, embarrassed. "I think we passed it, and now we don't know which direction it is. We went back and forth for hours yesterday, until it got dark. We slept on the ground down here. We've been wandering around all morning, looking for something. Someone." She looked at what he was doing. "Is it okay to drink the river water? We weren't sure. We did, but…"

"Always better to use a purifier," he told them. "Here." He handed them a full bottle, and they passed it around. He looked back and forth between them. "Do you guys not have any backpacks? Any supplies?"

The chubby guy shook his head. "We thought we'd only

be gone a few hours. Just down to the river and back up. It looked really close on the map."

Murph shook his head, dug into his backpack, and handed out two energy bars. All natural, no preservatives. "So where did you park up top?"

The skinny guy shrugged. "I don't know. We drove through a little town with a train and some cabins and a hotel."

"Maswik Lodge," one of the girls said around a mouthful of food.

"Grand Canyon Village," Murph told them.

"Yeah, whatever. But there were shit-tons of tourists there, so we kept going, found some side roads, and headed, um west. Like, half an hour? On dirt roads. Then the road we were on ended. But there was this awesome space to park on the side of the road, where we could see the canyon, and we followed this trail down here. But it took forever to get down. We went swimming, and got high, then we got lost, and couldn't find the trail that we came in on. We almost froze to death last night. I can't believe we haven't seen anybody, you're the first person we've seen."

Murph fought the urge to roll his eyes. "This park is huge. The closest place to here that tourists go is Supai Village, run by the Havasupai tribe. The Havasupai Lodge is very nice. But you can't even drive to it. You have to park and hike eight miles. Just to get to the hotel. I think you probably drove onto the reservation. But the canyon's no joke. You're lucky you didn't die. Seriously."

The brunette moaned. "Is that how far we have to walk? Eight miles? My feet are killing me." Murph looked at their feet. The whiner was wearing flat-bottomed Vans, a totally, completely horrible choice for hiking. The others were wearing various running shoes. Better, but still not good.

"To the Lodge?" He shook his head. "No, it's twenty miles from here, straight line. And there are no straight lines. It would take days to get there. I just mentioned it because it's the closest thing to civilization from here. But if you come with me, it's about an hour to the base of the trail I take up the south rim. There's this big spur of rock... Anyway, once we get to the top, which looking at you I'm guessing will take more than a few hours, my vehicle is another couple miles." On an unmarked reservation road that in many places was little better than a two-track. If the ground wasn't so hardpacked he never would have been able to get his RV down it, even with its all-season tires.

"Is that near our car?"

Murph shook his head. "I have no idea where your car is. But I know where the Village is, and from there you should be able to backtrack to your car."

"I can't believe there aren't police out here," the brunette said. "No cell service, and no police?" She looked around, then peered at him. It appeared she wasn't sure if they could trust him.

"Park Rangers," Murph told her. "And you're welcome to stay here. But considering all the dumb decisions y'all have made already, I'm guessing you'll end up dead before you get rescued. I'm Kelly. Come with me if you want to live." He smiled and cocked his head and waited. None of them seemed to get the reference, which was disappointing.

By the time they reached his vehicle the sun was down behind a ridge, the land in shadow but the sky still aglow. They'd spent hours working their way up the narrow switchback trail on the south rim, in shade almost the whole time, which was a blessing as three of the four of them were slow and out of shape. Laboring in the hot sun might have been too much for them. They still had to stop to take frequent breaks. Not quite halfway up the canyon wall was a flat-topped mesa that spread out for a hundred yards and could have been on Mars for as barren as it was, nothing but dirt and bare red rock. While they rested Murph walked out to the edge and enjoyed the view. The rest of them seemed to have lost their appetite for sight-seeing. By the time they reached the top of the south rim they'd gone through all the water and the remaining energy bars in his pack.

He'd learned they were college students and had just finished out the school year at ASU. Emily was the thick brunette—she'd just graduated, and would be going into nursing school after the summer. Rich was the chubby one, a junior getting a business degree. The skinny guy was Troy —more than a bit of a jerk, but his asshole tendencies seemed to be tempered by his physical exhaustion. His friends said he was really good with numbers, but he didn't know yet if he wanted to go into accounting or try something involving the stock market. All of them were smart, at least by normal standards.

The skinny blonde who'd caught his eye was Hannah. She handled the climb better than any of them, probably because she was in the best shape—she said she used to do track and field in high school, and still ran regularly. She had a plain, almost masculine face, but a pretty, shy smile.

"Where's your car?" Troy gasped, as they finally topped the rim. He looked around, then glared at Murph suspiciously. They all did. Their disappointment was palpable.

"I told you, it's another two miles," Murph said. He pointed. "But it's flat. At least, compared to that." He jabbed a thumb over his shoulder at the rim of the Grand

Canyon. "No more climbing, just walking." The canyon behind them was sparse and arid as a desert. The south rim, on the other hand, was covered with a pine forest, and the temperature had dropped significantly. It wasn't cold, not yet, but it would be. "Anybody needs to go potty, pick a tree to hide behind, and if you see any elk, don't try to pet them." There seemed to be more elk than squirrels in the forests around the east end of the canyon.

Rich pulled out his phone, and lifted it into the air. He thought for sure he'd have a signal, now that they were out of the canyon. He frowned at the display. NO SERVICE "Seriously?"

Forty-five minutes later they came around the side of a small rise and saw his RV, the glass reflecting the glow in the sky. It was parked at the end of a narrow dirt road, little more than a two-track, running between two low hills.

"That's yours?" Rich said. He'd been expecting a shitty, thirty-year-old Winnebago. Their rescuer looked like a dude with no money, one of those spacey surfer/hiker types who'd be in-between jobs his whole life. And he sounded like one too, talking about nature and some of the wildest conspiracy theories ever as they'd trudged to the top of the canyon. But what squatted in front of them looked more like Dave Matthews' tour bus than an RV. And Rich said as much, as they walked up and stared at it.

"Yeah, well," Murph said, and shrugged. He glanced at his ride. It was a Prevost bus conversion by Marathon Coach with dual axles in the back and a bombproof diesel powertrain made by Volvo. Brand new it had probably been a million and a half, easy, maybe twice that, but it was fifteen years old, and he'd bought it from the Miami Police Department in an online property auction for a fraction of what it was worth. His stupidly-low bid had been the highest the department received, and they'd set no minimum price, so.... It looked brand new inside and out with leather-wrapped couches and chairs, all-new appliances, and cherry wood floors in the bedroom. Likely seized from a drug dealer who'd bought it and never used it. Murph had spent a decent amount of money and a lot of time customizing the interior, although most of his efforts weren't meant to be noticed by casual visitors.

"You rich, Kelly?" Troy asked him, eyeballing the motorcoach.

"What's rich?" Murph said. "Define rich. Hundred years ago, if you had a house with floors that weren't dirt, with running water, with electricity, with central heating, you'd be considered rich. And nobody had air conditioning back then, not even kings. Maybe servants, waving fans over you. Now everybody's got all that, in addition to cable TV, smart phones, cheap antibiotics..." He shrugged again.

Rich nodded at the RV. "That's rich, to me." He pulled out his phone again, checked the screen—his battery was almost dead—and silently swore. Still no signal.

"To me, if you can afford to fly private everywhere, not have to deal with TSA and commercial airports, if you've got enough money to do that, you're rich," Murph said. Not that he'd flown anywhere in years. He ran his hands over the big door which fit flush to the body, then reached under it casually and pressed a concealed button. Then he dug a remote out of his backpack and hit it. The door slid open with a hiss of hydraulics. He looked at his companions. "I don't have that kind of money. Which is why I've got this. I've got cold water and Gatorade in the refrigerator," he told them. "But more important than that, maybe, is the shower, if you're feeling grimy."

"Oh God yes," Emily said.

"Can she shower while you're driving?" Troy asked Murph. He honestly didn't know, he'd never been in an RV before.

Murph shook his head. "I'm not driving anywhere until sunup. I'd break an axle or get stuck in the sand off the road, I tried to drive out of here tonight." There was a glow in the sky to the west, but the sky above them was black, the stars already coming out by the hundreds. Soon, there would be thousands of them. Too many to count. The sky at night was one of the best things about coming to the Grand Canyon.

"Are you kidding me?" Troy said, getting angry.

"Does this thing look off-road capable?" Murph asked. "Getting it to here, in daylight, is like threading a needle."

"We don't have to be anywhere until tomorrow anyway," Hannah said, looking back and forth between the two of them.

"You want to clean up, I can get the grill started. I've got steak, should be enough for all of us," Murph said.

"I'm a vegan," Emily told him.

Murph blinked at the chubby girl. "Then why are you here?" he asked, sounding confused.

"What?"

He waved his arm in the general direction of the Grand Canyon. "Out enjoying nature. A vegan diet is anything but natural. At least, for humans."

"What are you talking about?"

"Biology," he told her. "We don't have the stomach for it. Or the teeth."

"Humans don't have the teeth of carnivores," she said defiantly.

"Humans don't kill with their teeth," he pointed out. He raised his hands and wiggled his fingers. "Tool users."

"I am not having a debate with you," she said, hands on her hips.

"And it sounds like you're not having dinner, either," Murph said. "Because all I've got is steak. And weed," he added. "Marijuana is vegan. But I guess it only makes you hungrier, so…"

He put wood charcoal in the 12-inch Weber grill over a crumpled up tumbleweed he'd grabbed off the ground. It was dry as straw and made great tinder. He lit the fire and was giving the charcoal time to generate some heat before throwing the steaks on, rummaging around in the coach for another chair, so they could all sit outside, when the bathroom door opened and steam billowed out.

"Oh, I needed that," Hannah said, seeing his vague reflection in the foggy mirror. She had a big white towel wrapped around her. It reached from her collarbones to her thighs. "I've definitely got sunburn, though."

"Could be worse. Going to be throwing the steaks on in a few minutes," he told her, standing in the hallway. "I found some asparagus, and can grill that, if she's really not going to eat meat. I think I've got a few more energy bars in here…"

The blonde shook her head and rolled her eyes. "She just says she's vegan for attention. She'll eat whatever you give her. Ugh. I hate having to put back on dirty clothes, but…" She went to turn back into the bathroom, but she wasn't used to the tight spaces and banged her elbow on the door. She hissed, and grabbed at her elbow. The sudden move was enough, and the towel she'd wrapped around herself popped loose and fell straight to the floor.

Murph's eyes opened wide. "Wow," he said, looking her up and down. Then he realized that might not be the appropriate reaction. He looked away and moved down the corridor toward the front of the RV. "Sorry," he called back over his shoulder. Then he stopped, but didn't turn around. "Actually, not sorry," he said. "But...you know."

She stuck her head out the open door and called to him. "You don't think I'm too skinny? That I'm too flatchested?" It wasn't that her breasts were small, they were nonexistent.

He turned in place, and looked at her over his shoulder. "I did say 'Wow'."

She blinked once, then the corner of her mouth curled up. "Yes, you did." And it sounded like he'd meant it.

"No, seriously man, are you rich?" Rich was slumped deep in his folding chair. He took another hit and then passed the thick joint to Troy, then peered at Murph through the smoke. "How'd you afford this thing?" He stuck a thumb over his shoulder at the RV. "Looks like it costs as much as a house. Inside's nicer than my parents' house."

"Gravity," Murph told them. They stared at him stupidly. "I was working construction. A wall fell on me. On my head. Messed me up a little bit. But I got a lot of money out of it. Work comp."

"Cool," Troy said, nodding.

"Asshole," Hannah said to him, frowning. Emily tried to pass her the joint and she shook her head. They were arranged around the small grill, where a few embers still glowed. They'd eaten off paper plates, then fed them to the flames. A bit of heat radiated from the steel. The night air was growing crisp.

"What? What'd I say?" They were full of steak and exhausted, and the marijuana wasn't making them think any clearer. "Oh." He looked at Murph. Murph had a lot of sunbleached blonde hair above wide shoulders and a lean body. He was slouched in one of the cheap folding chairs he'd pulled out of the storage compartment on the underside of his bus-sized RV. "Not cool the wall fell on your head. Cool you got some cash out of it. You need a CDL to drive that thing?" He jerked his head at the bus-sized motorcoach.

Murph shook his head. "No, because it's a private vehicle."

"So you come here a lot?" The joint came back to Troy and he took a hit, then offered it to Murph. Murph shook his head. He had weed for guests, but rarely smoked it himself, and never right after doing peyote. It would completely mess with his clear head.

"At least once a year. I'm trying to hit all the national parks and monuments, but this is maybe my favorite."

"So you don't work? You just drive around?"

"I'm trying to teach myself to code."

"Code?" Emily was half-asleep, and having problems following the conversation.

"Computer code. Programming."

"Yeah, I saw that," Troy said. "You got a killer setup inside. I figured you were a hardcore gamer, all those monitors."

Murph shrugged. "I do some of that too." He leaned back in his chair and stared up at the sky. There was absolutely no light pollution—none—and there were too many stars to count. The night sky was so clear and bright he could see the Milky Way no problem. The stars looked close enough to reach up and touch. He raised his hand and grabbed at them. Emily watched him, frowning. Way off in the distance, likely several miles away, they heard a yip-yip-yipping.

"Did I just hear that?" Troy said. "Or am I that high?"

"The coyote? No, you heard it," Murph told him.

"Kelly your first or last name?" Troy peered at him with stoned eyes.

"First. Kelly Linklater."

"Kind of a girl's name."

"Don't be an asshole," Emily said.

Murph shrugged it off. "*Kelly's Heroes*. Machine Gun Kelly."

"The rapper?" Rich said.

"There's a rapper named Machine Gun Kelly?" Murph said.

"Who were you talking about, if not him?" Rich said, confused.

"The gangster. Used a machine gun. Back during Prohibition."

"Do you think that's where Machine Gun Kelly got his name?" Rich wondered aloud. "I mean, the rapper."

Hannah snorted. "You are so high."

"I need to go to sleep, and I don't want to fall asleep in this chair. I'll wake up paralyzed," Rich said.

"It is getting a little cold," Emily agreed.

Murph gestured at the RV. "That couch in there pulls out. And there's a foam mattress rolled up in that little closet next to the desk, you can put it on the floor. The chairs in front are nicely padded too, and the passenger seat reclines almost all the way. But the bedroom in back, the bed, that's mine."

Rich got up and staggered into the RV. Emily got to her feet and followed him inside. Murph was mellow, content and satisfied with a stomach full of steak and vegetables after a nearly four-day fast. He stared up at the sky. "You know, they say that if we ever do meet any aliens, they'll come from a planet that doesn't have complete cloud cover.

Like, they'd never come from a planet like Jupiter, which is always covered by clouds."

"Why?"

Hannah had asked the question. She was looking at him, her eyes glinting in the darkness. He glanced over. Troy was asleep in his chair. Murph gestured at the stars. "If there's never a break in the clouds, you'll never see what's up there. Out there. That there is a there there. You can't 'reach for the stars' if you don't know they exist."

She thought about it for a minute, then shook her head. "I think with any advanced civilization, eventually they'd wonder what was up there, in the clouds. Past the clouds. It might take them longer, but eventually...."

"Hmm. I guess that makes sense."

She pressed fingertips against the skin of her arm. "Man, did I get burnt. That shower hurt. I put on sunblock before we went down, but it wore off I guess. It's not supposed to last two days. What kind do you use?" He was very tan.

Murph shook his head. "I don't put that poison on my skin."

She blinked and frowned at him. "You've got to get your skin out of the sun, protect it, you'll get skin cancer."

"Horseshit," Murph told her. "Our bodies evolved to be out in sunlight as much as they were to breathe air, drink water, and eat meat. You ever hear of people in Africa getting skin cancer? The Middle East?" He peered at her.

"Uh, I guess not."

"Exactly." He sat quietly for a while, then added, "And if it is the sun giving people skin cancer, it's because it's interacting with something in them. I mean, it's the seed oils that are causing all the cellulite as much as overeating. So chemicals from food preservatives, maybe, interacting with the sunlight, the UV rays, to cause skin cancer. Maybe even fluoride. We are mostly water."

She blinked and sat up, wondering if she'd heard him right. "Fluoride? Like what they put in the water? To make your teeth strong?"

"Oh God." Murph sat up, and leaned forward. "They don't 'put it' in water," he told her. "Back eighty or whatever years ago when they first started treating city water to make it safe for drinking, they used all sorts of chemicals to kill the bugs. Including fluoride. But they discovered they couldn't get all the fluoride out of the water. At least, not cost effectively. It just would have cost too much money. So instead they began this huge PR campaign. Having doctors tell everyone that fluoride was good for you. Made your teeth stronger. Horseshit. Total horseshit. Fluoride's a carcinogen. Causes osteosarcoma, among other things."

"There's no way that's true," she said, frowning.

"Why not?"

"Doctors wouldn't go along with that."

He laughed, a short bark that echoed across the dry ground. Troy jerked awake and looked around. "Wha...?"

"Go into the RV," Hannah told him. "You fell asleep in the chair. You sleep out here all night you'll freeze to death."

The young man, still half-asleep, mumbled something, but then got to his feet and shuffled into the motorcoach. They watched him go. Then Murph turned back to Hannah.

"In the fifties, doctors were telling people cigarette smoking was good for them. Good for their lungs. Because the tobacco companies were paying them. Just like big pharma is paying them now to push pills for every little thing instead of exercise and eating right. Slightly irregular gut? There's a pill for that. Blood sugar not textbook perfect? There's a pill for that. Might cause your taint to fester and explode, but whatever. FDA started a massive campaign against ivermectin when it was shown to be a cheap cure for COVID, saying it was a horse dewormer and not fit for people. Except that was a flat-out lie, and doctors sued them, and won, and they had to take down all their bullshit lies. Didn't help the people who died because they couldn't get access to the drug, but whatever, right? They blame climate change for all the myocarditis, not the experimental gene therapy with spike proteins they were paid to push, and blame everything but the hundred vaccines they give to kids these days, for no good reason, for the sudden increase in autism."

"Ohhh," she said knowingly. She slowly nodded.

"Oh what?"

"Conspiracy theorist."

He smiled, his white teeth bright in the dark. "In the past five years, how many conspiracy theories have been proven right, versus how many have been disproven?"

Hannah shook her head. "I don't even...my brain is too fried to talk about this."

"I'll help—short answer, none have been disproven." He kept going. "And that's just the last five years. Then there's the classics. Operation Mockingbird, where the CIA infiltrated the news media. Cloud seeding. Operation Northwoods, a false flag plan to get us into a war with Cuba. TWA 800, which expert witnesses insisted was brought down by a surface-to-air missile. You want to talk conspiracies, how about the media's silence on what's happening in South Africa today, which is at least as bad as what went on during apartheid. South Africa is one bad day away from a Rwandan-style genocide. Directed energy weapons. Obama's missing student registration at Harvard Law

School. The non-existent plane that hit the Pentagon on Nine-Eleven. Area 51."

"Aliens?" she said dubiously.

He smiled and shrugged. "Maybe I just had one too many walls fall on my head." She grinned, and that turned into a yawn. He stood up. "Maybe we should go inside before we freeze. Find a place for you to sleep. I'd hate to have my rescue efforts all go to waste because of hypothermia." He smiled at her.

She stood up, and gave him a look. "You did say you had a bed in back," she said.

"Yeah. That's where I'm sleeping."

She stepped close to him. And was surprised how tall he was, she hadn't realized he was so tall. She was almost six feet, and he had her by at least four inches. She looked up into his face. "Maybe you saved our lives. Did you?"

He shrugged. "Maybe. I probably at least kept you guys from ending up in a hospital."

She bit her lip, staring him in the eyes. "Hmm. And you said wow."

He didn't say anything for a few seconds, then smiled. "I did, didn't I."

When he woke up the sun was shining in his eyes, again. He blinked, and saw Hannah was sitting upright on the bed, looking at him. It was the first time she'd gotten a good look at him in good light when she wasn't exhausted. "How old are you?" she asked.

"Thirty-five." She kept looking at him, her mouth twisted to the side. "Do I not look thirty-five?"

"You've got surfer hair, and a surfer bod, but you've got

a lot of wrinkles. Around your eyes. It's probably because you don't use sunblock," she said, one side of her mouth curling in a smile. "Your body is twenty-five. But you've got old eyes."

"I used to be fat," he told her. "Like, really fat. Four hundred pounds. Maybe more, but most scales only go up to three hundred, or three-fifty. When I lost the weight, I think it made my face look old."

She tilted her head. "I can see that, I guess."

They heard a groan through the closed bedroom door and looked that way. "Sounds like they're awake. I guess I better put some clothes on," she said.

"And that's a damn shame," he said. She turned away, smiling shyly, and reached for her shirt on the floor.

Once he carefully turned the motorcoach around at the end of the road it took just over half an hour of careful driving to reach the Maswik Lodge. From there he followed their (occasionally conflicting) directions, and backtracked along narrow dirt roads and forest service access routes for nearly an hour until their car appeared over a rise. It was dusty, but otherwise appeared unscathed.

The boys climbed down from the coach and checked the car out while Emily used the bathroom, leaving Murph with Hannah. "Where are you going to go from here?" she asked him, leaning an elbow on the front passenger seat. "Where do you live, Kelly? I never asked."

"I've got a place outside Columbia, Missouri," Murph told her. "I'm heading back there now."

She gave him another shy smile. "If you ever come down to Phoenix…you've got my number."

He smiled back. "I do. And you've got mine." They traded knowing grins. Emily came out of the bathroom and the two girls went down the steps into the sun. Murph gave them a final wave, closed the door, then drove past the car. He found a place to turn around a quarter mile on. When he came back, the car was gone. He stopped the coach in the middle of the road and stared down it, smiling. Eventually, his smile faded. He climbed out of the big driver's seat and looked around, out all the windows. He didn't see another vehicle, and wasn't likely to. They had wandered out of the national park onto tribal land. The Havasupai Reservation was the most isolated and thinly populated indian reservation in the country, entirely surrounded by the national park, and the road the quartet had found wasn't on the way to anywhere.

He pulled a set of replacement license plates out of one of the hidden cabinets and swapped out the ones on the vehicle. Then he woke up one of his computers and physically inserted a plug into the wall, connected his system to the hidden dishes on the roof, and thus to satellites. He waited five minutes, but he had no new messages—no emails, no texts, no voicemails on any of the accounts that were active. He pulled the plug again and got back behind the wheel. He drove out of the park, turned north, and not quite nine hours later pulled into a KOA outside Salt Lake City.

And got to work.

Grab your copy...
vinci-books.com/subsection

Author's Note

I have to thank Howard Toy once again for sharing his wealth of knowledge of Vegas. Before he retired, over the course of his career Howard ran several of the hotels on the Las Vegas Strip, and the stories he has are legendary. After listening to what I wanted in a Vegas steakhouse setting for a mob meeting, he recommended Phil's in Treasure Island. Ironically, I had a lovely steak dinner there once, with Howard and my better half.

Dr. Will Dabbs, M.D., answered a few of my questions about wound care in the field, so Bob would sound like he knew what he was talking about. Any medical technical errors are on me.

Once again, my sons Harrison and Barrett were my two best editors. Because of Harrison's suggestions I combined two chapters and moved them, and cut what I realized was a lot of extraneous detail out of another chapter, making this a better book. My better half told me I should do another novel just focused on Aaron…and I'm realizing that's not a bad idea.

Author's Note

This of course is a work of fiction, and any persons or places herein which might seem the least bit familiar is just a weird coincidence. That said, if you're a gunowner and are looking to get some defensive training, I don't know that there's a better place than Gunsite, in Paulden, Arizona. Over the last decade I've been lucky/spoiled enough to have been there well over a dozen times for various classes and media events. Everything I wrote in this book about the completely fictional Ravengard, the quality of that facility and its instructors, goes double for Gunsite. I would love to retire to nearby Prescott, but all the Californians doing the same thing have driven the real estate prices up beyond my ability to cope, at least until Hollywood takes an interest in one of my books....

About the Author

James Tarr is a regular contributor to numerous firearms/outdoor publications and has appeared on or hosted numerous shows on The Sportsman Channel cable network including *Handguns and Defensive Weapons* and *Guns & Ammo TV*. He is also the author of fourteen books (and counting), including the critically-acclaimed *Dogsoldiers*, *Whorl*, *Bestiarii*, and *Carnivore* (with Dillard Johnson), which was featured on The O'Reilly Factor. He lives in Michigan with his fiancée, two sons and three dogs.